Ann Devine, Ready for Her Close-Up

www.transworldireland.ie
www.penguin.co.uk

Ann Devine, Ready for Her Close-Up

COLM O'REGAN

TRANSWORLD IRELAND

TRANSWORLD IRELAND
Penguin Random House Ireland, Morrison Chambers,
32 Nassau Street, Dublin 2, Ireland
www.transworldireland.ie

Transworld Ireland is part of the Penguin Random House group of companies
whose addresses can be found at global.penguinrandomhouse.com

Penguin
Random House
UK

First published in the UK and Ireland in 2019
by Transworld Ireland
an imprint of Transworld Publishers

A CIP catalogue record for this book
is available from the British Library.

ISBN 9781848272460

Typeset in 11.5/14.5 pt Palatino
by Integra Software Services Pvt. Ltd, Pondicherry

Printed and bound in Great Britain by Clays Ltd, Elcograf S.p.A.

Penguin Random House is committed to a sustainable future
for our business, our readers and our planet. This book is
made from Forest Stewardship Council® certified paper.

1 3 5 7 9 10 8 6 4 2

For Marie and Lily and Ruby

CONTENTS

Ann Devine, Ready for Her Close-Up

1

A POCKET OF DISADVANTAGE

I bet Denis will have the beef.

He always has the beef. You'd swear he doesn't get it at home. I've tried to get him to give fish a go. The oily fish are supposed to be good for keeping the Alzheimer's away. *I had fish shoved down me when I was a small boy*, he says. *I don't want to take the risk. If I'm spending nearly twenty euro on a dinner, then it's a pure waste if I don't like it, Ann*, he says. Then when the children bought us the dinner that time for the wedding anniversary, he *still* went for the beef. *I don't want to be wasting their money*, he said. *Well, when are you going to not eat the beef?* I asked him. He even ate it during the Mad Cow panic. In fact, he ate more of it. *It might cure me*, he says. If Gordon Ramsay was cursing at him, telling him he was an effing so-and-so and the beef was like a boot, he'd stick to his guns. He has his principles. I'll give him that.

I'm not going to make a thing of it this evening anyway. We're having a special dinner for Rory's going away, so the less time spent talking about the menu, the better. I like it here in the Station House Hotel. It's an old enough place, and there aren't many of them around. There's the wood panelling and the carpet and a few books on a shelf, *Reader's Digest*s and a Jilly Cooper. They still have the old blocky tellies in the rooms, Geraldine, my sister, says. She works here a few days at the check-in. Not that they've much checking in to do. *Checking my phone most of the time*, she says. It's been in the owner Dinny Sheehan's family for years. Bianconi used to stop here with his coaches, but that didn't last long. There was a row in the road one time over a fare, so the story goes, and a couple of horses ran off into a wall and Bianconi pulled out. The only town he pulled out of. That's Kilsudgeon for you.

We're all out. Or all of us that were around. Myself and Denis and Rory, our niece Freya, who is almost a daughter because I mind her a fair bit while her mother, Geraldine, works. And my mother, Margaret. She's a good age and hardy enough, but her digestion is giving her fierce trouble and she's not backwards about letting all and sundry know about it. Deirdre, my eldest, is due in too. But she'll be late.

It's quiet in here tonight. Dinny is leaning against a wall with his phone. *Candy Crush, Ann*, Geraldine says. *He's obsessed with it*. In fact, we're the only people here so far. Apart from one fella sitting on his own in the corner. He has his back to me, so I can't get a good look at him. But I can't place the neck so he must be a tourist.

'Feck sake, Mammy.' Rory was making big dramatic sighs.

'What's the matter with you?'

'Why did we come here? I thought this was a special night for me. It's dead in here. Literally dead. Like, *removal* dead.'

'It's early yet. We'll have no problem getting served.' If we're eating out, we have to eat early because of Mam's innards.

'There's nothing on the menu.'

'There's pages and pages on the menu. What are you talking about?'

'Pages and pages of spuds.'

'And what's wrong with that? Don't be giving out now.'

'Shoulda gone to Winch.' He was sulking now.

Rory had wanted us all to go to the new place in Drumfeakle. Two fellas with beards run it. Slaughterhouse & Winch. We went there once. Actually, that was the only time Denis *didn't* have the beef, because he got mixed up when he was ordering. Written on a cornflakes box, the menu was. You can see right into the kitchen. They'd want to put up a partition. If I wanted to see my food being cooked, I'd cook it myself. And Denis hates the ceiling. *You can see all the wiring and the pipes. Does any one of them know a plasterer at all? If you had a wall like that long ago, you'd be mortified.*

'Ah, don't mind your whingeing now, Rory. Don't they have that pulled pork?'

'Pulled pork is yesterday's news, Mammy.'

'Is it gone off or something?'

'Once a fashion reaches Kilsudgeon it's time to get off the train. And pulled pork here means it should have been pulled from the menu.'

This is how Rory talks these days. And now that he knows he's going somewhere cosmopolitan, I think he's being even more Roryish. My charming tangler of a boy. What'll they make of him below in Cork? I wonder. What'll I do when he's gone?

My mother is glaring at the menu. I try and help her, or we'll be here all night. She's as deaf as a beetle.

'Well, Mam, how about you? What will you have?'

'AH, I DON'T KNOW. MY CONSTIPATION IS ACTING UP SOMETHING FIERCE.'

'Thanks, Nana, for the image,' mutters Rory under his breath, and he gives Freya a nudge. Freya looks a bit sad, actually. I suppose she'll miss her cousin. She wouldn't have a huge circle of friends.

'DENIS IS HAVING BEEF, IS HE?'

'I am, Peggy. You can't go wrong with beef.'

'NO, YOU CAN'T. GOD BLESS YOU THAT YOU CAN DIGEST IT. I CAN'T HAVE IT BECAUSE OF MY BOWELS.'

'Would you eat risotto, Mam?'

If the rest of the place didn't know my mam's views on risotto before, they know them now anyway. Risotto doesn't agree with her. Not much does, the poor thing. The IBS has her plagued.

'I'LL EAT A BIT OF MASH, AND WOULD THEY HAVE A RASHER?'

'I'll have a word,' says Geraldine.

We move on around the table. Freya is sighing now about the lack of a vegetarian option. She only puts it on for her mother because she mills into the burgers when she's down at our place. Which is often.

Nathalie comes over to take the order. I should have told her to go away, but I do what I always do and sort of pretend I'm ordering, even though I haven't read the thing. But I'd always go for a chicken supreme anyway. It's a handy one. Hopefully, the spuds will be simple enough, but the fella they have here goes mad with the sauce. They discovered garlic one day in here a few years ago and they can't leave anything alone with it.

Geraldine disappears off to have a word with one of her pals on the staff. She's back in a little while.

'Three in tonight.'

'Who?'

'Seanie Gillen and the uncle and some old crony. Down from the mountains.'

'Would they not know your roster at this stage, to know you weren't on?'

4

'They must have found out about the dinner.'

'Did you say hello to them?'

'I did. It would only be manners. They came all the way down and they won't take a drink for fear of being done by a checkpoint.'

Geraldine has a few admirers who often might come into the hotel just to have a look at her. There's no malice in them. They're just of a certain vintage and there wouldn't be many women to give them the time of day. Geraldine is heading towards a certain vintage herself, but you wouldn't know it. She's always minded her looks. And she'd be well blessed in front. Although that isn't a family thing. I think she had a bit of work done, although she keeps her cards close to her chest on that one, as I said to Denis. He thought I was making a joke. *It wasn't the medical card anyway*, says Denis. But I don't be encouraging him to be looking at Geraldine that way, although it's hard not to. Her rig-outs are fierce draughty. There's no fear of us borrowing each other's clothes anyway. Although I'd love to have her shape just to wear something red.

'I'm sorry, I'm sorry.'

Deirdre has arrived.

'Could *not* get that child to bed. I'm sorry he ever found out about that cursed *Minecraft*. A fright to Christ that I should be arguing with a small boy about killing a Creeper and then an hour later he has a nightmare about it. Women's Christmas, my foot. And Hughie sitting there saying, *Ah sure, isn't he grand, he'll grow out of it*. Have ye ordered? I'll eat a burger and a dose of wedges or something. I don't know when I'll be called away again, so there'll be nothing fancy for me. I'll find the girl. Is it Nathalie is on tonight, Geraldine?'

'I'll go tell her,' Geraldine says. 'Sit yourself down.'

'Anyway …' Deirdre sits down with a big breath. 'Hi!' She waves around the table. 'Hi, Nana, how's the pipes?' Deirdre leans over and gives her a big squeeze.

'Grand, girleen,' says Mam with a smile. Deirdre is her first grandchild born in the country and will never do wrong in her eyes. And come to think of it, Mam doesn't get many hugs.

My eldest daughter is in her usual tizzy, doing four things at once with a million and one things left to start. She puts more rearing into her own two than I ever did with four. *And* she's training the under-fourteen girls for the football, *and* she has a demanding job. I'm often exhausted just talking to her.

'Guess who I was talking to, Mammy?' says Deirdre. 'Stephanie.'

I feel a wave of panic. I'll nearly have to go home now and clean the house.

'Is she here?'

'No, on Skype, Mammy. I was on the phone above at Dooney's Turn. Relax. You're gone pale!'

I'm able to breathe again. Stephanie is my son's wife. You see, they've *fierce* notions. They've always looked down their noses at us because Denis drives a truck while Derek Rourke, Stephanie's father, was an auctioneer and they've never been short of money. I nearly had to get counselling after the wedding, I was so worried about letting the side down. Denis said it was like holding in a fart for a month.

Kevin and Stephanie are out in Dubai now with two grandchildren I've barely seen. The little girl is called Claonradh and Cathbad is the boy. There wasn't a peep out of Kevin when they named the child Cathbad. *It means 'trusted adviser of royalty'*, says Stephanie at the christening. *If you give a child a name, they can live up to it. The Rourkes were all in positions of trust.*

I wouldn't trust Derek Rourke to mind my chair. They say he was up to all sorts during the boom. Fake bidders and the whole shebang. Kevin means 'well-born', so they should be delighted with his pedigree, even though I know they're not. If Cathbad ever grows a beard, he'll get stuck in every airport for the rest of his life. Stephanie and Deirdre get on well enough, though.

'Well, how is my favourite daughter-in-law?'

'Oh, Mammy, you'll be gutted you missed out on chatting to her.'

'I don't know how you do it, Deirdre.'

'Ah, she's not the worst of them, Mammy. She has a good heart. But Dubai has her ruined altogether. She was bringing me on the phone around the new apartment they've moved into. There's a pool, of course, and a balcony, where I suppose you can watch all the poor brown lads. But you won't hear that from Stephanie. Telling me I should get a maid. Can you imagine having a maid in Kilsudgeon?'

'I'd watch that over *Made in Chelsea* any day.'

'Oh, har-de-har, Rory. So, smartarse, are you all set for going down south?'

'That's a very personal question, Deirdre, and none of your business,' and he starts laughing away to himself.

'WHAT DOES HE MEAN BY THAT?'

'Don't mind him, Nana, he's only being smart.'

I'm not quite sure what he meant, but no doubt it's about sex. At his age, it always is.

'Rory, Mam was trying to explain it to me, but I can't get my head around it,' says Deirdre. 'How can you transfer in the middle of a college year?'

'A stroke,' says Denis, as he wires into the bread. 'A pure stroke, I'd say. A Patsy Duggan special.'

'Denis is being dramatic.' Rory calls him Denis when he's trying to wind him up. 'Patsy is on the Special Higher

Education Reform Committee.' He takes a bite of bread and continues talking through the eating. I lost that argument a long time ago. 'The committee was interviewing professors from around the country about what's going on in their colleges.'

Denis interrupts with a laugh. 'What's going on?! I was watching it on the Oireachtas channel. It was a howl. The Teamsters'd have nothing on these lads. They were grilling this fella one day. High-and-mighty professor, you know. I'd say no one had said boo to him in donkey's years. They says to him, "Did you get a construction company in to renovate your offices?" "I did," he says, like he was surprised they'd even asked him. "And who owns it?" And the professor gave the name anyway. "And who's he?" says the fella doing the grilling. "My son," says the professor. Not a bother on him. "And what are you professor of?" they asked him. "Ethics," says the latchiko. John B. Keane couldn't write it. A pure skit.'

'So is it a stroke?' Deirdre asks.

'No,' Rory says. 'Patsy was chatting to one of the profs afterwards and it turns out there's a special scheme to transfer during the year. And Patsy knew I wasn't happy in the Tech. Stifled, he said I was.'

'What's the scheme?' It's the first I've heard of this bit of the story.

'Disadvantaged Area Restart Scheme. It's an EU thing.'

'It's always an EU thing. But are we disadvantaged? I knew there was something wrong, but I was blaming myself.'

'Kilsudgeon is in a pocket of disadvantage,' Rory says.

'My pocket is always disadvantaged,' says Denis, delighted with himself.

'Patsy got Disadvantage for Kilsudgeon. It was one of his election promises,' Rory goes on.

'So you just said you were from Kilsudgeon and they let you transfer?' Deirdre asks.

'Well' – Rory's a bit sketchy-looking now – 'not exactly. We *might* have had to be a bit creative with the disadvantaged thing.'

I don't like the sound of this.

'What do you mean, "creative", Rory?'

'OK, Mammy, first of all, chill. Promise you'll be chill.'

I don't like being told to chill. I'm frozen half the time anyway.

'What is it, Rory?'

'So we might have had to *imply* that I was a big hardship case. That there were ... issues at home.'

'Issues at home! What kind of issues?'

'You said you'd be chill, Mammy, and you're not being chill.'

'I'm not a white wine, Rory! Are you telling me the whole world thinks you're on the breadline and your father is on the drink or something?'

'It doesn't matter. No one's going to know. It's just a thing for a form. And it was prescription drugs – you know, benzos and all that? And it wasn't Daddy. It was you I said was having some issues.'

'*Rory!* Do you mean to tell me ...'

The restaurant is filling up now. Of course it is. Just in time for the Devines to have an *EastEnders* meal in the middle of them. We might as well be having a row at the top of Mass.

I whisper at him, 'Do you mean to tell me that the university in Cork thinks I'm on drugs?'

'It's only a box-ticking thing, Mammy. No one thinks anything.'

Sally walks past. I raise an eyebrow at her to let her know I'd have a story for her another day. She nods back. She knows the signal.

'You're here for the Women's Christmas, Sally?' I say to her.

'Donal is treating me.' Sally glances her head back at her son. Donal Considine is standing around. A big, awkward boy of nearly forty who could do with a woman now at this stage. Sally spent a lifetime looking after his father, who had arthritis, and she'll be looking after him as well.

'So I've free accommodation and all. Pretty sweet.' Rory is grinning at everyone around the table. 'What you think, Nana?'

He asks his nana because he isn't getting any grins back from us.

'I NEVER MET ANYONE FROM CORK I LIKED.'

'Nana, who did you meet from Cork?' Rory asks.

'THE FELLA WHO PUT IN THE BURGLAR ALARM.'

'Nana, that was ten years ago,' says Deirdre. 'You'll have to let that go, and you can't say it was his fault.'

'MY GOOD ROSARY BEADS WENT MISSING THE DAY AFTER.'

I get up to go over to talk to Sally. Donal ignores me. He's on an iPad. Sally glares at him.

'What do you think of my dinner companion, Ann? Brings his mother out for dinner and stares at his machine the whole night.'

'I'm working, Mam. This thing is 24/7. If you're offline, you're off the pace. And this place has some bit of internet, not like the dial-up you're paying for.' He's looking at Facebook, as far as I can see. 'Feckin Kyle!' he says.

'His cousin is always getting a rise out of him by putting up comments on Donal's business page, Ann. Videos of a bull going at a cow, that kind of thing. How many likes do you have now, Donal?'

'Forty-eight, Mammy, but I'm just doing the groundwork now.'

'I've no idea what he's doing, Ann, but he's not meeting any young ones anyway. Put that away now, Donal, please. I'm sure they can wait now, whoever they are. Your clients. How many do you have again?'

Donal snorts like it's a fierce eejit question. 'Obviously, Mammy, I don't have any yet. This is beta stage.'

'If you can't batem, join 'em, isn't that right, Donal?' Sally says, nudging his arm.

Donal doesn't say anything at that. I thought it was quite good myself.

'You'll be lonesome when Rory goes, Ann. The last boy out the door. I can swap, if you want.'

Something about Sally's kind face and the realization means I nearly start wobbling there and then. She doesn't continue. She just puts her hand on my hand on the back of the chair.

'I know, Ann. I know. He's a good lad. He's not gone for long.'

'That's true, Sally. I'll let ye get on with your meal.'

'Do so, Ann. As you can see, we're anxious to talk.' She throws her eyes at Donal, who's furiously swiping on something on his iPad.

I come back to the table, and Rory and Denis are still jabbing at each other.

'Patsy says I'm the son he never had.'

'And by all accounts I'm the father you never had.'

'Now,' says Nathalie, appearing out of nowhere, 'who's for the soup?'

The food calms things down. We wouldn't be a family that'd say much when eating. Denis always says it's bad manners to do both.

I feel a hand on the back of the chair. Dinny Sheehan is over.

'How's Ann? C'mere, your man's after asking me if we're doing anything for Veganuary.'

'What man?'

Dinny gestures with his eyes to the man over in the corner. He has a laptop out now and I can see a bit of his face. I see that he has a little beard and what they call a 'man bun'. He must have sensed he was being talked about because he turns around. I'm mortified, caught staring. Well, we all are.

'You're visiting!' shouts Denis.

The man doesn't reply. He just looks at Denis.

'Veganuary,' whispers Dinny again. 'They'll all be looking for that now. I'm only just after recovering from the euro. They're talking about putting the calories on the food. Sure I don't know how many calories would be on a thing. How do you measure the calories for mash?'

We look at Man Bun again. He's back at his laptop, tip-tapping away, drinking a coffee. Very late for coffee. He won't sleep tonight.

'Kefir,' says Dinny.

'What's that, Dinny?'

'Another thing he was asking me. *Where would I get kefir around here?* Do I look like the kind of fella that knows kefir? I said it about the kefir to Anton in the kitchen, because Anton came from London first after Romania so I thought he might know. *We've heifers, but no kefir*, says Anton.'

'You were busy over the Christmas, Dinny,' I say, changing the subject to something he loves talking about – how bad things are.

'Ah ...' That's all you need to hear to know that Dinny is sceptical about something. 'Not too bad now, but it was dead all year. Dead, dead, dead. Dead as a doornail. Only for the takeaway, we'd be gone under. The town's gone to pot since the bypass. Nothing. Dead. Rural Ireland, Ann. Don't believe what they say that the good times are back. Rural Ireland is rightly shagged. Well, enjoy yer dinner.'

We say nothing again until Dinny has resumed his position near the bar, the phone back out and the *Candy Crush* on again.

Geraldine gives a look. 'That's him on a good day.'

'What's eating him?' I whisper.

'What's he eating, more like it. He's a bit upset since the Kilsudgeon Festival hit the skids. I keep saying he needs to put on a bit of entertainment here, liven it up, but Dinny's in a slump, the poor man.'

'HE'S GONE HUGE.'

Mam's latest observation is half drowned out by Freya cursing. I turn around to look. Benny Courtney is at the counter. Or Lightning Benny C, as he calls himself onstage. Lightning was a good name for him. You saw him at his best after dark and then rarely in the same place twice.

Benny C isn't alone. Hanging out of him is a girl, and I mean 'girl', because she couldn't be more than twenty-two or -three. I can tell by her that she's in some sort of showbusiness.

Freya curses again as Benny spots us and starts to walk over.

'THAT'S NO KIND OF TALK FOR A YOUNG GIRL.' My mother looks around to see who Freya was looking at. 'OH, THAT GOBSHITE, AND WHO'S THE *PISCÍN* WITH HIM?'

Benny C is a good-looking boy who never grew up, and he's Freya's father. Although the parents are not together. Geraldine was away for years travelling, or, as Mam put it, *suiting herself*. She came back one weekend, went out with some pals from school, didn't come back for three days and, when she did, she announced she'd met the love of her life.

Poor Benny wasn't ready to become a father at all. He could hardly look after a car. No sooner had he found out that Geraldine was pregnant than he was gone off the scene. It was the band he said, Lightning Benny C and the Country

Blues Explosion – although no one else in the band called it that – they had to go on a big European tour, and Geraldine was left holding the baby. It was a bit of news around here because Mam was always a first-in, last-out sort of Mass-goer and she didn't speak to Geraldine for most of the pregnancy. But it's hard to be angry with a grandchild, and Mam transferred all her dislike to Benny.

Benny comes over and puts his hand on Rory's shoulder.

'Well, big man, you're off out into the world, out of the bosom of your family,' he says, throwing a look to Geraldine. 'How's everyone?'

'WE'RE FINE AND HAPPY. THE FOOD IS GRAND.'

'You're looking great, Peggy.'

'WHO'S PEGGY?'

'Peggy' is reserved only for a select group, like the public health nurse, the doctor and Father Donnegan, so when Mam hears an interloper use it she might as well have caught him wearing her nightdress.

'How's Freya?'

'Yeah, Benny, whatever.' Freya calls him by his first name, but she's not joking about. 'Oh, hi, is it Kayla? I think you were in my school, like, probably at the exact same time as me?'

Geraldine coughs into her black pudding.

'This woman is going to be massive,' says Benny, putting his arm around Kayla.

'IS SHE HAVING A BABY TOO?'

'Mam!' I had to intervene or she'd be throwing bread rolls next.

Benny wasn't put off. 'You should hear Kayla sing. I guarantee it, she'll be on the telly soon.'

'Benny is working on some arrangements with me,' says Kayla.

I gave Mam a look to say, *No more.*

'We're up on SoundCloud. Benny and Kayla. We're sort of like She and Him.'

Kayla didn't have a bother on her. Oh, what it would be like to walk into a situation like this and not give a shite? I'd say she and Freya could have been friends if, well, she wasn't carrying on with Freya's father.

Benny isn't sure how to leave the situation.

'Ye're having the dinner anyway,' he says. 'We're getting a bit of takeaway. Big night of rehearsing ahead.'

'Happy New Year to you, Benny,' says Denis, ever the practical man. 'And yourself, Layla, like the Eric Clapton song.'

Ah, Denis.

They went and collected their takeaway from Dinny, heard a bit more about the state of rural Ireland, and they were gone.

'He travelled thirty miles for a takeaway?' says Geraldine. 'That was very strange.'

'Now, the beef is for yourself Denis, is it?' Nathalie is back.

'We're all having the beef today,' he says.

My phone goes. I jump for my bag. There's a text I'm expecting.

'Is that your phone, Mammy? You've it on fierce loud.'

'I'm sorry, Deirdre, I have to. There's a text I'm waiting for.'

'You're worse than a teenager checking it.'

'I'm watching out for Tom Mullins. He's nearly gone.'

'You're like the Angel of Death,' says Denis. 'Are you going to be at the foot of the bed?'

'Stop that, Denis. Tom put it in writing he wanted me to be around to help with the arrangements. The poor man, he has no women in the country belonging to him. He specifically asked for me.'

15

I check the phone. NEW OFFERS HERE AT GALLIGANS LADIE'S BOUTIQUE. CHECK OUT OUR NEW ONLINE SHOPPING FOR ALL THE LATEST IN GREAT STYLE!!

Fecking Galligans. Always texting when I'm expecting another one.

'There he is, lads, the man of the moment, a young Frank Sutherland.'

Can no one let us enjoy our meal in peace?

'The scholar. Heading off to Cork.'

Patsy Duggan, Independent TD, walks over to us. Geraldine has gone to the loo, so Patsy sits into her seat without so much as a by-your-leave.

'Excuse me for sitting down. I've to take the weight off the leg.'

Patsy has a prosthetic leg. If you talk to him for longer than five minutes, he'll tell you how it happened.

They're all looking at us now around the restaurant. Patsy's entrances are always dramatic. Literally. There's a whole zoo of stone animals on the pillars at the gate of his house.

Rory looks at Patsy. A big smile on his face.

'Mammy was just saying how grateful she and Daddy were to you for ...'

Patsy waves his hands as if to shush Rory. 'There's no need for gratitude at all, Ann. That's not why I do what I do. I just believe in unlocking potential, and this fella is bursting to be the best he can be. And he won't do that in a Tech.'

'They're called Institutes of Technology now, Patsy,' says Rory, teeing him up.

'Ah, they're all Techs as far as I'm concerned. Institutes. Anyone can call themselves an institute. Four whackjobs with a box of teabags waiting for the media to ring them and it's an institute. I'd have sent him to Dublin, only I wouldn't have the same connections as Cork.'

Sent him. Me and Denis – well, mainly me – should be the ones doing the sending. Here's Patsy going around the place as if Rory is a poor orphan out of the slums needing rescuing. Needless to say, I say this all in my head.

Rory and Patsy have been as thick as thieves since Rory did transition-year work experience at Patsy's constituency office when he was fifteen. I blame Patsy for turning him. Or maybe it was always there and he unearthed something in him. Patsy rang me after that first Monday.

'My good woman, Ann, you've reared a special boy. He just got me out of a spot of bother there with his silver tongue. The boy is a voter-whisperer.'

From that day on, Rory has always been knocking around with Patsy. 'Voter research', he calls it. The school marks went out the window. He did two Leaving Certs and neither of them would set the world on fire. I didn't know what he was going to end up doing, but I knew he wouldn't be going off to be an actuary anyway.

The parent–teacher meetings used be gas. *Rory needs to apply himself* and *Rory needs to focus his energy* was all I'd hear. It was only Mr Carley, the maths fella, who had it right.

'Ann, don't mind what the other teachers say. Rory is a pure fixer. Whatever way you'll be measuring Rory's worth, it won't be in points for a university. I've a feeling he's going to make money, but I couldn't guarantee he'll pay tax on it.' And you know, I *haven't* worried as much as your average mammy might about their youngest. Maybe I should have.

Patsy is still singing the praises of Frank Sutherland and I look at Denis and I can see he's put out by this too.

'And how are you getting there, Rory? I can give you a lift down if you want, to save ye the bother?' he offers.

'I was going to get the—' Rory starts to say.

'We'll be driving him down, thanks very much, Patsy.'

17

Denis looks at me as if it's the first he's heard of it. Which it is. I know he doesn't trust the car to do big mileage. But we have to take some bit of control of our son back. This is getting ridiculous.

Geraldine returns from the toilet, having taken a good slow look at Man Bun on the way. Slow enough that he noticed her. Geraldine is not exactly an Apache at the stalking and of course she'd draw attention, the way she looks.

'Well, I'll love ye and leave ye.' Patsy stands up as Geraldine reaches the table.

'Bye so, Patsy,' says Denis.

'Before I do, can I make a small toast?' He says 'small toast' but he uses a big voice, and now the whole restaurant is raising a glass.

'WHEN IS HE MOVING IN?' says my mother.

'I'd like to make a toast,' he says again, clearing his throat. 'This is an auspicious occasion. Thanks to Denis and Ann for having me along. This young lad is taking a step out into a world that is more and more uncertain, but I am confident that he will be learning the skills needed to continue on the work I am trying to do for this area.'

I'm beginning to wonder whose son is Rory at all.

'To Rory!'

'TO RORY.'

There are gawkers toasting my son, having great sport, wondering what's going on, and they'll have it figured out before I will.

'C'mon, we'll have a selfie,' says Patsy. 'Dinny,' he calls out, 'come over and take the selfie!'

'It's not a selfie if you ...' Freya starts to say, but no one's listening to any of us now.

Dinny comes over and takes Patsy's phone and we all have to get in and smile. Patsy gets up from the table and I expect him to sweep out the door, but he stops by Man

Bun and talks to him and gives him the big two-handed politician handshake. Only he's not talking as loudly as he was with us. This is definitely not for everyone's benefit. The heads are down, they're both looking at a laptop.

'That rules out pervert,' says Deirdre.

Patsy limps out. We're all set to launch into him – apart from Rory – when the phone goes again. BE-BE-BE-BEEEEE-BEEE BE BE BEEEEP.

I read it out: *Ann uncle tommy v shook can u come tomorrow.*

'I suppose the nephew will get the farm,' says Denis, finally able to enjoy his beef.

2

BEST OF BREED

'We don't have to drive him down, you know.'

'We can't back down now. If we don't bring him down, we might as well change the surname to Duggan. How did we get ourselves into this situation, Denis?'

'Are you eating that sausage?'

'I was going to later on, in a sandwich. But Denis, is it not strange that he should be so independent of us and then dependent on Patsy? Is that normal?'

'Young lads work with ould lads all the time. He's nearly twenty, you know. Remember that actor, the one who killed Michael Collins? Wasn't he reared by a pair of gay farmers?'

'I don't know that that example works, Denis. And I think it was only one gay farmer.'

'I'd better go. Are you sure about the sausage?'

'Take it so. You've your priorities right anyway. We won't be having any more fried breakfasts after this, though. Christmas is over, Denis, old stock.'

'There's a yellow warning for cold from the weather forecast. I need the fat.'

'I don't know do you need it that much, Denis. You're not a penguin.'

'But I am faithful, though.'

'Go on, Emperor, waddle away out so.'

I hear the truck starting up outside. This is my favourite time of the day. I've a bit of time before doing my rounds. The house is quiet, so I can have a cup of tea and listen to the bad news on the radio.

My phone rings.

'Ann, it's Tracy. I want to talk to you. Can you come into the office this morning?'

'But I've to go see Tommy, Tracy.'

'You're not rostered to Tommy until the afternoon, Ann.'

'But he's on his last legs, he wants me to be there when he dies.'

'This is not what we are here for, Ann. We are not vigil-keepers. You are not rostered to Tommy until later. Come in for ten if you can. I have a few issues I want to work through with you.'

I pull on my old, battered coat and I get into the car and drive to Drumfeakle, where Mellamocare have an office. Tracy is my manager or, to give her her full title, the EMEA-Atlantic Midlands Regional Execution and Activation Lead. Honestly, the job titles that are on the go now. Mellamocare is a mighty big organization altogether. Freya keeps sending me articles from the internet about them being caught in America chaining people up, but that doesn't make the news over here. They're always winning awards here. Or so Tracy tells me. She has one on her desk. *Best Promotion of Inclusion and Diversity*. They say the sheikhs from the Gulf own half of it if you go up high enough. The diversity must be in the bit they don't own.

To think that, only a few years ago, it used to be just Ciss Hearn with a phone ringing up to see who was available to mind some old people. But then she got a stroke lifting a fella off a toilet – *and not in a good way*, she says, she's a scream – so she had to take a step back from the operation. Mellamocare bought her out and the old informal arrangement got fierce complicated with paperwork and health and safety. I don't mind health and safety, but it's gone mad with us. I've to nearly ask the High Court before wiping a bottom.

Out of nowhere then came Tracy Lee. She was a carer like me at one stage, but you could tell her heart wasn't in it. She didn't like the old people. But obviously Mellamocare saw the cut of her and liked what they saw. So, from her asking me to take on more of the high-dependence people, as she called them – basically, she couldn't stand other people's shite – now she was my boss. She went from changing sheets to spreadsheets, and she's delighted with herself.

Off she went, doing courses left, right and centre. New computer systems, management theory, conflict management, human capital management. And then we all had to go in for induction. Deirdre was going in to have Adam, so at one stage I was telling everyone both the mother and daughter were being induced at the same time, and I didn't know which was the more painful. I might as well have been in labour for all the notice I took of the stuff. It was very corporate. We had tasks now, and deliverables, and KPIs.

I dread going into the office. It's never to get a go off a box of Roses or get Employee of the Month. It's just Tracy in there, and whatever poor misfortunate little mouse of an assistant she has in there with her shaking in the corner, waiting to hear about Tracy's latest date. They don't last long. The dates or the assistants.

'Ann, did you have a good Christmas? That's great.'

It's like she got the training to ask the question but was off sick the day they covered Listening to the Answer.

'Tell me, Ann, how are you finding the current workplan? Do you find it challenging?'

What's challenging me now is that I can't get the zip of this fleece open because it's caught again, and I'm trying to answer this question and wrestle with a coat at the same time. And I'm around on the block long enough to know that when someone asks you how you are finding something, what they are really saying is that they don't think you are finding it very well at all and they have evidence to prove it.

'Ah, no more challenging than usual, Tracy. Why do you ask?' I say as I finally pull the thing off over my head, and now my hair is all over the place. It didn't have far to go to get into that state.

'Well, Ann, I have some concerns.'

She's rattling away at the laptop. Clicking here and there as if looking at videos of me acting the maggot. Clicking into 'The System', no doubt. She does it so she doesn't have to look me in the eye because we both know this is a pure cod. There's nothing wrong now. There rarely is.

'Ann, what do you think we do here?'

Click, click, drag, click. She types some letters. It looks like A S D F. Makes no sense.

She always asks these stupid questions. No matter what I say, it'll be the wrong answer. I might as well say, *We sit on our holes, Tracy, scratching ourselves*, for all the difference it would make. Denis says to me I should turn it back on her and say, *Why don't you tell me?* But this isn't *Murder She Wrote*. I'm not going to be finished this episode at nine on a Sunday night.

'We look after old people, Tracy.' That's the best I can manage.

'No, Ann. It's more than that.'

Of course it is.

'We are a systematic, holistic, end-to-end care facilitator, Ann, operating in a highly competitive market committed to driving efficiencies.'

And you know, she barely got honours in the Inter Cert.

'Oh, that's right. I forgot "holistic".'

'Ann, we charge thirty euro and forty-one cents an hour for these visits.' She sees my face. 'I know we don't see much of it, Ann ...'

She sees more of it than I do.

'... but for that we need to provide a service that is comparable to Best of Breed internationally.'

'Best of Breed. Grand, so.'

'Now, Ann, I am a bit concerned about your performance.'

'What kind of performance? Where did you see me perform?'

'I mean how you are doing your job. How you are performing in the tasks on your roster. How are you finding it, Ann? Do you find it challenging?'

'Challenging'. She's asked again. I have four old people to mind. Or soon to be three, if Tommy goes the way as expected. The Fab Four I call them. But not in front of Tracy, because that would be 'a level of informality unbecoming of my key deliverables', according to the last time I got into trouble.

'How are you interacting with your task allocations?'

'The task allocations? Oh, you mean the people? Ah, fine, I suppose.'

'*Ah, fine, I suppose* isn't good enough, Ann.'

Tip, tap, click, click, drag.

'I'm looking at the activity logs that have been uploaded to Themisto for the last few weeks. I'm looking at yours,

Demelza's, Patricia's and a few other girls'. Theirs are all one hundred per cent. Yours are incomplete, Ann. I don't know what you are up to half the time.'

'Were there any complaints?'

'You went to the chemist for Neans. Did you pick up her prescription?'

'I did indeed, yes. Was it not right?'

'I don't know, Ann, because it hasn't been logged on the system. Everything has to be logged now, or the next thing we'll be getting sued by Neans' children because Neans is after getting two doses of Eltroxin because she forgot she had it, and then they'll come back to us wondering why she's sitting out on the front lawn shouting at the bus because her thyroid is gone so hyperactive.'

'OK, I'll fill out the thing. Look, Tracy, I'm anxious to get up to Tom.'

'And that's another thing. You're going up there out of hours, Ann. You're not insured.'

'The poor man is dying. He's only looking for a bit of company.'

'And what am I to say if you end up inheriting the farm, like what happened with Colette? Forty-five thousand in legal fees that cost us. We have a duty of care not to be inheriting things. What's more, when you're up there you're not visiting other people. You visit the lowest number of people of any of our carers. Tina Deegan gets around to ten people each week.'

Tina Deegan doesn't stay long with them. She goes in and barks questions at them and gives out about them on Facebook, often while she's with them.

'Mellamocare Worldwide takes its responsibilities very seriously, Ann.'

'I'm sure the Saudis do all right.'

'Ann, not recording Neans' pharmacy visit is a huge procedural breach.'

'But where else is she going to get the tablets from? I don't see what the big deal is.'

For a second, she starts talking like a normal person.

'I don't know, Ann. Maybe one of her family will get up off their backsides and come visit her once a decade and decide to help. You know what families are like. Especially useless ones. When you don't want them around, that's when they turn up. Ann, we have to cover ourselves. All of this stuff has to be logged. Logged, Ann. Do you need a refresher course on the BlisterTec module in Themisto? I can send you off, if you want. They'll ask me why you need a refresher course so soon, but I can come up with something.'

'Tell them I'm gone addicted to benzos.'

'What?'

'Nothing.'

'So tell me about your weekly workplan.'

'Workplan? I mean, I suppose my plan is to work for the week.'

'Ann! That's more of it now. The WWPs were brought in six months ago.'

'But it's the same work every week. Go in, chat to them, make a cup of tea, clean them up, do a bit of washing. What do we need to plan?'

'Ann, this isn't easy for me. I don't like this aspect of the job. You know I'm a mother too. I'm not an ogre. I don't want to have to put you on a performance-monitoring programme, but I will. This job requires tough decisions.'

'OK. I'd better go and make a tough decision about an adult nappy.'

'Ann, I'm on your side here.'

I stop fighting her. She does seem sincere now.

'I know, Tracy. It's just ... I just have my own way of doing things.'

'Well, if you have your own way, then maybe you need to set up your own home-care company, Ann, because while you're at Mellamocare, you do it the Mellamocare way, do you understand? It's getting harder to work with you and I can't do it indefinitely. I'm putting you on a professional-development programme.'

That's shook me. I make some apology about being under pressure and get out.

This has not been a good week so far. I sit in the car for a while, examining my situation. The bloody fleece, I find now, has bits of scrambled egg on it. This is what happens when you don't have a mirror in the hall. *Sure we know what we look like*, says Denis.

With Rory going, these old people are all I have to look after. I suppose there's Denis, but he's at an age now when he can manage most things, apart from keeping an eye on his moles. As I say, I have four to look after. I couldn't manage ten. I call twice or three times a week. Sometimes it's just for the cup of tea.

There's Tommy, a bachelor farmer who lives with his nephew. I don't know who's minding who there. Noel is not going to manage well after Tommy goes. Tommy has bad lungs from the factories in England. He didn't wear a mask. *With the IRA acting up, they weren't inclined to be handing masks out to Paddy*, says Tommy. Tommy would be the last of the old stock around here. The kind that wouldn't let a red-haired woman in the door for fear of bad luck.

I do know my work plan. Tommy is Monday morning: today. Noel opens the door to me when I arrive.

'Ann, come in, come in. Come in. Don't mind the place. I'm sorry now it's a bit of a mess.'

Poor Noel is not able for this sort of situation at all. The house is back in a state after I cleaned it the day before. There are socks in the hall and a wellington boot near the cooker, and the cats are no doubt in and out because I can smell them and where they've been. Those cats have nothing else to do only watch for an opportunity when someone slips up. And then when they get in, they're not happy then either. We're all like that, aren't we?

'Ann, he's gone very shook,' Noel says again.

I walk through to the sitting room, where he's all set up. He's not long back from the hospital. He told them to go away from him. He wanted to die in his own bed. There's a hoist there, but Noel is lifting him. I don't think Noel knows the right way to lift him, but Tommy only wants the minimum amount of people touching him. They'd be like that, some old people. They wouldn't have been touched much over the years. Especially the bachelors.

He's wheezing away. By rights, he should have had it looked at fifteen years ago, but you don't find much hypochondria in the likes of Tommy.

I sit down on the bed. Noel is fussing around, picking up tea towels and putting them down again. An attempt at tidying. There's no point now, I want to tell him. I've seen the butter knife in the geranium pot.

'Ann ... come here, girleen,' Tommy calls me over to his ear. 'I've not long to go. Ann. I've done enough work now, but Noel ... he's not ...' The breathing is hard on him now. 'Noel isn't ... Noel, will you go out and get ... Ann the tea, like a good boy ...'

Noel goes out. I can hear the clattering going on out in the kitchen.

'He's a grand boy, Ann, but easily ... scuppered ... Will you ... mind him ... a bit?'

'I will, Tom.'

'And don't ... let him do anything with the Lios field. Don't ... want that interfered with for money. No one will have luck ... out of it if they do ... mark my words.'

The Lios field has the fairy fort in it. Tommy's generation have no problem being keen for Mass and paying respect to the fairies too.

The Pope would excommunicate you, he said to me once, a while back, *but only the fairies would give your cows mastitis.* I couldn't argue with that. There's no mastitis in the Bible.

They're not making any more Tommys these days. I wonder who'll be keeping an eye out for the fairies now. The vegans, maybe.

Noel comes in with the tea and I sit back down into the chair near the bed. The bag is still in the mug and the tea is cold. You know a household is up in a heap when they make a hames of the tea. It's the last to go, the last vital sign.

We say nothing for a while. Tommy closes his eyes for a bit. Noel stares at the wall. I should be going home soon to help Rory with the packing. I shift around a bit in the chair.

'Ann ...'

'Yes, Tommy.'

'You're ... anxious ... to ... go.'

'I have to bring the young lad down to Cork, Tommy.'

'Rory ... the tangler. I'll hang on until you come back, so. I have a bit of a thing to give you.'

'Oh, don't be getting me into trouble, Tommy. We're not supposed to be getting anything from the ...' I stop myself.

'From the dead, I know ... Tracy Lee ... the hoor ... I put the run on her ... before you were looking after me. She doesn't tell you that, I'm sure ... always in a hurry. Rough hands.'

'Don't mind that talk, Tommy. You're flying.'

'Ann, I'm ... not ... an eejit ... I know the game is up ... the breath ... can you pass me the sponge ... my swallow is gone.'

I dip the sponge in the glass and he sucks on it for a bit.

'Why … Rory … Cork?'

I tell him the story. I shouldn't have. When I mention Patsy, he erupts.

'BAD CESS TO THAT HOOR'S BASTARD.'

Roaring nearly broke him.

'Calm yourself, Tommy. Don't be wasting energy on him.'

Noel comes in and sees the state his uncle is in and starts crying.

'Ah, Uncle Tommy, don't be leaving me now. You have all the dockets. He does all the paperwork, Ann.'

'Mind yourself … with Patsy, Ann. Rory has … made a deal with the devil.'

'I will, Tommy.'

And just as I say that, I see through the window Patsy's jeep pulling up outside the hedge. He starts limping up the path. Tommy can't see who it is from his angle on the bed.

For once, Noel shows a bit of initiative and goes to the door. They're talking for a bit and I see Patsy limping out again.

'Who was … that … Noel?'

'Aaaam … the binman,' says Noel, his initiative running out and him panicking in the lie.

'Why'd the binman … ring the … doorbell?'

'Erra … he had the wrong house, Tommy. He was looking for the purple ones.'

'I didn't hear the … lorry …'

Noel is sort of pleading with his eyes now for his uncle to stop asking him questions he doesn't know the answer to. Tommy is silent. I'd say he's watching people closely these days, wondering who's lying to him. Old people get lied to a lot. White and black ones. Lies, I mean.

'I'll be away off then,' I say to the two of them. 'But I'm at the end of the phone, Noel, OK?'

When I get outside Patsy is still parked there. I walk past him to where my own car is parked.

'Terrible sad about Tommy,' he says out the window to me. 'A fine man. He had a fierce brain.'

'He still does, Patsy.'

And although I wasn't intending to look at him, I give a glance, and who should be sitting in the passenger seat of the jeep, only Man Bun!

3

COLD AROUND THE EDGES

So this is it. My Rory is leaving.

'The Hare Krishnas are on the bypass again, Ann,' announces Denis at the kitchen door.

That'd be the kind of news I'd eat up usually. They're Buddhists, but once Denis got it into his head they were Hare Krishnas, there was no changing him. We spotted these two fellas in orange walking the hard shoulder of the Kilsudgeon Inner Relief road a few times in the last while. I thought they were firemen at first, from behind, but they'd no helmets, and then when we looked in the mirror we saw it was two fellas with shaved heads. There was talk they were going to be starting a temple where the post office used to be. Whatever the story was, I'd say Geraldine would know more anyway. She's alternative that way. All about 'the East'.

But today, I've no interest in Buddhists.

Denis sits into his chair. I know the look he's giving me. It's the look to get me to say what's on my mind without him having to ask any tricky questions.

'Are you all right, Ann? Have you a bit of a cold?'

'I'm grand, Denis. Small bit of a sniffle. You'll have tea?'

He leaves it at that, of course. He wouldn't be the type to go poking around when it comes to feelings. Denis is a man who doesn't like investigating things without cause. I think it comes from the time he got done for the car tax, when the guard was only looking for green diesel.

We're sitting down with the tea, listening to Rory shouting at some Korean on the Xbox for the last time before packing it up. He's running the internet off his phone. A phone that Patsy got him.

'Come out of it, ya so-and-so, ya. Drive on ta ...'

'That tea is cold around the edges, Ann. Did you not scald the pot?'

And that sets me off. Sniffling and snotting and crying. If I can't make the tea ...

'What's wrong, Annie?'

He calls me Annie when there's emotion involved. So he must have understood I was upset.

'Ah, what do you think is wrong, Denis? Rory's bags are in the hall, ready to go, and then what? The house'll be empty.'

'I thought you were looking forward to that. You were talking about doing up a few of the rooms as guest rooms. I was afraid you were going to Airbnb the place out to continentals and I'd have to be dressing for breakfast.'

'I thought I was, too. I was very blasé about it, but ... all the empty houses I call into, Denis! Old people like Neans or Flash just sitting there on their own. Plenty of photos of communions and graduations around the place, but no visits. It's sad.'

'But, sure, that's what happens.'

'Aren't you upset yourself?'

'Ah, I don't know. It's not as if anyone's gone far away. Deirdre's only down the road. She's not going anywhere. And Jennifer's only in London – you could visit her any time. And Kevin – well, they'll surely finish building Dubai eventually.'

'I know it's not logical, Denis. I can't help how I feel. It seems like only yesterday he was waking us at five in the morning in his little nappy, wanting a cuddle, the poor little baba.'

'He did that last month when he came home balubas and got the rooms mixed up.'

I'll see the flash of lonely in him later, I'm sure, when he'll get angry at the telly. It comes out in odd ways. Like that time he couldn't do his tie for Deirdre's wedding, and it one of the easy ones, and he was blaming it for everything.

I go out to boil the kettle again and scald the divil out of the teapot. The sound of shooting has stopped above in the room and Rory comes thumping down the stairs. In twenty years I don't think he's ever taken one step at a time. It used to frighten the life out of me to hear him when he was a small lad, coming backwards down the stairs, pretending to shoot upwards as he went, like *Die Hard* or one of them fellas.

And now here he is, galloping down the steps like a small elephant for the last time, hitting his knuckle off every bannister.

'Well, Mammy.'

'Well.'

And then I was off again. My eyes all wet.

'Ah, Mammy, you're acting like I'm off to join ISIS.'

'You're joining Patsy Duggan. That's nearly worse.'

'Mammy, I don't know what you have against him all of a sudden. He's the only one fighting for rural Ireland around here.'

'Patsy Duggan fights for himself. Or he gets young lads like you to do it for him. I'm worried about you.'

'Well, look, Mammy, you're always worried about me and I've turned out fine. Look at the lads who got all the points. Seamie got 580 and he's after dropping out of medicine with stress. You need to let me fly, Mammy. Patsy's only looking after the next phase. And anyhow, do you know maybe I'm only using him too?'

'So my best hope is that you're more devious than Patsy Duggan?'

He puts his hands on my shoulders. 'It's all in the game, Mammy.'

We load up the car. Rory has the phone out, recording.

'OK, just getting the limo down to Cork with the folks. Take a snap there with me, Mammy.'

I look into the phone with him. I look very old, like his granny.

'Greetings, bitches. I'm off ta Cork. This is my mammy. She thinks I'm going to hell.'

And then he gives me a kiss on the cheek. He's not happy with it, though, and we have to do it four times more. Four kisses. It's as much as I've got off him in the last few years. I have to admit I've never seen him as happy. I didn't think he'd be so chuffed to get out of Kilsudgeon. He always seemed to be so happy here, but ever since he found out about the transfer he's ferocious hyper.

'My mammy. I love her, even though she's mental,' and there's a sound, QUSH, of him sending it up to the Web.

We hear *bing bing bing* for the next few minutes.

'They're all loving it, Mammy. I'm getting heaps of comments.' He shows me.

I love your mum.

She is sooo cute.

Not able for this snap of your mum Rori.

35

'What way have you spelled your name? R-O-R-I? Is that the latest?'

'It's more contemporary.'

'And will Patsy be P-A-T-S-I now on your advice, will he?'

'Whatever it takes, Mammy. The campaign doesn't stand still.'

We say nothing for a while after that. We leave the floor open to Denis to give out about other drivers and the state of the road.

'What hurry is on that fella now, I'd like to know?' says Denis as a Micra overtakes us, roaring. It has the big Nike thing on the back window. Deirdre calls them Nicras. Not the kind of micra that'd bring nuns to devotions. This Micra looked like it had fallen in with a bad crowd.

'Haha, that's Skitchy. Hang on, I'll snap him.'

'Skitchy, you beast, greetings from the slow-lane fam,' or at least I think that's what Rory says. It's not always easy to understand him now.

'He's driving. How's he going to receive that?'

'Don't worry. I'm sure he'll pull over when he finds a safe place to stop, Mammy.'

'He won't get it anyway for half an hour with the internet around here.'

'Oh, here he is, look, Mammy.'

He shows me a video of Skitchy laughing and saying, 'BRRAP BRRAPP KILSUDGEON MASSIF.'

'Well, thank God that you're not going down with that lunatic anyway.'

'I'd nearly be there by now if I was.'

We drive on for another bit, Denis not saying a word. When he thinks Rory is distracted he puts on a bit of Declan Shannon on the local radio with the old-time waltzes.

For I knew not how but I knew to fear ...

'Ah, Jesus, Denis, you're not in the grave yet. You're making me feel old with that stuff.'

'Put that on Snapchat there, Rory,' says Denis. 'Tom and the Strummers was massive himself long ago.'

Rory says nothing. Texting away like mad, as usual. Two hands. He'd have paragraphs of a response written to me as a reason why he shouldn't do the thing I asked him to do while I'd be struggling to find the full stop.

And there was my love, with her sailor dear ...

We get on to the motorway now. I'm glad Denis is driving. The motorway makes me nervous. Once you're on, you're on, and they make you go at a savage speed just to be not in the way. I look at my phone to see what variation of shag-all reception it'll tell me it has now. GPRS or E, I suppose. It might as well say, *Go away and don't be annoying me, Ann.*

Just as we pass a sign for Cork, it changes to 3G and I get two bars. And a load of texts start arriving. All from Noel.

Ann uncle tommy going fast enough i'd say you may come over ann

I was about to say to Denis that maybe he could turn around, but then the texts kept arriving.

Ann are you anywhere near hes asking for you

But I was too late.

HE'S GONE ANN. LHMOH.

'Ah, Jesus, the poor man! LHMOH? That isn't a very appropriate thing to say. Laugh my ...?'

Rory takes the phone. 'It's Lord have mercy on him.'

'You'd better bring me back, Denis. Noel can't handle this stuff at all. He'll have the body sold or something, and Patsy will be hovering, too. I don't know what he wants, but I don't trust him and Man Bun.'

'We're a good bit down the road now, Ann. I don't know how we're going to manage it.'

And that gives Rory the excuse he needs.

'It's not a problem. I'll get Skitchy to bring me, Mammy. He's not too far away from here.'

'What's Skitchy doing in this part of the world anyway?' I ask, but Rory taps the nose as if it's a secret, so now my mind is working overtime. Skitchy Ryan could be up to anything, from visiting a cousin to burying a body in the Galtees.

But we're miles down the road, and Rory needs bringing to Cork, and I need bringing to see a body and calm a nephew. And that's why we're in a layby, like something out of *Love/Hate*, parked behind Skitchy on the hard shoulder somewhere near the Bealnamulloch exit.

Skitchy gets out, all go.

'Mrs Devine,' he says, 'I'll take good care of your son. I will bring him to safety.'

'Don't tell her too much,' says Rory. 'She mustn't know.'

The two of them are laughing at me.

'Give your mother a hug so, you flute,' I say, and I kiss him a few times to take the wind out of his sails.

'I'll do the bags, Mrs Devine,' says Skitchy, and transfers them to his own car.

Denis shakes Rory's hand and Rory gets into the Nicra. The music starts up when Skitchy turns the key. Something about 'bitches' thumps out of the window. We get into our own car and watch Skitchy tear up the hard shoulder, sending gravel clanking off our bonnet.

'We'd better go back and see this body,' I tell Denis.

And on my wedding day, cold and dead he lay ...

4

THEY LOOK LIKE THEY SMELL WELL

Denis drops me at the door of Tommy's and I run in. We'd have been sooner, only we were pulled over by a Garda patrol car after someone reported suspicious activity on the motorway. I'll have to get a better coat if people are going to be thinking I'm in a gang.

Noel meets me. He does not look as cut up as I expected.

'He's grand, Ann. It was only a deep sleep he was in. I couldn't hear breathing, but the doctor came in then and said he was fine.'

Ah, for fuck sake, Noel! I very nearly say. *I've left my boy on the side of the motorway and tore up for this.*

'That's no bother at all, Noel,' I say.

I go to Tommy. He seems almost apologetic.

'Noel was ... telling me I was gone ... Ann, but if I could hear him ... then I mustn't be.'

'Ah, Tommy.'

'You seem ... disappointed ... but I've to wait for the sister as well.'

I can't be angry with a man figuring out when to die. I give Tommy's hand a squeeze, give Noel a smile and leave.

Denis drives us back home and when we get there the empty house hits me. I hoosh him out the door to the pub, or anywhere. We always agree I should do my crying alone.

The phone rings. It's Deirdre. She knows straightaway. I so rarely cry, she can tell it in my voice.

'Mammy, Daddy said you were up in a heap.'

Or else Denis had delegated, it seems.

'I'm not up in a heap.' But I am. I look around the room and see he's left his woolly hat on the back of the chair and I'm off again.

'Mammy, it's fine to be upset. After all, he's your last child out the door and you're probably feeling a bit rudderless. Without a purpose. It happens to a lot of women your age. And also the prospect of spending more time with Daddy.'

'OK, steady on there, Deirdre.'

'Well, I've one thing you can be doing anyway. I've tickets for Ryan Montana tomorrow night. That'll take your mind off things.'

'I don't know, Deirdre. He wouldn't really be my scene.'

'You'd be the only one around here thinking that, Mam. Everyone I know is going. There's even a bus laid on from the filling station. Ailbhe said Mrs Foley has them making banners.'

'I won't be getting the bus anyway. I don't know how long I'd be able to stick it out. I'd rather go under my own steam.'

'Do go, Mam. I need to get rid of the tickets.'

'Tickets? Aren't you going?'

'We were supposed to, but Adam is after getting a virus. Please, Mammy.'

Since she made the effort, I decide to do it, and I drive up and collect the tickets off her.

Who will I bring to it?

It's a fundraiser for renovating the church. Renovating again. It was done up about fifteen years ago and they put the altar going lengthways along the church. But seemingly Father Donnegan was saying that St Udgeon's was missing out on a rake of weddings because there was no aisle and brides want an aisle. *If they don't have an aisle*, he says, *they've no reason to have the Mass.*

So we're getting the aisle back. Ryan Montana really isn't my scene, but he's a big deal now on telly and everything. I wonder how Father Donnegan swung it.

You can't move for hearing that Montana song 'Roundabout' on the radio at the moment. I have to admit the tune is fairly catchy, although the lyrics – mother of God! They'll put anything into songs nowadays. *Momma, wanna be your round-about. / If you yield to what's right. / It's just a suggestion. / Through the night, / I'll ease your congestion. / I'm a roundabout, baby, / I'm up to the task. / Just indicate, baby, / That's all I ask.*

What kind of rubbish is that? I can't get over how the young wans and the lads are into country music. When I think of the gang I hung around with growing up, we wouldn't be caught dead listening to 'Country and Irish'. Of course, Country and Irish was a different story in my day. They'd be called Felix Fuohy and the Balers, or Johnny Jim and the Hardy Rockets, and you'd have some singer with a bit of a belly and a guitar and six gropey, sweaty lads on the stage behind him, going through the motions, imagining what kind of action would they be getting after. I suppose they were sex symbols in their day. But my gang back in Clonscribben were all into the rock. Not that we ever went to a show or anything, apart from one trip up to the Adelphi to see Rod Stewart.

I think they're nearly more conservative than we were. The crowd playing the country music now are very clean-cut compared to anything we saw on a stage. Young lads with fierce shiny haircuts and teeth. They look like they smell well.

I ring Sally, but she can't go because, of all things, she's at her book club. No Sally, so. I realize then I don't have a whole lot of people I can ask. Geraldine will be working, unless …

Do u want to go see Ryan Montana hun Dee is after giving me 2 tkts.

Freya is straight back. *Don't know auntie ann. Supposed to be putting pins in my eyes.*

Cmon hun u owe me I brought u to that play.

Omg are you still on about that ??? That was aeons ago and I brought you. You needed that more than me at the time.

I brought her up to Dublin to see that play about the women talking to their bits. The Monologues one. (Not the original. 'An intersectional reimagining, Auntie Ann,' said Freya as we took our seats.) Her mother had been supposed to bring her, but she got stuck with work and I ended up sitting there, speechless. It was very good, but I'm still traumatized, because she was only thirteen at the time, and I was afraid I'd be thrown out for bringing her. We didn't say a bit to anyone around here about it, but then Freya wrote about it in an English essay, but she said she went with her mother instead and the teacher was an ould wan who probably expected that kind of thing from the likes of Geraldine and said nothing about it.

I've had to mind Freya a lot down the years with Geraldine at work. To tell you the truth, I always look forward to seeing her. She's a pure tonic. The things she comes out with. You'd have to look them up after. Geraldine says she spends all day on these feminist websites, reading about all sorts of injustices. She'd put me to shame with what she knows. But you'd have to be fierce careful what you'd say in front of her because she'd be right back at you with some fact or correction. *Well, actually, Auntie Ann …* and I'd know then I was behind the times and letting the side down. Denis is ferocious fond of her, even though he's always trying to get a rise out of her. The Suffragette, he calls her, and she calls him The Cold Dead Hand of the Patriarchy. With love, of course.

I text her again. *I thought Ryan Montana would be your style all the young wans are mad after him.*

She texts straight back. *I am not fangirling a FAF country music singer auntie ann.* She put one of those little getting-sick pictures on it. Emotions, or whatever they're called.

Ah do. Ur poor auntie at a loss to no wat to do with her lif.

Quick as a flash she's back. *Emotional blackmail and 'wats wit de speling'. Stop trying to be cool.*

There was nothing from her for a while, but I figured I had her all the same. She's a kind little one. She took her time, though. I was even waiting by the phone. What am I like? Then it beeped again and I nearly knocked over an ornament reaching for it.

OK so I will go with you but I will totally hate it I know. Sorry for delay in replying just making you sweat. Not hard at your time of life lol.

That's my girl.

It's the day of the concert and I'm awful busy on account of the trip down with Rory. I've to visit my other three in the one day: Johnny, Neans and Nonie.

Johnny Lordan. There's a tale. The poor thing. He's not even that old, but he had a bit of an accident in the car a few months ago and made ribbons of his leg. There's no one at home with him the last few years. The wife was a bit of a rip. She took up with a fella selling burglar alarms around the place. Their alarm must have needed fierce maintenance because the van was parked there nearly every day, until Johnny found out. Talk about being caught on your own hook. Johnny got a text one day to say the alarm had gone off and he went home and found the two of them at it. They were in such a rush into the house, they hadn't the time to turn it off. The funny thing was, she was the one who'd pushed for the text alert, to give lover-boy an extra sales bonus. Bonus is right. Herself and 'The Installer' came in one day, took everything that wasn't nailed down and headed off. They were cute enough to switch the alarm off that day all right. Johnny has most of the farm let now, so he's idle enough, watching tractors go in and out of the yard. There's a daughter somewhere, but the wife turned her against him and Johnny is all by himself. A nice man.

They call him Flash Lordan because, up until recently, his main hobby was driving up and down the road, flashing his headlights at other drivers to let them know there was a speed van on the road. You might laugh, but he's saved a good few from getting penalty points. Even that's been taken away from him now, though, because people just put up warnings on the Spirit of Kilsudgeon Facebook page: VAN UP AT DEMPSEYS F*CKERS. Then there'd be a clatter of replies underneath about where else the van might be. And who might be driving it as well. There was talk he might be local.

Poor Flash. Technology was after taking away a job nearly before it had been invented. He still went out on the off-chance, to see if he could warn anyone, but often people would already have slowed down, so he got no kick out of it. That's how he crashed. He was looking at a white van in the mirror, thinking it was the speeding van, but it was just a builder parked up to make a phone call. Flash had his eyes off the road, clipped a pillar at the

44

bad bend and put the car on its roof in a field. He wasn't going fast, but now his leg's in a bad way and he needs me more than ever.

He's always pleased to see me. Struggling around on the crutches, looking in presses for buns. I eat the buns, even though I don't want to think about when he bought them. Usually I've to chip out mouldy bits when he's not looking. This is the sort of stuff you've to look out for, doing the rounds of the old crowd. Are they feeding themselves? But the main thing is the bit of company. They'd be peeled out for a bit of gossip or news. Especially the oul lads, sitting there during the afternoon, waiting for *Loose Women* to be over so they could watch a quiz. Shouting answers at the telly.

Johnny was all courteous when I was changing the dressing on his leg.

'You've grand hands, Ann. You must be getting manicures all the time.'

'I don't, but thank you anyway. It must be the soft water around here. Do you miss the road, Flash?'

'I do, Ann. I can only see out the window now and the hedge is getting high, so I only see the Land Rovers. I can't tell whether they're locals or not. The sister brought me out for a spin there the other day and I saw a car I hadn't seen before, with a Northern reg. I don't know how long it's been around, but I'd have seen it much earlier if I'd been up and about.'

'You'll be back out in no time, Flash.'

'Oh, I'm fierce sorry, Ann,' he says to me as I do the dressing.

'Sorry for what, Johnny? Oh, I see.'

Poor Johnny has become visibly excited by my manicured hands changing the dressing on his leg.

'Ah, don't mind it, Johnny. I've seen a lot worse.'

45

'And better, says you! I'm fierce sorry, Ann. It's just these tracksuit bottoms are too roomy altogether. My normal trousers would keep me under control more.'

'I don't know how you can even think that way with the pain from getting these dressings changed.'

He winces as I pull off another length of it. He's cursing his hairy legs.

'Multitasking, Ann.'

'We'll say no more about it, Flash.'

They could trust me to keep my mouth shut about these kinds of incidents. I won't be 'logging' this in the BlisterTec module of Themisto or wherever on The System I make a note of a man's vital signs.

'You're keeping me young anyway, Ann. I'll have a beard next, like your man.'

'What man?'

'The man in the Northern reg.'

'A beard and a sort of a thing on top of his head like a kind of a ...'

'Bun?'

'Yes, I suppose you could call it that.'

'Dark-haired fella, was he?'

'No, he was very fair.'

So there's two of them. Are they taking over or what?

'And a young one called in as well, in a different car with the yellow number plates. Head shaven on one side like she was protesting about something. They were wondering if I had any spare fields. I've a good mind to call the sergeant. What would this one be renting a field for? Scoping it out I'd say they are, for a home invasion. I saw it on *Prime Time*. They're using drones now as well. I must go looking for the cartridges.'

What's going on at all? There's nothing around here to be scoping out and now Flash Lordan is at the rear window, tooling up, as they say.

After Flash, I drive a mile down the Drumfeakle road to Neans Malumphy. A fella on a quad bike nearly ends me on the bad corner near her house. Neans is as hard as nails, a little sparrow of a widow. Actually, I should say she calls herself a widow. The husband ran out on her fifty years ago. *Before it was fashionable,* says Denis. She held on to the name because that's what you do and, as she says herself, it's handier for the post. But the whole thing toughened her up. She's a great old character, and full of gossip and a bit of history. It's very handy to talk to her because she fills me in on any old grudges or gripes from way back, so I can avoid putting my foot in it. Even though we're here thirty years or more, I'd still be a blow-in and mightn't have the background. She has the archive. She has one daughter, but she's not around much. *I don't blame them, Ann, they've full lives. But they could call in on their way somewhere. I only tolerate visitors for a small amount of time.*

I can't stay with her too long because it'll only give Nonie something to shout about. Nonie was sent to try me. So I finish up with Neans and get straight over to Nonie's place.

The husband opens the door. A saint.

'How is she, Brian?'

'Ah, she's herself. She was expecting you yesterday. I think she rang Tracy.'

'IS THAT HER, BRIAN? SEND HER IN.'

I walk in like I'm to the headmaster. Nonie is stationed in her armchair, looking fierce expressive. I see now that it's the makeup. Brian does it, and he's managed to make her eyebrows even more angry. Her own hands are too shaky with the Parkinson's.

'You're a day late, Miss Hoare.'

She uses my maiden name on purpose, to let me know I married into the place. She's the reason I don't take on more people, in case they're like her. A more unpleasant, sour, bad-tempered crone you could never hope to meet. She has pain, but she's not offering it up or thinking of anyone worse off than her. Father Donnegan told me once about a woman whose confession was a list of people who'd wronged her. He said it happened somewhere else, but I'm full sure he was talking about Nonie. He shouldn't have even said that much, but he knows I won't say a word. I think her therapy is to take it out on everyone else.

I do her blood pressure and check the drugs are being taken.

'I told your boss you weren't around, Miss Hoare. You'll be for the high jump.'

I ignore this. I had cleared it with Tracy before, but she knows how to get at people, does Nonie.

The husband still dotes on her, though. He walks me out.

'I thought she'd be worse, Ann, to tell you the truth. She's grand with me, believe it or not. I never go anywhere.'

'You're very good to her, Brian.'

'We don't marry who they turn into, Ann. Only who they are.'

'BRIAN, ARE YOU STILL TALKING TO HER?'

'That's her now. She'll be a pussycat when you're gone. No offence, Ann.'

'None taken, Brian.'

After a day like that, and with Rory gone, by rights I should be down in the mouth, but tonight I'm going out!

5

UGLIER WITH GIN INVOLVED

Freya walks in the back door. Early. Freya wouldn't be the typical fourteen-year-old, as she takes no time to get ready at all. I'm still getting dressed myself. I have to tell her to put on a screed of makeup.

'But why, Auntie Ann? I'm not trying to impress anyone.'

'Ah, do. They'll think you're making a statement about something. Just a bit, for me.'

'*For me*. Classic Auntie Ann.'

'And will you put on something check underneath that hoodie as well? It is country music, after all.'

'Mam says you have to be yourself.'

'Only up till age twelve, pet. Then you need to blend in.'

We pull up outside the convention centre, or The Mart, as everyone calls it. There hasn't been a convention there yet, it's just a sort of nightclub and function place, and then it's next to The Mart so there's an awful smell of Jeyes fluid and that sticky stuff, the Jägermeister, and in the background the smell of the cattle. They say Club Ikon is the only night-club where you'll hear and smell bullshit at the same time.

There's a big crowd there already. Freya sees two girls she knows from school. I see her almost shrink in front of me. Young Kylie Cafferty and the youngest of the Kennedys, I think.

'Hi, Freya. Hi, Mrs Devine.'

I get the impression they are only being nice to her because I'm there. There's a bit of giggling after we pass. I've a good mind to go back and find out what they're giggling about, but I know what young wans are like these days. I'd only get a smarter answer than I'd be able to think of a reply to, so I'd end up looking a gom in front of them. And the last thing Freya needs at school is to be laughed at because her aunt 'had an eppo', or whatever they call it now.

There are two bands on before Ryan himself is due to make an appearance. If I'd known that, I'd have stayed at home and watched the rest of the news. But Freya gives a little squeal as she watches the first warm-up act.

'Auntie Ann! It's the Honkythinks! I can't believe this is actually happening right now.'

'Who are they?' I was trying to see them, but they were almost hiding on the stage.

'They're, like, twins – a boy and a girl – but they, like, identify as a girl and boy? So they're, like, so amazing about gender and sexuality and how it's all mixed up.'

She skips off down the front of the hall.

The main mix-up is how this pair managed to find their way on to the stage at The Mart in Kilsudgeon, because they definitely wouldn't be the standard entertainment here. It's just these two waifs in big, baggy jumpers leaning over a keyboard and some kind of a machine with a wand and a wire from what I can see. Maybe Father Donnegan thought when they had 'Honky' in their name that they were going to be all about cowboy hats and trucks. Freya is dancing away on her own up at the railing. Everyone else is milling around doing selfies and queuing for drink.

'Awful stuff, isn't it, Ann?' says a voice at my shoulder. I turn and it's Phil Grogan. 'And who's that wan dancing up to them? Is she their manager or what, hah?!'

Freya has her hood up, so Phil doesn't recognize her.

I just mutter something like, 'Oh, sure, don't you know the way now, Phil ...' and then I feel fierce bad for not standing up for my niece.

'Thank you, Kildungeon,' the pair say into the microphone after about ten minutes. I think they're after getting a signal from Father Donnegan. They head off the stage. I imagine they're used to not getting encores in places like this.

Freya screams, 'Omigod, I love you, Honkythinks!'

Fair play to them, they look surprised to have a fan. They come down to her and have a quick chat, give her a hug and then go back on stage to pack their gear. Freya comes back all excited. Skipping. I haven't seen her skip in ages.

'I can't believe I actually, like, *met* them, Auntie Ann. That was, like, the most amazing experience of my life right now? Oh my God, I'm actually literally shaking. Look, they signed a set list for me.'

'To Freya, a special crazy spaceship – ready for lift-off!! xxx The Honkythinks'

'This is actually ... *lit*, Auntie Ann,' she says, as if trying out the word.

'I think I might even be able to watch Ryan Montana now. I'm, like, totally vaccinated.'

She's high as a kite on it. I'm delighted to see her so happy, because she's had her problems.

The sight of the Honkythinks leaving with their gear causes a few in the crowd to cheer and we're bumped by people moving down the front. The next band is more in the Ryan Montana mode. Another fella without so much as a sign of shaving about him, in a checky shirt and with a guitar. As it turns out, it's Montana's younger brother, Ryle. As soon as he starts up with some country stuff and a tale about how *lovin' you is like savin' hay in the June-time*, we make our way to the bar.

I decide to chance a wine, as it should be well out of my system by the time this is over. I could fit in two if I wanted, because a lot of the local gardaí would be at this, but wine goes straight on to my belly and there's enough wine there as it is.

The wine is freezing, of course. But you can't be telling people to keep their red wine out of the fridge around here because you'd nearly be read from the pulpit for notions. It's the kind of place where, when they ask you what kind of wine you'd like, they mean red or white.

Freya is sipping her fizzy water. We've moved a good bit back now because Ryle is very loud. Making up for the lack of a song.

'I'm glad I came, Auntie Ann.'

'That's great, pet. Imagine now that you saw that band of yours.'

'It's not just that. I like being out too.' She takes another sip. 'It's hard, isn't it, Auntie Ann?'

'What, pet?'

'Like, big crowds and knowing what to do.'

'You and me both, pet.'

'I, like, hated the first-year disco. I mean, like, where do you stand?'

'I don't know, pet. I always try and find a wall to lean against. And then after I met your uncle Denis, I'd just lean against him.'

'I was glad I wasn't alone at the front there watching the Honkythinks.'

'I was right behind you, pet.'

'No, not you, you were miles away – thanks heaps, by the way. There was another couple of people off to the side, a red-haired guy with a man bun and a woman – did you see her? She had her hair all shaved on one side like Mammy won't let me do.'

I'm about to reply, but then there's a huge cheer. It's Ryan Montana himself. The wans of all ages are going mad for him, taking photos and holding up banners. RUIN ME RYAN says one. I don't even want to know what that means.

'WHAT'S THE CRAIC, KILSUDGEON?' he says into the microphone. 'Are ye still knocking lumps out of Drumfeakle in the Junior B?'

More laughs. A few boos from a Drumfeakle ladies' football contingent, but they are booed back. Ryan has the crowd in the palm of his hand.

'How's Father Donnegan? Is he still looking for money for the roof?'

They go wild for that, and there are a few gestures made to Father Donnegan, who's standing at the back. He raises a glass to the stage. The crowd start chanting, 'The roof, the roof, the roof is on fire!'

Ryan Montana knows all about us. The likes of him would have someone doing a bit of research in advance. Every place would have a rival of some sort, so they'd ask whoever runs the hall. Although it can backfire as well. I remember Denis brought me to Canada Jim Murphy and the Mounties, and Canada Jim was all set to have a bit of forward and back about some local character, but he didn't know he'd died that very morning and it went down like a lead balloon.

After he plays the first song, 'PTO', which is about writing a love letter but also about a drive shaft, Ryan Montana brings Father Donnegan up on to the stage to make a speech.

There are boos. There'd be a strong anti-clerical streak around here, but if it meant seeing Ryan Montana, they'd nearly go to a Tridentine Mass.

Father Donnegan thanks the Honkythinks – *Fair play to them, most unusual. I must get one of them wire things instead of a bell* – and young Ryle.

'Thanks very much for coming along, everyone, and supporting such a worthy cause and while I have ye ...'

And doesn't he do the parish notices from the stage! Such a chancer. There's results from collections, news of a bus going to Knock, the whole lot. He'll never get a bigger crowd, apart from Christmas. Montana is giggling away with his band as this goes on.

'... and one last thing, a new organization has been set up – Kilsudgeon Tidy Towns. They are committed to making Kilsudgeon a jewel of the baronry of Castlestrokard, so there's a meeting tomorrow night in the parish hall and they're looking for volunteers. Right! I'll let ye back to the music. Take it away, Ryan.'

And Ryan is off again, launching into 'Roundabout'.

'Tidy Towns? What do you think of that, Freya?'

'They should bulldoze the town, not tidy it.'

The crowd are in a frenzy now for Ryan Montana. It won't be long before they're throwing underwear. I would say he does well for himself, although to look at him you'd swear he'd never been kissed, he's so clean. He gets one girl up on the stage to get a duet for one of the verses of 'Roundabout'. This does not go down well with a few who thought they should be up there instead. It looks like there's been a bit of drink taken by the crowd. Waiting for Ryan to start up, no doubt. And everyone's drinking gin now and I'm told the mood is uglier with gin involved. A small plastic glass goes flying across the stage. 'Roundabout' gets interrupted. A few of Ryan's heavies move in to the front of the stage. They're definitely not local. You wouldn't see them on *The Late Late Show* or on the cover of the album sitting on a bale. I think they might be Polish of some sort.

'MOVE BACK, LADIES. LADIES, PLISTO MOVE BACK NOW, 'MON TO FUCK PLIS.'

This calms them down a little bit. But Father Donnegan was already on his way up on stage to add his tuppence-worth and he starts them all off again.

'LADIES, CAN I ASK YOU PLEASE TO SHOW A BIT OF DECORUM.'

A man on a stage telling women how to behave – a man who isn't Ryan Montana – especially a *priest*. Poor Tony Donnegan hasn't a chance.

'BOOOOO!'

'PLEASE, LADIES, THIS IS A VERY WORTHY CAUSE.'

'YOUR NEW PASSAT IS THE WORTHY CAUSE,' someone roars up.

Then he makes the mistake of replying.

'I BOUGHT THAT CAR WITH MY OWN MONEY.'

'WHERE DID YOU GET THAT KIND OF MONEY? WAS IT RESTING IN YOUR ACCOUNT?'

I see a few lads hanging around the edges, throwing things and shouting. The kind of fellas who always do that. Out of nowhere a traffic cone comes flying in. Next, there's a hi-vis jacket wrapped around a Ryan Montana poster for his new album *Country Routes*.

Eventually, there's calm again as a few women are brought out to the edge of the room by friends and the odd boyfriend gone pure red. I hear one couple arguing as they pass me.

'Not worth it, Teresa. Montana's only a bollox.'

'I wanted to do the duet, Gary. I thought then he might play the wedding for us.'

'Why didn't you wait till the meet-and-greet?'

'I'd only be thrown in with all the other bitches then, Gary. I needed him to hear me sing so's he knew we'd be a good duet, like. Only that *wagon* Stacey Coffey throwing herself at him. Well, she's not invited now anyway.'

'There'll be no one from your side at this rate, Tee.'

Freya and me look at each other.

'I might stay for another bit,' says Freya. 'I want to observe your species, Auntie Ann.'

Ryan starts up again with 'Roundabout'. It's one of the verses I haven't heard.

I'm not looking for complication, I don't need a motorway interchange / Just something round and true, to bring me back to you.

Oh, for God's sake.

Montana is not his real name. I don't blame him for changing it. His mother married again and she married a Ryan, so he's really Ryan Ryan. I don't know how I know this. Freya is wearing a face now. Her happy feeling after the Honkythinks and the melee over the duet is wearing off. Ryan's next song tips her over the edge.

'Oh my God, Auntie Ann, it's like the last fifty years didn't happen? He's singing some song about roping his love like a young heifer. Like, hello? Consent issues, much?'

Montana finishes 'My Yearling Dear' and when he says the next song is about how he likes a woman who is an angel in the silage pit and a devil in the hay, Freya begs me to take her home. I'm just about done myself. But it was good to get out. Sometimes you have to go out to be glad you're going home.

On the drive home Freya's phone is pinging.

'Are you getting messages, Freya? You're very in demand.'

'Just some Snapchat stuff from girls in my school about the show.'

56

'I hope they're not cyberbullying you, Freya. I hear that's everywhere now.'

'Not yet, Auntie Ann. I'll let you know. No, like, they're just saying stuff about the show and they were there and all that. I actually got tagged. Which is, like, a major weird-storm for me.'

She's sounded more like a fourteen-year-old tonight than in a good while. Normally, she's carrying the world's problems on her shoulders.

'Did you enjoy that, Freya? Are you glad you went?'

Ping!

'OMG, would she actually stop.'

'What's wrong?'

'It's goddamn Lasairfiona. She's always sending me snaps or WhatsApps and wants to hang out, but I dunno, Auntie Ann. Like, she's even less cool than I am.'

'I didn't think you were a social climber.'

'It's not like that.'

I say nothing more, and neither does she. What I want to say is that I don't think she can be turning down too many friends. I turn on the radio. It's the local station.

'And a shout out to all at the Ryan Montana gig tonight in Club Ikon, and for those of you who couldn't make it, here's a song from his latest album, *Country Routes*. This track is called "That's All the Rotavation I Need".'

My love for you / Is a ploughed field / I been through some harrowing times / but my seed is ...

'TURN THAT OFF, AUNTIE ANN!'

6

ON THE SESH – SOUTH-SHTYLE

'... and she comes into me then. A grand-looking girl, mind you. With the hair kinda shaved. "Would these be ethically sourced?" "I don't know," says I. "I never looked at the label before." Hah? No, I don't know who she was. I mean, like, I know the man who brings them and he's sound enough, but I don't know beyond that.'

Leona Talbot is on the phone as I land up at the counter with my scones. She drops her voice down a touch out of manners, but I can still hear everything. Leona is an open book, unless it's about her own life. I've a day off today, before the roster begins again – according to The System anyway. It sends me a text. 'Hi Anne,' says Themisto.

And Tommy is still alive anyway. *Still waiting for the sister, Ann*, said a message from Noel. So I've a bit of time to dawdle in the shop.

Kilsudgeon has the Spar and Drumfeakle has the Lidl, but when I want the news I'll go into Talbot's Superstore first, for something cheap enough.

'... maybe they might be down from the Moonies. Scoping out, hah? Gwan, look, I'll talk to you. Bye, bye, bye. Just the scones, is it, Ann?'

Leona has half guessed what I'm up to at this stage. I never buy much at her prices.

'Just the scones.'

She changes the subject. 'Well, Ann, how's it being free and easy now? I was never free but I was always easy, says you. The young lad settling in well?'

I think back to this morning, when Deirdre forwarded on a thing Rory had put up, something about being 'on The Sesh – south-shtyle' and a picture of a pyramid of cans. I knew he should have been put into digs. That student accommodation is a pure cesspit, by the looks of things.

'He's settling in too well, Leona.'

'That's the way with young lads. Are you going to the meeting, Ann?'

'What meeting?'

'The Tidy Towns.'

'They're still doing it? After all the commotion last night?'

'They reckon it became more memorable. Ryan gave it a plug at the end. He says, by the looks of things, there's a lot of energy in the community. The sergeant had to bring him out there was such a scrum of young wans after him. I suppose they think Ryan Montana is their ticket out of Kilsudgeon.'

'Ah, I might go. I don't know. Didn't they try that Tidy Towns before?'

'Oh, don't be talking to me. I still have a leaf-blower that I never use.'

There've been numerous attempts, in fact. And a few arguments. The first time they only did it to get a grant and there was nothing done and they pulled out. Then there were the Boats. But the less said about that, the better.

Leona is packing up the scones. I don't even want the scones, but they'll be handy on my rounds.

'Someone else saw the jeep, Ann.'

'What jeep?'

'The one with the Northern reg. Lads in yellow plates driving around the place, looking into fields, cameras.'

'Would it be the Google van again?'

The Google van caused consternation that time. Actually, if you look closely, Skitchy Ryan's bare backside is facing out of one gateway. We still don't know if it was for the benefit of Google Earth or was that way anyway. I'm only grateful Rory was sick that day from school because it would have been his on view too.

'They'll hardly come around here again,' says Leona. 'There's nothing new here. There hasn't even been a new signpost.'

That's saying something.

The scones are verging on stale. They won't last another day. In fairness to Leona, she was never a stickler for best-before dates. I ring Deirdre without really thinking, because I'm at a looser end than I've been in a while. I know from the way she answers, 'Hello??? Yes? Mammy, yeah, what's up?', that she might be too busy to be interrupted and wouldn't appreciate eating a picnic of borderline scones in the car park of her work. But she hears me out anyway.

'How was the concert? I heard there were ructions?'

'The ructions were the best bit. Freya was delighted. She said she was going to come back and make a film about the place after she'd finished whatever therapy she'll need by then. I don't think she was joking.'

'That's our girl all right. Nice to see her happy, though.'

'She's lonely.'

'And no sister.'

'I don't think that's going to change.'

There's nothing on the other end for a second.

'You know, Mam, Auntie Ger, like, I don't think … I don't know about Auntie Ger sometimes, Mammy. She was the best aunt you could have, but …'

'Don't be starting now, Dee. Your Auntie Ger has had a rough time of it.' If anyone's going to be judging Geraldine, it's me. 'Plus, Freya is a teenager, and it's all very well being the best mother in the world of a five-year-old. You might be the worst mother of a fifteen-year-old. I always thought they should bring in specialists to do the mothering after twelve. Bring them as far as twelve, and then get someone with different training in.'

'Jesus, fine, Mammy, I won't mention Auntie Ger again. And thanks for the warning from the future. Anything else strange or startling from last night?'

Deirdre is almost down my throat when she hears about the Tidy Towns meeting.

'GO, MAMMY!' she says. She launches into another critique of my future life, saying that I'd waste away without a purpose and too many women just don't take life by the horns.

'OK, I'll go, but I won't get roped into anything. I'll go along to this meeting, I'll support them, I'll buy a few raffle tickets, but public stuff just isn't my thing.'

'You've spent so much time looking after all of us, Mam, you need a change.'

'But why would I want another crowd to look after? I thought I should be taking my ease.'

'But your type are always caring, Mammy. You'd be lost without something like this. But you'd be doing it for you.'

7

A BAD FEELING ABOUT YOUR BUNS

I don't know when I've been to a public meeting last. There was one over wind turbines a few years ago. They were all up in arms about it. It would kill bats, they said. I never knew so many people to be interested in bats before. The bats and the birds got a good airing. But the wind-turbine fella never turned up, and it turned out they'd withdrawn the application. We'd had the calmest year ever that year, you couldn't dry a line of washing, and they reckoned the turbines wouldn't make any money. All the bats died the following year when a farmer knocked down the shed they all lived in. They didn't last half as long as the row the Turbine Committee had about spending the money that was raised. The treasurer was a teacher and she bought a load of books on birds without telling anyone and people are still not speaking to her over it.

This is why I generally stay away from committees. It seems like you're only ever one misunderstanding away from someone getting their nose out of joint.

'C'mon, Mam. If I'd known you were going to take this long, I'd have come later.'

Deirdre is coming with me, and she's sitting in the kitchen tapping her watch.

'It's hard to figure out what to wear to these things, Deirdre. It was easier when we used to go to Mass. You'd have your best for Sunday because of the daylight and the second best for evening because of the dim light. But now we don't go to Mass I don't know which outfits go where. Say what you like about Mass, but it put a bit of structure on the day.'

'It put plenty of structure on all our lives too, Mammy. Structure we could have done without. It's not a gala. Look at what I'm wearing. Now put on that fleece or we'll be late.'

I don't know who's the mother and who's the daughter half the time these days.

After all our rushing Deirdre and myself are the first there, apart from Mary Funshion, who looks after the place. We make a beeline for the radiators because it's freezing. Mary appears now and then, filling the burco. She refuses any offer of help, as usual. She's about two stone and five foot tall and it would give you heart failure to see her carrying anything bigger than a mug, but there she is, dragging chairs around like a fella loading a plane.

We move away from the rads for fear of chilblains. Deirdre and I are in the chairs, kinda leaning against one another. I like these little moments where you can feel the physical contact with your child. Isn't it a funny thing, you hug the absolute stuffing out of them for years, and then one day they tell you to stop and not be embarrassing them? The hugs dry up then, unless there's a funeral, or some bit of a strop over a boyfriend or a girlfriend, and then their wedding please God. So the lean is nice.

Eventually, people start showing up, late. That'd be the way around here. Don't show too much respect for a thing by being on time in case the thing turns out to be a dead loss.

'Who's running it?' I whisper to Deirdre as I watch a few stalwarts meander in.

My question is answered in a minute. We hear the sound of leather-soled shoes as Gordon Patterson walks in carrying a black, technical-looking bag.

'Ladies,' he says, 'you're here before me.'

'We are, Gordon,' I say. 'All set for Tidy Towns.'

Deirdre looks at me. 'You're gone very enthusiastic all of a sudden, Mammy,' she says as he walks away from us.

He's a different cut of a man compared to a good few around his age. I don't mind saying I like looking at him. He's tall, but not lanky. He can hold himself well. He was in the FCA for a while, and it shows in the bearing of him. They had no children either, and you can tell. They're not wrecked like the rest of us. Denis knows I keep an eye on Gordon. He says he doesn't mind. *I'll carry on with Mary Richardson*, he says. Mutually assured destruction, he calls it. He has a soft spot for her since she admired his jumper the one time he got up the courage to go for a pint in the golf-club bar. He likes her because she's a Church of Ireland sort of a Catholic. I think that means posh.

Gordon wouldn't necessarily be that popular around here. Nothing to do with him actually being Church of Ireland. Although that's probably part of it. It's just that his wife, Flora, has a bit of a reputation for turning her nose up at people. There mightn't be any truth in it whatsoever, but once you get a name some people would have nothing else to do except keep the name alive. That's why I'm so careful about saying a bit about the wine in the pub or at a concert.

It would be a different matter now if you got cold *tea* somewhere. You could bring a magistrate in to look at that. It's more of a civil rights thing, tea.

And then in comes Flora. Immaculate as well, like himself. Boots nearly up to her knees. A kind of a brown skirt. All good stuff as well.

'Why don't we ever wear anything like that, Mammy?' whispers Deirdre to me.

'I don't know, Deirdre. It's not really our style, I suppose. But maybe it could be yours.'

'But it could be yours too, Mammy. You see them on the makeover shows. *Here's Bernie. Remember, before, she looked like the arse of a donkey? Well, we've hosed her down and told her to cop on and now look at her!* But they always look miserable afterwards. I'd say they go back to the old fleece straight-away. I think it's a confidence thing.'

'But you've bags of confidence, Deirdre. Look at you, organizing left, right and centre with the camogie. Running the show.'

'In certain things, Mammy. Camogie, work, mammying. In my comfort zone. But it's a different story putting on a display.'

Flora and her pair of displays arrive over with a Tupperware thing full of buns.

'Can you taste these for me, ladies?' she asks. 'I think they're too dry. I hope you don't mind being my guinea pigs. Haha.'

'I'll always risk it for a biscuit, Flora,' says Deirdre.

'Don't be afraid to tell me they're too dry, Ann. I don't know what happened to them. I had them in and then the phone rang, or else the mixture is wrong to begin with. Taste them there and tell me are they too dry.'

The buns are grand, and I tell Flora so.

'Thanks for saying so, Ann, but they are too dry.'

I knew she wouldn't believe me. If you get a bad feeling about your buns, nothing is going to convince you otherwise.

People are trickling into the meeting now. Mostly sitting down the back. I realize we've sat too far up the room. I'm a bit exposed. This is what happens when you're early. We'd have been late if I was busier.

The crowd are a few of the usuals you'd expect to be at this kind of a thing, and then a few I don't know who must be out of the new houses.

The Nolan twins arrive in. Liam and Larry work with Denis. A double act. Nice lads, but fierce indiscreet. Denis always warned me to say nothing to them that you wouldn't put in the parish newsletter. I wouldn't need to see them to know they were on the scene. They're always either finishing a joke or coming up with a new one just as they arrive. They come in the door with the tail end of a laugh, like the last puff of a smoked fag blown into the room.

'You'd be well able for it, Nuala, I'd say, hah?'

'Well able is right,' chimed in the other one, and I see now that the current object of their attention is Nuala Costigan. She is swept into the room at faster than her normal pace. Fending off the joke.

'Oh, goway outta that, Liam.'

That would definitely not be Nuala's way of doing things. If Flora might have notions, Nuala has convictions. She waves stiffly at me. For some reason, she has fixed on me as a person to tell all the great things that are happening to her. A cruise was the last thing. *You should go on a cruise, Ann.* I always reply that *Oh yes, I should*, as if the only thing stopping me is I keep *forgetting* to go on a cruise.

The Nolan brothers spot me and head over. I can see from their faces that the two minds are up to ninety over what line of attack to open up, nearly rubbing their hands to see what kind of craic can be knocked out of us.

'The two sisters are here,' says Liam.

'Oh, thanks a million, Liam,' says Deirdre. 'I lose out on that compliment, though. Unless you're saying we both look thirty.'

'Jays, you can't say anthing now,' Liam replies. 'With the feminists.'

'If you think I'm bad, you should see what's coming after me,' says Deirdre.

'Good turnout, Ann,' says Liam.

'Good enough.'

'How's the boy below in Cork? The final one out the door. You'll be going mad with the nightclubs now, Ann, will you? Will she, Liam?'

'She will, Larry. Mad with the nightclubs.'

'House music, is it, Liam? All the drugs they'd be on. Legal highs, is it, Ann?'

There's no stopping them when they get like this. We're just sitting here, yet they're going on like we have specifically asked for a load of comments. I let it wash over me with the odd reply – 'Tis you said it', 'That's the way' – just acting my part in a play I didn't ask to be in. But I do it for an easy life. And they're good lads, really. They just can't stop acting the eejit.

'You'll get the drugs now up from college, will you, Ann? Will she, Patsy?'

'Are these two troublemakers bothering you, Ann? Will I have them escorted from the premises?'

Now Patsy's joining in the 'banter', I suppose you'd call it.

They move on and Patsy has his hand on my shoulder.

'It's good to see you here. You're the sort of woman this thing needs. Have you heard from the boy wonder? He sent me a WhatsApp today. He's flying.'

I haven't heard from him at all, but obviously he's been in touch with his new dad. I don't let on, though.

'Oh, yes, Patsy, flying. Throwing himself into college life.'

He pats my shoulder and heads up the front and sits with his arm around the chair next to him, and he half turns to face the room so he can get the measure of who's there. You'll never sneak up on Patsy. If a burglar went in, I'd say Patsy would be ready for him and have his vote by the end.

I turn around to see who he might be surveilling. Gary Cushin is at the back. That's no surprise. He'll turn up to any community thing and then cause trouble, that fella. He used to be the Kilsudgeon Communist Party. Cushin the Russian, they call him. He has run for every election, and the highest number of votes he's ever got is fourteen. They say he was able to work out after a while that not even his mother was voting for him, so he's not speaking to her or anyone in the family, especially after his younger brother went off to Kazakhstan, working for the oil people. In the last few years he's formed a new party called the Workers' Anti-Globalization and Exploitation (WAGE) Movement, and he's doing a bit better. That's when he got the fourteen votes, with all the cuts during the recession.

Half past seven it's supposed to start. Eventually, after a load of chat and messing about, at half past eight Gordon stands up to talk. He's half crouching, trying to click buttons on the computer at the same time. It makes him look a bit awkward.

You can tell he isn't comfortable. Standing up locally isn't easy. Fellas start clinking their tea cups and saying, 'Speech! Speech!' and muttering small insults under their breath.

'Hello, everyone. It's great to see such a strong turnout.'

'We're only here for Flora's buns!' says Larry.

Don't mind them, Gordon, I say in my mind.

Gordon carries on. 'Well, whatever reason you came here for, I hope ye'll leave with the same intention. A bit of pride in Kilsudgeon. Because we need it.'

He clicks on the laptop and the screen lights up. It's a slide show of rubbish around the area. He's made it like a video. There's even a bit of sad classical music playing over it. That shuts them up. Mattresses over a wall at Plumber's Cross, a pram by the river near Quigley's. Oh, and – the mortification of it – three bags of rubbish in the ditch just a few yards from my own house. I remember walking past them, thinking, *Someone should do something about that.*

Then he presses another button and there's another set of photos, of Drumfeakle Grandest Towns. Big gangs of them out in their hi-vises, cleaning up rubbish. Thumbs-up for the camera. Ould lads acting the goat with brushes. You'd swear our place was cursed by comparison. Funny I should have thought that, because the next thing the words 'AND NOW IT'S PERSONAL' flash up on the screen.

Someone has put a photo on the Drumfeakle Facebook page of Chernobyl, with 'MEANWHILE, IN KILSLUDGEON' in big writing underneath it.

Gordon is on his feet again. 'I think it's called a meme. This is liked no fewer than thirty times, including, I'm sad to say, by people from this very village. So, my friends, I think we need to establish a bit of pride in Kilsudgeon. We have been left behind for too long. All roads lead to Kilsudgeon, they say, yet no one stops here. We have to put Kilsudgeon on the map. To restore our old glory. Who's with me?'

That's when Gordon makes his mistake. He opens it up to the floor for suggestions.

'Now, have we any suggestions for what we can do in Kilsudgeon? Just little steps to start off with?'

'This is where I get my ulcer completed,' says Deirdre. She'd be more of a doer than a talker, and the talkers up her blood pressure.

Sure enough, Phil Grogan grabs the microphone. 'The first thing, Gordon, with the greatest of respect to yourself – and thanks very much to you for organizing this ...'

That is a bad sign. There is going to be a *but* and a few *all very well*s coming up for sure.

'But, you see ...'

Once you give people any kind of a stage at all, you're asking for trouble. I think the mistake is having a microphone. There's no need for it, but when someone gets a hold of it, they have it in a death grip. It's like a load of wedding speeches where everyone is the father of the bride.

'... we have been down this path before, trying to get things done around Kilsudgeon. But you see, the problem is that ...' And he's off. I'd say he's ten minutes or more going on about the pointlessness of everything. 'It's all very well to be theorizing about ...' Nearly everyone got a mention as to why this isn't done and that isn't done.

Gordon steps in then. 'Thanks, Phil. Lots to think about there. Yes, Breda?'

Breda has nearly ripped the microphone away from Phil. She wants something done about the smell, but it's nearly five minutes before we can figure out what she means. It turns out she has a blocked drain.

'I'll fix it, Breda,' says one of the lads at the back. Liam and Larry look like they're about to say something, but they can't think of it fast enough because there's a shout at the back and it's Gary Cushin.

'COMRADES, COMRADES.'

He doesn't need the microphone. They say he developed the voice up in Dublin, shouting on the street, when there was more demand for communists. I can hear groans around the place. *Comrades?* Maybe Kilsudgeon is closer to Chernobyl than we thought.

'Comrades, I agree that what we need is an active citizenry. But not to plant flowers. Flowers are only window-dressing to distract people from the fundamental inequalities in society. We need to fight for our rights, which have been subjugated underneath the boots of the landlord class.'

I suppose this is a dig at Patsy Duggan, as he has a few houses around the place.

'It's about a grassroots revolution of the rural working class, a sorely neglected constituency, the descendants of farm labourers of generations of old, not that far out of the mud cabin.'

That doesn't go down well. Most of us would rather forget where we came from. You could see why he wouldn't get many votes reminding people of their humble beginnings, especially if you're thinking of joining the golf club.

'But planting flowers? Comrades, you are just playing into the hands of the neoliberals. By doing this voluntary work you are taking work away from men and women who could be paid to do it.'

'But the council have no money for it,' says someone from the other side of the room.

'They would have enough money if the multinationals paid their fair share of tax, and that man there could do something about it. And half of his family on the council as well.' He's pointing at Patsy, who's laughing away to himself.

'There're no multinationals around here. We barely have foreign nationals.'

'You are deliberately misrepresenting me, Patsy. I'm talking about the neoliberal—'

'There wouldn't be many liberals around here, Gary.
Didn't Kilsudgeon vote against divorce twice?'

'Neoliberals, Patsy, you know well what I'm talking about,
because you're the worst of them. Taking jobs away from
working men and women by manipulating people into
volunteering—'

'I thought Stalin was all about the volunteering, Gary?
Didn't he volunteer the whole country to go farming? Are
you going to help out, or are you just going to eat the buns
and give out, Gary?'

'I didn't eat any buns.'

'Well, you should, they're mighty. My compliments to
yourself, Flora.'

I look over at Gordon. He's rubbing his chin nervously.
It's nearly nine now, and there hasn't been so much as a
geranium agreed on.

'Thanks, Gary, for your … contribution.'

Gary sits down. He probably thinks this has been a fairly
successful intervention by his standards.

Patsy has the mic now. It's a different one. I think he
brought his own. He pauses before speaking.

'Here comes Churchill now,' whispers Deirdre.

'Obviously, as the independent representative for this
constituency, I can't show any favouritism between towns
like Drumfeakle and Kilsudgeon. I see us all as a unit
within the River Fleekra catchment area, battling for sur-
vival in a country that has turned its back on rural Ireland.
That said, I'm a Kilsudgeon man going back generations,
and I will do everything within my power to give the
Kilsudgeon Tidy Towns campaign my full backing. I will
be lobbying the minister over a few other matters raised
here as well.'

Lobbying the minister is a Patsy line when he's not going to do much about a thing.

He is expecting applause after that, but then someone shouts out something about rural crime. Now, microphone or not, everyone wants to talk about crime.

'They were around the other week again. Travellers.'

'They aren't Travellers, they're down from Dublin.'

'They can't have been from Dublin. They had a yellow reg.'

'I saw them too. Looking in over at Tom Mullins's field.'

I look over at Patsy. Not a peep out of him. The face doesn't change. He catches me looking at him and smiles, and I blush. How is it that I blush? And I was up to nothing. Some people just have no blush.

'They say Horans are after letting wind turbines in as well.'

'Are the turbines from the North?'

'Plenty of wind up there.'

'No, the Northern-reg cars are separate to the turbine crowd.'

Deirdre is starting to fidget. 'It's always the same at these meetings, Mam. It's no good for my stress levels.'

From the talk in the room, there is so much crime going on you can see people getting nervous in case their own houses would be broken into while they're at the meeting. I start to worry if I've locked the door, as Denis is on a long trip up the country and won't be back till late.

Flora appears again, asking if anyone wants more buns, trying to break the spell. But it's no good. We're halfway through speculating on a Dublin crime-gang feud when it becomes too much for Deirdre and she is on her feet before I can stop her.

'IF I COULD JUST BRING US BACK TO THE POINT,' she roars. 'Can we just focus on what we *can* do instead of complaining about things we can't do anything about? I can't redirect a motorway, Phil. Can you? There's been one robbery around here in two years, but to listen to ye, Kilsudgeon is like South Chicago! And what is a committee in a parish hall in the middle of nowhere going to be able to do about tax havens? Let's plant a few bulbs, try to pick up the rubbish and just get on with the bloody meeting! This place is freezing, and I'm not waiting here for spring to come. So can we just try and get some sort of committee together?'

It is a thing of beauty, watching her in full flight. This busy woman with no time for *ifs, buts, maybes* or *what are the council going to do?*s.

She shuts them up anyway. I'm looking around to see what kind of reaction she's getting. Maybe I could head off a bit of backchat with a look. But it's all smiles. I think they're relieved she's put a stop to it and people can get home to watch the end of *Prime Time*, which, now that I think of it, is about rural crime tonight.

Gordon clears his throat. 'Thanks, Deirdre, for that … eh … strong contribution. And I think we should start assembling a committee to figure out what we want to do, so—'

'I nominate Ann Devine for vice-chairperson,' says Deirdre beside me.

'What are you doing, Deirdre?' I'm trying to whisper and look honoured at the same time.

'You've loads of time, Mam. Now's your chance to make your mark around here.'

'But I don't want to make my mark. I'm happy enough with whatever amount of mark I have.'

'I second it,' says a voice at the back of the room.

I didn't even know the fella who seconded me. I don't like being seconded without getting a good look at them. Mind you, I'd never been seconded before, or nominated, for that matter.

The upshot of the night is that Gordon is going to be the chairperson. People thought that was only fair, after the buns and the projector. Various other positions are filled by some of the local worthies. Father Donnegan seems to have a floating advisory role. Once people are given actual jobs, the meeting gets a bit back on track, and I'd say after only another five minutes we've agreed to do our first clean-up in a few weeks' time and then every other Saturday after that.

As we walk out to the car I let Deirdre know I'm still not happy with her.

'What did you have to go and do that for, Deirdre? I only went along there for a look.'

'You went along to have a look at Gordon, Mammy. Well, you got your wish. Anyway, I knew they'd nominate me, and if I end up on one more committee the White Coats will take me away. I'll help you, don't worry.'

I can't help worrying, though. I'm out of my comfort zone, and it isn't just a pair of nice boots.

8

MOIST ENOUGH NOW

'Keep your hands out of it now, Tommy. You'll get them all dirty.'

I'm in my comfort zone now anyway. It's the following day, and I'm cleaning Tommy. Noel is helping me and has the legs raised up a bit while I give the poor man a bit of a wipe down below. He's in mighty form. Or as good a form you could be in if you were being wiped by a neighbour.

'Nasty oul job, Ann ... I'm ... sorry ... I've no control any more ...'

'We could all end up this way, Tommy. Don't worry.'

'Just hanging on ... now for my ... sister.'

'She'll be here, I'm sure, Tommy.'

'If I'd known ... I ... was ... headed this way I'd have ... driven off ... a pier, Ann ... and that's the ... truth. But we don't go ... downhill fast ... do we? We go slow ... and then ... before we know it ... we've no choice.'

I tell him about the night before, just to distract his mind.

He is silent for a while. Then he waves his hand to tell Noel to lean into him.

'Listen to me ... now, Noel. You know you're getting ... the house ... and the bit of land. I ... want you ... to make sure ... the Tidy Towns get the ... use of the fairy field. Do you ... hear me? They're ... to have ... the use of it. They can make ... a heritage thing out of it ... or something.'

I hear it all but pretend not to hear it. My heart is racing. Tommy calls me close. His voice has strengthened.

'So I'm going to give ye the field, Ann. Well, I'm giving it ... to Noel, but he's to lease it ... to the Tidy Towns ... to make a nice thing out of it. Isn't that right ... Noel? You're to make ... arrangements. Give them ... . the field to use ... for half nothing. A lovely field. A special little field.'

'That's right, Uncle Tommy. But that won't be for another bit yet. You're as strong as anything.'

'Since you're so ... good to me, Ann ... in my ... final few days. Where is that ... sister of mine? Are you ... sure you called her ... Noel?'

'I've no reply yet, Tom.'

I barely hear their conversation or notice the work I'm doing. I mean to say, when you're cleaning an ould lad's undercarriage you tend to zone out anyway, but still, I was up to high doh inside. I was only in the job of vice-chairperson twelve hours and I'd already discovered land! Gordon would be delighted with that now. I wonder will I text him straightaway or play it cool?

'I'd say he's grand now, Ann. Ann?'

Noel is looking at me. I've nearly scrubbed poor Tommy clean away.

I put the cloths into the waterproof bags. We talk a bit more about the field. I hear myself telling them that we'll turn it into a park and there'll be a bench for people to sit on and an information board about the ring fort. I don't know where this comes from, but I seem to have found hidden depths in my excitement.

The rest of the day is great. Even Nonie can't bother me. She tries everything to get me to give a sigh or express some other type of dissatisfaction. But it's no good. I'm in too much good form.

'I've spilled the meals on wheels, Miss Hoare.'

'That's no bother, Nonie. I'll clean it up.'

'I might spill it again.'

'Will you? You'll be hungry then, and Brian will have to make more.'

'I'll do it, Ann.'

'Do so, Nonie. If that's what you want to do.'

And she doesn't. She's still looking at me as I say goodbye to Brian, who can't make it all out either, and head out the door.

There's a text from Rory. *How are u mam.*

I don't even reply. I haven't time now, young man. I'm a busy woman.

'That's great work, Ann. I never knew you were such a fast mover.'

I'm sitting in Gordon's study exactly three hours after getting Tommy's offer. We could have done this over the phone, but I was dying to see the house so I let myself be invited over to discuss the next steps. Imagine, they have a room for studying or reading. No telly. Just books. It's like being on *Midsomer Murders.* The things you can do when you've no children.

'Is this it now, Ann?' Denis had joked as I headed out the door. 'Thirty-five years of marriage and you're throwing it away over a fairy fort? I haven't even seen that jumper before.'

'Would you stop, I was wearing it last week.' But that wasn't true. That was a cheaper one.

'It's a beautiful room, Flora,' I say to her as she comes in with more buns.

'Thank you, Ann. These should be moist enough now. It's a different batch. Now, can I leave you two alone? I must go and do a bit of admin for the book club.'

She leaves again. Another lovely outfit as well too. As if she got dressed up for admin.

'Patsy's very interested in Tommy's proposal as well, Ann.'

'You told Patsy already?'

'We'll need planning approval from the council before putting anything in there, Ann. As soon as you put up so much as a sign people come out of the woodwork to ask you about paperwork. They'll need to be with us every step of the way. It could take a while.' He sees my face. 'Is that a problem?'

'No, nothing.' I couldn't explain to Gordon why I have a bad feeling about Patsy knowing something. But he's just been in and out of our family this last while. He's worse than the Church.

I put it to one side and sit back into the armchair. We've planning to do.

'We'll need archaeologists to do a bit of digging around, Ann. There are a couple of standing stones buried there.'

'Neans told me the old people used to say it was the entrance to the fairies' world.'

'We'll need planning permission from them as well so.' He laughs.

We're both excited by our new couple of acres. By the end of two cups of tea and four of Flora's buns – I made a bit of a pig of myself – the ideas are flying out of us. We've a piece of paper with *Kilsudgeon Town Park Proposal* written at the top of it and a clatter of bulletpoints.

'I'll type this up if you'll do the email addresses from the meeting, Ann.'

'Right you are, Chairperson,' I say, a bit girlish. But feck it, what harm? It isn't every day you change your village.

9

TOOSDAY

'I'm sick of … this … Ann.'

It's the following week now, and Tommy is still hanging on, but he's getting very down in himself. It should be strange to say that the dying are down, but I've seen plenty who are in great form up until the end. As if they have no list of things to do. No worries. But Tommy is down. He's depressed the sister hasn't showed up. Sally told me that Tommy was always talking about the sister in America, how she was making a great fist of it and sending him photos of a ranch.

'How is … Tidy Towns going … Ann? Will you be putting … flowers around … the fairy fort?'

'We're just planning and plotting, Tommy. We wouldn't dream of going near the field until—'

I realize again what I'm saying. It's very hard when Tommy is so on the ball about his own death.

'Until I'm gone … I know … Ann. I'm just … waiting for Una. No … reply yet, Noel?'

Noel looks at his feet and mutters that there wasn't any reply and he would try her again, and then we hear the sound of a car stopping on the road outside and a door opening, and he looks up and I cannot believe the change in his face. The colour is draining out of it as I'm looking at him. The mouth is open. I look out the window to see what he's gawping at.

A fine figure of a woman is striding up the path towards the front door. She looks like she means business. She looks familiar, but I can't place her. I glance at Tommy, and that's where I see the resemblance.

The doorbell goes. Noel doesn't move. He's wincing, as if he's just thought of a bad memory.

'Are you ... going to get ... the door, Noel?' says Tommy.

Still no stir from Noel, apart from taking out his little Nokia and rolling it around in his hand.

'Ann ... will you answer the ... door there, please. Noel, what's ... the matter with you?'

I go out into the hall and down to the door and open it. It's swelled with the damp weather, so I'm struggling with it for a while and it's a grunting me that opens the door to a woman with a bouffant of blond hair and a big long leather coat.

'Can I help y—' I start to say.

'Who the hell are you? I wanna see my brother!'

She goes right past me into the house. I follow her in slowly as I start to twig what's happening. There's a scene already developing in Tommy's room.

'UNA! ... You ... made it ... at last,' says Tommy.

'Whaddya mean, AT LAST? I only found out you were sick on Tuesday and I took the first flight I could get.'

She says 'Toosday'. This was the sister all right.

'But Noel's sending you ... messages for days.'

'Tommy, I have not received a single goddamn message! The first I heard you were sick was when your local

81

representative reached out to me – that guy Duggan? Real go-getter. While I was on vacation. He said it wasn't his business to say but that I should know my brother wasn't well. I said, "Why hasn't anyone told me?" and Duggan tells me I should ask my nephew Noel about that.'

'Noel … what do you … have to say … for yourself?'

Noel stares at the floor and checks his little phone to see if anyone would rescue him. There'll be no help from a Nokia. Not even an iPhone would help Noel out now.

'Noel?'

'You said you were holding on for her. It would kill you.'

'What?'

'You said you wanted to say goodbye to her before you went, so I didn't tell her because you'd go then sudden and I'd be on my own.'

'Noel … Noel … you can't keep … me alive. I have … half of one lung … I would have died anyway … Oh, Noel … you gobshite … come here to me.'

Noel leans over the bed and Tommy hugs him into him so much that Noel falls over on top of Tommy. It isn't grace-ful, but it's lovely in its own way. Noel is crying.

'This is so beautiful, you guys, a teachable moment,' says Una, and then she notices me again.

'I'm sorry, what was your name?'

'Ann … Ann Devine.'

'Ann, thank you so much for what you are doing for my brother,' and she sort of leaves it like that. Una is telling me in an American way to go.

I pack up my bag as they're talking. I take my time, like a player being substituted when his team is leading. Una makes herself at home very quickly and hooshes Noel out of the room to bring her bags in and make her tea. Tommy looks happy, but he catches my eye at one point and I see a small doubt. Or maybe it's his cataracts. Una is asking him how he is and telling him about herself and giving out about her flight.

I walk down the hall to the front door. I chance a look at the luggage label. OONA MULLINS. So that's how she spells it. Noel comes past as I'm snooping on the label. I straighten up quickly, but he looks at me and says something in a voice I haven't heard out of him before, firm – sort of hard, you could say.

'There was another reason I didn't ring her, Ann.' And then he hears her call for him inside and he scuttles back up the hall with one of her bags. I let myself out and I'm full of questions about Noel's mysterious admission, only Rory rings me and hangs up straightaway. If I don't call back soon he'll use that as an excuse not to call for months.

He answers. It's noisy in the background.

'Where are you? That doesn't sound like college.'

'It's a study room, Mam. We're doing practicals.'

A voice that must be from a telly says: 'You know not the things in which you meddle, Assassin. I spare you only that you may return to your master and deliver a message.' There are lads swearing in the background. I recognize the music.

'*Assassin's whatchamacallit?* Ah, for feck sake, Rory, are you wasting time with computer games as well?'

'Just unwinding, Mam, from the stress of the course.'

'And how is the new course going?'

'Great, Mam. They're only messing in the Tech. Uni is where it's at.'

'Uni? You're in uni now.'

'Oh, relax, Mam. Culchies can say "uni" too. What's going on in your life anyway? Are you pining without me?'

'I'm having a great time. Just back from Tommy's.' And I tell him about Oona arriving.

'Oh, his sister is home. He'll be brown bread soon so.'

'How did you know about him waiting for her?'

'I don't know. You must have told me, Mam.'

'Oh, right. Will you promise me you'll do a bit of work now? You can't be failing this year as well. You'll be a mature student by the time you leave.'

'No fear, Mam. I'm actually interested. Patsy was spot on about this course. It's politics and auctioneering. It's a fascinating combination.'

'C'MON, RORY, LAD, WE CAN'T PAUSE IT ANY MORE. THE AZERBAIJANI LAD IS LOSING HIS SHIT WAITING,' says a voice in the background.

'Better go, Mam. Bye.'

'Hang on, Rory, I never—'

But he's hung up.

I'm almost certain I never told him about Tommy waiting.

It's different up at Tommy's in the week since Oona arrived. Tommy is rambling a bit more. He's not happy. He looks at me suspiciously when I go near him and he does be shouting a bit about thieves and bastards. And Oona is installed there in his room on the good chair, which Noel must have brought in for her. She watches me like a hawk. Suggesting things. I very nearly say to her, *Oh, do you have training in this area, Oona?*, but I don't because she might be straight back to me with a sharp reply and I'm never as good with the second answer. So I don't enjoy it as much at all up there now. Even Denis notices I'm a bit down over it and, on a Friday afternoon, when I'm at home making a stew, I get a text.

ive a surprise for you annie

Denis texts me about twice a week and usually it's 'grand' or 'what time?' So this text has me intrigued. What can he want? I wonder. Denis doesn't usually do surprises. *I'm spontaneous as the next man*, he says, *as long as I've a bit of notice.*

I hear the lorry park outside. If I were a houseproud type with a lovely garden, I'd probably have words about him parking a big Iveco outside the wall, but it doesn't bother me.

In he comes with a big bundle of brown bags. The smell hits me.

'I've stew on, Denis.'

'The stew will keep, or you can dip it, if you want. Forget about Oona now for a while. There's no better way to celebrate your Tidy Towns job, Ann, than a rake of takeaway wrappers. We should throw them around the road to make work for your first clean-up.'

I look through the bags. 'Did Nawaz give you the extra shovel?'

'Only when I said it was for you.'

'Battered sausages and onion rings. Three bars of Dairy Milk! Jesus, Denis, are you trying to make me fat so no one else will want me?'

'That's the plan, Ann. I've been putting myself beyond reach for so long now. Anyway, Nawaz had them three for two euro.'

'He's still pushing the bars, so?'

'Not even telling Joe about it. Joe doesn't want chocolate in a chipper. He's a purist. Nawaz plans to show him the big ball of money he's making off it.'

Nawaz is the *Indian Pakistani from Bangladesh*, as he calls himself, because no one ever gets his country right. He has three brothers working in Topazes up and down the country and they're all of them doing a roaring trade in selling chocolate cheap with the petrol. They pretend to be Turkish some days, to get rid of the Turkish Delight and the Caramello, because no one eats them, only oddballs, apparently. For years he's been trying to get Joe Barry to do the same in the chipper, but no dime, as the fella said.

'And ... De-daahhh!'

'Cans, Denis? You're sweeping me off my feet. Making me feel like a young girl again.'

'C'mon, sure. We've the house to ourselves. Throw on the Netflix there while we're eating and it might have warmed up a bit so we can watch it.'

The internet is chronic still, even with Rory and his gaming gone, but we've convinced ourselves if we load it up a bit in advance and don't surprise it there'll be enough Netflix to get us through an hour before it knows where it is. It makes it very tense to know if it'll get to the end of an episode. We're nearly more tense about that than the thriller we might be watching.

We dole out the chips and the quarter-pounders. Denis orders me to turn off the phone.

'You're not paid to be on call, Ann. Tommy will hang on another bit. Show me over a can of beer there till I ruin it.'

We're in high spirits. Date night – is that what the young people call it? We never dated. We were just going together. Which kind of makes it sound like we happened to be headed in the same direction and said, 'Why don't we travel in the one vehicle?' Which in a way is what our marriage is. Nothing fancy. But happy out.

The Netflix looks like it might be good to go for a bit anyway. We even chance another episode, but it falls apart halfway through a murder. We turn on the proper telly then, but it's all depressing. Another report on rural Ireland. We're emptying, apparently.

'I don't know how we're still alive at all,' says Denis.

Normally, this kind of combination might lead to a bit of carry-on, but when we're off to bed the burgers and chips have us handicapped rightly. We should have done it the other way round. We promise we'll get back to it later. The following day is Saturday anyway, and we look forward to the lie-in.

10

CASING THE JOINT

It's halfway through the Saturday before I remember the phone. Just as I go looking for it, there's a knock at the door. It's Sally.

'You lock the door these days, Ann, do you? You're dead right. There's all sorts of latchikos doing the rounds now. I saw some crowd with yellow number plates around earlier and I going to the shop. Casing the joint, I'd say.'

We're all up to date on the crime lingo now.

'You can't be too careful, Sally. You're out early yourself.'

'I thought I'd get a few bits done because I'll be out at the rosary later.'

'Wait a minute now. What rosary?'

'Tom Mullins ... Ann, didn't you hear?'

'Tom MULLINS? When?'

'Last night, Ann. I thought you'd have been up there.'

I let on I'm on the way out and half usher Sally out the door. Then I go mad searching for the phone. It's dead. 'C'mon, you usless yoke!' I shout at it and I wait for the thing to charge. Never mind a watched kettle never boils, is there a slower thing than watching a phone wake up?

What possessed me to switch off the phone? They're all on about it now. Digital Detox. Well, it's good to tox sometimes. Wait! Here she is up now with the apple.

Bzzz bzzzz bzzzz Bip Bzzzzz

Nineteen missed calls from Noel. And then one text: *He's gone Ann. Where were u. Auntie Oona is making all the decisions. Can u come around. Patsy here too.*

'*Shit!*' I'm shouting by myself in the kitchen as all the buzzes and beeps from all the other things I've missed come through. Tracy texting about updating the Defecation Logs. Geraldine looking for minding for Freya. I'm cursing Denis now for his date night and myself for turning the thing off.

I get into the car and speed up to Mullins's.

Straightaway I can see the lie of the land has changed. There are people in and out of the house that I don't recognize, and certainly none of them is those who called around when Tom was wheezing his way through the last three months. Noel is standing outside. Adrift. More assertive people than him are walking right past him. The man is not able for this kind of thing at all.

'He's inside, Ann.'

Noel produces a fag from behind his back where he had his hands. I'm on the point of asking him when did he start smoking, but I leave him off.

'You need one sometimes, Ann,' he says, reading my face, and he horses the last of the fag and flicks it against the concrete dog.

Tommy is laid out on the bed where I'd left him before. Even though I'd been saying goodbye to him for weeks, it's still a shock that he isn't there, watching and gasping out an instruction or apologizing for the state of the place and gently blaming Noel. I don't know what Noel will do. He's not exactly a practical man. A bit innocent, and no match for his aunt.

The sister is holding court. Taking whatever condolences are going for herself. They can't have been that close. She hasn't been around in a good while and, by the looks of the clothes, she could have afforded to come back more often. And Patsy Duggan is there as well too. As I walk in, she's talking about *opportoonidies* with him. That man is haunting me. I look at Tommy, almost to see whether he'd give a scowl to have Patsy so close to him.

The undertaker comes in with a brochure and she's not happy with the choice.

'My brother will not be buried in any of these cardboard boxes, Eugene.'

The Americans are great for finding out a name of someone they want to give out to. I don't believe we ever knew the names of the men who buried Daddy. She'll have poor Noel's money spent before he's out of fags if she can't find a coffin in that brochure.

I sort of edge my way forward and put a hand on Tommy's arm.

'Is there anything I can do to help?'

'WE'LL TAKE IT FROM HERE, MS DEVINE.' The voice has got louder the longer she's been around.

'Oh, it's just, you know, I knew Tommy well, and if there's anything ...'

'We'll be really sure to call you, dear.'

Only she said *rilly*. And *dear*. That doesn't sound friendly. Patsy doesn't even acknowledge me and goes back to talking to Oona as I leave. I'll be the last to know, as usual, but watching Patsy and Oona, heads bent together, talking away, I suddenly get a pang of worry about our little fairy field.

11

CAT MALOGEN

'Mind your nice coat, Sally. You'll destroy it with that cement dust.'

Sally is with me in the car. Denis took the Skoda, so I'm stuck with his Polo, the yoke he uses to get to and from the truck if it's parked over in the yard. I can barely see out the windscreen for the dirt from the gravel pit. Before Sally can sit in, I have to throw Declan Nerney tapes into the back seat.

Would you not have had the car washed? I'd said to Denis.

I didn't know your mother was going to need her corns pared the same day.

Mam was going to a different funeral tomorrow. It's all funerals these days. She's convinced it's the water is doing away with people. She read it in one of her magazines. But while she's still alive she wants her feet right so that she can stand. *I don't like going to a funeral and having people looking at me thinking, I suppose you'll be next.*

I bring a rug for Sally to sit on. She likes a funeral. But only if she has the right person to discuss it with.

'Are you lonesome after Tommy, Ann?'

'I am. But I don't let myself think about it too much.'

'How many of your people have died now, Ann?'

She means how many I've cared for. I have to think about that. I've been doing this for fifteen years, once Rory started school. I was trying to count the funerals. They sort of blend into one another unless something out of the ordinary happens, which it rarely does. I come up with twenty over the years.

'Do you get used to it? You see them a bit more than the rest of us.'

'I don't know. I miss the routine of visiting them, and some of them were lovely people, but some would be hard enough to like, like Nonie. And then there's the fear that one of them would go leaving you something.'

'Wouldn't that be lovely?'

'Lovely if there wasn't a family gunning for you with solicitors' letters and the whole lot. I've avoided it, but Demelza, one of the Filipina girls, was left only a handbag. The daughter went after her as if she'd done away with the mother.'

'I wasn't a bit sad when Donal died, would you believe, Ann? I got sick of minding him. Am I awful?'

I don't know what to say to that.

'Ah, Jesus, Ann, don't go silent on me now.'

'I'm not gone silent, Sally. I just don't have anything to say.'

'After I said I didn't miss my husband? That was some time to go dry.'

'Well, it's a big thing to say.'

'I know.'

And then she goes silent. Luckily, the funeral is huge, which gives us something else to talk about. The traffic

91

outside the church is cat malogen. There's men – relatives of Tom, I suppose – out directing traffic in their hi-vises. Some poor Learner is having an awful time trying to park and one man in the hi-vis is going balubas with the effort of the signalling.

And into this fuss I drive. The new vice-chairperson of the Tidy Towns committee with the dirtiest jalopy in the place. We go past all the finest of cars. I thought they were part of the funeral cortège, but there must be money on the Mullins side. There's a few old cousins who are bachelors. They're the kind to change their cars once in a generation, but when they buy, they buy well. And this must be changing year.

'Not many of this crowd will have the NCT test for a while,' says Sally, looking at all the new number plates. 'You must need a cert for this car nearly monthly at this stage, would you, Ann?'

She's still sore, so.

'Tom was a man of faith, a man of God. His faith was simple, but it was strong,' says Father Donnegan.

He says that about everyone. I remember we were all smiling when he told us Jimmy Toolan was a man of faith. Jimmy Toolan, who was Kilsudgeon's only confirmed out-and-out atheist. But he died young, and his mother ignored everything he'd said for thirty years and buried him with his father with the full-kit-and-caboodle ceremony.

I'm not sure about Tommy's faith either. He never asked for the priest when he was feeling close to the end. He never went to Mass that I knew of, and any conversation I had with him he was always giving out about how a priest never died during the famine. I didn't know enough about the famine to disagree with him.

'A great man for the local community, and his generosity will be remembered by future generations.'

Now that's more like it. Obviously, Father Donnegan is hinting at the field. I see Gordon further up across the aisle and look at the back of his head. He straightens up a bit.

Father Donnegan announces that Oona Beauregard would like to say a few words. I have to think who he means for a second. She stands like she has no fear of this sort of set-up. She strides up to the altar as if she was a priest or a server. Not the way locals would. I did a reading at Kevin's wedding and I nearly tripped over the two steps, I was so bamboozled at being at that end of the church. It's the height. You'd think you'd like to be looking down on your neighbours until you see them all looking at you.

'Thank you, Father Donna*hew*,' says Oona. She makes a big fuss of adjusting the microphone, pauses and then looks us all dead in the eye – however she managed it, like the *Mona Lisa*.

'My fellow mourners, it's October twentieth. A little girl and a little boy are walking along a road. A road that neither of them knows what is at the end of it ...'

'What's she talking about?' whispers Sally next to me.

It turns out to be the story of Oona and Tommy, she just tells it in the American way.

'... we frequently wrote one another. He would tell me how all of you were doing, our beloved neighbours. I read these and smiled from my office on the thirty-fifth floor. I guess you could say I came up in the world.'

She smiles after this and looks around. We don't know what to make of it. There's definitely more people thinking about her than Tommy anyway. Maybe that was the plan. She goes on and on about how great America is, but how she misses the simple life back home.

'... and the little girl has come back to bury,' she wipes her eye, 'the little boy.'

And that was the speech. No mention of Noel, the care he had given, the neighbours, nothing, and Father Donnegan has to kick off the clapping because we're too stunned to stir.

'We should make some sort of a move outside,' says Sally, 'for the shake-hands, after as we missed it at the start.'

But as they pass after Tommy down the aisle Oona looks right through me and even Noel doesn't seem to want to look at me. What's after happening at all? I get afraid then that I'm after making a bags of something of Tommy's care. Did they find a complication? Tracy would love that. Thank God she's not here. Funerals are definitely not her thing. *I haven't time to be going to funerals, Ann. I need to replace the client.*

I see Noel after and go up to give him a hug, but he seems a bit stiff in it.

'I'm so sorry, Noel. How are you at all?'

'Ah, grand, Ann. You know. I'd better go now, Ann. You know.'

The poor man is in shock, I think, and then I see him being wrapped up in Patsy's entourage. Patsy and a few more Duggans, like a pack of beagles. It's not like Noel is my son or anything, but I feel the same feeling as when I hear Rory talk about Patsy. I don't have time to think further about this because I hear familiar voices behind me.

'Ann and Long Tall Sally, hah?'

The Nolans are there again, ready for action.

'Good turnout, Ann,' says Liam.

'He'd have been happy with that, Ann,' says Larry. 'And he wouldn't have been the most popular.'

'Not wan bit,' agrees Liam.

'Is that what they're saying, lads, is it?' I'm not saying anything because Denis says, as sure as anything, you'll be the one caught saying something if the wrong person walks past.

Sally isn't up to speed, though, and she gets sucked in. 'Why is that, Larry?'

But they're not interested in Sally. They act like they haven't heard. I swear they're like midges. And I've sweet blood.

''Twas your crowd that tipped him over the edge, Ann,' says Larry.

'Oh, right?'

'The Tidy Towns. There's talk you're getting the field. And then he's gone straightaway. People would be looking at that suspicious.'

'Ye'll probably need to make a statement.' Liam is winking away at the brother. They're getting into their stride.

'I heard they've brought Gordon in for questioning.'

'File gone to the DPP, I'd say.'

'Out on bail, though. Everyone gets bail in this country.'

'Bags of rubbish taken away as evidence.'

'Would be the first bags taken out of here in a while.'

'They'll dump them back again.'

'Oh, ye lads are hilarious altogether. Will I see ye at the clean-up on Saturday, anyway? It's the first one so we need a big turn-out.'

'We'll be there with the trucks, Ann. As long as we don't prejudice the inquiry, hah?'

'Good luck, lads. C'mon away, Sally. Before we die laughing.'

We walk towards the car.

'Are we going to the graveyard, Ann?'

'I don't know that we'd be welcome. They'll go past the house first. But I can't get home without passing it. But I can't get past it now because we're blocked in.'

After all the stress of getting parked, the L-plate woman has us blocked in, so we're stuck now. We sit in and wait for a while.

'Do you mind if I smoke, Ann? Would Denis be bothered by it?'

'You can do mushrooms in this car, Sally. It won't make a blind bit of difference. It might take some of Denis's smell out of it.'

We sit for a while saying nothing, looking at the cars leaving.

'I'll give it a go now. Surely it's gone in the lane to the cemetery.'

But it hasn't. We're three or four hundred yards down the road when the procession comes into view again. Stopped dead in the road, with no sign of movement. I weave out a bit into the other side to see what I can see.

What I can see, before I pull back in, is a quad bike on its side. Yet another bearded fella, no man bun this time, is standing around looking shook.

'Who would drive a quad bike into a funeral?' says Sally.

It's a fair question that I think anyone would ask in the circumstances.

The hi-vis lads are out again, directing traffic. Thankfully, he didn't drive into the hearse, so that was able to go on. He went into the car with Oona in it, of all people. I'm thinking she'll have the army called in, but no, she's just there talking to Patsy and it's all very civil.

We drive past, as signalled by the hi-vis man. A little bit up the road, near Tommy's house, there's a fella taking photos. I thought first he was from the *Kilsudgeon Sentinel*, not able to believe his luck to see a car crash in a cortège. But as I get closer I see he's pointing the camera in the other direction, away from the accident. Towards Tommy's fairy field.

12

THE HEDGES HAVE MOUTHS

'Well? How do I look?'

  'Are you supposed to look a certain way?' says Denis.

  'It's a public occasion.'

  'Aren't ye picking up rubbish?'

  'I know, but people would be looking at me.'

  'Ann, you go around most of the time with the same fleece on anyway. Why are you getting all het up over it now?'

  I leave him be. I'd need Deirdre for this kind of discussion. Denis has two good jumpers – the one Mrs Richardson liked and then another one from a charity shop that he tells everyone proudly that he paid two euro for. He never has or never will be a help when it comes to my outfits. There's *Say 'Yes' to the Dress* and then there's *Say 'Grand' to the Jumper*. I miss the daughters around the place. Rory, actually, in fairness to him, was surprisingly good to tell me an opinion. Unfortunately, he was far too critical and nothing I owned *worked in this century*.

  'What time are you kicking off?'

'Are you not going as well?'

He blows out through his lips and focuses on the television. As if to suggest I should continue to leave him be. I'm surprised at Denis. He's always saying how there's no one around the place who'd do a bit and then, when presented with the chance, he's in his socks flicking between wrestling and Brexit.

'It'll look odd if I'm there and you're not there.'

'Why will it look odd?'

'They'll be saying, why should we support that when she's not even getting any support from the husband?'

'Who's *they* that'll be saying this?'

'Who is *they* ever? Just *they*. The hedges have mouths around here, Denis. C'mon. You weren't doing anything anyway.'

'I was looking forward to doing nothing.'

'The exercise will do you good.'

'What do you mean by that?'

'You're putting on weight, Denis, we both are. The bed is getting small.'

'I didn't notice.'

'Well, I did. And it's my job to notice these things and mind you. I see enough old people who need to be lifted with hoists. I'm not going to be lifting you, so get out of those slippers now and turn off the television or we'll be late. You'll thank me when you don't have gout.'

'I don't have gout now.'

'That's thanks to me.'

He gives a big, exaggerated sigh and after a few seconds drags himself out of the chair with a big groan and a stretch.

'Right so, Sir Humphrey.' He always says that when I've bested him.

We arrive at the hall and already there's a crowd gathering. It was called out at the Masses, apparently, and in the school, so a good few have been shamed into it.

Actually, I shouldn't say 'shamed'. There's a different sort of spirit about this. Excited. Something I haven't seen in a while around here. People are even a bit giddy. Gordon has a box on the ground in front of him and he's handing out bibs.

'Put these on, team – everyone is starting up front today, haha.'

'No subs, Gordon?'

'No! Everyone is getting their game.'

'I'm injured, Commissioner Gordon,' says one of the twins. I couldn't make out which one.

I pick out two bibs for myself and Denis. As I unfold mine and hold it out to get a proper look at it, I stop. Drawn right across it, in huge print on both sides, it says DUGGAN ENVIRONMENTAL, and KILSUDGEON TIDY TOWN tiny on the front, stuck on at the last minute, by the looks of things.

'What's the story with the bibs, Gordon?' I say to him, out of earshot of the group.

'Aren't they great?'

'Gordon, for ffffffff—' I just about hold it in. I wouldn't want to be starting off a clean-up cursing at Gordon. I doubt he gets cursed at much at home.

'What's the matter, Ann?'

'Gordon, we'll be walking around the roads like billboards for Patsy's cousin's waste place. Duggan Environmental. You know the rumours about them and the dumping and the smells up there?'

'Ann, I think you're letting your personal feelings against Patsy get in the way of what we're trying to do here. They've been very good in helping us get off the ground.'

'Gordon, the man a pure snake and he's ...'

'Ann, there's a great crowd here now. Are you going to spoil it?'

'Give me the bib. But I'm not a bit happy about it.'

Denis isn't happy either, and just wears the bib I brought with FUN RUN FOR CANCER written on it.

I get over myself, though, because there is a great crowd there, in fairness. There's all sorts. For all the messing, the twins turn up. A few of the golf-club set as well, no doubt spending the morning looking for clothes bad enough to wear out and still managing to look better than me at the doctor's.

'The spirit of Kilsudgeon lives on!' Gordon is standing halfway up the ditch in a pair of expensive-looking wellies. He has just given us all another little speech. He got a bit carried away. Apparently, he used to be in the drama groups before.

The 'spirit of Kilsudgeon' might be a bad choice of words. It comes from the time the IRA were supposed to have driven the Black and Tans out, but the real story is that there were about five Tans around and the IRA were mainly going around Kilsudgeon burning Protestants' houses. But maybe it's an act of forgiveness on Gordon's part.

'Today is our Independence Day ... the hi-vis army is on the march!'

I decide to jump in gently.

'We might start with the clean-up there, Gordon, before it gets dark,' I say to him, and whether it's the spirit of Kilsudgeon in me or being annoyed at having a Duggan name on my back, I get a rush of blood to the head and start organizing. Me! Sending high-powered prominent local residents off to the different areas around the town. Professionals, no doubt, with all sorts of job titles, like facilitators doing dynamic this-and-that. And me ordering them around Kilsudgeon like a general.

'Doctor, will you go towards Dooney's? And take Derek and Sarah with you,' I can hear myself saying it, but barely recognize it. The doctor and the accountants go off to pick choc-ice wrappers out of ditches.

'Sounds good, Ann,' they said, like they expected to be told where to go. It was like figuring out how to train a dog for the first time. No fear. Don't let them know you're afraid, Ann.

Someone gives me a light kick in the back of the leg.

'Where'll I start, Ann?'

Neans! There in her wheelchair, with the picker across her lap. She hasn't been out of the house in ages. And she's with the carer she doesn't like. The sour-faced wan, Tina from Dransha, who does the weekends with her. Normally, Neans tells her to go out to the car and have a fag and she'll ring her if she needs her. That's completely against the rules, but it's the only way they'll get on. But today there is Neans, with the still-sulky Tina standing behind her wearing the hi-vis, probably disgusted it doesn't go with her nails.

A photographer has turned up from the *Kilsudgeon Sentinel*. He's all bustly and full of chatting and silly little jokes to keep people from noticing he's getting them to act the eejit. Neans and Tina are in his firing line first.

'Put the picker across you there – Neans, is it? Like a sword. That's it. Now, act like you're fighting the litter louts. Good woman.'

'I'll throw this at them!' Neans points to 'the bag'.

'There's no stopping you now … Ah, Tina, give us a smile. It might never happen, hah?'

Tina forces out a smile. I'd never seen her teeth before. She's a bit like myself. We could have both done with the free dentist growing up.

He's moving around, trying to get people to jump up and put on quare poses. I don't fancy his job. Kilsudgeon isn't a high-jinks sort of place. We have a reputation for being cagey. But there are enough youngsters here today to play-act a bit and loosen us all up. Before long we're practically on Broadway.

I don't know would any of us talk to each other if we hadn't had children.

Then the photographer comes up to me and starts chatting about the whole operation as he's writing down the names for the photos. I'm a bit flustered. He's asking me what the plans are long term and I talk about the Tidy Towns and mention that we might have a place that we can make into a little garden.

'A sort of a town park, would you say?' He's scribbling a huge amount of names. I don't know how he has the memory for all of them.

'That would be lovely, wouldn't it? If we want something done, we're going to have to do it ourselves, especially as the politicians are doing sweet FA, if you'll excuse my language.'

'Thanks very much, Mrs ...'

'Ann Devine.'

'Ah, yes, I have your name already. That's great, you've given me plenty.'

Given him plenty? What a strange thing to say.

'Where'll you go, Ann?' asks one of the twins, who, it seems, have been standing there all along. 'Will you be directing operations from your trailer?'

'Hands off, I'd say she'll be.'

'Three-hundred-and-sixty-degree view they call it.'

'Full circle, that's right.'

'I will not be hands off. I'll do the boats.'

'Good girl yourself, Lady Vice-chairperson.'

I'm telling you, there's nothing like a bit of a title to make you stick your neck out. And I *was* sick of those boats.

The boats. If ever there was a sign that this wasn't our first Tidy Towns attempt, it's the boats. The council brought in eight of them years ago. They were planted with fierce swanky flowers, and all was grand until a man arrived with a low-loader one day and tipped over one of them, spilling the earth and all the plants out on to the road. Anyone who was nearby said he was just roaring at the ditch, saying they were his boats and the council shouldn't be buying stuff from receivers, and he was going to come back for the rest of them and drive the digger into the council offices unless he got a few bob. Then he knocked over another boat. Seemingly, Patsy turned up in a jeep and handed over an envelope and yer man went away cursing. And then the sergeant nabbed him for tax and drink on the way out, fined him on the spot and got the whole envelope back again. Someone threw the earth from the boats over a ditch, but there wasn't much inclination to go on maintaining the boats after that.

I park near the worst of the remaining boats. It's a sight. It's full of dead grass from last year, and leaves and all sorts of rubbish. A crate of those small beer bottles you get thirty for half-nothing up in Lidl. I even found a bag of old computer CDs. *Final Masters Thesis* was written on one of the ones that fell out of it. I hope they got a job out of it.

Then there are the coffee cups. Does anyone bring a flask these days?

There is worse than coffee cups in there as well too. I'm glad they're all taking so many precautions around here.

It's dirty work, but you'd get lost in it. Mindfulness they call that now.

A 4X4 with a sort of big rump at the back pulls up beside me while I'm all Zen. The window winds down. A man leans across. He looks comfortably off, although the 4X4 has muck all over the side of it. He has sort of a golfy tan. He looks at me in all my finery, with my old duds and battered runners and up to my elbows in topsoil and Coke cans.

'That isn't a bad day to be out doing a good deed,' he says. 'I was wondering if you could direct me to a place called Edenmere House? Patrick Duggan's place? He gave me the house name and I was going to put him in the sat nav, but the thing's given up on me.'

'That'd be right, with the internet around here.' I give him the directions, but I'm fierce anxious to know a bit more without seeming nosey. Which is what I am.

'It's a fine house, Edenmere. He made a nice job of it.'

'Aye, right enough.' His answer is no good to me.

'He's some operator is Patsy.'

'Aye, you could say that, aye.' There's a sort of smile in the side of his mouth now. We both know what's going on here.

'Would you know Patsy well?' I just come right out and say it or we'll be here all day.

'Aye, a bit. First time down here, though.' That's as much as I'm going to get. 'By the way, what's the story with all the signposts? I never saw so many signposts for one town in my life. You'd end up in this spot whether you wanted to or not.'

I have to laugh. 'That's right. All roads lead to Kilsudgeon, they say.'

He isn't the first visitor to mention all the signposts. That was another Patsy special. He was councillor around here before he was a TD, and he said he was going to put Kilsudgeon on the map. Every junction for about thirty miles around has a signpost for Kilsudgeon on it. It's a wonder you don't see it at Dublin Airport after you collect your bag, he got so many of them put up. Jennifer told me she's found leaflets for *Visit Kilsudgeon – the Beating Heart of Ireland* in her airplane magazine a few times because Patsy has a niece who's an air-hostess. More than a few times tourists have wandered into the town expecting something to be there because of all the signs. But they'd drive off fast enough. And now with the bypass, even though there are about forty signs up, people just go right around the place.

Of course, while he was putting up all these signs, the mobile library closed down for the want of a few bob.

I leave all of this out of what I told yer man. You don't know who you'd be talking to. He closes up the window and drives off. And I look at the reg to see the age, but the number plates are yellow. So *that* must be one of the Northern regs everyone was talking about. What was Patsy up to with a load of Northerners? Had he got mixed up with the IRA or what? There was a filling station done for green diesel a while back in Drumfeakle, but that was one of the few businesses around here *not* run by a Duggan. And then my mammy's mind starts running away with me and worry leads to worry and I start thinking, *What if Rory is in danger if there's paramilitaries around?* And nearly before I've recovered the run of myself I have already sent Rory a text.

Northern fella looking for directions to patsys house I hope u are not mixed up with ira

The phone beeps. A picture message from Rory. It's a baby with 'ARE YOU HIGH?' written on it in big white writing.

13

RIDING THE JUDGE

'They're kicking off again up in the North, Denis.'

No reply. Denis is buried in the paper. His boots are off and the big thick work socks that he doesn't wash often enough are up on the chair. He looks the picture of relaxation, but I've worries to share and he's the nearest, so tough luck, Denis.

'I said they're kicking off above in the North.' I point at the news on the telly. One of the Orangemen is giving out about, of all things, an Irish-dancing competition.

A provocative militant dance commemorating Republicans in battle ... affront to the Orange people ... 'Siege of Ennis' is clearly a crude and insulting metaphor for a thirty-two-county socialist republic.

'Stone mad they are,' I say.

'Stone mad is right,' he says, repeating without listening, and he rattles the paper up around him again to show he thinks he should now be considered off-duty.

'And if they do kick off again, there'll be carry-on down here too. Rory could be dragged into it. Do you remember during the Troubles they arrested students for making bombs?'

He says nothing.

'Denis?'

He puts down the paper with a big sigh.

'They were engineering students, Ann. They had the education for that. Rory can't even change a plug. What is it he says? *I'm the vision guy, Denis.* Anyway, didn't he say he wasn't involved in anything?'

'He said, *Are you high?* and sent a picture.'

'There you go, so.'

'I don't know. It's not an outright no. And it mightn't be up to him. They might be doing propaganda on him, like ISIS would, telling me it's all rosy in the garden. Or Patsy might be putting in a word.'

'No self-respecting paramilitary is going to get involved with Patsy Duggan. Even paramilitaries have to be careful about the company they keep. And if they are, they're not going to be sending a fella down with Northern number plates asking directions of someone on the road. Unless they have completely dropped their standards.'

'I know what makes *sense*, Denis, but we know so little about what he's up to these days. He could be involved in *anything* and we wouldn't know. He's drifted away from us. I get one text once a week. Where is it now?'

I search on my phone.

'*Story mam? And if I go back further. well mam? how's it going mammy?*'

'And how do you reply to him?'

'The usual. *All fine here.*'

'You're not exactly *War and Peace* yourself, Ann.'

'Yes, but it's not up to me to have news. He's the one away from home. He should have the news.'

'Haven't you been elected as vice-chairperson?'

'Deirdre will tell him that kind of thing. The point is that I don't know what he's up to. I have to find out from Freya what pyramid of cans he's after building. He could be drug-dealing or anything.'

'Is he a drug-dealer or a Real IRA bomb-maker now? Which is it? I'm glad he's busy anyway.'

The paper goes up again, though this time with less certainty. His right foot is wiggling.

'I don't think you're taking me seriously, Denis. It's always the same. I do all the work of the worrying and the thinking. At least do me the courtesy of listening.'

'I am listening, Ann. But lookit, he's twenty, Ann. Thirty years ago the likes of Rory would be gone to America, illegally up a scaffolding and making huge money, and probably working for much bigger gangsters than Patsy and getting into fights with black fellas in Hell's Kitchen over turf. And we would have got a letter once a month saying, *All is grand. They have lovely cars here*. I was mad as anything about Patsy making him go away to college without our say-so, but do you know something? Let him grow up a bit. Now, can't you turn off the news? You're upsetting my bit of a routine.'

His Thursday-evening routine is reading the local paper. Denis gets the *Kilsudgeon Sentinel* most weeks. *The world is your oyster. But Kilsudgeon is your home and you can't live in an oyster.* That's their slogan. There doesn't be much in it, but Denis likes to read the court cases.

'It's a very handy way of keeping up with the neighbours,' he tells me, and he opens a can. 'Look, here's a good one, Ann, to take your mind off our son the paramilitary. Just think about what some other poor mothers have to worry about. Listen to this now.' He reads out the headline. 'YOU'RE ONLY BUT A FASCIST PRICK. But they have the I crossed out. LOCAL MAN IN ANGRY RANT TO JUDGE. Davey Finnerty again.'

Davey features in the court cases about twice a year. He usually gets away with a fine because *he comes from a respectable family*, although they're getting sick of him. The last time there was no one in court for him. The mother has given up. This could be his last rodeo for a while after what happened. Davey had been part of the Kilsudgeon Communist Party – or rather, he was the other fella in the Kilsudgeon Communist Party – before a split with Gary on ideological grounds. I think the ideological difference was that Gary wasn't a headcase and Davey was. Nowadays he'd have got looked at, but they weren't looking out for much in Kilsudgeon Primary School in the eighties. They'd have him seen much earlier these days, or at least he'd be on a waiting list.

'Will I carry on?'

'Go on, so.'

'A Kilsudgeon man was threatened with contempt at a sitting of Castlestrokard District Court today and remanded in custody after he refused to recognize the authority of the court. David Finnerty with an address at The Pines, Meelart, hurled abuse at members of An Garda Síochána, the judge and his own solicitor.' Denis pauses. 'Davey's after taking things up a notch, isn't he? *Stating that he believed the constitution of 1937 was invalid as it was signed under duress by de Valera under pressure from a disgraced archbishop ...* and it goes on like that.'

'What did the judge say to him?'

'It says here, *He warned the defendant, "Don't be coming in here with your AERTEL law degree."* Then Finnerty started roaring that he was dismissing his solicitor who *"must have been riding the judge"* and would be defending himself under the Brehon laws of the country. That's when he told the judge to eff off, that he was a fascist prick.'

Denis takes a slurp of his can and then fairly shouts, 'WOULD YOU LOOK WHO IT IS?'

'I nearly dropped my tea, Denis. Who is it?'

'You! In the *paper*!'

'Me! In the courts bit?'

'Kilsudgeon Tidy Towns Vice-chairperson Accused of Land Grab.'

'WHAT? Show me!'

He angles the paper away from me. 'A prominent figure in local life is reeling ...'

'What?' Then I see his sly smile. 'Denis! You put the heart cross me! Oh God, I was seeing Tracy's face!'

I grab the paper off him and it's just the photos from the clean-up. The headline is *Killing the Sludge in Kilsudgeon*. There we all are, gathered around Neans in her wheelchair. Of course, my hair is all over the place and my mouth is open like a pure gom.

'He could have turned off the flash.'

The hi-vis was reflecting out so much we were like an apparition.

'I think he took this with his phone, Denis. I remember now he was all shapes with the expensive camera and then at the end he started looking at it and then he said, *One more for luck*, and he took that one with a phone.'

'Mightn't have switched it on. You're quoted as well. *Ann Devine, vice-chairperson (pictured), said, "This is only the beginning ... we hope very soon to be able to announce that we are going to be working on a town park on a piece of land near the centre of Kilsudgeon."* I was only joking about the land grab, Ann, but you're serious?'

'I never said no such thing.'

'Well, it's in the paper, so it must be true. You were *urging* the council, they said. Great to see you still get the urge, Ann. Well now, Annie, I hardly recognize you with your campaigning in the paper. I'd better up my game if I'm to be the First Husband.'

'But I never said anything to anyone about it. There was no reporter.'

My phone rings. It's Deirdre.

'Mammy, since when are you urging the council? I never took you for an urger.'

'I swear, Deirdre. I'm just after saying it to Denis here, I wasn't talking to any reporter.'

'You didn't say a word to anyone?'

'No. I was only chatting to the photographer.'

'What did the photographer look like?'

'I don't know. A photographer. Whatever a photographer looks like.'

'Did he have kind of mousey hair, not that washed-looking?'

'That's the one.'

'Yeah, that's the new editor. He's pulled that before. Borrows a camera and then gets people to chat away, thinking they're talking to a freelance photographer who's only doing it for the money. He was up at one of the tabloids before. I'd be surprised if he even knows how to operate a camera. He caught out the Minor trainer before, Shane. Chatting away to him. Before we know it, Shane is in the paper. *This is only a load of bollox* was the headline.'

Denis has gone out to the hall and come in with the land-line, talking away to whoever's on the line.

'Hello, Gordon. She is. Yeah. Just planning her urges now.'

'I'd better go, Deirdre. I'd say I'm in trouble with the bossman.'

I swap over the phones.

'I know, Gordon. I didn't know he was a reporter.'

'Ann, my dear woman, don't worry at all. It might get a bit of buzz going around the place. People are always looking for a story to latch on to. You might have just kickstarted something. Leave it with me, Ann. I've an idea I want to look at. Oh, and how is it coming along with the email addresses? It's been a few weeks now, Ann.'

'Grand, Gordon. We're flying.'

'Could you have them across to me tomorrow morning? I want to send out a few notes.'

I'm lying. We've done nothing with them. Because I'd been all keen when I agreed to do it but then I saw the amount of them and … oh, just the thoughts of that yoke of a computer we have made me keep putting it off. Denis is not going to be happy. He's opening another can now and wiring into the Lincoln biscuits. I decide to break the news to him indirectly.

'We're just going through it now as I'm talking to you. Right so, Gordon.' I hang up.

Denis looks at me. 'What are we going through?'

A separation, I think. He's a man with his rituals, and if there's an interruption …

'Look, all you have to do is read email addresses out to me and I'll type them in on the computer.'

He seems OK with that, as he can do it and hold a can at the same time. To sweeten the deal I bring out a Twirl I've been hiding. But the handwriting is chronic. And he wouldn't be used to the flow of an email address.

'Stevie Bee at YAHOO DOT … ah, I can't make this out at all. Panal R I J A N. Who's Panal Rijan? He sounds like some class of an Indian. Would Nawaz know him? I wonder.'

'Show it to me here. Ah, that's Paul Ryan, Denis.'

'*Him?* You'd think he'd have nicer writing. I'd be better than that and I've no education.'

If it wasn't the handwriting, it was the strange email addresses. You can tell a lot about people from their email address. We came across the most respectable people with madhoor31 and hitthediff10 and all sorts.

113

'Trust Noone – is that one of the Noones at Aghagubba? If it is, they've nobody in that family called Trust anyway. Unless one of them married a Nigerian in the last while. But I think we'd have heard.'

'What are you on about, Denis?' He hands the sheet across to me again, smiling.

'Trust No One – ah, you're taking the mick now, Denis.'

It was Sally's son, Donal, with his trustnoone234@gmail.com. He was in good company if there were another 233 fellas as paranoid as him out there. He won't get anywhere with that attitude, and him trying to apply for some FÁS course in digital marketing.

'Are you deliberately being useless, Denis, so I won't ask you to do it? That's an old trick, young fella, and I'm not falling for it. C'mon, keep going on that list and stop your messing.'

14

PURE DULL ROUTINE

It's Deirdre who suggests the table quiz.

We're out on our walk. Deirdre and me have a mammy–daughter walk when we can. Denis calls it the Security Council. Insecurity Council more like it. Deirdre gives out gently about Hughie. I listen and tell her she's after marrying her father. Then I tell her I'm worried about Rory ending up on *Reeling in the Years*, Jennifer never getting married and Kevin never coming back from Dubai. Or worse, Kevin coming back from Dubai and bringing Stephanie.

We meet up in the village and park outside Leona's. We walk out of town, past the church and the graveyard. But this time we take a right and decide to loop up around the fairy field.

'A fundraiser is the way to kick things off, Mammy,' she says when we've talked out our irrational fears. 'Lets people know you're serious. Continuity. That's what it's all about with voluntary. People need to know they won't look like a fool if they turn up. So *you* have to look like a fool for a while, to show them that they can jump in, the water's fine, so to speak. You see Father Donnegan there. What do you think keeps him going? Is it the Holy Spirit? No,' she says, answering herself. 'No, Mammy, it's all about the fundraising.'

'We had a great turn-out for the meeting and the clean-up.'

We have to stand in as a tractor comes flying around the corner. We're used to leaning against ditches.

'Means nothing, Mammy. The first thing of anything is easy. A few free biscuits and a microphone. That's heaven for some people. It's the bit after that when you find out who the properly committed are. That's how the Church got such a hold. They had one Mass, and then they had another one the following Sunday and they never stopped until you couldn't ignore them.'

'I think it was a bit more complicated than that, Deirdre.'

'No, Mammy. Routine. Pure dull routine. Church. GAA. Macra. Someone gets up out of their chair on a Monday evening and goes down and puts on the heat in a freezing hall and finds mouse dirt in the teabags and carries on and just does it. I'm telling you, the next thing now is the fundraising.'

'What did ye do?'

'What haven't we done? Coffee mornings, brunches, table quizzes, a comedy night.'

'Comedy night? I don't remember that.'

'That was when you were sick. Oh, Mam, stop, the mortification of it. We couldn't get anyone to come down for the money we were offering. And then this fella, he's a brother of one of the girls above in Dublin, said he was a comedian. Oh Mammy, it gives me the shudders still, thinking about it. No one laughed for the fifty minutes. He started off with something about fisting.'

'Fisting? As in a handpass? Wouldn't that have done the GAA grand?'

'Em ... yeah, Mammy, that's what it was. Don't google it. Don't watch any videos anyway. It got worse. I wake up sometimes and I see the crowd looking at him while he was screaming about his mother. There was another girl with one of these small guitars and she was just as bad, going on about her vagina and the boyfriend not wanting to, you know, go down ... How am I even talking to you about this, Mammy? The point is, you need a table quiz, Mammy, with handy small prizes that you can get for nothing. And Kilsudgeon has a bit of a name for table quizzes because the internet is so bad here people can't cheat like they cheat everywhere else. Johnny's is a blackspot, so now it's a hotspot.'

We have left the town and are back on to local gossip at this stage. Deirdre is updating me on the goings-on in her Mammy WhatsApp group. There is, it seems, a rake of rows brewing beneath the surface.

'And how do you know the two of them don't like one another?' I ask her about one particular pair of mammies.

'Whenever Aisling posts anything Laura changes the subject straightaway. It's weird. I could show you a hundred examples.'

'And what do you do?' I'm struggling to understand the politics of these new ways of falling out with people.

'I just post camogie training news and if I hear of any burglaries. Otherwise, I'd say the wrong thing, I know it.'

Soon we're up at the fairy field. I feel self-conscious about going in there, but Deirdre is up on the low fence and into the field with no hesitation. It hasn't had cattle in a while, so the fence isn't maintained. The gate is tied with rope. I scuttle down from the ditch. I haven't been in it in ages. It feels strange to be trespassing. We don't do that now like we used to. Long ago you'd go into nearly any place as long as there wasn't a sign about a bull. Tramping around the

117

countryside, exploring, getting scratched and stung and cow-dunged. When I think of all the compo we missed out on!

'C'mon, Mam, we'll have a look.'

We walk towards the fort. It's a small mound in the middle of the field, covered in trees. A good few of the stones out of it are on the ground nearby, kicked around by cattle over the years. We climb up the little slope. I slip in my runners and have mud on my knees like a small boy.

'That's the door there, where the two whitethorns are, Deirdre. Will we go in and see what kind of a set-up do the fairies have in their world?'

We walk over to it. Deirdre walks in and out a couple of times, and so do I.

'Do you feel anything different, Mam?'

A draught is all I feel. But then there's a kind of a humming, a vibration. I wouldn't be someone who'd have 'experiences'. Geraldine would be in her element here. There's definitely a sensation.

'Do fairies hum, Deirdre?'

'Only if they don't know the words, Mammy.'

'No, I mean … there's a humming sound.'

'I hear it too now. It's sort of up in the air.'

We look up, and there's a drone over the field. I wave at it.

'Why did you wave?'

'I don't know. A force of habit. Trains, buses, boats. You just wave at them, don't you?'

The drone doesn't wave back. It just flies back over across the field and appears to land behind Tommy's house, where a number of cars and jeeps are parked. I don't think they are post-funeral visitors.

Then I get a text. It's from Noel.

oonas watchig ye ann shes after getting a lend of a small plane.

15

AN ERROR HAS OCCURRED

'Ah, I'll break your lid off, I swear to fffff— I DID UPLOAD
IT!!! WHAT DO YOU MEAN, *NOT RECOGNIZED*? I DON'T
FFFF— I DON'T RECOGNIZE *YOU* … DENIS, COME IN
HERE AND STOP ME BEFORE I THROW THIS LAPTOP
OUT THE WINDOW!'

This is how I normally talk to the computer. I'm trying to
put in information.

I'm after finding a voicemail from Tracy from last Friday.
She loves emptying her mind of all the week's worries on
a Friday night by ringing to inform you of whatever bad
news has been bothering her all week.

'Can you call me when you get this, Ann? I am having
difficulty understanding,' she says on the message, 'why
there are still gaps in the data.'

And I am having difficulty with this bloody computer,
which keeps going doolally when I want to do the simplest
thing with it.

'What's wrong, Annie?' Denis comes into the bedroom where I am.

'I have to put a whole spiel about Tommy into the care system.'

'But he's dead. Isn't that the main thing? He's fairly carefree.'

'It still has to be put in, and I'm trying to add in bloody Oona as a care "entity". WHAT DO YOU MEAN, I DON'T HAVE THE REQUISITE PERMISSIONS LEVEL? And I can't do that without being an Admin and Tracy wants the whole thing tomorrow or there'll be another black mark against me.'

'Put in what you can. They'll have to file that away somewhere,' says Denis, looking at the screen, like, as he says himself, a dog looking at a phone.

He's right, though. I'll save what I have and that'll have to do for now.

HONG, says the computer.

I click it again.

HONG HONG.

CLICK CLICK.

HONG. *An error has occurred.*

'AN ERROR HAS OCCURRED? WHAT ERROR, DENIS?'

'I don't know what error, Ann.' Denis scratches behind his ear. 'Maybe it's the biscuits.'

'WHAT BISCUITS, DENIS?'

He means cookies. He must have heard me talking about them before. I have to laugh.

'Bring in the biscuits so, Denis. We'll draw a line under it. It'll keep until the morning.'

'The System is the same for everyone, Ann.'

I'm sitting in her office the following day. She has called me in: *I'm struggling to make sense of what you are saying.* Poor

Tracy and her struggles. When I get in and show her, she isn't having any of my explanations about errors and permissions.

Then she sighs and does exactly the same thing I was trying to do last night, but it takes less than ten minutes. I'm standing behind her desk going red and praying the computer will say HONG, but it doesn't. She calmly breezes through all the steps. The System sings for her. It might as well be laughing at me.

'I can't keep doing your job for you, Ann,' she says. 'This is unsustainable. Do we have a problem here?'

'No, Tracy, no problem,' I say, my voice getting lower and lower. I walk out of Tracy's office and start breathing out, *phoo-phoo-phoo*, just to get my bearings.

'Ann! Aaaa-annn!'

It's Geraldine, coming out of another unit in the same estate.

'What's the matter with you, Ann? Your shoulders are down.'

I tell her my story. She practically orders me to follow her in the car back to her house. She sits me in one of her odd-looking chairs that, might I say, is ferocious comfortable, and I don't know why I didn't sit in them before. She plugs her phone into a thing that looks like a bottle of perfume. Soon there's the sound of waves and she asks if I mind if she practises on my head.

'Women are very hard on other women,' says Geraldine. 'Very judgemental.'

I can't tell if she's hinting to me or not, but the head massage is working a treat. I must teach Denis how to do this.

'Do you want your ears candled?'

'Does that put the wax in or take it out?'

'It clears them out. You'll be able to hear the fairies with this thing.'

'I heard that it was supposed to be bad for your hearing in the end.'

'Then you heard wrong, Ann.'

I let her put in the candles.

'Technically, you're supposed to lie on a bench for this, but I don't have a bench. Maybe if I open up a healing centre. And I can tell Dinny and the men of the mountain and they'll have to come and pay me for their therapy. That's what you should do too. Just tell her to shove her job where the sun don't shine. Do you need the money that much?'

'I need it some bit.'

'You have Denis.'

'He doesn't make much, and I want my own money. Remember Mam would tell us to have our running-away money.'

'Tell me five good things that are happening now, Ann.' She lands that one on me.

'Well, there's the table quiz ... Oh, that reminds me!'

I'd forgotten to collect a prize from the butcher.

'Well, I'm glad I took your mind off things anyway,' says Geraldine as I get my things together and leave in a hurry.

16

FIZZY WATER AND SHANDIES

I'm up to ninety with this table quiz. I know there's mammies organize things in their sleep, but everything is taking me ages to do. I have to pluck up a bit of courage to look for prizes. I went into the golf club and came out with golf balls from the manager and a voucher for a four-ball, whatever that is. But I was outside in the car for half an hour beforehand, composing myself. But I'm discovering unknown depths. I designed a poster. I was very proud of my efforts, although it won't be winning any awards. And the computer worked fine for me to make it. File – Insert Picture from ClipArt – no bother to me. Change Font to one of those 3D ones – a piece of cake. Johnny's logo from the Facebook? Right-click (I only learned about right-click in the last week, after Freya showed me) – Copy – Paste. I'd say my computer just doesn't like Tracy or her system. By the time the night comes around for the quiz, two weeks after we announced it, I'm fairly tense.

I'm the first to arrive, at seven o'clock. I push open the door of Johnny's a bit nervously. I wouldn't normally go in on my own. It's not like in Dublin, where you could be meeting someone or going in to read a book, like they do in the films. What would I be meeting someone in here for, the worst place to meet them? Everyone listening in. They'd probably turn down the telly to hear us. So it's not something I'm used to. Normally, Denis is with me, and he knows the *geography* of the place. When I go in, I get half stuck in the two doors carrying stuff in from the car and I'm generally just all in a fluster.

All I see first is Johnny not there, but there is a screen, for some reason. I'm standing there with the box of paper and pens and raffle tickets in my hands. There are no tables set up. Just the usual suspects watching a match. Another United match.

'Waste of money, that bollix! He doesn't want to know about it. Doesn't want to throw a leg at it,' says Dave Mooney, barely needing to support the pint resting on the belly of his jumper. It's been a while since Dave threw a leg at anything other than a couch.

Johnny appears from behind the bar.

'Oh, Ann,' he says. And then he sees the box. You can see the look on his face as he realizes that I'm not in there for a Coors Light in a glass with ice.

'I clean forgot,' he says.

'But it was all over Facebook. One hundred interested. It said on the event.'

'That's the nephew. He's handy at that. I've taken a step back from promotions.'

I should have a conniption when I see the state of the place. I should shout, HOW COULD YOU FORGET AND YOU STARING AT A POSTER ACROSS FROM THE BAR AND WHERE IS YOUR NEPHEW, SO? HOW COME HE DIDN'T SET IT UP SINCE HE WAS *ALL OVER IT*? But I don't feel comfortable shouting in a pub. *And* he's giving away a good few drink prizes tonight, so he can kind of do whatever he wants. He starts to explain to me that this is a big match and he doesn't want to move the lads. He suggests maybe we could go in the back room, which he brings me into. It's cold. Cold like a house we all grew up in. They won't be able to hold their biros in it. The biros mightn't even work. We might need pencils. Like the Russians.

Johnny doesn't care about anything. One of the few people around here who doesn't care about money. His money is made. He doesn't want to upset the lads in the pub, especially the ould ones.

'I'm the only one they have,' he says. 'I'm like a counsellor. They would have made arrrangements to be in here for this.'

He looks at me again and sees I'm troubled.

'I tell you what I'll do. We can turn down the telly for the questions and then turn it up again.'

I thought we'd have the whole pub, but I don't want to be seen to be difficult.

'OK so, that's grand. Where might we set up?' I can hear myself agreeing to all of this, even though it's a cod.

And then Deirdre comes in. Johnny's face changes. I think he knows he won't get away with it.

'I'm early for once, Mam,' she says, and looks around. She sees my face, sees the place, sees Johnny with his tea-towel looking dumb and goes into full Deirdre.

'Johnny, what the fuck is going on here? Where're all the tables?'

'Well, as I was explaining to your mother, Deirdre, there's a big match on and—'

'Fuck the match, Johnny. More Champions League, is it? First leg, second round? I know well what match is it. United against Turks, and they'll win. We've the whole pub booked. There's a huge gang coming in. There was supposed to be fifty tables set up. Jesus Christ, Johnny, do you want to make any money at all? Move these lads on or put them in a table. Surely they've spent enough time talking shite now to have the answer to everything.'

The ould lads look around from their barstools like hens who think there might be a fox. I do feel sorry for them because I know their situation. A lot of them are lonely. Apart from Dave Mooney, who's surrounded by loved ones and just plain red useless.

Not for the first time I watch my daughter with a sort of mixture of admiration with a bit of guilt. They're always on about this sort of lioness we're all supposed to be, lifting cars to get a child out from underneath, but I don't think that's me. I'm a plump ould tabby looking for a quiet life in front of the fire. Luckily enough, this tabby is after somehow rearing a lioness.

'Well, Johnny, what do you have to say for yourself?'

Johnny moves as fast as if it's two in the morning and the gardaí are at the door. Tables are scraped across the floor, chairs arranged around them.

People start arriving. And arriving. The tables that were set out optimistically by us are already full. The lads on the high stools are surrounded as more tables are brought out from the back room. It's a real mix of people, a lot of whom I don't recognize at all. I go around collecting the money.

'What's the team name, lads?' I ask one group. Three men in their fifties and a younger man I take to be a son or a nephew. They are not from here, but they're from somewhere like here.

'Champions League,' says one of them. I notice now that they're nearly all dressed the same. A blue or a navy jumper and jeans.

'How did you hear about us? I only put up posters around the village.'

'TableQuiz.com,' says the young fella. 'Every table quiz in the country automatically goes up on it. We're here for the record.'

'What record?'

The older men give him a sharp look. But I don't think he's seen it.

'How are the results published?' he asks me then.

'Published? I don't know. Do results be published? We write them up in marker on the board.'

'You'll need to submit the results to the website. We're going for ten in a row. It's an all-time consecutive table quiz victory record.'

His team mates are not happy with him at all, and when I move on to the next table to get the money I can hear, 'What did you go telling her that for?'

The next table is teachers from the primary school, arguing over who has the better handwriting. They're calling themselves The Wicked Blues.

'Make sure you spell that right now, Mrs Devine,' says Miss McDermott. 'Wkd, as in the drink. Because we'll definitely be winning that tonight.'

She says she has Junior Infants in the morning, because she lost a coin toss with Miss Grogan, and they'll all be told to *Téigh a chodladh*.

There's no Blue Wkd for the men in blue jumpers. Fizzy water and shandies is the round.

I'm confronted next by three long-haired fellas with beards and a quiet-looking boy who doesn't look straight at me.

'Give him the pen,' they say to me, 'he's our man with the answers.'

They call themselves Pretty Loki. They say they're tourists. They seem to know the other trimmed-beardy types at the next table. Man Bun is there and a few others like him, and the woman with the half-shaved head. That gang of four are having a good old look around the pub and smiling about us. They're not country people, by the looks of them, or if they are they left it behind them in college. Where are they out of at all?

I come back to my own area, which is a mess of paper and pens and raffle prizes, and finally Gordon shows up.

'Sorry, Ann. I had to meet Gerard off the train.'

Who's Gerard? I'm wondering, but I've no time to ask that because Geraldine arrives in all flustered.

'Can I leave Freya with you, Ann? I'm trying to do a few more shifts this week. The car insurance is after going up again.'

Deirdre catches my eye as if to say, *That's more of it*, so I can't get cross with Geraldine now and, anyway, I need the help.

Freya stands awkwardly next to me. A crowded local pub is not her natural habitat.

'Sit down, Freya. You can help me with the registering and the correcting.'

We are at the corner of the lounge, behind a large table.

'Oh, here's Gerard,' Gordon says, and he goes off to talk to a man who has just arrived. He has a small leather bag. I haven't time to get the measure of him; there are more people coming in.

When there's nearly thirty tables full Gordon starts talking into the mic, trying to get them all to order. That takes a while. Whatever smartarses were at the meeting, they're multiplied now by drink.

'Ladies and gentlemen—'

'There's no ladies here!'

'You totally should be doing quizmaster, Auntie Ann, after you doing all the work,' Freya whispers to me as we watch Gordon in a battle of wills.

'I'm in the background, Freya, that's my style. Pulling the strings.'

'You're invisible, Auntie Ann.'

'As far as I'm concerned, propped up behind this table I'm visible enough. Too visible. And they can see under the table. I should have worn better shoes.'

'We had this talk,' Freya says. 'This woman came in about doing IT and tech in school who's all like, *You can't be it if you can't see it*. If women don't go into computers, then they're going to make robots that only work for men.'

I wonder are these the sexbots they were talking about on local radio?

'Do you think there should be more girls getting into table quizzes, Freya?'

Gordon is still struggling with the crowd.

'Nooo, Auntie Ann, you know what I mean. It's about stepping up.'

'I know, pet.'

'Ladies and gentlemen, there'll be no quiz until we get a bit of hush,' says Gordon, sounding a bit frazzled.

The professionals start a bit of shushing and it spreads, so even the smartarses quieten down.

'Now, there will be ten rounds of ten questions. The quizmaster's answer is final. There will be a picture round and also a puzzle round. And there's no point trying to use Google, as there's no internet here. After each round, we'll call the questions out again and go around collecting after a few minutes. Please put your team name and table number down. We'll have a break at half-time for the raffle. Now, are you ready?'

'Question number one ...'

Even with all the joking, there's a tension that takes over as soon as the first question is asked. Everyone thinks they're in with a chance. I've seen enough of these quizzes to know how it goes. It settles down after a while, after most tables realize they haven't a bull's notion about anything. And then the tension turns into bitterness. There's a special kind of madness takes over people at a table quiz. You could be giving away coupons for a fiver off a box of Daz and people get agitated over it and start complaining. I've heard of couples not speaking after one said to go for one answer and the other wouldn't write it down.

'Wait, wait, wait!' Miss Tealy runs over with a gin and tonic to the teachers' table. 'I'm doing the writing.' She's a bit of a gas case. Went in for the Rose of Tralee a few times already.

'All right, then. Question one. What is the capital city of the state of California?'

And we're off! The groans of the average and the aww-yeahs of those who know. The professionals barely flinch, like when the big man on *The Chase* has it. I look down at the answer. I wouldn't have picked that myself. Sacramento. That's hardly a city, is it? I thought it was out of a Western, or a song.

I don't have time to think about the answers because soon enough the first round is over and they come in for correcting. We haven't time to scratch, me and Freya. And then I have to tot up the scores as the rounds go on. And would you believe it, the ould lads have a table between them! There's six of them on it, above at the bar, and Dave Mooney is doing the writing. Last of the Summer Wine they called themselves, and for all their lack of interest, somehow they are in second, only one behind the professionals. By the interval, they're ahead by one.

Freya and myself are at the pin of our collar to do the correcting. I only hope we get the scores right. Honestly, the answers out of some people. The teachers are near the bottom. The handwriting is appalling and they don't even know the name for a group of crows.

Freya shows me a bit of paper from a team of GAA lads. Minors. It has a willy drawn on it.

'They know I'm correcting it, Auntie Ann. Sickos.'

Deirdre spots this. Without a word, she goes over to the young lads' table and talks to one of them until he blushes, shrinks into his shirt and starts to smile but is then nearly crying, and as she leaves he takes a big, nervous gulp out of his pint and we know there won't be any more trouble.

'No marks for them in that round,' she says to me as she comes back. 'They won't complain.'

Dave Mooney passes on the way to the toilet. He should be well oiled at this stage, but men like Dave can go for days.

'Ye're flying, Dave,' I say. 'Who's the brains of the operation? I didn't know you were a Rihanna fan.'

'Who?'

'Rihanna, ye got her bang-on in the picture round. I don't even know who she is myself.'

'Ah' – he hesitates – 'we'd keep up to date. Philly has the Sky now.'

'Philly! Fair play to Philly.' He's the oldest of them.

One of the professionals appears next to me.

'Excuse me, are you in charge of the questions?' he says. 'What was the answer to number seven in the third round? *What man-made object can you see from the moon?*'

'Hang on a second there … oh, yes … the Great Wall of China.'

'But it's wrong.'

'Is it? That's the answer I have here.'

'You can't see any man-made object from the moon.'

'And what did ye put down?' I know well what they put down. I'm doing the correcting.

'That you couldn't see anything, that it was a trick question. That's what we thought it was.'

'Well, you'll have to take it up with the organizers.'

'You are the organizer.'

'OK. I'll see.'

'Are you going to give us an extra mark?'

'The quizmaster's word is final,' says my daughter, and glares the jumperman out of it.

He's still giving out and throwing his hands up dramatically as if to say to all and sundry, *Look at what I'm dealing with*. My eyes get a little wet with the confrontation so I go back behind my table.

'You'll have to be firmer with these types, Mammy,' says Deirdre. 'You're a *vice*-chairperson, not a *nice* chairperson. They'll run rings around you.'

'But I never wanted to be a vice—' but I'm interrupted when I see the man from the *Sentinel*. He smiles at me, like butter wouldn't melt in his mouth. I'm going to go over to him right now and ask him what business had he pretending to be a photographer, when Sally intercepts me.

'Ann, Donal thinks there's a wrong answer in the fourth round with the pictures. He thinks it's Zsa Zsa Gábor.'

'Sally, tell him it's not, and that it wouldn't matter anyway if it was.' I'm fairly short with her, which I feel bad about because there's only two on their table and it's a mournful enough looking one, as well as being near the bottom. Bilderbergwatch, Donal Junior has called them, for reasons best known to himself. I decide to give them an extra few marks along the way.

We go through round eight. There's still nothing separating Last of the Summer Wine and Champions League.

Another jumperman is up to me.

'There's something funny going on here,' he says. 'We have won our last nine quizzes and those fellas are like no other crowd. And they're mouldy drunk.'

I mutter that there's a lot of local talent, but the scoreboard shows the rest of the locals are miles behind. Even Man Bun and his college buddies and the hairy fellas can't touch them. But Pretty Loki don't seem to mind. Or three of them don't anyway. They are topping their drinks up from a bag of cans. The fourth fella seems to be doing all the work. He's passing at one point and I ask him how he's getting on. He seems shocked to be spoken to.

'Eh, grand, yeah ... grand.' He stands there for two long seconds then he continues walking.

Gordon comes back to the table. 'Right so, Ann, pass me over the last two rounds. They must have fallen off the back of the staple.'

'I've no rounds, Gordon.'

We search around the ground for the other sheets. Father Donnegan wrote the questions. Gordon rings him. The crowd are starting to notice the gap. No reply. Gordon gets a text.

Am at cinema is it a death?

We're looking at each other, trying not to text the F-word in a message to a priest.

Where's rounds nine and ten?

What rounds nine and ten? It's eight rounds. Remember we said?

We didn't say. Gordon has to stand up and tell the crowd it's over and there's a tie-break. Them professional lads won't be happy with that. They've spent fifty euro on the table and the prize is only two hundred euro and a hamper. Except we've no tie-break question.

Patsy arrives up to the table, wondering what's going on. Who *hasn't* been up by the organizers' table at this stage?

Gordon explains the problem. Patsy makes out that he will sort it. We're kind of happy to pass it on. A TD gets blamed for everything anyway. They don't take it personally.

'Only thing for it, a local round. That'll separate the men from the boys.' Patsy grabs the microphone. 'LADIES AND GENTLEMEN! We have a TIE! Between Dave Mooney's Last of the Summer Wine and Champions League. For this one, we will have a local question.'

Champions League look disgusted. They can see their goose is cooked.

'To the nearest five,' says Patsy, 'how many signposts are there for Kilsudgeon along the N64 between Dransha and Drumowsa? We're counting all the signposts for the turn-off, and all the promotional signs as well.'

There is a bit of ceremony as I go over and collect the two bits of paper. Dave Mooney wraps his in a beer mat and says, 'SHHHH! DON'T TELL ANYONE.' Jumperman practically throws it at me. There's a low boo at this.

Patsy makes a great show out of opening them.

'Now, the correct answer is thirty-four. I should know, as I was instrumental in getting them put up.'

He is shameless. Absolutely shameless. I can't help but admire the impudence. But we like the bit of the trickster in him, I suppose. That's what we vote for.

'Champions League, you said there were fifteen. But the winners are Last of the Summer Wine, who said forty-five. Now I applied for forty-five, but you are the closest, so Dave Mooney's Last of the Summer Wine are the *winners*!'

17

GRAND PRIX FOR SYNERGIES

Now I don't know how to run a show. But I know how not to run a show, and trying to bring on an architect at the end of a table quiz to talk about his *vision* is one way not to run a show. But Gordon is insisting.

'Ann, I want to introduce you to someone.' Gordon is standing at the table with the man who had the little bag. From a different direction, I see the Champions League team approaching. 'Gerard is from GCM Landscape Architects.'

'Hello, Gerard. You're an architect? Isn't that a great profession to be in? I thought my eldest would go for architecture because she was great at drawing, but she just hadn't the points.'

He looks blank. Maybe I came on a bit strong.

'Ann, Gerard is an old school pal of Flora's, and we persuaded him over a good bottle of wine to give us a bit of advice about bringing a proposal to the council for a town park for Tom's field. I felt if we went to the council with some input of our own, it might stop them making a mess of it.'

'Well, it's a bit early to talk about ... I mean ... Tom mentioned it ... but Noel ...'

Gordon ignores me and takes up the mic.

'IF I COULD HAVE YOUR ATTENTION, PLEASE! Thanks very much to all of you for your support and for travelling so far to help us. We have some very exciting projects lined up. Not least, we hope to have a town park in Kilsudgeon!'

The crowd cheers. And just at that point, I see Oona standing at the door to the women's toilets. It's no exaggeration to say she has a puss on her.

'To give us an idea of what that might be like, I've invited a good friend of mine, Gerard Callaghan Morley, an architect, to give us some impressions of what we might do. Take it away, Gerard.'

'Hello, everyone. My name is Gerard Callaghan Morley of GCM Landscape Architects. If you haven't heard of us, you've probably seen this.'

He presses the clicker and a photo comes up on the screen. I'm not sure what we're looking at. There are some shrubs and then ... to be honest, it looks like a huge metal backside with a tree growing out of the middle of it.

'This is *Epiphany*. It's probably our most high-profile work and' – he gives a little chuckle – 'our most controversial. No doubt you read about it in the *Irish Times*.'

The shop only sells the *Sentinel* and the *Independent*. There wouldn't be much call for the *Irish Times* around here. Unless Kilsudgeon was mentioned in it, which was never.

'Could I have a word, please?' It's one of the Jumpermen. He's holding the bottle of Jamesworth whiskey – I think it's Lidl Jameson – that was part of their runners-up prize. I don't think he likes its vintage.

'*Epiphany* has won a number of awards internationally, including the Grand Prix for Synergies at the Exposition Architecturelle in Rouen.'

He pronounces 'Grand Prix' with a French accent. No grand pricks for him. I can't warm to him.

He clicks again a few times. More photos of *Epiphany* appear. It looks more and more like a backside.

'So, I've been doing up a bit of a mood board for your town park at the ring fort. The ring fort is a unique opportunity to encapsulate Ireland's heritage in a sympathetic urban space ...'

Jumperman doesn't seem to care about *Epiphany*.

'This is a joke of a table quiz,' he says to me, 'and we'll be complaining to Table Quiz Ireland so that you won't be able to hold one again and call it a table quiz. There are standards, you know. And you can take this back as well.'

'Can you put the whiskey down, please, or take it away.' That's Deirdre, fanning the flames.

'A load of bollix.' Jumperman is not happy.

The words KILSUDGEON: THE GATEWAYS OF THE PAST BECOME OUR FUTURE appear on the screen.

'A LOAD OF BOLLIX!'

Click.

'COME OUT OF IT, DADDY! IT'S NOT WORTH IT.'

'... creating flow through empathy with our greatest resource ...'

Click.

'... our people.'

'IT'S A SHITHOLE, THIS PLACE. IT'S TRUE WHAT THEY ALWAYS SAID ABOUT KILSUDGEON – CORNER BOYS AND SCAMMERS IS ALL YE PRODUCE.'

Click. The screen shows a load of people walking around the park. They aren't locals anyway because they're all skinny and dressed nicely. I wouldn't have qualified.

'DADDY, COME OUT OF IT. YOU'LL LOSE US THE FAIR-PLAY AWARD.'

'... a continuum both in time and space ... to breathe ...'

Click.

'... a sweep of landscape and story ...'

Click.

'CHEATING BASTARDS! WE WERE GOING TO MAKE HISTORY ONLY FOR YE CONNIVING C—'

'... knitting together a tapestry of history ...'

Click. A picture of Newgrange and a Druid.

'... and your story ...'

'DADDY! TONY, GRAB A HOLD OF HIM THERE, HE'S LOST IT.'

Click. A load of Chinese schoolchildren doing peace signs.

'A FIX!'

'PETER, COME OUT OF IT. C'MON TO FUCK.'

'A FUCKEN FIX!'

'If they only knew the half of it,' says Patsy, watching Peter being dragged out, shouting.

Patsy and Dave Mooney, who'd be a distant cousin, are laughing and sniggering fit to beat the band, so I've a fair idea how Last of the Summer Wine happened to score so well and how a team of five crabbed pensioners and one waster knew who Kerry Katona is married to *now*.

Gerard has finished up. He never wavered while the row was going on. He asks for questions. There aren't many people listening now. Distracted by the row and pints and relieving babysitters or themselves.

'Will there be any swings?' asks one woman.

'Swings?' He looks offended. As if the swings were interrupting his *vision*.

'For the young lads. Or a pitch to puck a ball around. They're going five miles up the road to train. My daughter is spending a fortune on diesel.'

'I ... well ... the brief was to redevelop a moribund site. I suppose there could be space for ... swings ... while retaining the character of the original vision. But—'

'And slides too. Once you put in a swing, you'll have to put in slides. Children expect one when they see the other.'

'And a climbing frame for the older children,' someone else chimes in.

Gordon steps in. 'Well, obviously, there are a number of considerations, but I think first of all we should give Gerard a round of applause for coming down here and showing us what Kilsudgeon can achieve.'

We clap then, of course. No sense in being rude to the man, but he's a bit deflated. He didn't get any Grand Prix de Eiffel Tower from us and he's used to getting them, I'd say.

And no applause from Oona. She's talking very animatedly to Patsy. But we raised thirteen hundred euro and things are never straightforward raising money, are they?

Gerard seems happy. He mentions a fact-finding mission, but I don't take any notice.

18

SCARY WOMAN. MANY SHOUTING

I should have taken notice, because it turns out he's being foisted on me the following day. Gordon rings to tell me Gerard needs a guide and he's on his way to me. Flora drops him down and I intend to meet him at the door, but he ends up in the house because I can't find the car keys.

In he comes, and straightaway I can see him twitch. The place must offend him. He's dying to say something, and he can't help himself.

'You could open up through here and let in the light.' He's walking around as I'm turning the place upside-down looking for the keys. 'This is a very dark hall. There is a lot of scope for opening on to the southern aspect. They really were afraid of the light when they built houses in Ireland years ago.' And he gives a little laugh. 'It was part of our insular identity, keeping things hidden.'

I find the keys in the coins jam jar. I'm certain Denis hid them in there because that's not where they go.

'Yes, the southern aspect,' he says again, stroking his chin.

There are lots of aspects of this house I want to change before looking at the southern one. I hustle him out the door before he has a chance to rip into the seat covers and the dado rail.

Gerard wants to walk the site at Tom's field. I'm not sure, given the drone episode last time, but Gordon is fierce gung-ho about the whole thing. He reckons it's a done deal, but that's only from talking to me, and I'm not that certain.

We drive along the twisty roads. I mention that we're trying to get the council to take away a few of the bad bends. Gerard thinks that bends add to the *bucolic charm of an unspoilt hamlet like Kilsudgeon* and tells me how, where he has a holiday home in Wexford, they've taken away too many bends.

As we round the last bad bend before Tom's house, something looks different. I lose my bearings for a second. A ditch is gone from the side of the fairy field, a bit of a bend has been removed and in place of the ditch there's a couple of workmen putting up a big wooden fence. Like it was a building site.

'I didn't realize work had started,' says Gerard. 'This will interfere a little with the visualization process, but maybe I can just compartmentalize my vision and reconfigure and …'

I'm hardly listening.

'We're not doing anything, Gerard. This isn't us. I don't know what this is.'

My phone is ringing. It's Rory. Not now, Rory! Though I'm dying to talk to him. I haven't even had a chance to worry about him being involved with the IRA in a while. That'll tell you how stressful the table quiz was.

We park the car and get out. I go up to one of the fellas in the hi-vis. A big tall fella. He has a look of a Pole about him.

'Excuse me, what are you doing here?'

141

'Putting up fence.'

'I know, but whose fence is it?'

'So many questions. But maybe I don't tell you because not your business, missus.'

He goes back to hammering nails into the plywood. He glances back at me.

'Who are you?'

'Eh ... Ann. Ann Devine.'

'Ann Devine. I do not know this name. Are you famous? Are you politician?'

'No. Just Tidy Towns.'

'Tidy Towns. What do you do? Do you tidy a town? Is this a town?' BANG BANG. 'Looks like field. In Poland, town is fifty thousand persons.'

'No, it's just ... it's a community, it's ... a small town.'

I didn't expect I'd have to describe the Tidy Towns.

'Maybe forty thousand, but is not a town. Lots of towns in Ireland. I go to Kilkenny, they call it a city. Not a city.'

Bang bang bang 'FUCK SHIT!'

He sucks on his thumb. He must have hit it with the hammer.

'Are you OK?'

'Look, missus. I have many, many fence to put around field. If I don't finish today, fucking President Hillary Clinton will break my bollox.'

'Hil— but, it's just that we're from the Tidy Towns, and we were promised this field.'

'Who promise field?'

'Tommy.'

'I know only woman. Very scary woman. Many shouting. I don't know this man Tommy.'

'Tommy died a few weeks ago.'

'Dead man don't keep promise. You have legal paper for this field?'

I haven't anything of the sort, of course.

'Is he husband?' he says, pointing at Gerard as he paces around the fence and peeks in at the field. 'Hey, man! Who say you could measure? Step back. Not safe for professors.'

Gerard was visualizing a bit too much for the fence man's liking.

'OK shit. She comes now. I go back to work. Maybe you explain your town tidy to this woman.' And he turns around and starts hammering more than ever. It's the first time he looks nervous.

'MRS DEVINE.'

Striding along the roadside from where she's parked Tommy's old Jetta is Oona. She seems even bigger and more formidable than the last time I saw her. And she's wearing wellingtons. Noel gingerly gets out of the passenger side. He scuttles a little to keep up with her, and maybe he had a notion to try and get to me first but realized it was pointless.

'Surprised, Ann?'

It's Ann now.

'Oona, hello. Noel.'

'Ann.' Noel's face is strained. He won't look at me straight. I want to say to him that it's grand.

'You have a query with my workman, Ann?'

I go to jelly in front of her.

'No, it's just that we were under the impression ... you see, Tommy said to Noel that he should let us ...'

'Well, it's not Noel's say. The field was left to me, as it turned out, in the will.'

'But Tommy said that he left it to ...'

'How do you know? Were you present when a will was being discussed? You, a paid carer? Who is your superior? Don't bother, I'll find out. I'm sure Patrick Ignatius has all the details. Anyway, FYI, even though it's none of your business ...'

BANG BANG BANG. Her 'workman' is working his way down the fence away from us.

'... there were a few changes after I came home. I heard this guy last night. This guy' – she points to Gerard – 'talking about a goddamn park. TOWN PARK, MY ASS! Do you think I would let a prime developmopunidy be used for a couple benches and a bunch of tulips?'

Toolips, she says it.

I'm blabbering now. And my phone is going again and distracting me.

'... and you see, then we got an architect, or Gordon did ...'

'WHO'S GORDON? THE WET FISH IN THE GREY JUMPER? IS HE YOUR HUSBAND? SO HE GOT AN ARCHITECT? YOU WERE PLANNING ON ARCHITECTING ON SOMEONE ELSE'S PROPERTY, WERE YOU?'

'I envisage a beautiful town park here, Mrs ...'

Gerard is not helping.

'Oh, I misunderstood. I thought this was a big cheese. Turns out he's full of baloney.'

Now I'm defending Gerard.

'Gerard has done a lot of stuff with the Europeans, according to Gordon.'

'I DON'T CARE IF HE'S GODDAMN TY PENNINGTON FROM *EXTREME MAKEOVER*. THIS IS *NOT* YOUR LAND. ARE YOU GUYS BRITS? DO YOU GRAB PEOPLE'S PROPERTY?'

'No, it's just that the Tidy Towns, we had a meeting, and then there was the table quiz—'

'I KNOW. I was at your table quiz. And I enjoyed seeing your local alcoholic get it handed to him. That was cute, but anyhow … I mean. No-el and I got BIG PLANS for this place. Big ones to start, even bigger ones after that, so why don't you and your little hi-vis gnomes scoot off and pick up some trash?'

'But the town park …'

'There won't be a GODDAMN TOWN PARK. I'm not having my ancestral home a place for TEENAGE FORNICATION and a CESSPIT FOR GOD-FEARING FOLKS. The country I left has taken up with the Devil and I'm fixing to make it a bit more Christian.'

Oh, I see. She's a 'Christian'. That sets off the alarm bells with me. There's no reasoning with an American Christian. My phone is buzzing again. Who rings when you're in the middle of a row?

'Now, Mateus has a lotta fence to put up, so if you don't mind permitting a man to do an HONEST DAY'S WORK? That's the thing with you volunteers. You think that just because you've decided this is the cause, then you're auto-matically in the right. Well, that's not how the world works, OK, HONEY? No one made you guys the TOWN COUNCIL.'

We edge away. The penny seems to have dropped with Gerard too.

'It's a difficult situation, Ann,' he says when we're out of earshot. 'The American sensibility can be somewhat funda-mentalist and brutalist.'

'I'll drop you back to Flora and Gordon's, Gerard.' He looks like he needs to sit in a study for a while.

Another buzz from the phone.

'I'm sorry, Gerard, I'll have to answer this.'

It's still Rory.

'What is it, pet? Are you all right?'

'Didn't you hear the news, Mam? *Game of Thrones* is com-ing to Kilsudgeon.'

'Game of Who?'

'Thrones. The one you said was all dragons and hooring. OK, Mammy, it's not them exactly, but something like it. They're going to be filming in Kilsudgeon. Patsy was instrumental and I was doing a bit of the paperwork. I wasn't allowed to say until it was confirmed. But it was just announced today. They've a site picked out and everything.'

I look at the fence.

I bet I know where they're going to be based as well.

19

TO PLAY THE TEMPTRESS

A week has passed since the fence row, and it hasn't been a good one. We had a smaller turnout at our clean-up because of a GAA match. Then I had to spend two afternoons with Nonie after swapping with Demelza. Nonie is delighted with this. It's like a double helping of dessert for her. And her sainted husband has a bit of respite. I don't know why he doesn't leave the country.

'You're putting on weight, Miss Hoare,' she says on the second afternoon.

It's all I can do not to tell her to eff off out of it and bring herself to the toilet.

WHAT'S YOUR STORY, NONIE? WHY DO YOU HAVE IT IN FOR ME? WHY WOULD YOU WANT TO LIVE YOUR LIFE LIKE THIS, YOU MISERABLE SO AND SO? I shout at her in my mind.

But you have to be very careful. She or Brian or both could start crying and make a complaint and then it's elder abuse. I feel sorry for her too, because I presume she can't help herself. Although Neans says she was like that as a younger person, too, and that the only bits of her brain that got addled were the nice bits. Howandever, it's not my place to be giving out yards. So I offer it up.

'How does that husband of yours put up with you? Liam? Liam is a fine man. A doctor as well. And how did he marry you and you with three children by another man?'

She has me mixed up with somone else, which is a comfort, thank God. I'd hate to be the other woman, though. Married to a doctor. The pressure!

By the time I'm done with her and back up to Flash for a few more stale buns, I'm all done in and glad to go home. When I get there, Deirdre's car is outside and the two youngsters are out playing around the place.

'HELLO, GRANNY ANN,' is all I get and they're back to kicking a bush.

Denis and Deirdre are in the kitchen drinking tea.

'All set for an audition, Mammy? Would you like to be a Celtic warrior?' She's pointing to the *Kilsudgeon Sentinel*.

Denis reads it out to us.

Kilsudgeon could be the new Hollywood is the headline. '*Kilsudgeon could be going to the movies! Talks are at an advanced stage for Kilsudgeon to become the location for shooting the pilot of an epic TV show. The Celts is described as an exciting journey into the mystical past of the Irish and another gamble from the hugely successful online TV provider Gubu.*'

'They must have been extras at the table quiz, so,' says Deirdre.

'Who?'

'The hairy lads and the oddball. I was talking to them after and they said they were here for some filming. Hardy boys the lot of them, apart from the pale fella.'

'And did anyone think to tell me that before I went up fighting a Polish lad over a fence?'

'It completely slipped my mind. Sorry, Mammy.'

'*One of the original Hollywood come-back kids, Cody Bryan, has put his recent legal troubles behind him and signed up to play the chief warrior Fionn McCool. Up-and-coming star of I.Am.Not.Able., Shelf McKinnon, is rumoured to play his beautiful temptress, Morga.* The Celts *was originally due to be filmed in the North of Ireland but, with the uncertainty surrounding Brexit, it is one of a number of productions that could be heading south of the border. And the North's loss is Kilsudgeon's gain. So get your casting couches ready. You could be going to the Emmys!*'

'See?' Denis says. 'Northern Ireland. That's who you saw driving around. It was a fella from the telly. Not an IRA man. Unless it was the Reality TV IRA, hah? Now, isn't that a turn-up for the books? You might play the temptress, Ann, if yer wan Shelf is up the walls. Is that your phone going there?'

It was another picture text from Rory. Does he type words any more? It was just a selfie of him holding the newspaper with the page open at the headline about *The Celts* and a little caption that said *Original IRA*. How did he know to send that? And that wall looks familiar.

There's a knock at the window. I turn around, and Rory is looking in at us, laughing, a bag of washing slung across his shoulder.

I run out and give him a hug. I need it more than he does.

I look beyond him and Patsy is there, waving from his jeep. He shouts out, 'The boy has become a man, Ann!' whatever that means.

'What does that mean, Rory?'

'I don't know, Mam. He's in flying form these days since *The Celts* was announced. He picked me up and asked did I want to go for a spin. We've been discussing strategy all the way up. And he says he'll drop me back down on Sunday.'

'GREAT JOB ON THE TABLE QUIZ, ANN.'

I go up to him and ask him about the field and Oona.

'We'll find another field,' he says. 'And you leave Oona to me. She's ... hahaha ... a feisty one.'

I'm glad Freya isn't around to hear the f-word. She goes ballistic whenever anyone says 'feisty'.

'Right so, Ann, I'm off. Rory, enjoy your little break. We'll talk soon.' And the jeep speeds off.

'You'll eat a fry, Rory?'

'Prodigal son,' Deirdre says from the doorstep. 'She'll be killing a fatted calf with her own hands now.'

'Good to see you too,' Rory says with a grin.

'Come on away in, all of you,' says Denis, looking delighted with himself. 'I know where she hides the Twirls.'

20

SUSSED IN A HEARTBEAT

My mother is not happy. 'I DON'T LIKE THAT NEW FELLA AT ALL. HE DIDN'T EVEN MENTION THE SAINT'S DAY.'

We're on our way home from Mass. It's not a regular Sunday, as we don't go to Mass that much any more, but we've to bring my mother.

'THEY WOULD ALWAYS SAY THE NAME OF THE SAINT BEFORE.'

I've never heard of St Peter Damian before, but my mother has them all in her missal. I don't think he's a regular with her, but she has a soft spot for forgotten saints. She usually gets brought to Mass by one of her cronies but the arrangement has fallen through, so we're giving her a lift. Denis has to come along as well because Mam said, *Oh, did you get evening Mass, Denis?* and Denis can't lie to her because he says she sees right through him. So he's heading to Mass as well, for the first time in ages.

We're a merry band of pilgrims going into the chapel. I have to accompany her to her usual spot, far up the church, while Denis sneaks into a cubbyhole under the stairs where the problems of the world get sorted out by lads wearing jumpers that smell a bit of silage.

'NOT ONE BIT!' says Mam again.

I don't want to get too deep into this in case I'd have to reveal I haven't exactly been Matt Talbot these past few years, so I let her alone with her opinion.

I used to be a better Catholic Mammy – you know, the usual, hunting them all into Mass when they were growing up. You kind of had to, even if you weren't the total Holy Joe yourself. It was part of the job, wasn't it? One bit you had laid out straight for you to follow. And Mam is a divil for devoutness. There was no way I was going up against her.

I did the whole Catholic deal when the kids were growing up. 'Well,' I'd say, 'who said Mass?' But then I'd have the follow-up questions to trick them. 'What did the priest talk about in his sermon? Who was there? Was so-and-so there? Was she? That's strange, because they're gone to the Canaries.' I used to be like Matlock, trying to catch them out if they were lying. Deirdre told me they ended up going to Mass because it was too much effort otherwise to get the story straight. The best lie is sometimes the truth.

'NO, NOT ONE IOTA,' says Mam again.

I bite. 'Why don't you like him, Mam?'

'I DON'T EVEN MIND THAT HE'S POLISH,' Mam says, as if I had asked her. She's a bit deaf now, so she assumes people are listening to her and, if they aren't, it needed to be said anyway. She's talking about the new priest who does a bit of subbing for Father Donnegan when he's off.

'HE'S IN TOO MUCH OF A HURRY ALTOGETHER. HE DOES THAT SECOND EUCHARISTIC PRAYER AND IT WOULDN'T MATTER WHAT SUNDAY OF THE YEAR IT IS. IT'S JUST BECAUSE IT'S SHORTER. HE'S PROBABLY

OFF HOME TO WATCH A MATCH. I NOTICED SINCE THE SATELLITE TELLY CAME IN, THE MASSES DON'T GO ON AS LONG. I DON'T EVEN THINK THE PRIESTS' HEARTS ARE IN IT THESE DAYS. AND WHERE DOES THAT LEAVE THE LIKES OF ME? THE ONES WHO STUCK WITH THEM THROUGH ALL THEIR TROUBLES WHEN EVERYONE ELSE LEFT?'

She catches my eye in the mirror, as if she has her lapsed children and pagan grandchildren sussed in a heartbeat.

'MAYBE I SHOULD BE A PRIEST. CUT OUT THE MIDDLEMAN.'

She's a feminist when she wants to be is Mam.

'I DIDN'T HEAR MUCH PRAYING OUT OF YOU, ANN.'

As we drive along through the town, I get a text from Jennifer.

Facetime?

'Facetime, Denis. Jennifer wants to Facetime. Where'll we go to get reception? Will we go up to Dooney's Turn?'

'We might as well. It'll be quiet up there now. We'll have all the signal to ourselves.'

'WHAT'S FACETIME?' asks Mam. 'IS IT ABOUT MAKEUP OR WHAT?'

'It's a phone call but you can see the person, Mam. But you need internet.'

'WHY CAN'T SHE JUST RING? GOD BE WITH THE DAYS WHEN SOMEONE WOULD RING HOME FROM LONDON AND WOULD HAVE TO CALL THE SHOP BECAUSE THEY WERE THE ONLY ONES WITH A PHONE AND YOU'D GO DOWN CHRISTMAS EVE AND EVERY GOSSIP IN CLONSCRIBBEN WOULD BE LOOKING AT YOU TO HEAR THE NEWS. WE USED TO LET ON THAT WHOEVER WE WERE TALKING TO WAS MAKING HUGE MONEY OUT THERE AND A REAL SWELL AROUND THE TOWN. BARNEY LORDAMERCYONIM WAS A HOOT

153

FOR THAT. "A ROLLS ROYCE, UNCLE GERRY?" HE'D SHOUT DOWN THE PHONE, LOUD ENOUGH SO THE WHOLE SHOP COULD HEAR. "BUT WHAT'LL YOU DO WITH YOUR OTHER CAR?" IT USED TO DRIVE DYMPNA CLOHESSY WILD. BUT POOR DYMPNA HAD HER TROUBLES TOO, WITH THE SON MARRYING BADLY AND YOU KNOW—'

'Oh yes. God be with the days, Mam.'

I thought I'd better cut in now. Once Mam remembers something from the past, there'd be no stopping her for half an hour.

'Jennifer just likes Facetime. Stay quiet a minute till I hear what she has to say.'

Jennifer likes Facetime because she says she can read me if I'm making a 'puss' about something she says. She wants everything out in the open, that girl.

Well?

Jennifer doesn't have much patience. No doubt she has to go out and do something Londony and is in a hurry. A play, maybe.

If u give us five minutes we'll be in position.

And back she comes straightaway: *Roger that.*

Denis was right. We are the only ones up at Dooney's. Mam says Jennifer must have got early Mass, though she knows well the truth I'd say. But we're always better off not being explicit, I find.

Boop boop beep, says the phone.

'Up she comes,' says Denis.

'Well, Jennifer?'

'Mammy.'

'Jennifer, in case you're going to say something scandalous from London, we're out in the car after bringing Nana to Mass,' I say, plenty loud enough.

'Did they recognize you up there, Mammy?'

'Jennifer, your nana is in the car with me, so you can keep your normal smartness to a minimum. Say hello to your nana.'

'Hello, Nana. You look great.'

'I CAN'T SEE HER. WHERE IS SHE?'

'She's there on the phone, Mam.'

'IS SHE IN A CLOTHES SHOP OR WHAT? ON A SUNDAY AND ALL. A DAY OF REST.'

'That's my bedroom, Nana.'

'WHAT HAVE YOU DONE TO YOUR HAIR?'

'Nana, my hair was always like that.'

'YOU'VE IT ALL SHORT AND MANNISH. WHY DID YOU GO CUTTING YOUR GRAND CURLS?'

'Mam, that's Deirdre has the curls.'

'Thanks, Nana. Now I know my style is mannish. Maybe that's what I've been doing wrong. Scaring the men off with my mannish hair. They must have thought they were looking in the mirror.'

Mam was taking the conversation off track. I wanted the news.

'How was your trip to Dubai?'

'Busy, Mammy. Lots of meetings during the day and then all this networking at night to *actuate the leads* we might have made during the day. You know the drill at this stage, Mammy. Bolloxology.'

'Did you bump into my long-lost son out there?'

'I did. We went for evening brunch one night.'

'What's that?'

'It's like a buffet.'

'Why don't they call it buffet?'

'Mammy, buffet now means wrapping ten sausages in a hankie underneath your *Sunday Independent* at a hotel breakfast and taking it away to a match.'

'Nothing wrong with that,' says Denis.

'And how is your brother?'

'Ah, Kevin is Kevin. He can send a thousand Bangladeshis out into fifty degrees of heat but he couldn't wipe his nose without Stephanie's permission.'

'Deirdre was telling me Stephanie is gone cracked with the place.'

'Stop, Mammy. You should see her Instagram. Non-stop Prosecco and shops. Completely unreal, and the children are gone spoilt. Kilsudgeon National School won't know what hit it if they ever come back. And they've no respect for the nanny either. I don't know, Mammy. It's just full of culchies who think they're the Wolf of Wall Street, and there's Kevin's big innocent face in the middle of all the gloss.'

'What's the story with yer man? This fella you said you were seeing?'

'Feck, Mammy, that was a quick change. You'd make a great interrogator.'

'Just answer the question, Jennifer.'

She laughs. 'That's over. Anyway, how are you? Rory tells me that you're involved in a land war.'

'I'm not letting you off that quick. So you were free and easy out in Dubai, so?'

'Free and uneasy, Mam. There is no way I'd be interested in anyone out there. The locals are princes and all smiles when you meet them first, but I knew well if I got any way serious with them, it'd be shutters down for me. *Here's your palace, oh, and here's my other three wives, best of luck.*'

'What about the Irish lads? If they're out there, they'd have a bit of money.'

'They're worse. You wouldn't know who'd have another family back home. I see lots of white tanlines on wedding fingers. Or maybe they're into a bank for big money at home. I heard of a Swedish girl who married an Irish lad and now this vulture fund is after her for a ghost estate in Leitrim.'

'So, no story, no? No bit of scandal to keep your old mother dreaming of hats and fascinators?'

'I'm not even close to a whiff of scandal, Mammy. I don't know what's going on at the moment. I must be giving off a weird chemical. Every man I meet these days is problematic. I meet them first and they seem normal. And then it turns out just awful. They're Scientologists or Evangelicals.'

'Don't talk to me about Evangelicals,' I say, thinking of Oona.

'AND WHAT'S WRONG WITH THAT?' Mam pipes up from the back seat. 'IT WOULDN'T DO EITHER OF YOU A BIT OF HARM TO HAVE A BIT OF RELIGION.'

'Not your kind of Christian, Nana. These fellas are fundamentalist. They'd think you were a holy terror with your set dancing.'

Mam chews her teeth a bit at this news. Anyone who'd come between her and a little dance is not doing God's work.

'Where do these fellas turn up in London? I thought there was no religion there.'

'They turn up everywhere, Mammy. In pubs and online. Terribly charming at first. Promising the sun, moon and stars. I'm telling you, Mam. The Christians are worse than the Muslims for fundamentalism. At least you can tell the Muslims from the name.'

'So what happened with His Nibs – was he in the Moonies or what?'

'Well, Mam … no. It was a different problem with him … you don't want to know.'

'Oh, I do now. What was it?'

'I can't really discuss it in public. Can you get out of the car?'

'I'll get out of the car and leave all ye women to yer filth,' says Denis. He gets out and walks around the layby, looking in over the ditch, blowing on his hands. Denis always does this when the Facetime gets a bit personal.

'Mam, take me off speaker a second. I can't really say it in front of Nana either.'

'CAN'T SAY WHAT?' says Mam. 'IS SOMEONE ON DRUGS, I SUPPOSE?'

Mam thinks everyone is on drugs. And she's on more drugs than any of us.

I turn off the speaker. 'OK, you're on a secure line now, pet. Go ahead.'

'It just felt routine, you know?'

'No spark there, as they say on *First Dates*?'

'No, Mam. The physical aspect of the relationship was not good. He was very uptight, he didn't like it when—'

I have to interrupt. Jennifer is way too frank for me, and listening to her with Mam behind me is like watching telly when a quare bit comes on.

'I suppose the physical thing *is* important, Jennifer. In fairness to your father, he always had great stam—'

'MAM, AH JESUS! What made you think it was OK to start telling me anything like that?'

'I DON'T CARE WHAT YOU'RE TALKING ABOUT, BUT TELL JENNIFER I DON'T LIKE TO HEAR HER TAKE OUR LORD'S NAME IN VAIN.' This was Mam again in the back seat. I hope that was the only bit of the conversation she'd overheard.

'Where did you meet him again?'

'The cuddle workshop.'

'*Cuddle workshop?* Is that the hugging place?'

'This is different. You meet and there's cuddling lying down and it's all supposed to be a safe space, but it doesn't mean the fella you'd meet there wouldn't turn out to be a waste of space after.'

'And are you on this Kindling thing?'

'Tinder? Yeah, but that's no good for finding a relation-ship. It's just hook-ups.'

'Hook-ups?'

'Sex, Mammy.'

'Leave some bit of mystery, Jennifer. Or I'll start talking about your father again.'

'OK, Mammy. Anyway, as I always say, I don't need a man. Maybe I'll go for a woman. That'd get Nana going!'

'As long as she was Catholic, I'd say she wouldn't mind.'

'AS LONG AS WHO WAS CATHOLIC?'

'It's good to keep your options open anyway.' I'm going along with her because I'm assuming that she isn't, but I hope she isn't because ... not that there's anything wrong at all, Paudie Doran's youngest is ... it's just, I was reading it costs the couples a fortune to have a baby.

'And how are things back home?' Jennifer interrupts me as my thoughts run on to surrogacy and court cases. 'I forgot I was talking to the vice-chairperson of the Tidy Towns. Is Nana taking the minutes? And by the way, where's your chain of office?'

'I'm getting it Brassoed.'

I tell her about the table quiz and the clean-up, but I don't mention arguing on the side of the road with fencing Poles and angry sisters.

'I'll have to go, Mammy. Me and Neelam have tickets for a matinee at the South Bank. Sounds like you need to sort out three generations there. Put me on speaker again so I can say goodbye to Nana and Daddy.'

I knock on the window to tell Denis to get back in. He gets in eagerly. He's frozen.

'How are you, Daddy?'

'Ah, the same as ever. Your mother probably has you filled in.'

'That's it, Daddy? Nothing to say to your favourite daughter?'

'She's not here to say anything to. Are you seeing any matches over there?'

'It's the other side of London, Daddy, and they've stopped winning now that the recession is over.'

'That's the way. And the car. How's your Beamer?'

'Flying, Daddy. Passed the MOT.'

'A fine car. You should bring it over here on the ferry to let the locals know we're in the money.'

'But it's a 2008.'

'With an English reg you could tell them it's new and they wouldn't know.'

'And Nana, how are you?'

'I'M VERY BOUND UP.'

'Thanks for letting me know, Nana. How are you otherwise?'

'I'M NO WAY OTHERWISE. WHEN I'M BOUND UP, I CAN'T THINK OF ANYTHING ELSE.'

'Are you getting plenty of fibre?'

'I'M SICK OF FIBRE. NO TASTE AT ALL OFF IT.'

'Right so, Jennifer. Anyway, I'd better go home and get your Nana settled.'

'I THINK SOMETHING'S HAPPENING DOWN BELOW,' says Mam.

'Giving out always loosens her up,' says Denis under his breath.

'I've never felt more homesick in my life than right now.' Jennifer is as dry as sandpaper sometimes.

'I'll hang up first so, to make it easier on you, Jennifer.'

'Bye, Mammy. Mwah mwah.' And she's gone.

21

CRUELTY IN A WRAPPER

Whats the internet like in your place Auntie Ann it's medieval here

This type of text from Freya is a common occurrence. However bad the reception is with us, you'd be better off sending pigeons from the little cottage where she and Geraldine live. Geraldine rents it from Ollie Twomey, an old farmer who I'd say has a soft spot for her, because she pays shag-all rent. And sometimes she doesn't bother paying it. I've warned her Ollie won't be around for ever, but she says she'll cross that bridge when she comes to it. The cottage used to be called Willow Cottage before, but Geraldine renamed it Tig Síle na Gig. She was big into all this Celtic stuff after she saw Clannad around the time they did the *Robin Hood* theme tune. She covered the front wall in carvings of women's bits. Although the hedge has grown over them. Not that I'd be a bit prudish, but poor Freya used to get a fierce mocking over it when the school bus picked her up. Pussy Willow they called her. Anyway, the cottage is in an awful hole in the ground so it'll never get more than one bar of internet, they say.

i don t know

can you do a test?

Half the town is telling the other half to do a test for internet speed. You go on to a website and press a button and this needle measures how much internet you have. It's a form of masochism, if you ask me. Sure we know it'll be cat. I go on and test it. As usual, the poor needle barely stirs.

its no worse than the usual

its still better than ours needle wont move ill be down asap

She arrives on her bicycle with her mother's laptop. I knew it straightaway because Geraldine had painted it. It smells when it heats up.

'Does your mother know you have that?'

'She's not talking to me right now. And I'm not talking to her, so that works for me.'

'Why not?'

'I might have said some stuff and she lost it.'

'What kind of stuff?'

'That ... she was a waste of space and a terrible mother. OK, I know, Auntie Ann, but she was just being sooo annoying.'

'What were ye rowing about this time?'

'Guardian angels, Auntie Ann. How can a single mother who was, like, straight up excommunicated by her mother and given out to by a priest for getting pregnant believe in angels? I'd rather she was Catholic, then I could totally slate her on feminist grounds, but this angels stuff ...' Freya taps her head.

She's being dramatic. Mam was *upset* at Geraldine and the priest was a bit awkward, but he was only enquiring whether she was OK for money, but that's not as good a story when you're fourteen and everyone else is a gom.

'I'm there with cramps and she's all like, *Your armpits are blocked with negative prana* or some shit, and I'm like, *Ger, just give me some Panadol already, I'm on my goddamn period.*'

'Listen to me now, Freya. Your mother isn't perfect, no more than the rest of us.'

'Omigod, such a hypocrite. I *know* you think she's less perfect than you, though. I see your face when I'm telling you the latest thing she's said or that she's into. Anyway, can we please stop talking about her?'

She opens the laptop and immediately lets out a shout. 'Oh, noo!'

'What's wrong?'

'Her laptop is locked. I thought I turned that off. And I don't know the password. I know it's something to do with her reiki stuff. Oh, what's the name of those shaka things we're all supposed to have for healing?'

I'm only half listening to her. I'm on the phone. There's only so much you can be interfering with in another woman's family.

'Geraldine? It's Ann. Yeah, she's here with me.'

Freya's trying to drag my hand away from the phone. 'AUNTIE ANN! You are such a backstabber.'

'What? Yes, she told me about the row. How did that grab you? Oh, I know, I've heard worse from my own. Listen, what's the password for your laptop? Freya has it here. You knew? Yeah, I know, very dramatic. OK, hang on … Freya get a pen there. *chakramamma14* all lower case? Two m's in "mamma", thanks a lot, Ger. Yeah, I'll talk to you properly later.'

I hang up.

'Does that password work?'

'Guess so.' She's bit sulky now, typing fierce hard on the keys.

'What are you here for anyway? I was so distracted by your drama I forgot to ask.'

'I have to do a thing for school, Auntie Ann. Just pointless stuff. Junior Cert technology is dire. I've to research the internet for an essay about cybercrime and I'm like, *I'm already coding, hellooo.*'

'Would you eat apple tart?'

'No, I'm not supposed to. I'm just disgusting right now.'

She's as thin as a lath, but there's no point in trying to convince her. I put a Denis-sized slice of apple tart near her and sneak a biscuit in as well.

It's like leaving food out for birds. She doesn't stir at first, but eventually she takes a pinch off the crust, and then a nibble, and soon she just mills into it. There's bits of it on the keyboard and she's licking her lips as she types. I love seeing a young one destroy an apple tart. It makes me feel better about doing it myself.

'C'mon, would you … omigod, this stupid laptop. I don't know why we don't have a tablet. Mam is just the worst.'

There's further typing and cursing. I go out and leave her to it and get my things ready for my rounds tomorrow. After a half an hour I come back and she seems finished and is looking at me as if she's got plans for me.

'Still can't believe they stole your field, Auntie Ann.'

'Strictly speaking, it wasn't my field. It was just a promise, Freya.'

'But the way they humiliated you, Auntie Ann. Oona, that American woman, such a dick move. Total patriarchy thing.'

'Patriarchy? But she's a woman, Freya.'

'They're the worst, Auntie Ann. When you're a hostage to the patriarchy you can become an internalized misogynist. Self-haters. It's a thing.'

I'm finding it hard to keep up. It was easier when men were supposed to be a shower of shites and we were in the right. Which wave was that again? Freya tells me there were four in total.

I sit down with tea and some of the lesser biscuits. She has left nothing on her plate.

'Would you like a few sausages?'

'Eugh, Auntie Ann. Cruelty in a wrapper.' And she takes a few of my biscuits.

'No one died for these, Auntie Ann,' she says, crunching.

I don't tell her where gelatin comes from. But it's nice talking to her, so I open up a bit more than I might with a daughter.

'I mean, like, I was a bit upset about the field thing, Freya.'

'Tell Auntie Freya, Auntie Ann. Spill it. You'll feel good,' and she starts rubbing my hair.

'Cop on, you! And mind my hair. It's useless enough as it is. One head massage from your family is enough for me.'

'Your self image is worse than mine. What's your excuse? Menopause, is it?'

'No, I'm gone beyond … hold on a second now, I'm not discussing my hormones with a young slip of a thing.'

'You're just jealous cos all my hormones are brand new, even if they're making me insane.'

We laugh a bit. I fill up the mugs again.

'To tell you the truth, the worst of it was that everyone seemed to be in on this TV thing and know about it before me. And they let me go and make a mug of myself in the paper.'

'We'll have to get you on Facebook so, Auntie Ann.'

'I am on it, but I'm afraid of my life of pressing the wrong button and putting out a picture of my bra or something. You wouldn't know what you'd catch off it. They'd hack you as soon as look at you. I prefer getting my news the old way.'

'So you're going to the meeting?'

'What meeting?'

And she shows me the Kilsudgeon *Celts* Appreciation page, which has a big Information Meeting tonight. The first I've heard of it. The news is passing me by. The old ways are letting me down.

'Look, I'll set you up as Kilsudgeon Tidy Towns, then you can be friends with everyone, get all the news and say nothing to no one about your bra.'

She takes my phone and starts tapping away like mad.

'How did you get into my phone?'

'Zero, zero, zero, zero is your password, Auntie Ann. Now what's your app store password?'

'What store? I haven't gone near a store.'

Freya does the sigh she normally does when trying to explain technology to me. 'What passwords do you use anywhere else?'

'I don't know.' I type out my email password with my fingers in thin air to test it. 'Try Ann1210.'

She types it and makes a snorty laugh. 'Omigod, Auntie Ann, how are you not hacked already? That's the worst password *ever*. Your first name and your birthday. That's it?'

'How would they know my birthday? Denis hardly does.'

'It's on your Facebook. Your birthday is on it.'

'Ah, no one would be interested in the likes of me. What do I have to be sharing?'

She shows me the phone. 'OK, it's downloading now.'

'There's no sign of it stirring, Freya.'

'Just wait, Auntie Ann. It has to load. It's going to take more time with the absolutely tragic internet here.'

I don't know why I need it on my phone at all, but Freya says to run a successful page you need to respond quickly, and apparently I'm one of the administrators as well. The only administrator I know is Tracy, so I wonder does that mean I'll become a pain in everyone's backside.

My smartphone doesn't know what hit it. I got it two Christmases ago, but my lot are always giving out to me that I don't use its 'full potential'. *What's the point in having a smartphone if you're only texting and ringing and checking Rip.ie?* says Deirdre. But that's all a phone used to have to do and we got on fine. I say that now as if I don't remember the landline or not having a phone at all. How quick you get used to something.

'Now it's ready. Put up something.'

'What'll I put up? Eh, maybe write … Hello, everyone … this is our Facebook page for the Tidy Towns. I don't know. What do people write on these things?'

'Hello? That's going to win the internet. Here, show me the phone and I'll do a bit. Are there photos of the clean-up somewhere?'

'I don't know. They were in the paper that time.'

'You're a disaster. Maybe let me take it over for a while, Auntie Ann. I have plans for it. I mean, *I'm* not actually on Facebook much, but it's useful for the old folks to find out what's going on. Just remember, Facebook are totally taking your secrets, so don't say anything on the phone because Messenger might be listening, but for this you should be OK, as long as you don't go throwing any local shade.'

I recognize all the words she's using but I have a feeling they don't mean what they used to mean.

'Look, all you have to do is take a few photos of rubbish and people in hi-vises and I'll do the rest, OK? Trust me, Auntie Ann. Now, you should get dressed for the meeting. I'll mind the Facebook for you.'

22

WOULD THEY BE NEEDING MEAT?

There's a sniff of money in the air as we gather for the meeting in the hall. People from every shop and small business for miles around are in. A few of the young lads have Viking hats on. This is different from the Tidy Towns meeting. No one is saying what they should be doing or complaining about anything. They're there to listen.

It starts only ten minutes late, which is a record. There's no waiting for stragglers. There are no stragglers.

Sitting up the front are Patsy and Father Donnegan, as usual, Dinny Sheehan, the man who organizes most things; Man Bun is there, too, and Oona has also wangled her way on to the top table, sitting right next to Patsy. Proud as punch and dolled up as well. There's just about enough room for Gordon.

Man Bun is looking very much at home.

Patsy takes to the stage. We're all ready for a big long rigmarole of a speech, but it's not.

'Before we start, I understand that our wonderful Tidy Towns group has a few concerns over the location of the production, isn't that right, Ann Devine?'

'Habvuh.' A sort of a noise comes out of me that doesn't make sense.

'Round of applause for Ann, everyone.'

'Emfff,' I say. You see, all it was was that I was on the phone to Gordon about them taking the town park and I just happened to mention we were worried about the rubbish they'd bring, and he said he was going to do up a 'letter of concern' and I didn't hear any more after that. He must have sent the letter and now I'm supposed to talk about it. Meanwhile, Patsy is still praising us away to beat the band. Which is a bad sign.

'They're doing sterling work, mighty work, out there on the highways and byways, making our little town spick and span, and I'm sure that's one of the reasons why it was picked as a location for the historic filming. Now, the floor is yours, Ann.'

I want the floor to swallow me up. 'Epff,' I say.

Gordon puts his hands on his chair like he's going to stand up, but Patsy places an arm on his.

'No, we have to hear from one of our local heroes. You don't want to be accused of mansplaining, do we, haha?'

I don't have Deirdre beside me to give me a nudge. I get to my feet. Patsy is doing this on purpose. Oona is looking at me, through me. I keep babbling, though, at least I'm saying words.

'Ah well, no, Patsy, no, it's just that we were hoping, you know, you see Tommy was going to give us the field … I mean … no, we just wanted to make sure that there wouldn't be any rubbish and then, like, I suppose, you know, it's just that, we'd be concerned that … *cough* … and like, I suppose like … amm …' My throat goes dry.

Oona sees her chance and interrupts. 'Oh, come on, Patrick Ignatius, and with the greatest of respect, Mrs Devine, we're talking about the greatest investment this communidy has ever seen. Can we get on with finding out about the TV show, amirite, people? Amirite? Amirite?'

She's rite it seems, because there are a few claps around the room. I shrink back into my chair.

Someone pats my arm. It's Sally. She must have snuck in behind me. She whispers into my ear, 'She's a sharp one, Ann. I'd stay away from her. Them Mullinses were a dark lot going way back.'

I turn around and Freya and Geraldine are standing along the side. They must have arrived in late. Freya looks annoyed.

Patsy stands up, pats Oona's arm a little too long and puts on a show of acting as the peacemaker. 'Now, ladies, we're all on the same side here.'

Then he pauses, long enough to make people think he's got something big to say, but not so long to allow anyone else to get a word in.

'My friends, neighbours, hardworking people of Kilsudgeon, this is potentially the greatest thing to happen to our little village. *The Celts – Hound of Destiny* promises to do for Ireland what *The Romans* did for the Brits. There will be renewed interested in our Celtic heritage. From a government point of view, I will be lobbying for infrastructural improvements – a direct link road to the motorway to facilitate the busloads of fans that this series will no doubt generate. Busloads of dedicated fans paying money to have photos taken on the site. I understand the concerns of good people like Mrs Devine, but did you know that *Game of Thrones* is after bringing one *billion* euro to the North of Ireland, going to benefit Orangemen? Well, this time it's all going to the green side, no disrespect to yourself, Gordon.'

Gordon looks a bit put out. There's always a bit of that under the surface around here. Even though Gordon's grand-father fought in the War of Independence.

'Would anyone deny us that opportunity?' Patsy shouts.

They're all looking at me now. Like I'd burnt a billion euro in front of them and danced a jig around the flames.

'The money will be reinvested in the area, bringing jobs and prosperity, finally, to one of the most ignored regions in the country. Look at *Star Wars* and Kerry. They are gone stone mad for Skellig Michael. We can build our own Skellig here. We have the technology. There's children tak-ing Luke as a confirmation name don't know one iota about gospels or Mass. Isn't that right, Father, you were saying that before?'

'As long as they don't be coming up with Obi Wan Kenobi I don't mind,' Father Donnegan says with a laugh.

'The opportunity this presents for us could be huge. We'll have money for ten town parks!'

After a few more minutes of telling us about the jobs, film school and shopping mall that we were going to get in the next fortnight, he brings Man Bun into it.

'I'd now like to introduce you to Malachy Stevenson, from Gubu Productions. He is the official location scout with the production.'

Man Bun stands up. He looks less shifty now that we know what he's up to.

'Kilsudgeon, thank you for being so perfect for us. We love the site. There's no way we'd have gone to Drumfeakle, with their bullshit standing stone.'

They love him. He's a pure charmer. Like Ryan Montana, he has all the local jokes.

'Kilsudgeon's fairy fort is the real deal. We'll take good care of it, don't worry, Mrs Devine. All our litter is biode-gradable,' he says, and they all laugh. Ann Devine and her litter. That's what I am now. I can feel my face just burning.

'Picture the scene,' he goes on. 'The armies of the North lined up against the armies of the West. Queen Maeve against Cúchulainn ...'

'I thought it was about Fionn mac Cumhaill,' pipes up Gordon, but he's shushed down.

'Fionn mac Cumhaill is in it as well,' says Man Bun.

The Celts – Hound of Destiny seems to be about Cúchulainn and the Fianna and Queen Maeve and whoever else they can throw in it, by the sound of it. They have monsters and seabattles and the devil knows what else. Maybe the Devil as well.

'But it all starts here at the Kilsudgeon studios. Right here in Kollywood.'

Kollywood, everyone starts muttering, like it's a prayer.

'Why Kilsudgeon?' asks Malachy Man Bun. 'Why not Kilsudgeon? The underdeveloped jewel in the crown of the heart of Ireland. Unspoilt. Pristine. The true beating heart of Ireland.'

He's good, I'll give him that. I'm nearly carried away myself. There's cheering now in the room. Patsy is back on his feet. He looks a bit miffed that he doesn't get this kind of reaction, so he wants to claim the stage back again.

He launches into a list of things he has got for the area – signposts, medical cards, including one for Mam. Although she would have got that anyway, but he claims credit for it and for a list of other things that he probably had nothing to do with, but that's the game, isn't it? Claiming credit.

There are questions from the floor. None of them is about town parks. Only about what kind of money you could make out of the TV people.

'Would ye be needing meat?' asks Alan from the butcher's.

'Where will ye be getting yer sheet metal from?' says a fella next to me wearing a Moore's Fabricators fleece.

Every business is wondering if *The Celts – Hound of Destiny* will be needing something.

'Celtic hairstyles?' shouts Frances Deegan, the woman who does my hair. Now, no disrespect to Fran, but she can just about manage my mop. I don't know what kind of a fist she'd make of the Queen from the West.

Geraldine even sticks up her paw and asks if there would be a need for a reiki or alternative-therapy centre. I give her a *you as well?* look. She mouths *What?* at me.

Just after a local farmer asks whether there would be any market for hay and silage and *maybe a few sucklers*, Gordon chips in that we'd love to have the place looking as nice as possible for the film set in advance of the Tidy Towns, which I think is what I was trying to say.

Oona makes a big show about rolling her eyes. 'Aw, come ONNN,' she says.

But Man Bun is ever the diplomat. 'That would be super-amazing,' he says. 'We should totally reach out to you guys. In fact, we'll be setting up a liaison committee to tie in with local community representatives.'

Local community representatives – that's more like it now.

'So we're hoping to start filming in a few weeks' time, but it's going to get exciting around here in the next while as we build our outdoor and indoor sets. We'll be looking for locations, accommodation and, who knows, maybe a few sucklers, haha.'

Man Bun seems to think he's finished, but he's still holding the microphone so the meeting gets a little derailed by rumours of a Buddhist centre and *where will they get planning permission for that?* and *the Muslims will probably be next, I suppose?* Patsy rescues him from having to answer anything on that and he wraps up the meeting.

Gordon comes up to me afterwards.

'We'd better fill out that form, Ann. We can't call ourselves a Tidy Towns group without a Tidy Towns application. I'll call up later in the week.'

Freya is standing by my side as we file out after the meeting.

'Don't worry, Auntie Ann, I won't let you be humiliated like that. I'm going to sort it.'

'But Freya—'

'We have to fight back, Auntie Ann.'

She looks fierce determined. I don't like the sound of this.

23

MAD LADS ONLINE

'LEAVE THEM BISCUITS ALONE, I'M WARNING YOU!' I roar in at Denis from the kitchen after I hear the rustling.

'I was only going to take the one.'

'There's only nine in it. One will be missed!'

'NINE? That's about a euro a biscuit, Ann. I hope this fancy man is worth it.'

It's two weeks since the film meeting and we're finally getting around to filling out the form for the Tidy Towns. Gordon arrives after eight. Denis is dispatched to the telly to watch his wildlife programme while we work at the table. I spread the biscuits out to make them look more. There are only seven. Denis looks guilty.

'I'm sorry again to be interrupting you both,' says Gordon when he arrives. 'It's just that Flora has her book club tonight and ... well, it gets a bit raucous. Sally is there, Ann, so you should definitely come along next time. There's going to be a lot of wine. I'd say I'll have to go in the back door when I go home.'

Denis starts laughing from the couch. I don't know what's that funny about antelopes.

'I still think we're a bit early to be entering the Tidy Towns, Gordon.'

'We have to enter the competition, Ann. It's our whole *raison d'être*.'

'My *raison d'être* is to stay out of trouble now, Gordon.'

'People expect it, Ann. Drumfeakle are making a big push. *Voice of the County* did a roadcaster from there.'

'I never really cared what they did in Drumfeakle before.'

'That's rivalry what you're feeling now, Ann. It's what keeps a community going.'

'But the turn-out for the clean-ups is drying up.'

We had three people at the last one. I felt an eejit putting all the pickers back in the car.

'They'll get behind a competition. You saw what they were like at the table quiz.'

'OK, look, it's grand, we'll fill out the form, but we should tell them it's our first time and to go easy on us.'

'That's the spirit, Ann,' says Gordon as I bring over the laptop.

Don't let me down now, I say to the laptop in my mind.

Installing updates one of eighteen. One per cent complete, is how it replies to me. We sit looking at it.

'Denis, were you messing with this?' I know well he wasn't, but I have to say something. 'We'll have to get a new one of these,' I say as it goes up to fourteen per cent complete. 'I'll freshen up the tea.'

Eventually, this teenage computer of mine drags itself out of bed and says hello.

'What's it saying now? YOUR COMPUTER IS AT RISK. BUY NORTON ANTIVIRUS OR RISK LOSING EVERYTHING. I haven't much to lose.'

I find the Tidy Towns form on the internet and we stare at it. I thought it would be along the lines of *Here's a picture of a flowerbed. Here's rubbish we picked up. What do ye think?* But it's page after page of stuff you were supposed to have done that they'd be looking out for, like special areas of conservation, presentation of heritage buildings, squares, parks, landscaping, paving, wildlife habitat restoration.

'Gordon, they'll laugh us out of it.'

But he's all optimistic. 'Rome wasn't tidied in a day,' he says. 'Don't give up just yet. Go back to the start and see what we have. Right. *Outline areas of special conservation.* What about the boats?'

'Oh, don't talk to me about the boats.'

The boats are breaking my heart. I think they've started entering my dreams. We were flying at one stage. The boats had all been cleaned out, new topsoil put in, bulbs planted, and every one of them got a new lick of paint. The children wanted to go painting names on them and we thought that was a good idea until the more 'patriotic' of them started putting anti-Drumfeakle graffiti on them.

Then there was retaliation. Probably by someone from Drumfeakle because they wrote *Titanic* on one of them and *Kilsudgeon is only a loada gays* on another, plants were ripped out and one of them even had the soil stolen from it. Can you believe that? In the countryside you'd think there was no shortage of earth. I know well where the plants have gone. Gary Cushin's mother suddenly has a great little flowerbed going, and she hadn't so much as planted a seed of doubt in twenty years.

'*List of initiatives relating to accessibility,*' Gordon reads from another page. 'Have we done anything here?'

'There's that bit of plywood going up the step into the post office. That's about the height of the accessibility now. We haven't a hope of getting any marks out of this crowd, Gordon. I'd rather not enter than bring the place into disrepute. Drumfeakle got three hundred and something last year.'

'We'll just put "Not Applicable" for that. Click next there and see what else there is.'

Tidiness and Litter Control pop up on the screen.

'Now we're back in the game,' he says. 'Our specialty. *How many clean-ups?* Put down thirty.'

'But we've only done four.'

'How are they going to know how many clean-ups we've done? By their very definition the evidence is thrown away. We've a load of photos from the first one. We can let it be known, without saying anything, that they're from a myriad of clean-ups.'

'That's lying, Gordon.'

'It's only lying if they ask us a question.'

'Are they going to think we got exactly the same weather each time? What about this bit – *Waste Segregation*? What did we do with the rubbish after, Gordon, by the way?'

'Duggan Environmental took it away.'

'Gordon, that'll be dumped in a lake! The EPA are around his place more often than the VAT man, and that's saying something. We won't say a bit about segregation.'

'Then put down that we are interested in exploring waste segregation strategies.'

'Fierce interested.'

'Right, what's the next category after segregation? *Inclusion. Outline how your group has reached out to disadvantaged and marginalized groups.'*

I don't tell Gordon about how I'm supposed to be an alcoholic disadvantaged mother whose son had to be rescued from me.

'I suppose they mean foreigners. Have we reached out to anyone else?' Gordon says.

'I was going to send an email to that prayer group of the born-agains. What are they called again? The Christ the Redeemer of the Son of God and His Cousin John the Evangelist. But Father Donnegan said to stay away from that crowd, that they'd only be trying to convert us. *And I can't afford to lose any more of ye, Ann, or I'll end up being transferred to somewhere mediating in a gangland feud*, he said.'

'That won't scan well on the form. I'll put down the litter clean-up for it anyway.' He edges me off the keyboard gently and starts typing flowery language about *endeavouring* to do this, that and the other.

'We can't put down "litter clean-up" for everything, Gordon. How is it inclusive?'

'Doesn't it attract a wide range of people? Wasn't Neans there in her wheelchair?'

'So Neans is representing the foreigners, the old, the disabled and the disadvantaged?'

'Look, Ann, we have to use our ingenuity here. The thing about these competitions is that they're supposed to motivate a town to do something. It's aspirational. Let's go back to the environmental one. *Raising understanding and awareness of natural amenities, creating an appreciation of how species and habitats should be best protected and managed. Provide evidence of good co-operation with expert groups and relevant authorities, especially in carrying out work in sensitive areas. Provision of access to natural areas and interpretation of key aspects.*'

'So?'

'Did I see somewhere there were meetings about badgers a while back?'

'The last meeting about badgers was about killing them over TB.'

'We'll have another one and get an environmentalist along. Gerard might know someone. Build it and they will come, Ann.'

'Jesus, Gordon, you're gone very blasé.'

'It's all about gestures, Ann. Seeing that Malachy man a couple of weeks ago was a revelation. Just put in the big words and fill in afterwards. Otherwise, we'll get nowhere. Right, next is *Communications*. What's our communications strategy, Ann? We'll have a look at our Facebook page.'

Gordon is silent, and then lets out a little yelp. 'Ann, what's this? Aren't you supposed to be running the Facebook page?'

'Well, I haven't got around to doing much yet. Freya is looking after it for the time being.'

'She's looking after it all right. Look at this. We can't have this, Ann.'

'What am I looking at? *Geraldine Hoare has shared a link on your page: Twenty-one signs that you may be an Earth Angel.*'

'No, Ann, the thing above. Not the mother, the daughter. Your niece.'

I follow where his finger is jabbing at the screen.

Kilsudgeon Tidy Towns page has signed DoSomethingAnything. org's campaign to stand with Freya Hoare to save Kilsudgeon Tidy Towns Committee's Campaign for Kilsudgeon Town Park.

'Ann, what is she playing at? You need to delete this straightaway.'

'I can't delete it. There's no button. She must have locked me out, Gordon.'

We look at the rest of the page. There's one set of photos of a clean-up and the rest is … very 'political' I suppose you could say. I watch Gordon read it, and I almost laugh. He adjusts the glasses on his nose as he sees *Twenty-five Microaggressions Perpetuated by Men and How to Spot Them*. I wonder is *Taking over a keyboard* on the list?

'This won't do,' he says. 'I don't think it's in keeping with our ethos. I mean, I admire her … well, she's feisty, but there's a time and place. And what's this?' He's pointing at an article that Freya has shared about mooncups. *Women of Kilsudgeon – this is the sustainable and safe way to manage your flow*, she's written above it.

'What's a mooncup, Ann?'

Denis is coughing away again on the couch. How does *he* know what a mooncup is?

It appears Father Donnegan doesn't know what a mooncup is either because this post is liked by Kilsudgeon Parochial House. Unless the housekeeper is secretly sustainable.

'I'll talk to Freya and sort it out.'

'Please do, Ann. It's just as well we've very few people liking the page at the moment.

I decide to stage an ambush.

I'm outside the Mercy school now, waiting for her. Not exactly outside, obviously. I know how far away to park from the days of my own three. Up around the corner, not opposite the shop. Down a bit. I told Geraldine I would collect Freya as a thank you for the head massage. I can be devious too when I put my mind to it.

I see her approaching. She looks like a young woman and a little girl at the same time. Head in phone. There's another girl walking near her, talking, but it's hard to tell if Freya is listening. She's a biggish girl, but I've seen bigger. She seems friendly. But I see the look in Freya's eyes and I don't like it.

'Hi.'

'Hi, Freya. Who's this?'

'Hi, Miss Hoare.'

'This is my aunt, Lossie, not my mother. My mother couldn't be arsed.'

'Would you like a lift anywhere, Lossie?'

'Lossie's fine, Auntie Ann.'

Lossie looks like she'd love a lift, but she says no. 'I need the exercise,' she says, and smiles down at the ground.

'Don't self-deprecate, omigod, Lossie,' Freya gives out to her.

'Yeah, OK. Sorry, Frey. OK, bye, Auntie Ann.'

I don't say anything yet. I'm struggling to remember teenage girl politics. It's been a while.

'I need to talk to you, miss, about our Facebook page. Sit into the car there.'

Freya sits in. She looks like she's been expecting this.

'OK, before you say anything, you have to understand what I'm trying to do. I'm trying to get social media on our side.'

'And how will that work? What'll social media do?'

'We need to go viral, Auntie Ann. When you go viral, you get loads of memes and likes and shares and retweets, and then the papers and the radio and the telly get interested cos that's all they care about now. Once the world hears about this injustice, there will be pressure on to get your town park back.'

'I think the world has other things to worry about.'

'It does, but this is the kind of thing people decide to get angry about. It's easier.'

'I think you're being a bit optimistic, Freya. It's just a town park. And we might get one eventually. Or a few garden seats to sit on. Or a few more boats.'

'Do you really believe that, Auntie Ann?'

'Well, no, but still, sometimes there's not a whole lot you can do about these th—'

'C'mon, Auntie Ann. Nothing is going to change around here without direct action. You know this council are just, like, the worst, and we keep electing them, but maybe it's time to stop.'

'But that TV show might bring some money in.'

'That TV show is just going to be boobs and axes and sex scenes with consent issues, Auntie Ann. Is that what we want Kilsudgeon to be known for?'

'It's nearly known for that anyway, if you read the court reports in the *Sentinel*.'

'We have to get the word out, Auntie Ann. We need to get everyone involved. We need to get militant.'

'You'll be hacking next, Freya, wearing a mask. Is that where this is going?'

I don't want to be negative. It's nice to see Freya so awake, or however she puts it, but I think she needs to live in the real world.

'Get me into the page, Freya.'

There is a 'pinned post' at the top of the page. *An Open Letter to the Council from Gary Cushin – Activist on behalf of Kilsudgeon Tidy Towns.*

'Oh, Freya, what did you go inviting him on for? Sure, he's a pure communist. Are we communist now?'

'He's not, Auntie Ann, he's just on the side of the workers. That's just name-calling to blacken the name of the class struggle.'

Where is she getting this language from? No prizes for guessing where.

'Read it. You'll see.'

Today was a dark day for democracy. Once again the people of rural Ireland, the plain working-class people, so often caricatured and patronized, have been oppressed by the heavy hand of nudge-and-wink politics, the sleeveen plámássers who were descended from the land agents that oppressed us under a different flag. Ancient Celtic land has been trampled on, and for what? A cartoonish production that will pillage more than our ancestors ever could have. Now is the time for Antifa Kilsudgeon to stand up!

'Antifa? Who's fa?'

'Fascists.'

'Have we got fascists? Wouldn't you see them marching around the place?'

'Fascists aren't marching, Auntie Ann, yet,' she says, and pauses for effect. 'They are marching online.'

'You'll have to delete it.'

'You are just a slave to the establishment.'

'But I thought you'd love a bit of establishment. That's what you're always giving out about your own mother, and her what is it you call it – her cray-cray ways?'

'She might be a bit OTT, but at least she lives her life her way.'

'Log me in and delete it, Freya.'

She reluctantly shows me where to go.

'I'll hack it, Auntie Ann.'

'Seriously, Freya, leave it or you're off the team. I can't have you doing a Jim Larkin on a page about litter, of all things. Jesus, have you nothing better to do? Like a normal—'

'Like a normal what? What do you mean, Auntie Ann?'

'Nothing.' But I knew she knew what I meant.

'Say it.'

'Well, have you friends to be spending time with? You know, people out in the flesh, besides talking to mad lads online about Antifa.'

'Thanks. Yeah, thanks for that.'

'Ah, Freya, you know what I mean. I just mean that ...'

'*You're* my friend. Or at least, I thought you were anyway. What else am I going to do around here, a weirdo like me? You *know* what it's like being me. I can't believe you said that.' She starts to cry.

I wall her up in a hug before she can get out of the car.

'I'm still your friend, Freya, sweetheart. You'll just have to put up with your weak ould aunt who's in the establishment even though there's no money in it for her.'

She's half laughing and crying and snotting into my shoulder.

'You can be my woman on the inside,' she says. 'We'll tear it down from the inside out.'

'I'll go undercover so, Freya.' I laugh. 'I'll be in deep. They won't even suspect me.'

'Auntie Ann, the one-woman resistance movement,' Freya says, smiling, and I know I've been forgiven.

24

PUT A CHANGELING IN

Jennifer hears me sigh down the phone to her.

'Oh, no, Mammy. What happened?'

'Nothing happened. Anyway, how are you? How's work? Your place got a mention there in the news. Sally was saying she heard it too. Were they fined by someone over something? Money-laundering, was it?'

'Never mind that, Mammy. What's wrong with you? Tell me what happened. Open up to me.'

'I prefer to bottle it up.'

'Mammy...' She winkles the story out of me – the promise, the field, the sister, the shame.

'She sounds like a right piece of work, Mammy. I meet the likes of her up high in buildings all the time. We'll have to do something about her.'

'And what are we going to do? We're not the John Guccis. We'll leave her be, thank you very much. It's her field and she can do as she pleases. How come you're back on the phone?'

'OK, Mammy. It's John Gotti, but whatever, you shouldn't bottle this up. Bottling it up is what got the country into the state it's in. So what's the story with the telly?'

'Ferocious excitement around the place, Jennifer. The golf club has put in a plan for an international convention centre, would you believe? International. Maybe your company could have a conference here. Patsy Duggan is going around telling everyone he secured the whole thing personally. He got thanked by the minister on the telly, even though they hate each other. The primary school are non-stop *Celt* this and *Celt* that. There's a festival planned for them. There's talk of auditions. A traveller called to the door there the other day with souvenirs.'

'What kind of souvenirs?'

'A kind of a keyring. Wood with varnish on it and *Kilsudgeon Celtic Experience*, and I'd say he got a small child to draw a kind of a spiral thing, a Celtic-looking yoke, on them in Tippex. In fairness, he was quick off the mark. He had eggs as well. And pillows. Such a combination. It was like Lidl in a van. I bought the eggs and they were all right, although you wouldn't know where he got them.'

'Mammy,' warns Jennifer, 'don't be like that now. You always told us not to judge other people.'

'Did I? Why did I tell you that? OK. I won't so.'

The car shook as a lorry went past. Which reminded me.

'The traffic, though, Jennifer. The traffic is a pure fright. Big trucks carrying gear up to the fairy field. And they've set up an office in town, in the church car park, and lads driving around in jeeps like they own the road. It's nearly as bad as when the silage is on. And they'll be filming during the silage as well. They've dug up a good bit of the field with it. It's in an awful state. The fairies'll go mad.'

'The fairies! Jesus, I remember being scared for a whole week because there was a rumour went around third class that if you looked at the Mass rock after six o'clock, you'd be dead within seven days. Do you remember? A fox was barking out the back one night and I had to come and sleep with you and Daddy because I thought the fairies were going to take me away and put a changeling in instead of me.'

I remember it well. I get a little pang. A small sleeping child in the bed is the most gorgeous thing, as long as they don't make a habit of it.

'And then we used to go drinking cans up there back in the day.'

'I know. I could smell it off you coming in.'

'You didn't say it at the time. We thought we were being very clever with the Triple X.'

'Oh, I remember. No one needs that many mints. Your father and me would be laughing downstairs when you came in and suddenly now you were a huge fan of brushing your teeth before a toasted sandwich. What children forget, Jennifer, is that mammies are like the Revenue. We know everything, but we only go after the big crimes. I picked my battles.'

It must be hard realizing Mammy isn't so thick after all. She changes the subject.

'So will you go for the auditions, Mammy?'

'I don't think they're looking for a Tidy Towns person. There wasn't much of that in those times.'

'You're a village elder now, Mam! They were basically the original "Tidy Towns people". Sticking their noses in, giving out to people about the state of their middens.'

'Less of the elders, if you don't mind.'

'Is there any behind-the-scenes news, Mammy? The actual show itself? Any sign of the stars? C'mon, Mam, I've been trying to explain Kilsudgeon to all the nobs I work with here in London and they think it's some sort of Martin McDonagh place, full of lads with slash-hooks sticking out of their heads ...'

She must be talking about Willie Callinan. Although he calmed down a good bit since he made up with the brother.

'... and now the first time it's in the news and you're all cagey.'

'We're kept in the dark as much as anyone, Jennifer. All I know is there's a Welcome Festival coming up and they're going to make a point of introducing the stars then, with a load of razzamatazz. That's when we'll see yer man Cody Bryan and the woman, what's her name, Wardrobe or Cup or whatever.'

'Shelf, Mammy, Shelf McKinnon. Cody Bryan and Kilsudgeon – oh, Mam, that's a combination I am definitely looking forward to seeing!'

'Why do you say that?'

'Cody Bryan is a drinker, Mammy. And whatever else he can get his hands on. He's been off the rails for a good while. This is his comeback, since the *Robot Future* films ended. Remember, Rory used to have a poster on his wall.'

'Maybe they got him for good value so.'

'I don't know whether Kilsudgeon's the best town for him, Mam. Johnny wouldn't be the most sensitive barman around when it comes to alcoholics. He'd serve anyone as long as they had the money. And Cody'll introduce the locals to all sorts. He was done for ketamine last year.'

'What's ketamine?'

'Horse tranquillizer, Mam. They found it on his ranch.'

'The vet will be delighted so. C'mere to me, you still haven't said what you're calling about.'

'Nothing. Just checking in. I might be home soon, that's all. I'm making some changes.'

'You're as bad as Geraldine on Facebook. *Big news but can't say anything* or *Amazing how you know who your friends are.* Spit it out.'

'Harsh, Mammy. Maybe I'm fragile.'

'You are in your eye fragile. Are you pregnant? If you're pregnant, I'll be delighted. Come away home and I'll raise him or her, and I'll get it right this time around after practising with you.'

I'm only half joking at this.

'Mammy, I'm so unpregnant it's not even funny.'

Jennifer has been in London for eight years. She has a big job in one of these multinational finance places. I asked her once exactly what she did for a living. She started to explain but then just said, *OK, Mam, you know on the news when there's a coup and the crowds are throwing stones and some fella with a load of stripes on his uniform is escaping in a helicopter? Well, someone has to manage that fella's money, and that's who I work with.* 'High-net-worth individuals' is the official phrase.

I just tell people she works in a bank. It's easier. I don't like to ask *exactly* how much money she's making, but I'd say she's doing well because I never hear her mention a lack of it. And she always has the nicest of clothes. They don't *look* expensive at first, but you'd know they were. The way the royals do it.

Jennifer is probably the one me and Denis would rely on if we were hard up. Don't get me wrong, we'd *hate* to be a burden, especially after looking after *his* mother – a fierce difficult woman. Still, it's a comfort to think there might be a safety net. Deirdre has the ability, Jennifer has the money. Kevin has the wife that isn't speaking to me. Rory has ... well, I hope it'll be a good while before I'm depending on Rory. Not that I'd ever say that to any of them, of course. They don't need reminding of their obligations before it's due to them. It's hard on the young people now. Long ago the old people died off much faster. Now we hang on till the bitter end.

'Mam ... MAM! You're zoned out. Are you still there?'

'Always, pet. So you're not going to tell me any more?'

'I'll explain properly soon.' She hangs up.

That's something new to be thinking about. Jennifer coming home. Whatever about the town, I'll have to tidy her room.

25

THE TALIBAN THEMSELVES

'Why won't you go, Denis?'

'Them festivals are always a dead loss. It's just an excuse for putting pints in plastic glasses. And then they're not even the full pints. The whole thing is a racket.'

Denis still has PTSD over plastic glasses since he dropped a round of them at Puck Fair years ago, before we were married, and the whole crowd was laughing at him. He was nearly in tears, with Guinness all over his new trousers. I think that's when I fell in love with the man. A man that was able to express his emotions, even about spilled pints, was a rare thing back then. He goes over the story of it every so often, when he feels like torturing himself. *I was squeezing them in and one of the bastards popped up on me.* Since then, plastic glasses are his symbol of everything that can't be trusted.

'Would you not go up and see what it's like now that Dinny has a bit of money to run it? Just come down with me for an hour. I want to have a quick gawk, that's all. I'll buy you a plastic pint, two if you want to make up for spillage.'

I get my way and we set off on foot. It's a fine spring day and there's a feeling of activity in the air. Everyone gets a bit of madness in this weather. Lads are up on roofs hammering and building walls and tuning cars and just celebrating the fresh air. Denis grabs my hand on the way down. The spring has got into him too. Although he lets it go as we approach the village.

A great day to have A Thing on in the Town.

There was always some sort of a festival in Kilsudgeon, with Dinny Sheehan at the heart of it, and no matter what the weather or lack of money, he pushed on with it. Even when it was cancelled because of the foot and mouth, it took a court order to stop Dinny from doing it. If the Taliban themselves were camped out at the Roundabout, Dinny would still try and put on a festival, and maybe rope them in for the skit.

No matter what the weather, he was up on that flatbed lorry doing the raffle.

I remember one year it was lashing rain and the crowd had drifted off to the pub before the raffle. He was shouting away numbers and no one collected the prizes, the poor divil. I felt so sorry for him, so I just said I'd won and brought my ticket up, even though it was the wrong one. *You can give me the worst of the prizes and I'll put it back after*, I said to him. He looked at me, very grateful but defeated. *Keep it, Ann. I'm fed up of this. Rural Ireland is dead.*

But he was always very dramatic. The following years the weather was good and the festival was thronged.

That was until last year, when there was an accident at the 1916 commemoration festival. They didn't have enough hi-vis people minding traffic and an English tourist drove into the flatbed truck with the dignitaries on it. Not only did an Englishman halt the Rising festival, every Tom, Dick and Harry within a mile of the incident put in a claim for whiplash. The court cases are still going on and the council wouldn't let him put on anything again. Obviously, all that's changed. We see Dinny as we arrive. He's rushing around with a walkie-talkie and looking awful stressed. There's a lot more on his mind now. He would have struggled to get so much as a bit of plywood and crates for a stage and a vase for a raffle prize before, but he has different problems this time.

We salute him as he flusters past. He stops, though he looks like he can't afford to.

'Mind a while, Pavel,' he says into the walkie-talkie.

'You're under pressure, Dinny,' says Denis.

'Pressure is for tyres, Denis,' he says, but he turns down the walkie-talkie and leans against a van to talk for a bit anyway.

'I'm used to having nothing. Now they're ringing me up, asking who's going to provide security for Cody Bryan. The fella putting in the sound system says it'll be heard in Limerick and he hasn't put in one like that since Springsteen. A *PR* company girleen – she looked about twelve, Ann – is saying to me, *Who's the engagement lead on social?* Engagement lead! Herself is now asking me should she get Instagram put in, and this is a woman who finds the new teletext fiddly. *You need to maximize your reach*, this slip of a thing says to me, like I was making toothbrushes. Be careful what you wish for is all I'll say, Ann. I'll never give out about the festival not being supported again.'

The light flashes on the walkie-talkie. He can't ignore it any longer.

'Nameajaysiswhatdisfellawantiwonder,' he mutters, and turns it up. 'STALL THE DIGGER, CLIVE, WILL YOU? I'LL BE UP NOW. TELL THAT BOLLOX STAY WHERE HE IS.'

We can see what has him so stressed. It's a different operation entirely to other years. There is a big stage in the church car park. Proper-looking crew with uniforms are setting things up. There are banners going across the street. *Kilsudgeon Welcomes the Celts. Symbols of Our Ancient Heritage.* We have an ancient heritage now, apparently. For the first time, there's a sponsor. Legitimate Fears, the monitored burglar alarm people, are shelling out money for a bit of a funfair, bumper cars and the sling thing that throws you up in the air. There are Legitimate Fears reps handing out sweets and leaflets to the children. I get one of them. *Don't let a sweet day be soured when you get home and the door is broken,* it says.

All across the front of the stage they have big banner ads. Slogans like *But can you trust your locks?*, *What if they're already inside?* and *We'll see the men in the white vans so you won't have to see the men in white coats.* We were never burgled ourselves, thanksbetogod. They knew we had nothing, although the telly is newish. Or was. Maybe we have been burgled and we didn't notice with the mess.

We'll soon have an army of Celts to protect us anyway.

We wander down to where there's food. There are a few chip vans, but they're not mobbed. They have competition.

'Artisans,' says Denis. He almost spits it out. But he goes a bit closer and he sees there are free samples. 'This chutney is the job, Ann,' he says with the mouth full.

I whisper at him to control himself. 'You can't be eating the whole thing, Denis, or we'll have to buy something,'

'How much?' Denis asks the woman at the stall. 'EIGHT EURO!' he says before he can stop himself.

'It's all certified organic,' says the woman. She looks worried about her cracker supply.

We mumble about being back later and slip away. I look back and she's breaking up the crackers into smaller bits.

'Lovely crackers too,' says Denis.

'You're a disgrace.'

I see Freya and Geraldine. She's back from a reiki course, so she should be all healed, but she looks uneasy. Benny C is standing there. Probably too close to her aura. I knew he'd be sniffing around.

Benny and me are civil, but not friendly. I think he's a flake. He thinks I'm boring.

'I'm sorry I don't fit into your pigeonhole, Ann,' he said to me once at a funeral. 'People like me threaten your cosy world because we know that life's not simple and controllable.'

All I'd said to him was did he want the last of the cocktail sausages. But there was drink involved. He had taken too much and I hadn't taken enough.

Now here he comes, over to annoy me.

'Well, Ann, what do you think? Finally, Kilsudgeon's got something going for it. Man, it needed it. Too stifling for a creative. Always has been. You know this TV show could be bigger than *Game of Thrones*, don't you, Ann? This might actually be a place I'd like to move back to. You could get a part in it, Ann, hah? Invading land. Fighting the fairies.'

They all know so.

'You should audition, Ann. Put yourself outside the comfort zone. It's good to try something you can't control. That's what being a creative means.'

Creatives, my eye. Creatives need to wipe their backsides too. And what does he know about me? I hate the people who claim to be free spirits and then tell the rest of us we're all closed up.

I open my mouth to say some of this to him, but there's a screech out of the speakers that has everyone making a face. Dinny wasn't joking about this sound system. He steps up to the microphone. He's nervous. There are dignitaries

196

with chains of office on a viewing gallery, and over in another area it looks like a bigger group of TV production crew. It's easy to spot them, they have a bit of a circus look about them. Confident. You could see by the way they walk around that they already feel they own it. Measuring us up for their lenses.

There are lots of speeches – Dinny, the chairman of the council, the minister, Father Donnegan – the crowd are getting restless and a child raises a laugh when she screams about wanting ice-cream and that this is boring.

'And now a special treat,' says Dinny after half an hour. 'The Kilsudgeon Dancers!'

The dancers fly out on to a plywood platform, choreographed by a woman about my age who must be their teacher. They clatter away for a quarter of an hour and then the teacher gets up and wants us all to do a set. She has one of those mics you wear around the head, and she's barking at us to get into position. I back away, but poor Freya gets sucked in as a group of people move forward. She looks back at me, horrified.

Help me, she mouths as the music starts up and there's ould lads twirling her around. I have to dance in and rescue her, and we twirl our way out.

Malachy Man Bun jumps in, high-kicking and whooping and cheering. Acting up for his crowd. A woman with a phone on a stick nearly falls over laughing when Catherine Shea's Scottie runs in among the dancers and then up the steps on to the stage and is barking at the squeezebox. The musicians take this as their cue to wind down, and there is plenty of laughing and trick-acting. The teacher is not happy, though.

'I had her for two lessons, Auntie Ann. She's pretty hardcore about dancing. Mam ran out of money so I stopped going. I was sooo not sorry.'

Dinny comes back on stage. He's a bit more comfortable now.

'Now, ladies and gentlemen, the boys and girls of fifth and sixth class have a little play to put on. And who knows? Maybe they might get a part in the movie. What do you think, Malachy?'

Malachy throws up a thumb. I'm beginning to warm to the lad.

The boys and girls get up. Master Timmons, the teacher, is over in the corner directing them. He's retiring this year.

'I am going to make Kilsudgeon great again,' says a little boy in a Donald Trump wig. He starts off going around the stage, chasing the girls in blonde wigs. I look over at the telly people. They're shocked.

'Omigod, he is, like, mental, Auntie Ann. I'm so glad he's not my teacher any more. Do you remember the St Patrick's Day parade when I was in school? We had people dressed as ministers in guillotines and I was holding a sign saying *Revenge for Education Cuts*. He is low-key mental.'

They stopped the parades then, after the 1916 commemoration accident, so we've been spared a Timmons special, but he must have persuaded Dinny to let him into this.

Young Trump is building a wall now, and he's trying to stop people from Drumfeakle getting in. 'GET OUT, MEXICANS!' he shouts.

We are relieved when the third and fourth class replace them. Deirdre is one of the mammies ushering them on. They are dressed as Celts. They do a short play about Oisín falling off his horse. 'And so, Oisín, you cannot return to Tír Na Nóg. The world you left is gone and strange. You will die soon.'

They know how to get the mood going. Oisín dies and gets carted off and the narrator makes a little speech at the end.

'We are the ancient people of Ireland. We are proud and free. We are Celts. The best that can be.' The narrator then changes tone. A little nine-year-old girl shouting, 'AND FOR TOO LONG WE WERE UNDER THE HEEL OF THE SAXON BOOT. WE HAVE THROWN OFF THE HEEL AND TASTE FREEDOM'S FRUIT!'

Timmons again, I suppose.

They get a big cheer as they come off. There is a break then, and Freya and myself go back to the food and I buy a chutney from the artisan woman out of sheer embarrassment.

'Put that in your jacket, Freya, and have it with a few crackers.'

I don't know where Denis has gone. When I said I would buy him a couple of pints, I meant of course that he had licence to buy himself a few. I hope he's OK now.

'Look at Benny,' says Freya sourly.

Her father is trying to make conversation with the camerawoman.

'Eughh. What a sap. I just wish that he was just, like ... you know ... there. Like Uncle Denis. It's so much work, Auntie Ann. Just ... being, like ... I dunno, me. And I get so angry with Mammy and it's not her fault – some of the time ...'

'Ah, pet ...'

We grab a tiny sample of brownie and on the spur of the moment I buy the full one.

'You know, Freya, he's still your father, and maybe he can help. Sometimes.'

'But you think he's a sap too, Auntie Ann.'

'Yes ... b–but, no, I don't ... we're just different people and maybe we rub each other up the wrong way.'

I'll have to stop throwing my eyes to heaven in front of her when her father is mentioned. A girl still needs her daddy. It's just that he always manages to say something to annoy me.

'Uncle Denis, he's, like, just … there. Whenever I call in the evening, he's just there or else he's working. He's not going to be running off with a singer.'

'That's true. He'd probably find singers too dear to keep. He's very practical when it comes to affairs, your uncle Denis.'

'How do you, like, I don't know …'

'How do I what?'

'How does anyone … how do you avoid the gimps?'

'I don't know, Freya. I suppose the thing about Denis is a thing that another woman might not like. You know what he's going to do. There isn't the constant worry about what he might get up to next.'

SCREEEEECCHHHHHH.

'Those speakers are a human rights violation,' says Freya.

Dinny is up there again. There is a new banner now, saying *Miss Celtic Kilsudgeon*. A beauty competition that's normally called Miss Road Frontage.

We continue walking and nibbling bits of food. I take the chutney out of Freya's bag again so they know I'm not a scrounger.

'That's the thing all right, Freya. He's predictable.'

And the next thing I hear laughing coming from the main stage and an announcement: 'AND OUR NEXT CONTESTANT IN THE SPECIAL "ALPHA BALE" COMPETITION IS … YOU KNOW HIM WELL … DENIS DEVINE!'

Oh, the Lord save us! Himself! He's there in his ould vest, flexing his muscles.

'I want world peace, Dinny,' he says in the interview, and the crowd are falling over laughing.

'What do you want in a man, tell me, Denis?'

'I want a big, strong man, Dinny,' he says, 'with a clean artic licence and can drive a low-loader.'

The crowd is howling.

Freya looks at me. 'Yeah, Auntie Ann, sooo predicable. You can read him like a book. The girls still waiting to go on must be so fuming, though. It's hard to follow that. Weird that it's Uncle Denis should be the one to make a beauty pageant non-gendered.'

'I'm boycotting the swimsuit competition, Dinny,' says Denis. 'I'm against body-shaming.'

'Omigod, has he actually been listening to me this whole time? I'm not able. I'm deceased,' Freya says, pretending to be horrified.

Eventually, after more eejitry, like saying people should recycle more and save the endangered otter, Denis is cheered off the stage. Some of the other girls aren't a bit happy. This would be a warm-up competition for the Rose of Tralee. Girls'd be practising their pitches, so they take it very serious.

We walk away as the more predictable entrants come on, but then after a few minutes there's cheering.

'AND THE WINNER, BY POPULAR VOTE, IS … DENIS DEVINE!!!!'

There's even more of a puss on the would-be Roses now.

He comes up to us afterwards, all excited with his hotel voucher.

'There's powerful stuff in them plastic glasses, Ann,' he says, putting on his jumper.

'The last safe space for women gone. So proud of you, Uncle Denis,' says Freya, half mocking, and gives him a hug.

Then the moment we'd all been waiting for: Cody Bryan is ready to make his first appearance. There's a ripple through the crowd as the director and him are ushered up by the hi-vis people. A good few young lads Rory's age are looking for selfies. They know him from all the *Robot Future* films. I hear one of them ask him if he *really rode all them young wans, tell the truth now, lad.* Cody Bryan doesn't seem to have understood what was asked.

They have it set up as a discussion panel. The host is an RTÉ fella called Fintan Moore. He's on when there's a strike. He's from not too far from here. He always gets dragged into these kinds of local functions, judging welly-throwing or wife-carrying. The RTÉ man introduces the historian Desmond Farragher, who has been on non-stop since the 1916 commemorations. They must have paid big money for him because he has to be introduced as *proudly sponsored by Be Double Sure Locking Systems.* Cody Bryan is sitting in the middle and there's a local comedian fella, Billy Books, he calls himself. Not that local, though, because I've never heard of him. The RTÉ man explains that Shelf McKinnon is unavailable due to filming commitments. There's a boo from some of the Minor lads from the table quiz.

Cody Bryan is a fine cut of a man, there's no doubt about that. He claims to have Irish roots. You can see the bit of Irish all right, but it's what an Irish person would look like if they had minded themselves over the generations and got a bit of good food. Someone has managed to put the Kilsudgeon Emmet O'Rahilly Wolfe Tones GAA shirt on him, but it doesn't do him any favours because he has a lovely black shirt, a bit of grey in his beard. A *pure* rogue, I'd say. A look of a young Kris Kristofferson about him.

But as soon as I see him sit down I can see he's legless. Absolutely scuttered.

Fintan, the RTÉ man, doesn't seem to have noticed.

'Cody Bryan, you've a lot of fans out there in the audience. Are you excited to be here in Kilsudgeon?' he asks, chirpily enough.

'Isss that where I am?' he says. He sounds fairly shook as well. A few in the crowd laugh, but unease trickles across the car park too. The RTÉ man chuckles and clears his throat. He thinks it's a joke, but he's starting to realize something is wrong.

'Ah, you're a terrible man, haha. Cody, what's it like working on a project like this?'

Silence.

'Cody?'

'FFFFFUCKKKKK YEAH KILSPUDGNON!!! YOU ROCK!!!!!!!' And he starts kissing the badge on the GAA shirt.

His fans are delighted, but I can see the mammies holding on to the small ones.

Cody is smiling now, thinking this is all great gas. Lightning Benny C turns round to look at me, giving me the 'rock-on' salute.

Freya appears beside me. 'All-male panel,' she says to me. 'Where's the female star? She's just sex-fodder anyway.'

'Jesus, Freya, give it a chance. We don't know what the story of it is yet.'

'They all end up the same way, Auntie Ann.'

The RTÉ man is trying to get the panel back on track. He goes on to the historian fella, asking about *significance.*

'That's right, yes, Kilsudgeon was scandalously left off the Ireland's Ancient East map. The *lios* that forms the backdrop to *The Celts* could be four thousand years old. This is the beating heart of Celtic Ireland. The ley lines of the culture and story run through this town.'

'Two grand they're paying him for that, just to talk shite,' whispers Denis.

'... a production like this, with historical verisimilitude ...'

Cody Bryan wakes up again for that bit.

'VERY WHAT?' he shouts.

Then the comedian tries to make some joke about Cody Bryan looking forward to going to Johnny's and Cody just says, 'Who are you? Are you a comedian? Because you haven't made me laugh yet.' He's starting to warm up now.

'But if I could get back to my original point,' says the historian.

'Where's his point? Has anyone seen his point?' Cody starts looking around the stage.

The RTÉ man is pure flustered now. He's never had to deal with this kind of thing outside the Labour Court.

'C'MERE ... LET'S HUG IT OUT, BRO, YOU SEEM TENSE.'

Cody has him in a bear hug now, and he's struggling to get to the microphone.

'... to leave the discuss—'

'GOTTA OPEN UP, DUDE ... LET LOVE IN.'

'Ladies and gentlemen, Cody ...'

'ANYONE GOT A TOKE?'

The hi-vis people are back to help him down from the stage. Young lads who loved him before are in ecstasy now. They're chanting, 'CODY, CODY!'

Dinny introduces the director of the TV show. The same fella that stopped me on the road when I was clearing the boats. And just like Man Bun, he lays it on thick for us.

'I don't have much to say. I think Cody has said it all, really.'

'KEEP FIGHTING THE FIGHT! LOVE YOU TOO, BRO!'

'Good man, Cody. I won't say much. I want to let you guys get back to your dancing. But I will say this. You know, I've filmed in a lot of locations, but already I can feel Kilsudgeon is special to me. This is your home. I hope to make it the home of television production in Ireland! But you can't arrive into a home with one arm as long as the other. And so we bring you a gift. But it's not a box of chocolates or flowers. We are bringing the world to you. In agreement with the council, we are providing a 4G hub right here in Kilsudgeon. WE ARE BRINGING HIGH-SPEED BROADBAND TO KILSUDGEON ONCE AND FOR ALL!'

There is a cheer as if he'd driven out the Black and Tans.

'In fairness to them, Freya, that's not bad now. You'll love the new internet. You can be learning all about feminism.'

'I know all about feminism, Auntie Ann. I don't need high-speed for that. You're getting bought off, Auntie—' She is cut off by an announcement from the stage.

'We will also be holding auditions next week. We want to get the best people from Kilsudgeon to be in the best show made in Ireland. Who knows, we might find the next Saoirse Ronan right here in the village.'

Freya's face changes at this news. She looks at me.

'Saoirse Ronan, omigod, Saoirse Ronan. Could you imagine being even, like, one millionth of a per cent like her? Obviously, the script is going to be limited, but I could bring so much to it. I could, like, research and stuff.'

'But I didn't think you were into drama, Freya.'

'Auntie Ann, I'm fourteen, my *life* is drama.'

The director isn't finished. 'And a final, very special surprise. You can't have a Celtic army without bands of warriors. Introducing the finest battle actors working in these islands, veterans of *Game of Thrones*, *Vikings* and at least twenty programmes about 1916. Let me introduce the men who will be the core fighters in our battle scenes, which will be filmed right here in the fairy field in Kilsudgeon. I give you … the Berserkers!'

About fifty of the hairiest lads you ever saw come running from both sides of the stage. Not a stitch of clothes on from the waist up. It's very early in the year for that. It's the Pretty Loki table quiz team by twenty. All tattoos and leather

205

necklaces, leather trousers. The crowd let out a *woo-hoo* as two more step forward with full-grown wolfhounds on leads nearly the size of Shetland ponies.

They meet in the middle and start play-fighting, battering shields with swords and axes. They have to stop for a bit as Catherine Shea's dog is back, hurling abuse at the wolf-hounds, followed by her granddaughter, who's only two, and her daughter, who's only mortified. They regroup and do a chant about being *The Sons of Erin defending the land of the Celts.*

As we all drift home, there's only one word on our lips. Broadband. Apart from Freya, who's still in a Saoirse Ronan fantasy. She even smiles at her father on the way out the gate.

26

HE *IS* THE BROADBAND

I feel the vibration in my jacket and put down the little trowel. It's Jennifer again.

'Jennifer! Again! And on a weekday! Are you OK?'

'I'm fine, Mam. Are you outdoors?'

'Would you believe, Jennifer, I'm here planting hibiscus and *Pieris japonica* in the boats in the big car park next to the church.'

'*Pieris japonica*, Mammy. Get you, Charlie Dimmock!'

'Gordon told me what to get and I went to the nursery and got them, but it's a start, isn't it?'

'You've changed, Mammy. You've got over your hump.'

'I did, as it happens. After seeing the Welcome Festival and all the children up on the stage, it made me think maybe I might get over myself. Recognize it. Own it. Move on. That's what Geraldine sent me in a thing on Facebook yesterday. So that's what I'm going to do.'

'All the management guru books talk about it, Mammy. Taking back control is the key to fulfilment.'

'Switch on the Facetime there till I get a look at you.'

'Facetime! You mean you're not hiding from me? Did you get Prozac as well? How have you the reception in the church car park? That's a blackspot. But you're as clear as day. I can see the topsoil on your face and everything.'

'Oh, now. Wait. Till. I. Tell. You. They're after putting an internet hub here in the last week.'

'So you've all been bought off for thirty-two megabits. And why is it in the church car park? Did Father Donnegan get the broadband?'

'Jennifer, he *is* the broadband. Have a guess where they put the receiver? Somewhere high? Have a think.'

'You're joking.'

'Up on the church steeple.'

'The man is a genius. He'll have ye all converted so ye can watch your porn.'

'I watch no porn.'

'Not yet, Mammy. Father Donnegan, the man with the password keys to the gates of Heaven.'

'He blessed the construction with a holy water bucket and the sprinkler and doused the teleporter. It was the biggest crowd we've had, bigger than a confirmation. Have a look at this.' I wave the phone around to the sign.

'Login saintudgeon. Password jesusloves. Oh, Mammy. My home town. You could not make it up.'

'And when you log on, Father Donnegan has set it up so that you can click to donate to the church. Silicon Valley has nothing on this fella for thinking outside the box.'

'Goodbye to Dooney's Turn, so.'

'This spot is much better, Jennifer. Full bars on the reception all the time, no matter how many's up here. The place is packed. When *Game of Thrones* came up on the dodgy website there were so many here Joe Barry in the chip shop sent Nawaz up in the van. Even the boy racers turn off the engines when they come in. And two nights ago the squad car was here, trying to get into their computer system, and the car next to them turned out to have been stolen. They only had to go out of their car to make the arrest. The lads never saw them coming.'

'And now, thanks to you, they'll have lovely plants to look at too.'

She's silent for a while then. I do a bit of digging with the trowel, to give her a chance to explain what the phone calls are about. No stir. She must be waiting for me to ask.

'Go on so, Jennifer.'

'Well … I'm thinking of taking a leave of absence for a while.'

'Are you sick?'

'No, but I will be. The work is just toxic.'

'I thought you were flying.'

'It's not me any more, Mammy. I'm afraid I'm going to lose my soul.'

She goes silent again, and I go back to digging a hole for the next plant.

'I just flipped about three months ago. At a planning meeting. They were all going on about the pipeline and how all these countries are very hot right now and I'm looking at these countries and they're all dictatorships, Mammy. I'm thinking, *Is this what it's about?* And Stuart, my boss, he's always bigging me up – in fairness, he's a nice fella – and he's saying, *Dublin is great because rents just go up and up and the returns are huge and Jennifer here has tipped us off on a lot of potential*, and they look at me as if I'm supposed to be proud of myself, and then I go back to my desk half an hour later and I'm reading the news from home and there's a big report on homelessness. I'm wondering, *Did I contribute to that?* You know, Mammy? And Stuart was saying, *Maybe we should go on a little fact-finding mission to Jennifer's home town.* I'm supposed to show them around, bring them to Copper's and all the rest of it, but am I part of the problem?'

'But every job has some knock-on effect, Jennifer.'

'Not really, Mammy. You mind old people and try to keep them safe and warm and happy. I'm throwing people out of their houses.'

'Don't lose the job now, Jennifer. It's a good job. The money is good. Have you savings?'

'I'm going to come home for a bit in a few weeks' time anyway. I need to think. Look, I've another call coming through. I'd better go in case they suspect I'm gone soft, ringing my mother during the week. Bye, Mammy.'

'Bye, pet.'

I try to go back to digging and planting, but I'm not in the zone any more. Jennifer and her soul have me in a small tizzy. I hope she knows what she's doing. And, as I say, I was hoping she'd look after us in our old age, with a few bob. I feel guilty thinking it. Maybe I'll talk it out with Sally. I owe her a confession. I decide to throw in the trowel and head home.

There are two letters on the mat when I get in. They are both addressed to Ann Devine, Vice-chairperson of the Kilsudgeon Tidy Towns Committee. I open the first. A cream-coloured envelope with *Damage Control PR* written on the outside and a logo of a hearse backing into a gravestone.

Hi, Anne!

They seem very excited already. Too excited to get the spelling right, but I'm used to that all my life.

My name is Winnie Tolan-Harrington.

Everyone has a double-barrelled name these days. Before it used only be The Quality. So they'd be able to show that they'd married well. I wonder is it on account of the women not changing their names after getting married? I don't mind that, although I was glad to be shut of mine. Hoare – such an awful-sounding one. My mother said that was the best thing about me marrying Denis, that I went from a Hoare to Devine. Could you imagine me being Hoare-Devine? Where will it end, though? If you were double-barrelled and you married someone else who was as well, you'd have three dashes in your name. You'd be like a bus route.

Anne, I hope you don't mind us reaching out.

As a significant influencer in your area, we are writing to you to investigate the possibility of working on our Celts Community Liaison Steering Group. *This would enable you to shape what we hope will be a very exciting engagement going forward. The* Celts Community Liaison Steering Group *is a group of like-minded individuals – influencers and others with significant social media profiles – who would work to bring about exciting opportunities for the people of Kilsudgeon as regards working with the* Celts Production *family.*

Community is our watchword, so we would be very excited if you could join us on this awesome adventure.

In addition, would you be interested in hosting one of our key staff in your house? Hilary Henderson-Fitzgerald will be our videographer and will chronicle the incredible journey of the creation of The Celts *in a documentary called* Hound of All Our Destinies: The Making of Ireland's Greatest Story. *To better assist Hilary in bringing what we know will be an awesome story to life, she will be embedded in the local community. We would be delighted if you would consider being part of that project and journey. Hilary is a super-experienced videographer and has worked on some of the biggest productions around the world.*

I like the idea of being an influencer. But a stranger in the house? I don't know how I feel about that. What does embedding entail? I wonder. It took thirty-five years to get my children out of the beds and into their own houses. And then with a name like Henderson-Fitzgerald? We'd have to get the house done up and everything. She could be from a horsey crowd.

A rent of 500 euro per week will be paid for a minimum of four weeks.

Well, that's a different story, of course. I would always be anxious to do a bit for the community.

This would be payable via EFT on a weekly basis.

I'd prefer cash in hand, but you can't always get what you want. I ring Denis, to see what he thinks, but he's in the truck and the reception is chronic so he can hardly hear a thing, just beeps and buzzing and his oul country music playing in the background.

'A WHO?'

'A videographer, Denis, in the house.'

And I'm just hoping this ole lonesome cowboy ...

'A VIDEO WHO?'

'TURN DOWN THAT TAPE, WILL YOU?'

'IT'S A CD.'

'TURN IT DOWN.'

Finds a space in the saddlebag of your heart ...

He turns it down only a smidge and I'm still shouting details at him over the truck.

'I'M POURING CONCRETE HERE. I DON'T KNOW WHAT YOU'RE SAYING, BUT GWAN AWAY ANYWAY. I'M SURE IT'S GRAND.'

That's how I get agreement on a lot of matters, and he hasn't complained yet.

That money *would* be handy. I can't put her in Rory's room, that's for certain. That place would need to be fumigated, or maybe just knocked. How that fella generates so much smell I'll never know. There are runners in there that cost about a hundred euro and you'd need a HazChem suit on them after a week. No, she'll have to go into the girls' room. I send Jennifer a quick text joking to her not to be arriving home unannounced, that I've found a replacement for her. There's work to be done.

Now I open the other letter.

Dear Chairperson and Vice-chairperson

Welcome aboard! Thank you so much for your application, which we received with interest. We are delighted to have Kilsudgeon join the Tidy Towns family. It also means that every town in the River Fleekra valley is now on board.

The next steps for completion of the process are as follows:

- *Payment of registration fee – see attached schedule. Please pay this at your earliest convenience. Failure to pay on time will result in immediate disqualification. We now accept Apple Pay and PayPal!*
- *Scheduled visit of Tidy Towns judges. This will take place on a day of our choosing and without notice. We want to see the town as it really is, in its natural state. This can take place any time from mid-May to June inclusive. We would advise committees to be ready from April onwards.*
- *Interim results – not published*
- *We may undertake a second visit at our own discretion*
- *Judging process*
- *Final results – published*

We will be in touch with some more detail on these timelines shortly.

We are so excited to see Kilsudgeon and all the great work you are doing! Your application was so comprehensive. The list of achievements it detailed is a real credit to

*you and your community. We look forward to seeing all
the efforts, particularly in the area of habitat restoration.
It really sounds like you and your group are performing
heroics. Well done!*

Oh God, what's Gordon after getting us into?

27

YOUNG GIRL, BUXOM

I'm just in the door from visiting Flash, and Freya is on the couch. She has a key. It makes sense for the amount of time she spends here.

'Where were you, Auntie Ann? We'll be late for the auditions.'

'Auditions? What auditions? And what's this *we* business, Paleface?'

'Mam said you're to bring me to the auditions for *The Celts* for today. Please say yes, Auntie Ann.'

'Excuse me for a second there, Freya.'

'You're going to call Mam, aren't you?'

'Well, what if I am?'

'Auntie Ann, just let her do her thing.'

'But she can't just do her thing. *You're* her thing.'

'I don't mind. I've always been free range.'

'Free range! You're not an egg. I'm giving her a ring.'

I ring Geraldine.

'I know what this is about, Ann.'

'Well?'

'I texted you, Ann, asking you.'

'I got no text.'

'I WhatsApped you.'

'I haven't got the hang of that yet, and you could have rung.'

'You should get the hang of it. I've you in the siblings group. It's just you and me until we figure out if we want to add the others or not. What's the big deal? I'm only asking you for a few hours.'

'And what if I do? Maybe I want to spend it doing other things.'

'Free-range parenting is what it's all about. It takes a village to raise a child.'

'But what if everyone said that? There wouldn't be enough village to raise all the children!'

'You're very stressed, Ann. And when you're stressed you get judgey.'

'I am *not stressed* until people tell me I'm stressed.' I clench my fists and kick the lower step of the stairs, but the tack strip gets me in through the slipper. I nearly let the C-word out of me with the pain. I hold it in.

'All OK, Auntie Ann?' Freya appears at the door, putting on the pre-teen smile that she uses for charming.

'What is it you're planning on opening up anyway?' I say back to Geraldine.

'I'm thinking of a yoga retreat.'

'I thought it was reiki.'

'Reiki is slightly out of fashion. Yoga will always be now. Kilsudgeon could be a centre of Eastern Learning. Especially if there's actors. I want to get in before the Buddhists. They're all men. Not that it's about the money. But everyone's looking after their mental health now and with my qualifications ...'

'What qualifications?'

'The Pittsburgh Institute's highly rated Mindfulness and Nowness Diploma, if you must know.'

'Since when were you in Pittsburgh?'

'It was online, Ann, as you well know.'

'I don't well know. I never heard of that place, Institute of Mindfulness and Newness.'

'Nowness, Ann. If it's not the Tech, you haven't heard about it. Look, are you going to take Freya or are you going to judge me for being an entrepreneur? We don't all take the path of least resistance, Ann.'

'At least I took one path and stuck to it. And there's nothing easy about my job. You lift a twelve-stone woman out of her bed to change a nappy and she shouting at you that you've stolen her bicycle and tell me that's the least resistance.'

Geraldine ignores that.

'C'mon, she loves when you bring her places. And you love bringing her, too. Don't pretend you're not ringing just to have a go at me. You know you can be a very negative person at times, Ann. It's not healthy.'

She's done it again! She asks me to do her a favour and then I end up trying to defend myself. That's the thing about family. Even when they're being a pain in the arse they know enough about you so that they can knock you down even when they haven't a leg to stand on. She hangs up.

'Well?' says Freya, sticking her head around the door again.

'Gwan so, I'll bring you. You knew I would anyway, you brought your bag, you scut.'

She shows me a costume in her bag. A big gown of a yoke.

'Is that what they wore – the Celts?'

'I dunno. It's from Bunratty Folk Park. Benny gave it to Mam one of the times he was around. She never wore it, though. Classic Benny present.'

217

'What role are you going for anyway?'

'I want to make my own role, but I'll have to pretend I'm going for one of the other ones.' Freya has the role description printed out from an email. *'Young girl, buxom servant girl. Stands in background. Looks wistful during the fighting scenes. Actions will include – crouching, screaming, running away from warrior, shouting "LOOK OUT!" at Fionn/ Cúchulainn.'*

'It'll be hard to make a lot out of that, Freya. And what's this about buxom? I don't think that's suitable for a girl of your age. Plenty of time for buxom. And to be honest, not to rain on your parade, but I'm not sure you will ever be. We were never big up top on our side. Although Uncle Denis is doing his best.'

'Mam is pretty stacked.'

'Eh … I don't know, maybe she's a throwback.'

I'm not going to be the one to tell her about Geraldine's extension.

'I want to redefine the role, Auntie Ann. This is the only one they'll let me in for that I'm closest in age to.'

'OK, you're the boss, but I'll have to change.'

I go up to get changed and Freya follows me up and sits on the bed.

'Ah, feck sake, Freya, a bit of privacy.'

'Body positivity, Auntie Ann. You are a beautiful, mature woman who—'

'GET OUT WITH YOUR POSITIVITY.'

When I'm finished I follow her downstairs.

'Are you sure about this, Freya? Sex and swords, you called it. I don't think it's suitable for a young girl.'

'All of these shows have young stars. Look at Arya Stark.'

'Who's that?'

'She's a total badass of *Game of Thrones*. She's awesome. She has a kill list.'

'We could all do with one of those. But I thought you hated the very thought of it, Freya.'

'Remember what we said, Auntie Ann? Reform the system from the inside.'

'I thought you said tear it down.'

But as it happens, maybe it's just as well she doesn't want to tear it down. With that videographer coming to stay, me and *The Celts* are getting on fine. There's a bag of wallpaper rolls in the hall. Ready for Denis to put them up.

What wallpaper would a videographer like, Ann? said Denis when we were walking around Toner's Interiors. *Something tasteful. I don't know. The man here will tell us,* I replied. The man there suggested, just to be on the safe side, we should buy wallpaper that costs a fortune.

The auditions are at the hotel. The car park is full, including a few tractors. One of them has a seeder on the back of it. Imagine that. A beautiful spring day and a farmer in auditioning to be on telly. The town is gone mad. I wonder what father will be wondering where the son has gone with the seeder, but when we go in it turns out it *is* the father.

It's Petey Welch – a mountainy man.

'You're going for the big time, Petey,' I say to him, joking. I assume he's waiting for someone, but no, he's auditioning.

'It was the girleen who said I should go in for it. *With the beard*, says she, *Daddy, you'd be sure to be a warrior.* There's supposed to be big money in it. The cattle prices are gone to fuck, so I might as well.'

'But where'll you find the time for it?'

'If I can squeeze it in between the silage and the barley I'll be grand. She does most of the work now anyway. And she still finds time to be snaptalking or whatever you call it. Typing away from the tractor. Taking photos of herself with the calves. I'd be telling her not to be letting the gangs know what kind of machinery we have, but she takes no notice.'

Petey hasn't bargained for the wait. He's sitting there with the other bewildered locals while the young actory types and starlets do their vocal exercises or *omigod* at each other. There's no sign of a move in the queue. I see him fidgeting and looking at his watch. After a while he knocks on the door and goes in. He comes out roaring about *a shower of Northern bastards* and that he *didn't come down here on a fine day for setting grain to be laughed at* and *they can shove their* Celts *up their hole.*

Freya nudges me and shows me her phone. It's Isla Welch, his daughter.

'On Instagram,' she whispers.

Isla has put a photo of Petey and it says: *So proud of Daddy. Taking a big step in his new career. #love #daddy #mountainman #celticwarrior* and about fifty more #es.

'Laughing at us, Ann,' says Petey to me as he passes us, his heavy boots making a fierce racket on the carpet. He pushes through the door with more cursing. There's the sound of a tractor revving outside. But then he returns a few minutes later, looking sheepish.

'Sorry to bother ye, but does one of ye own that Mini with the eyelashes? I can't get the tractor out with ye.'

A young wan puts her phone away with a big sigh and gets up.

Two more hours pass. There are long periods when no one goes in. A few more people get up and leave. The general feeling is that this is a pure cod. But eventually the door opens and Freya's name is called. I go in with her although, strictly speaking, it's performers only.

The director is sitting on the other side of a table, in one of Dinny's cleaner meeting rooms in the hotel. There is a faint smell of bleach. There are two more people there – a youngish fella holding a script and a woman twiddling with a camera. Freya is directed to stand on a spot. I try and lean out of the way at the back of the room.

The director looks up at her. 'Now, Freda, what age are you, darling?'

'Sixteen.' Freya gives me a look to say nothing.

'Now, sweetheart, we just need to see you walk, stand, maybe do a bit of gasping.'

'OK, but can I just try something? It's a spoken-word piece.'

They look at one another.

'Gwan, darling. Make it quick, all right, my love?'

'I thought that I would show where you could take one of the characters.' Freya does a sort of hoppy-dance and then launches into it. 'Arise, women of the Ivernia ...'

Oh no, Freya, I think, not one of your spoken-word bits. I can barely look. It's the protest at the Farm Open Day all over again.

'ARISE! You are the fighters of a new age. You are more than vessels of a civilization. Awaken and shake off the yoke of ...'

'OK ... Freda. OK ... how do I put this? OK, sweetheart – is this your mum?' He clasps his hands together and puts them to his mouth, like he's praying. 'We have our speaking woman, OK? We have Shelf for the main role and we have someone for the mother figure. We just need a few women, mainly as servant girls. We don't need any of that shouty-woman stuff. Anything else you can do? Somersaults, swordplay, anything?'

'I just thought maybe she could be your actress's friend. You know, someone to talk to.'

'She's going to be fighting warriors. She won't have time to talk.'

'But women have female friends in real life.'

'OK, I see what's going on here. Someone's been reading some Bechdel test. Look, Freda, here's the thing. This is *The Celts*, OK? People want to see men fighting. We have Queen Maeve. She'll be cool, a warrior. She'll do some martial arts, OK, but look, the thing about it is, people want it simple. Not, like, *Orange Is the New Black* or something. So do you want to do a few poses there as a servant girl?'

'But—'

'Look, sweetheart, it takes a while to get through a village, OK? Now, do you want to do something or not?'

And Freya just does a few screeches and gasps and says, 'Look out, Fionn,' but her heart isn't in it. She walks down to me without even looking up. As we leave I hear the director muttering, 'That's the best thing about am-dram – if they're nutcases, you can tell straightaway. The professionals hide it until it's too late.'

I drive her back to her mother's.

'Are you OK, pet?'

'We have to tear it down again, Auntie Ann. Promise me you'll help.'

I look at the text that I got while waiting.

Hey ann looking forward to seeing you at the Celts Kilsudgeon Liaison group Meet and greet next week

'OK, Freya,' I say, 'we'll tear it down,' but I'm thinking, *If we could just wait a week or so …*

28

AS IF WE WERE ALIENS

'Do you want much off, Ann?'

'Just a wash and a bit of a tidy-up.' My phone beeps. 'Excuse me, Frances.' It's a text from Freya.

Cant BELIEVE you're still going auntie ann Judas

Freya wants me to boycott the liaison committee after her audition. Ah, pity about her. We all have to move on. Anyway, I'm mad curious to see what's going on down there this evening. That's why I'm getting my hair done. The town is talking about nothing else. The big question anyone you meet has for you now is: who are you getting? Because there's so little accommodation around the place, they're putting them up with as many local families as possible. Every spare bed is in use. I'm fierce proud of my videographer. I can't wait to tell them.

'Who's staying with you?' Frances asks me.

Play it cool, Ann.

'Would you believe I'm getting the documentary-maker? She's making a show about the making of the series. You know, those programmes are often more famous themselves.

I was reading about *Apocalypse Now*. They had one for that and it was a holy show.'

Fierce cool, Ann.

May Hanaphy next to me butts in. 'They do the extras on the DVD, isn't it? I never watch them, but himself does.'

Everyone is an expert on film-making around here now, it seems.

'You lucky duck, Ann Devine,' says Frances. 'I got nothing out of it. They bring their own hairdressers around with them to do the hair. Wouldn't you think they'd support the local community now that they're here? I told them I could learn to do the corn braiding. They've tutorials on YouTube and everything. How hard could it be, like?'

Too hard for you anyway, Frances, I think to myself. You've been giving out the same hairstyles since you opened up. I don't think you're going to start corn braiding now.

'Very bad form, Frances, you'd be well able for it. Maybe they have them on the staff anyway, Frances, and they had to use them?'

'Maybe ...'

'And have you anyone, Frances, yourself, staying with you?'

'Two, but they'll be bringing in no money. It's a sliding scale, seemingly. My two are what they call runners and they only make the tea, so I'm getting half nothing for them. You must be doing well out of the documentary-maker?'

'Ah ... you know ... not too bad. But it's all gone on doing the place up nearly.'

It isn't true, but it's only manners in Kilsudgeon to deny doing well out of something. If the Sultan of Brunei came in for a short back and sides and someone said, 'You're doing well out of the oil,' he would be expected to say, 'But it costs a fortune to dig it out.'

'I've two key grips,' says Laura Nevin. 'There's a higher rate for them. I've two young lads in college in Dublin and I'm telling them not to be in any hurry back at the weekends since the rent on their place is for the full week anyway, and they're saying, *Mam, we haven't a stitch of clean clothes. WASH THEM*, I said. I'm not losing my two movie lads for nothing. It's the only way I'll be able to pay for the new boiler.'

She's well able to pay for the boiler, but again, it's all about manners.

'Cody Bryan is staying up at the hotel. There's no fear he'd be staying in a spare room looking at new wallpaper.'

'He's in town plenty,' says Frances. 'He's taken a fierce shine to Johnny's since he arrived. He told some paper in America that Kilsudgeon has given him the peace he's been searching for all his life and he's never been happier.'

'I never thought of Kilsudgeon like that. A place of peace.'

'The director lets him drink away there,' says Frances, as she snips away at the back of my head. I know well she's taking too much off somewhere. There's always one place she takes too much off. It just depends where she is when she gets into talking.

'You see, Johnny keeps in touch with him about the kind of state Bryan is in and gets him to learn the lines as well.'

Have a totally amazing time LIAISING with the enemy

Freya's texting me again.

I drink my tea and have the little biscuit. *You need to chill out and let your Auntie Ann get on with her own life, and come down off your high horse and make friends*, I text Freya, in my imagination.

We meet Winnie Tolan-Harrington in the church car park later that day and pile into a minibus. There's Gordon, myself, Father Donnegan, Dinny Sheehan, Catherine Bennet (a councillor) and Andy Walsh (the chemist). They must be wondering what the likes of me is doing there, but I have my new haircut anyway – even if it's the same as the old one, only less.

We turn up at a big shed. Winnie is turned around to us in the minibus, all excitement, explaining what's going on. The site at the fairy field is nearly ready for the battle scene, but there's a lot of heavy machinery so it's not the best place to show us around just yet. We are at the Warehouse Studio, where some 'green screen' and indoor things will be shot. The Warehouse Studio turns out to actually be the big shed owned by Phil Duggan of Phil Duggan Farm Machinery. Except there is no Phil Duggan Farm Machinery any more, not since Phil ran off to Brazil with their cleaner and left Philomena with a pile of debt. Imagine a Phil married a Philomena. The joke around the place was they called the house The Petrol Station because, no matter when you went up, you'd get a Phil. (They were both Duggans, although not related to each other. We think. She's yet another of Patsy's cousins.)

The shed was transformed inside. There were film lights hanging from the ceiling and a beam going across with cameras on it. On the floor they'd laid down train tracks, with a little trolley on it that you could put a camera on, I suppose. I feel a bit of tingle on my neck just to be there. It all looks so strange to have it here in Kilsudgeon. Something so unusual going on right on our doorstep. We used to watch the tour buses passing through Clonscribben on the way up to see the castle at Grugue, and they'd be looking out at us as if we were aliens. There was never a reason for tourists to stop anywhere I've ever lived, but now here was a magical thing right in our scruffy little town.

The director gives us a tour. He doesn't seem to recognize me from the auditions. God, is the haircut that drastic? He shows us where they'd be filming some of the internal shots. They have a room that was supposed to be the inside of the king's hut. You'd think watching on a telly that these would be complete rooms, but no, it's bits of rooms. So there's a corner where they've a cooking pot and a fireplace and a few doors that people go in and out.

It feels odd to see the tricks they get up to. It's like the time we went up to RTÉ to be in *The Late Late Show* audience and Denis and me found the *Fair City* set and we realized it was all a front. We couldn't watch it any more after that. It wasn't believable.

'This is the portal to the Otherworld that you'll see if you go through the fairy fort. We'll use this for when Fionn and Cúchulainn unite to travel to Hades. And this is the underground lake they must cross. It's just a water tank, but we'll make it look like a lake at the end, don't worry. This is the green screen, so when Cody is fighting the Spider God, we'll put the Spider God in afterwards in our SFX studio.'

I didn't think Cúchulainn and Fionn mac Cumhaill met one another, but maybe we didn't learn it in school. They seem to know what they're doing anyway.

'The reason we've invited you all here is to build a relationship with our local community. We hope that you will spread the good word about the production.'

I don't think there's much fear of that at the moment. They're selling Cúchulainn burgers in the chipper, with an extra five euro on them because there's a tiny hurley stuck through the bun.

'We hope also that you can help us with the logistics. We would like to hear about any other possible locations for shooting in the area that you can recommend. We are in particular looking for brushland or woodland. We will send on our requests by email but, for now, ladies and gentlemen, let's eat.'

He brings us into a room off the main warehouse floor. There's a kitchen in the process of being set up in there. You should see the spread they've laid on for us! The director is apologizing that they had to order in the sandwiches, but then I see the sandwiches. It's a shame to eat them. They came in from Slaughterhouse & Winch. The bread is all crusty. Hotel soup bread. No Kitchen Essentials White Sliced Pan for us, I can tell you.

There are blue crisps and black crisps and so many dips it's like a tray of poster paints. I try them all, but I don't ask what they are in case I'm the only one who doesn't know. There's wine in plastic wine glasses and it's the right temperature and, between you and me, it goes down very easy.

'They do really good guacamole, don't they? It's Ann, isn't it?' The director is next to me at the table. 'I almost didn't recognize you with the new hairstyle.'

'They do mighty guacamole,' I say, not sure if I've had the guacamole or not.

'It's the organic avocados.'

'That's what I was thinking myself.'

I don't let on it's the first time I realized guacamole comes from avocados. Any community liaison person worth their Himalayan rock salt would be expected to know that.

'I might be able to sort you out for land.'

The wine has loosened me up a bit. I'm almost blasé about discussing filming locations with a director.

'Flash Lordan, he has a lovely little spot just outside of town. You should go into him.'

'The man's name is Flash?'

'Well, it's John, actually,' and then I tell him the story of the name. He gets a great chuckle out of it, and I chuckle as well, even though I'm well used to it. But it seems funny to tell an outsider about it. Then I feel bad for laughing at Flash, but I take another slug of wine and the wine says, *Don't worry about it, Ann. Flash will thank you.*

'We went to him already, but he ran us out of it, saying we could go back to Dublin and that we wouldn't be stealing anything today,' says the director, when I describe the location.

'He's nervous with all the activity around the place. Flash'll be grand. I'll talk to him.'

Ann Devine 'influencer' all right.

29

THEY STOLE A COMBINE?

I'm not the only one drinking tonight. Denis is out too. But long after the minibus drops me back, Denis is still nowhere to be seen.

He comes in the door steaming. I know by the look of him he's had more than his usual amount. Denis is a man of regular drinking habits. I wouldn't say he sticks rigidly to the guidelines from the World Health Organization, but he rarely gives his system a shock. I can nearly tell by him how much he's had when he comes in after a few in Johnny's. It ranges from two and a whiskey to four and a whiskey, but tonight he's unsteady.

First, there's the long conversation with the taxi-man, most of which I hear one side of through our bedroom window, but I gather it's about potholes.

AH TIS A FUGGINDISGRACE THE CUT OF IT, HAH? USELESS. A TEASSPOON OF TAR, HAH? THE COUNCIL WASTINGYOURTIMETALKINGABOUTIT   RIGHTSO G'LUCK, HAH? OH SURE YEAH HE DIED YOUNG TOO, HAH? YEAH ...

Now he's cursing the keyhole for not staying still. I get up before he rings the bell and wakes the whole place up. I open it as he gives the keyhole one last chance to cop on and he half falls in.

'Annie, baby, c'mere, you dirty girl.' He makes a grab for me.

'Get off me, you flute! Get in out of the road. You had a good night so, did you?'

'Johnny's was hopping, Ann. Hopping!'

'You had five or six, did you, Denis?'

'I might have.'

'And more.'

He fishes around in his anorak.

'I brought you a few cocktail sausages.'

He has them wrapped up in a bit of toilet roll. SafeFood would shut us down if they saw the hygiene here, but I eat them anyway. We're still standing in the hall eating sausages. It's a nice gesture. Shows he was thinking of me anyway, while getting mouldy.

'I got talking to the extras. Fierce men altogether. Tattoos, Ann. Stop the lights. Maybe I'll get a tattoo. I was asking them. They said I should get the truck done on my arm. A sleeve, they call it. The proper job and all.'

I don't argue about the tattoo. I don't want to be firming it up in his mind. He'll forget most of this anyway.

'Did you know a few of them worked on *Braveheart* and they were so good they nearly had to rewrite history for them and have Mel Gibson win the final battle?'

'Is that what they told you?'

'They're wild, though. The extras were fierce men to drink altogether. They were drinking shots to bate the band. I'd a Jägerbomb, of all things. Only the small glass fell out on me. I wouldn't be used to that kind of apparatus for drinking.'

That's true anyway. He'd think a wine glass was over-complicating things.

'The stories they had, Ann, you wouldn't believe. One fella, tattoos on his face, would you believe it? Well, he was talking about the time they were all working on that film they made last year, *King Arthur and the Sacred Spoon*. It was filmed in Wexford, do you remember? Well, one night they had some sort of a party and a few of them I think were on the wacky backy and another lad had found mushrooms and they all went up Mount Leinster in a stolen combine.'

'They stole a combine?'

'No! That was the thing. The combine was already stolen and abandoned by, you know, the usual suspects. They couldn't drive it or they panicked or I don't know what, but these buckos found it in a shed and thought they'd borrow it and drove it halfway up Mount Leinster. Ten of them hanging off the thing. One fella was sitting on the auger, hanging out over a ditch, and he was knocked off by a branch. They found him after and he ended up having to play an injured knight for the rest of it. Then the combine conked out on them, and the strange thing was, they ended up bringing it nearly back to where they'd got it, unbeknownst to themselves. The guards found an ID in the cab, but it was all hushed up because the film was bringing in huge money.'

'These are your new friends? And I spend my days worrying about Rory. Do I need to be worrying about you too?'

'Cody Bryan was playing darts with some big lad in a vest. You should have come up.'

'I didn't want to cramp your style.'

'I'm fairly cramped now anyway. You could loosen me up, girleen.'

The romance.

'Ah, sure you're up now anyway, Ann.'

'You're up too, I see.'

'You have to strike while the iron is hot at this age,' he says.

'Where's my Milk Tray so?'

The following morning is fairly rough. Denis is snoring away, dead to the world, and I have to drag myself up. I've made a promise to a film director, so I go up and see Flash, even though it's not my day.

He's delighted to see me. The leg is better, so he's going around a bit cleaner and in better form. But he's chancing his arm with the extra requests.

'My toenails are gone to the dogs, Ann. I can't get near them with the scissors.'

'Now, Flash, it's not part of the deal, you know that. OK ... C'mon so ... Where's your scissors?'

I find his scissors with jam on them. I use my own scissors. I shouldn't be doing this really, as I'm not covered, but no one is going to tell Tracy and she won't come here, that's for sure.

'Christ, Johnny, what are you eating? These nails are like lino. You've no shortage of B7.'

'I eat the tinned fish, Ann.'

'I know, Flash, I know.' That's what the smell was around the place.

A big truck passes along the road and the windows shake a little.

'One of the TV people, is it?' he says. 'The speed they do down there. No speeding van, I notice, since they came around. Them hoors are all over the place.'

'I was going to talk to you about them, Johnny.' And I talk to him about it.

He's not convinced. 'And what would they want with me?'

233

'You wouldn't have to do much, Flash. They just want to use a bit of the farm. Maybe they'd park a few vans here. They said they called into you before.'

'I remember them well. I put the run on them, Ann. When I saw the van I went for the shotgun, but I couldn't find it and all I had was a pike. They got the message anyway.'

He says nothing for a while. He's thinking it over.

'You might give me a trim, if you don't mind, Ann. If you give me the trim, I might think about the TV.'

'Look, Flash, it's no skin off my nose if you let them in or not. I only said I'd pass on the message.'

'If it was no skin off your nose, you wouldn't be here on a Sunday, would you? You're well in with them. Give us the trim anyway.'

I look for a cloth to put around his neck.

'Would there be money in it?'

'I'm sure there would. They're supposed to be spending it like there's no tomorrow around the town. What do you want doing?'

'Make me young again,' says Flash, 'and your film director can have the field.'

'I'm not a surgeon, Flash,' I say, but I gave him a decent haircut all the same.

30

THE DANDELIONY LOOK OF IT

Here you go Needy McNeederson everyone thinks you're a ledge
Freya has taken a photo of our Facebook page, and it's
Nuala Costigan saying *Fair play, Kilsudgeon Tidy Towns, you
have the place looking lovely. Ann Devine, you're a treasure.*

I know, commented Jackie Seery. *Not all heroes wear capes.
Sum wear Hi vis.*

I read it over and over again. I'm not used to public praise.
My old people say thanks – except for Nonie, who says don't
let the door hit you in the backside on the way out. Over the
years I got the odd mention in the *Sentinel*, but it was usually
related to the children – graduations and the like. But now
there was someone – a number of people, in fact – thanking
me for planting flowers in boats around the town. And these
would be well-off people. Always changing their car.

Things are flying this past couple of weeks with the Tidy
Towns. Freya won't admit it, but *The Celts* is spreading the
word. A couple of the hairy lads turned up for one clean-up
and we cleared out the Black Ditch, a notorious dumping area.

The flowerbeds at the broadband are looking great and the boats – well, you should see the wildflowers and seed bombs now. I was learning about horticulture myself. What to plant and where and when. Denis got me a grand book, *The Tree and Shrub Expert*. It just goes to show, it's never too late to start something. I'd always been ashamed of our own garden. It was never really made for looking at. Denis parks the truck across the front of the entrance, to hide the dandeliony look of it. Maybe I could tackle that someday.

My phone goes *beep beep beep beep*. Four messages at once. I'm feeling like a VIP now.

Hey Anne it's Winnie. Your homestay will be arriving in a week.

Hello Ann, Susan Clarke from the Sentinel. We're doing a piece on local heroes and we'd love to feature you.

Hey Anne, Winnie again, you and a guest are invited to come and watch our first film day and watch us shoot the rehearsal!

Hi Ann, Tracy here …

Ah, shag off, Tracy. I'm not interested in whatever whining you're doing. I'm going to be in a profile. I'm getting noticed. I had a taste of it at the first meeting, lost it, got it again. Wine, location-scouting, eating organic guacamole. Things are looking up. I text Freya: *do you want to come watch a rehearsal?*

I park the car and Freya and me walk up to the fencing around the fairy field.

'You're not going to start shouting now, Freya, are you? About fascists? Am I going to see Gary Cushin throwing petrol bombs?'

'It's OK, Auntie Ann. I swear I won't say a word. We have this project for the Junior Cert, like, short film and stuff. So it would be cool for me to see how it's done.'

'What's your film about?'

'I think I'll be doing, like, female role models for the twenty-first century? I'll be shadowing a strong woman, showing her struggles. Just a few minutes, but I'll need hours of footage.'

I ignore the hint.

We are met by Winnie, who brings us up to an area on a little mound behind the cameras. The place is transformed. Half of it is covered in metal roadway, I suppose for the diggers and the transporters. There's scaffolding for a platform overlooking a village. They've made a village of stone huts and reeds or mud. It's very realistic. They're nicer than anything built around here during the Celtic Tiger, and there's probably more people living in them.

We go to an area behind the cameras and wait. And wait. There is a lot of standing. Then the director starts talking to one of his assistants. There seems to be an awful lot of hanging around in this game altogether. You could nearly put on a wash or go visit your mother during the break. No wonder them actors are all a bit unhinged. It's all the waiting.

The director seems cross at something because he keeps asking for things to be Reset and there are a lot of EFFs out of him. Eventually, though, he seems happy, and it looks like we're off.

'QUIET ON SET. EXTRAS READY.'

Hup, I think they're starting now.

'AUDIO ROLLING.'

'Here we go, Freya. It's exciting, isn't it?'

She rolls her eyes. One Junior Cert project and she's an old pro.

'CAMERA ROLLING. ACTION.'

'I thought it was "Lights, camera, action,"' I whisper.

'That's only a cliché in the movies, Auntie Ann.'

'This is a movie, though.'

'I mean movies about movies.'

There was very little happening as far as I could see, but then the director starts shouting, 'AH, FUCK ME, WHO THE FUCK IS THAT? I THOUGHT WE CLEARED THE SHOT?'

We all look off into the distance. One of the Buddhists is walking the far inside boundary of the field, minding his own business. He looks like he's picking something.

Someone goes off on a quad bike to talk to the Buddhist fella. By the looks of the little beard on him, it's Timmy. Timmy's his old name, according to Sally, who was telling me all this the other day:

'They get a new name when they sign up, Ann. I only found this out because Donal was after getting chatting to one of them on the internet and was thinking of joining. He was all caught up, thinking he'd get a name that meant "Lightning" or "Beautiful Horse" because no one took him seriously with Donal. I thought they'd brainwash him, but he decided against it when he found out there was no sex outside marriage or eating meat. I was worried I'd have to be calling him Srinavas Conundrum or something.'

The chastity would have been no problem for him, the poor slob, but there's no way he'd be giving up his kebabs.

Timmy came up on the back of the quad bike, smiling at everyone.

'Sorry about that,' he says. 'I was just picking herbs near the ditch.'

The director has a word with him for another five minutes.

He comes over to where we are all corralled and stands next to me.

'Timmy, is it?' I whisper.

'QUIET ON SET.'

'Actually, it's Vajrashura, but Timmy'll do,' he says.

'What did the director want with you?'

'OK, EXTRAS, GET READY TO START SHOUTING.'

'He asked me did I have the robes, the Buddhist robes.'

'AUDIO ROLLING.'

'He wants me to play a time-travelling ninja.'

'CAMERA ROLLING.'

'I tried to tell him that I'm from Tubercurry and I'm no more ninja than yourself, but he wants me to appear in it anyway.'

'Will you do it?'

'CAMERA ROLLING.'

'I don't know if I'm allowed under my religion, but I'll see.'

'And where does it fit into the plot?'

'He didn't say.'

Then he walks off, with a small Lidl bag hanging off his arm with the herbs.

'SILENCE ON SET, PLEASE.'

This is a bit of a fly-by-night operation, if you ask me.

'EXTRAS, READY AND ACTION!'

The extras are supposed to roar and shout, and they do. I recognize a few of them from Slaughterhouse & Winch. They had a headstart with the beards, I suppose.

'CUT.'

'Lads and ladies, take off the watches, and I can see earphones as well. C'mon! Ye were told.'

He starts them off again and then, 'AND FOR FUCK SAKE, EVERYONE STOP SWEARING. WE NEED CLEAN ROARING. SAVES TIME LATER. THIS IS NOT *GAME OF THRONES*. I'M HEARING AT LEAST THREE PEOPLE SHOUTING *GWAY OUT OF IT, YA FUCKER*. THEY DIDN'T HAVE THAT IN THOSE TIMES.'

After about five bits of shouting he seems happy with that, and then it looks like they are going to do a fight scene and someone shouts to get Cody Bryan. More delays. They send someone else to get him because the first young lad can't rouse him. Eventually, he comes down arm in arm with some young wan. He's looking shook. She isn't local, but she doesn't look too far away. I don't think she is part of the plot, although if she hangs around long enough she probably will be. They have him doing a fight scene, but it's the quarest fight scene I ever saw. He's just waving the sword around, shouting and fighting nothing. Jumping from rocks on to a mattress. Rolling around.

'What's he waving the sword for? There's no one there,' I say to a fella from the crew standing next to me.

'Eh ... yeah, it's Fir Stromach, the Spider God, summoned by Balor of the Evil Eye. He's trying to take over Éireann of the Free.'

'What Spider God? I don't remember any spider gods in anything about the Fianna we learned growing up.'

'I know, right? But the audiences in the States lap it up. If there's even so much as a sniff of it being based in Ireland, there'll be ten million Irish Americans will go for it. But we need spider gods for the teenage boys. There's a whole herd of monsters in this. I think they'll probably put a war-elephant in as well. There's big demand for those now. But it won't be real.'

There's a break for lunch and we decide to slope off. The director catches my eye. He's a bit more stressed than he was the last time, so I give him a bit of good news.

'Ah, Ann. And Freda, is it?'

Freya glares at him.

'I had that word with Flash. Yer man with the farm. I'm sure he'll hear ye out the next time you go down.'

'Ann, you are an absolute *diamond*. That is fantastic. You really are proving yourself invaluable. We should just hire you right away.'

So now I'm a diamond on set and a legend on Facebook. I'd better be careful it all doesn't go to my head.

31

PIERIS JAPONICA

'Just turn your head slightly, Auntie Ann. I want a framing shot of you but not your face.'

We're outside the house. Freya has me coming out the door numerous times until she's happy with it. I'm making out that it's a pain but secretly I'm chuffed with the attention.

'But why does it have to be me, Freya?' I ask her. 'Haven't you a million and one things you could be filming?'

'I want to film a strong woman I admire, Auntie Ann.'

'But what about your mother?'

'I don't admire her. Like, I *love* her, obviously. But we're fighting most of the time and it wouldn't look good on camera. Pleeease, Auntie Ann. I just need to shadow you on a typical day. You won't even know I'm there.'

But I do know she's there because she's very particular about every shot and she wants to know *everything*.

'What are you doing now, Ann? Where are you going with that, Ann?'

'What happened to "Auntie"?'

'It can't look like I'm interviewing my aunt. Supposing this went to the Cannes film festival?'

'Hang on till I get a cleaner set of scrubs.'

'What are you doing now, Ann?' she starts off again when I come back. 'Who are we visiting?'

I tell her the plan for the day.

'How do you feel about your job?'

I start to tell her about trying to get all the information on to The System. I forget about the phone she's holding. I'm halfway through telling her what a wagon Tracy is when I catch myself.

'That's not going in the video.'

'It's only a school project, Auntie Ann, it won't go anywhere.'

The old people are delighted to see her. Flash finds her a Club Milk which, miracle of miracles, isn't gone off. Neans is entranced with her. She brings her in to show her old photographs and tell her about who's dead and who's in America and who was no use at all *but don't put that in the film*. I sit back and have a nice cup of tea and watch them.

I mean to leave her in the car for Nonie. No one needs that at this stage of their young life, but she wangles her way in and softens Nonie up a small bit. Or at least, Nonie likes her enough to give out to her about me. Which is a start.

'Your aunt doesn't want to be here at all, Fiona,' she says as I check her blood pressure. 'Put that in the film. You're a nice girl, not like your aunt. Your mother is a good woman. I don't like her lipstick, but she's not the worst of them. But this one here' – she moves her head at me – 'oh, a *real* wild one.'

Freya is trying to keep her laugh in. But the phone camera is up all the time. This film will be need three sequels if she keeps recording.

'Did you get enough?' I say to Freya as we leave.

'Omigod, like loads,' she says. 'Don't worry, I won't put Nonie in.'

It's the evening by the time we're back. A balmy April evening and there's a bit of a stretch to it. We're coming back, past the turn into the village or to our house, and I decide to swing by to see how my new plants are doing. And that's when it happens.

There's a crowd around the boats. A crowd of the Berserkers cheering and a few other fellas I don't recognize. Surely they can't be watching the plants grow? I pull into the layby and the crowd moves slightly to let me in. Some of them. But enough so that I can see what's going on.

Cody Bryan is in a boat, with his top off. He appears to be rowing. I get a bit closer and I hear him singing.

'"ROCK THE BOAT …"'

He's crushing the flowers, the lilies I put in, the delphiniums. My *Pieris japonica* is out on the ground.

'"ROCK THE BOAT, BABEEEE,"' sing the crowd. They are absolutely fluthered as well.

'"ROCK THE BOAT …"'

They're trying to roll the boat up a bit and it's in danger of tipping over.

I push my way to the front. They become aware of me. Somewhere within me, it rises. I feel a kind of rage I haven't felt since the priest gave out to Jennifer or any number of times when my family was wronged. *My poor plants.* Not doing any harm to anyone.

'Excuse me, Mr Bryan, would you mind getting out of the boat, like a good man?'

He's laughing. 'OK, OK,' he says, but he doesn't get out of the boat. He lets some soil go through his hands on to the ground along with a battered ranunculus. I don't know what he's on. I struggle to keep calm.

'Can you please get out of the boat, you're ruining my plants. Excuse me now, you. I won't ask you again.'

'Lady, you gotta chill.'

'Chill' must be my trigger word because this sets me off. 'I. Won't. Fucking. *Chill*.'

'Ooooohhhhhh,' says the crowd.

'Oh, man, you're too much. I love your energy, but you gotta harness it. You gotta chill.'

'I'LL GIVE YOU CHILL, CODY BRYAN, YA BIG HOLLYWOOD GOBSHITE. GET OUT OF THAT BOAT THIS MINUTE OR I WON'T BE HELD RESPONSIBLE FOR MY ACTIONS!'

I'm screaming at this stage. There are more 'ooh's from the crowd.

He looks. He gets out of the boat. There's no one singing now. It's silent. I go back to the car. I sit in the car, breathing heavily. My legs are shaking.

'What have I done, Freya?'

'Called the patriarchy a big Hollywood gobshite, Auntie … I mean, Ann.'

'I better get up to the office. I can't have them lads ruining my boats. I've put enough work into them.'

'Do it, bossgirl.'

I am just about able to drive up to the production office. All the while, Freya is quizzing me about what happened.

'Freya, you'll have me off the road with the questions. Why do you need to know? Didn't you see?'

'It's technique. I'm reflecting on what just happened. I want to know what makes you tick Aun— … Ann.'

'Cody Bryan ruining my *Pieris japonica* makes me thick.'

I park at the production office and knock on the door, quietly.

'Punch it, Ann. Break it down.' Freya is egging me on.

I give it a harder rap. The director opens the door of the Portakabin. His mouth is open. He's not expecting me. I don't think he's expecting anyone. He seems to be in a meeting with Patsy Duggan and a foreign-looking fella. Indian or Middle Eastern.

'Ann, sweetheart, what can I do you for?'

I start to go into the room, with Freya behind me. He doesn't exactly block me but doesn't move very far to let me in, so I'm still standing in the doorway. Freya is on the step behind me. I explain how Cody Bryan has destroyed my flowerbed in a boat.

'Ann, I can assure you that we will deal with it. If there's been a misunderstanding—'

'There's no misunderstanding about it. He's made shite of the boats and the Tidy Towns will be here on a random visit one of these days. I've put too much work into that to have him feck it up on me.'

'Ann—'

'Have a word with your Hollywood star, please.'

I go back down to the boats. The crowd seem to have moved on. But it's all ruined. I'm nearly crying.

'FREYA, WILL YOU PUT DOWN THAT BLOODY PHONE BEFORE I THROW IT OVER THE DITCH?'

And she does. And that's the end of the day's filming.

32

QUARE EYES

I'm still in my dressing gown when the landline rings. It doesn't ring as much any more now, only Indian lads telling me I've a virus.

'Mam, what's wrong with your mobile? I've been trying to ring you all morning.'

'I turned it off for once. What do you mean? Is everything OK?'

'Mam, I have two children, I'm up the walls with the camogie and work and now, besides all that, my mother is going viral.'

'What are you talking about?'

'Look yourself up, Mam, and ring me back.'

No sooner have I started to type *Ann Dev*—... than Google completes it for me, as if it was expecting me. *Ann Devine Irish mammy Cody Bryan.*

I click Play on the video.

The World's Number 1 Celts Fansite presents in association with The Celts: The Fightback – The Natives are Revolting.

And there I am. Calling Cody Bryan a big Hollywood gobshite. Freya had recorded the whole thing. It's only a snippet. *My aunt the hero* is the title on it.

I look underneath. There are only a few thousand views, so maybe it isn't so bad. The comments are what you'd expect.

Is she/he spekeing English?

I earned 3423 dollars an hour from my house.

I no her she is from wear im from no word of a lie she is mental.

Who is that last comment from? I wonder. Protroll34? With the spelling, it's definitely someone from the town.

I ring Deirdre.

'You saw it? You called Cody Bryan a gobshite, Mammy. I turn my back for a minute and there you are, reading the riot act to a half-naked Hollywood star in boat filled with bark mulch. This is going to be big, Mammy.'

'But there's only a few thousand have seen it. It'll blow over.'

'That's YouTube, Mam. No one watches that any more. It's three hundred thousand on Facebook. LadzBantz have shared it as well. I'd say more watched you than went to Mass last week in the country. And there's more than one video. They've done remixes.'

'Remix? Have people nothing better to do? What's a remix?'

'That's the internet now, Mam. It *is* all there is to do for some people. Here, I'll play it for you down the phone. Wait now … there.'

They'd put an echoey effect around my voice and I was shouting, 'I'LL GIVE YOU CHILL.' And then a load of boom boom music. Dance music. The kind of music there'd be stabbings at. And a kind of repeat. Do they call it a loop?

'CODY BRYAN, YA BIG HOLLYWOOD GOBSHITE! BIG HOLLYWOOD GOBSHITE! GOBSH-SH-SH-SH-ITE ...'

It didn't sound too bad, actually.

'Where did all of this start?'

'You'd want to talk to Freya. She put the first video on her Instagram under *My aunt the hero* and said it was about how even just one local woman can fight back against the mainstream.'

'But I don't want to fight the mainstream. I like mainstream.'

'Well, you're fighting it now anyway, Mammy. To be fair to Freya, she's very talented. She has it edited nicely. I was watching and thinking, *This is very well done*, and then I remembered that I was watching my mother shouting curses at Cody Bryan.'

'What am I going to do, Deirdre?'

'Get an agent, Mam. The offers will be flooding in. I've to go to a meeting here at work, at which I'm sure you'll come up, but I'll talk to you later.'

I hang up and check my phone. It's flickering with texts.

Sally, Gordon and Galligans Boutique texting me personally to ask if I'd like to be kitted out for interviews.

Hi, Ann, this is Rachel McAndrew, I'm a researcher for The Late Late Show ...

ANN THIS IS EILEEN FRIEND OF YOUR MOTHER. SHE IS VERY UPSET ABOUT YOU MAKING A SHOW OF YOURSELF SHE HAS CHIROPODIST TOMORROW CAN YOU BRING HER ALL WELL OTHERWISE TG EILEEN

It goes on for some time. I can't stir outside. Deirdre sends me things over the next few days. A big long article in the *Guardian* – the English one – about The Glorious Multifunction of the Word 'Gobshite', written by some Irish fella who looks about nineteen. And then just stupid stuff that isn't even English. *This Irish Mammy is giving us life!* What does that mean? *This Irish Mother reaction to Cody Bryan is Everything.* How is it everything? *What this story tells us about Ireland.* What does anything tell us about Ireland? Rory tells me a crowd in Cork are making T-shirts that read, 'I WON'T CHILL'. At least they're useful. You could wear them, although I'd probably wear it under something.

There are a lot of phone calls from the radio and the telly, but I won't go anywhere. Denis is annoyed. He wants to try out the green room at *The Late Late Show*.

'A fridge of beer, Ann. You just go in and they give you what you want at the afterparty. The place is full of dryballs who wouldn't know what to do with it. Bedads, I'd know what to do with it.'

'Would you go away out of that, acting like Oliver Reed? You'd be on your ear after five or six.'

'I'd pace myself.'

'You won't get the chance because I'm going nowhere near it. Once you give yourself away to people they'll always have a piece of you, and then the next thing you do, they'll play it back to you in your face. I don't want any fame. And you'd get no luck in your own job, Denis. They'd say everything you did was because Ann did this and Ann did that.'

'What would you have to do with me driving a cement lorry? I think you're losing the run of yourself.'

But I'm firm on it, and I won't be doing anything in public. And besides, I've nothing to wear. I'd have to get a stylist. *Get Queer Eye, Mam,* says Deirdre. *They're the lads.*

There's enough quare eyes around here watching me.

33

I COME IN PEACE

That's the thing about all this viral business. Once a story goes out into the world, you lose all control over it. There can be good and bad about it. It doesn't do our Tidy Towns entry a *bit* of harm. We organize a clean-up. Or, actually, Gordon takes charge and he must have given everyone else a different start time because, when I get there, there's a large crowd already. I get out of the car and they are all waving their pickers and shouting, 'CODY IS A GOBSHITE LA LA LAAA LA.' It's pure comical. I'm a bit embarrassed, but this is all the recognition I want – from the locals.

Freya comes up to me, because Geraldine is there as well.

'Haley and Caley want to know if they can get a selfie with you.'

'Who're Haley and Caley? Are they a band or something?'

'No, Auntie Ann, they're in my class. They're over there.'

'What's their surnames? They look familiar.'

'Bailey. They're sisters.'

'Them two? Weren't they the ones sending you the texts? Do you want me to tell them to feck off?'

'Yeah, they were WhatsApps. No, Auntie Ann. They're actually OK. Anyway, I need the credits. Money in the bank, isn't that what you call it?

'But I don't understand. Why would they want to be in a photo with me after me making a show of myself?'

'It doesn't matter, Auntie Ann. You went viral. That's all anyone wants now. It doesn't matter for what.'

'Even for being a clown?'

'Especially for being a clown. Do it, Auntie Ann. They've been sound enough to me since.'

'OK, I will, but I won't smile.'

The two girls do the selfie anyway, with the stupid face they all have for photos now. They call Freya in, and even she does a bit of that hip thing, although not as bad as the two Baileys, posing like Lady Gala. And I know for a fact their father is driving around doing sheds with watered-down paint. I couldn't do the hip thing or I'd put my back out. Anyway, it wouldn't make much difference to my hips. It'd take more than that angle to undo the damage of pushing out four babies, I can tell you. Lossie is there as well. I make a point of going over to her, and I look at Freya, to give her the message that this is the friend she should be making.

'You're, like, my hero,' says Lossie, and I give her a squeeze on the shoulders. Her mother is a lovely woman. Much nicer than the Baileys or Kylie Cafferty and the Kennedy girl, who are floating as well. If I'm a celeb now, then I endorse Lossie. I practically order Freya to bring Lossie to the house the next time she's around.

Gordon is the next person to come up to me.

'You've started something, Ann. You're showing that local rights won't be ridden roughshod over. I've already heard from another group in Wicklow who are concerned about the filming that's going on up there. They cut down a one-hundred-year-old tree, would you believe, because they needed access for some machine for the filming of *Fast and Furious 15 – Escape to the Country*. I'm telling you, it's a grassroots movement.'

'I never thought of it that way. A grassroots movement is right. Which reminds me, we'll need to spray a bit of Roundup around the new flowerbeds, if Cody Bryan hasn't sat on them.'

'You never stop. By the way, we've a new recruit.' He looks around him. 'He says he wants to speak to the chief of the natives. I assumed he was talking about you.'

The words are hardly out of his mouth when I hear this shout from across the road.

'Aye, there she is, the woman herself. THE WOMAN WHO DON'T FACKING CHILL FOR NO ONE! Oh my days! The legend that is, I behold it before my own eyes.'

This big tall lad comes up to me. English fella. No socks on and a sort of leather waistcoat and bare arms. He shakes my hand in a kind of a complicated way, so that our elbows are touching and it's a kind of a half-hug. I wouldn't be one for complicated handshakes. I hate complicating a basic thing. And I *definitely* don't like being hugged without knowing the person. But they're all hugging nowadays. No wonder all these superbugs are thriving.

He has tattoos all over his arms and up around his neck. I have a fair idea he isn't doing too many interviews for a job in the bank. One of the extras, no doubt.

'I come in peace, Leader of the Tidy Towns Dé Danann.'

'Actually, Gordon is the chairperson. I'm just the vice-chairperson.'

'Who's Gordy? That wee Victor Meldrew geezer over there? Fack me, Ann, he's just the civil servant. In this business, you need warriors.'

'For your information, Gordy – I mean, Gordon – set up this group, so he very much is the leader, thank you very much.'

'Sorry, my liege.' He puts his arm around Gordon's shoulder. 'I'm only facking wiv ye, Gordy mate. Heart and soul of the community. Isn't that right, geez?'

Gordon was half smiling. He wasn't a fella that was manhandled that much, I'd say. He was mostly in insurance before he retired.

'Anyway, I come in peace from *The Celts*. To help the natives clear up their kingdom. We are a civilised race. Let us fight the common enemy together. The Saxon litterers. What do you say – bury the hatchet? Say sorry on behalf of the production?'

'Ah, there's no hatchet to bury. Put on a hi-vis as well there. We don't want you getting knocked down on the road.'

'That would be bad, wouldn't it? A mighty Celtic warrior getting whiplash from a Vauxhall Astra.'

'They're Opel over here, but good enough so. Here's your picker and a hi-vis and there's gloves around here somewhere, so best of luck.'

'Right you are, teeshock. AND IF IT ISN'T MY OLD MUCKER DJ DEVINE ...'

He runs over and gives Denis – DJ? – who has just got out of the car, a big hug.

'This geezer here drank us under the table. You need to come dahn again next week, mate. Cody wants a rematch.'

Denis – predictable Denis. I've been obsessing about myself this last while and Denis is going up on stages in his vest and is best friends with a man who has a banshee – naked, of course – going up behind his ear.

Just then Oona comes by and seems a little rattled by all the commotion. I haven't seen her out walking before.

253

'Oona,' says Gordon, innocent out, 'are you joining the clean-up?'

'I don't want to take away the glory from your star attraction,' she says, and it seems like a compliment but it doesn't feel like one, and she gives me a smile with her teeth and walks off in the direction of Tommy's house.

'Could be a good thing, Ann, this bit of publicity. You know, adversity brings people together. Kilsudgeon, the tidiest Celtic town in Ireland. And it's all down to you, Ann!'

I hope he's right. The whole thing looks to have blown over a little anyway.

34

A BEELINE FOR ME

When Denis comes home on Thursday with his few cans and the paper it's clear from his face that something's happened.

'What is it?' I ask before he's even taken off his coat.

'Nothing,' he says.

'If you're lying, it can't be good.'

'It's just … you'd better take a look at this,' and he hands me the *Sentinel*.

LOCAL WOMAN'S VIRAL VIDEO HEAPS PRESSURE ON CELTS PERMISSION DECISION

It was a case of Devine intervention today as the Castlestrokard Urban District Council met to review the circumstances under which permission was granted for the filming of The Celts – Hound of Destiny *following an expression of concern in the Dáil and from the Film Planning Board.*

The video of local woman Ann Devine upbraiding Hollywood star Cody Bryan has caused quite the stir locally and led to much attention being focused on Kilsudgeon.

However, it appears that the increased attention has uncovered some problematic details with the shoot – attention which has currently suspended the shooting schedule.

An initial inquiry from a national newspaper journalist was rebuffed by the district council last week, and it was revealed the letter outlining the refusal inadvertently included a handwritten Post-it that read 'TELL THEM TO EFF OFF BACK TO DUBLIN WITH THEIR QUESTIONS.'

A freedom of information request was sent and it was revealed that there was no notification to either the local authority or the gardaí, and that gardaí may have taken an ad hoc approach to the filming. No Garda spokesperson was available for comment.

'I'm too busy with the crime scum,' said an unnamed sergeant.

More worryingly, there are allegations that there may have been financial inducements paid to 'grease the wheels' of the production, though this has been denied by councillors.

Independent councillor Eiriú O'Dumhaltaigh raised the question of how the town had granted unlimited permission to the production company Gubu to film. He asked that financial records relating to the deal be released, but this motion was ruled inadmissable and outside of the order of business by the acting meeting chair Danny Duggan. When Councillor O'Dumhaltaigh raised the matter further he was ordered to leave the chamber, with the Chair saying that if he couldn't learn to behave, he'd be better off trying out for a job as an extra on the movie.

A spokesperson for Gubu declined to comment in person to the Sentinel, however they have released a statement *saying they are committed to Kilsudgeon, 'a great little town to make TV in', and they would be working with the local community to address any issues that had arisen. Damage to the boats has now been repaired and the boats restored to their former glory.*

Denis and me decide that no one will notice it and it doesn't matter, but they do and it does. The mood suddenly changes. No filming means no business, and the locals aren't happy. Freya rings me to tell me the Facebook page is being bombarded. A farmer who wants to know when they're going to use his sucklers for the cattle raid hurls abuse at me in a comment. *UR a disgrase Ann Devine.* I *know* him. I went to school with him. 'Who's going to pay for the redecoration?' some woman whose homestays haven't arrived yet asks. *You owe me Anne Devin.*

My name is at the top of the page. How did she spell both halves of it wrong?

Not everyone is unhappy, though. Johnny is delighted because the extras are hanging around the pub most of the time now. He writes up on the page: *Business is booming. Thanks, Ann LOL.*

One person is very unhappy. Patsy Duggan. He sends me a text. *Your little stunt will blow up in your face Ann.*

Oh feck.

I'm trying to keep a low profile, avoid everyone, but we're out of gooseberry jam and Denis won't have breakfast without it. So I decide to run into SuperValu. I'm definitely not going to Leona's, but I should be able to duck in and out of SuperValu quickly. I even park near the exit, like I'm a getaway driver. In my own town.

I'm around by the bread when I hear him. He's on the phone.

'Oh, a pure disaster, but look, we'll get through it. They'll move on eventually, hah? I'll talk to you. G'luck. Byebyebye.'

He turns and sees me looking at him and makes a beeline for me.

'Ann, the very woman.'

'Patsy.'

'How are you enjoying your new-found fame?'

'I'm trying to lose my fame, to be honest, Patsy.'

'Well, that's the way with fame. Once you go too close to the flame, you get burnt.'

'I didn't go too close to any flame. It was a pure accident.'

He's looking at me. Smiling first, but he kind of turns it into a sucking sound with his teeth. He looks around the aisle. Takes down a packet of detergent and seems to take fierce interest in it. I don't know if he's still talking to me or not.

'And you're well, Patsy?'

He doesn't seem to hear the question.

'What's your evaluation of me, Ann?' he says then. 'What do you think of me? Do you think I'm a bit of a chancer?'

'Em ... I don't ... I mean, I, you know, like ... I don't ...'

'It's fine, Ann. As a matter of fact, I know what you think. Rory told me you said I was a crook.'

'Rory said that? ... I never ... I might have said that ... I'll kill him.'

Rory! The scut. No loyalty to his mother. But then, he's only just out of his teens. Well, I'm going to clear out his room and put Jennifer in it and put the most girly wallpaper on it to remind him of where his bread is buttered. He can sleep out in the shed when he comes back.

'Well, it doesn't matter what you said or what anyone said. I'm a one-hundred-per-cent man. What you see is what you get. Don't judge me until you know me.'

'But I'm not judging you.'

'You don't know the half of it, Ann. You only know what you see when I'm in campaign mode. But I have hidden depths.'

I thought he said, 'What you see is what you get'?

'I know you're looking down your noses at me. You and the Dublin media. You're just part of the establishment.'

What does he mean, 'establishment'? How am I the establishment? Driving around in a zero-nine Skoda.

'Dublin media, Patsy? Who's that?'

'You don't know where I'm coming from. Why do I do what I do? Why do I do it?'

I think he's going to answer this one himself.

'I do it for the love of this village. For Kilsudgeon. For the people who elect me. Do you know how this happened?'

He's still holding the Daz, so I don't know *what* he's talking about. Then he taps on his artificial leg and I know what I'm in for. He's told this story about his leg at every council meeting, every election. Even in the Dáil when they wanted to bring in divorce.

'When I left Kilsudgeon first, in 1972 or 1973, I can't remember which year ...'

He can remember it well. He put it in his autobiography, *Kilsudgeon to the Core*.

'... I went over to London, working for an uncle of mine. We were doing the kerbing. Fifteen years of age, mixing cement for the Murphys. I went over a few years, got the mail boat to Holyhead and then the train: Chester, Crewe Stoke, Rugby, London Euston and wound up in Camden Town. A lonely bastard of a place. I hardly knew anyone and only that I had a bit of a way with words I got a bit of female company, do you understand me, Ann? Rows of houses with boarding rooms in them and oul lads in there, sitting on beds, writing home with a few pound, and no one talking to each other. Street after street with no neighbours. English people in watching telly and no one to puck a ball. And one fateful day, I remember well, it was a Friday, because I was looking forward to a dance that night ...'

Here we go. The story of the leg. He is quoting almost word for word from the autobiography now.

'... I'll never forget the pain, Ann. But there was one pain worse than that, Ann. The pain of the place that I was convalescing in. A home for poor oul Irish lads with no one to visit them. You know what being alone and old is like, don't you, Ann, from your job? And I swore that I would never let that happen to my beloved Kilsudgeon. I won't let it die, Ann ...'

'Patsy ...'

'No, let me finish. So you'll excuse me if I don't mind pulling a few strokes to get things going in this town, and if that means bringing a television show in here and a couple of fucking shrubs get broken when Cody Bryan lies on top of them, then so be it. You should be putting up a plaque. Towns all over Ireland would be falling over themselves to have Cody Bryan lying across their shrubs.'

'But I only told him get out of there. I didn't know it was going to be viral.'

'Oh, you're being very cute now. You know all about the lingo. *Viral*. Since when do you know about viral? Your own niece recorded it.'

'She was doing it for school. She was just out with the phone.'

'And then recording a private meeting.'

'What meeting?'

'I was in the middle of a very important meeting when you came up and interrupted.'

'I'm sorry about that. I wasn't looking for you. I was only talking to the director. I didn't know you were going to be up there.'

'And now the reporters are asking about money changing hands.'

'But I didn't say a word to any reporter.'

'There's a new editor up at the *Sentinel*, thinks he's fecking Robert Redford doing Watergate. He started the whole thing and then the Dublin crowd took it up. Well, my man at the *Sentinel* is back from holidays next week and he'll put a stop to his gallop.'

'I said nothing about money. I only wanted him out of the boat.'

'Well, fuck it, money did change hands, and what of it? If you want something done quickly, you need to lubricate, do you understand, Ann? Lubrication.'

I hope he's still talking about money.

'Denis knows what I'm talking about. Where would Denis's lorry be without oil, hah? And it takes a mechanic with vision to know who and what to lubricate. Now listen to me, Ann. Nothing's changed out the country since the time of the high kings. When strangers come to an Irish village, they look for the local leader. Who is that, Ann? Is it you with a couple of begonias?'

Not much I could say to that. They weren't begonias, but now isn't the time.

'Is it Father Donnegan, worrying about his roof? His days are gone. The old magic doesn't work any more for the Church, Ann. Is it Gordon? That's a howl. No, they come to meet the chieftain. That's how it's done.'

I'm about to reply when someone comes around the corner pretending to buy dogfood. I know she's trying to eavesdrop because I know her and she has no dogs.

'Now, I'm looking at you and I'm thinking maybe you had nothing to do with what happened, but I'll thank you to stay out of our business and get that niece of yours to turn off her camera. But I like her style. She could work for me one day, like her cousin. But I'll make one thing clear, Ann, stay away from *The Celts*.'

'But I'm on the liaison committee.'

'Liaise away, Ann, but don't break anything, do you hear me?' And he walks out, still carrying the Daz.

I am fairly rattled after that, I can tell you. I am not going to do a single thing out of the ordinary now.

35

BUTTER ON THE SOFA

The filming is still suspended, but Winnie gets in touch to confirm that Hilary is still coming. She's going to film the nothing happening, and then she'll be there when it all starts up again. So she's due at twelve today, and now I'm looking forward to her coming. It'll get me back on track with the film crowd. Denis is looking out the window from half eleven. I think he's a bit excited at the prospect of another woman around the place. Denis likes to have someone to impress. Not that you'd know it from the cut of him.

'Denis, have you no better trousers than them?'

'What's wrong with them?'

'There's butter on them. You can't be meeting a Henderson-Fitzgerald with butter on your trousers.'

He half wipes it off with a tea towel. I don't have the mental energy to give out any more. I've been up since dawn cleaning the place.

'And what harm if she did see me?'

'Ah, I don't want her thinking we're on tenterhooks waiting for her.'

'But we are.'

'But I don't want her to know that. It'd give her an advantage.'

'We're not in mergers and acquisitions, Ann. We're not negotiating with her.'

'Just, can't you get away from the window anyway?'

In the end, we both missed her coming in. Denis turned his back and there was the car in the yard.

'That's her! I didn't hear her come in at all.' He squints out through the net curtains. 'An electric car?' Denis doesn't like them at all. *What's the point in driving something if you can't hear it?*

'Oh, she's a grand-looking girl,' says Denis. He chooses his words carefully when describing the physical appearance of any girl around his daughters' age. *Grand-looking* is safe enough. 'Come over, Ann, and look at her.' I go to the window and peer out. It's not Hilary.

'That's Winnie, Denis.'

A man gets out of the passenger seat. A tall, slim man with a kind of a square head and glasses. He looks very familiar. He speaks briefly to her and she seems to encourage him on. Winnie comes to the door with a folder in one hand and he starts to take bags out of the boot of the car. I can't remember where I've seen him, and then it hits me. It's the boy from the table quiz. The one who knew the answers while the hairy lads had the craic.

We meet her at the door.

'Oh, Winnie!' says Denis, getting the wrong end of the stick. 'So are you staying with us?' He sounds a bit too enthusiastic.

'No ... um, so, that's the thing. There's been a change around with some of the arrangements. Sorry, I meant to get in touch with you, but it's just been so manic around here with setting everything up, so anyway ... um ... . this is Declan!'

Declan.

We look over to the car, where Declan is picking up his bags and coming towards us wearing a jacket and shirt and jeans that I might pick out for Rory if he'd ever let me dress him. He stops at the door and looks awkwardly at us. I stretch out a hand and he shakes it. Denis does the same, but Declan doesn't see it because he's looking at Denis's map in the hall.

'I saw you at the table quiz, do you remember, Declan? You were with your friends with all the hair.'

'They're not really my friends.'

'OK so.'

He's holding his bag and seems anxious to go away.

'Is the room ...?'

'Of course! Sorry, young man, I should have shown you. You must be tired.'

All the surplus mammying I'd been storing up for a while pours out on top of poor Declan. 'Would you eat a fry or a burger? Denis, run down for chips there.'

But he has sort of edged his way up the stairs and, whether he's an expert on embossed wallpaper or not, has somehow found the right room and closed the door.

I look at Winnie and she looks away.

'Yeah, so, is that OK? Declan was, like, a last-minute change because his other accommodation wasn't suitable, and then Hilary needed to be closer to the shoot site so ... we had to change a couple things and ... Look, if there's an issue, we can find somewhere else. I totally know this is short notice, but ...'

I think of the money. I look up the stairs where Declan has gone. I wonder what on earth Jennifer will make of him when she arrives back to find him sleeping in her room. He looks like someone she'd have a shocking bad first date with.

Declan comes back down the stairs and goes into the sitting room without saying anything. Winnie seems anxious to go. Her phone rings and she walks a bit away from the door.

'Poor Winnie seems to be stressed,' says Denis.

'Never mind poor Winnie, Denis. What are we going to do with this fella?' I whisper to him. I can see Declan inside in the sitting room, looking at photos on the walls.

'Oh yeah, OK ... sure, yeah ... right away ... hold on. So, Mrs Devine, what do you want to do?'

'Well, he's practically part of the furniture now, I suppose. Lookit, he can stay, but is there any chance of an increase in the amount for the inconvenience of ...' *What inconvenience?* I say to myself. The inconvenience of him being odd? Where would you put that on an invoice?

Winnie says she'll look into it, but I'd say she'll look into nothing. She leaves, and we go back into the sitting room. Denis sits down on the seat near the telly. Declan looks at him and sort of gestures.

'The butter.'

'What's that, Declan?'

'You have butter on your trousers, Mr Devine.'

'Oh, right. Is that what it is?'

'And on the sofa.'

We look at the sofa. He's right. How did I not spot that? It must be recent. Or I'm gone butter blind.

'Ah, for feck's sake, Denis. Butter on your trousers,' I say, as if it hasn't happened before.

Denis goes out to get a J-cloth and starts going at the butter. There's only one thing for this situation.

'You'll have tea, Declan?'

I don't wait for a reply. I leave the fry and the burger and chips for a while. He doesn't look like he eats many of those. But when I come back in with tea and biscuits, I sense his unease. I pour the tea and ask how he wants it and it turns out he doesn't want it at all.

'I don't drink tea.'

A few years ago, this would have been like a death in the family, but with Freya in and out like a draught, I am better equipped these days. I bring out the box of what Denis calls 'quare tea' and Declan flicks through it before taking out the only jasmine one. I don't know how long it's been there or what hotel it came out of, but it gets me over the hump. I'd better go to the shop straight away, though.

'What did you think of your room, Declan?' asks Denis, anxious to get some bit of praise.

'It's grand.'

'It's not too girly for you?'

'No, it's grand.'

'You see, we were expecting a woman,' Denis blurts out. 'We were told we were getting a woman.'

Declan doesn't know how to react, and neither do I.

'Ehh ...' says Declan.

I should get down to the shop.

'What happened in the other place, the other accommodation that fell through?'

'Denis! You can't be quizzing the man.' Though I am dying to know too.

This is the first time he looks a little different. Declan looks away and has a small wince on his face. Denis looks sorry he asked.

'Don't mind him, Declan. Will you eat a sandwich or something?'

'Is it gluten-free?'

'I'll go to Lidl now so.'

'I'm going to look at my coins,' says Denis.

'I collect coins too.'

Denis brightens up at that news. He springs out of his chair and scuttles into the other room. We can hear him rooting around. I'm trying to think of something to say, hoping he'll be quick.

'What do you do on the filming then, Declan?'

'I'm a trainee boom-operator.'

'That sounds like a big job.'

'It's OK. You just kinda get on with it and not too many people are ...' He trails off.

'And you don't have to talk to anyone.'

'Yeah.'

'I'd like one of those jobs too.'

Denis brings out his coin collection. The folders, the boxes. It's a bit of a mess. He sweeps newspapers off the coffee table.

'What do you think, Declan? I'd say it would be worth a fair bit. There's a few beauties in there.'

Declan looks through it and lifts up coins and examines them closely.

'They're all fairly common, really. I don't think it's worth much, Mr Devine.'

Poor Denis. He looks deflated.

'Yeah, I thought that. It's only a silly thing. A bit of a cod.'

'Yeah,' says Declan.

Declan doesn't seem to notice that he's upset him. As Denis packs up his coins, I slip out of the house. Where's our grand double-barrelled videographer gone who'd be telling us stories about all sorts of carry-on on movie sets with famous stars? And who have we landed ourselves with?

*

I hear her before I see her. She's in the next aisle, on the other side of the chainsaws.

'Yeah, so I said to the guy, I want it all out – the kitchen, all the old cupboards. How much ya think he tells me? Guess. Higher … higher again. Right. Isn't that *insane*?'

I try to head over behind the veg aisle where the boundaries are higher, but it's too late.

'WELL, WHADDYA KNOW, IT'S ANN DEVINE, TIDY TOWNS HERO.'

There's a woman with her who also has a shopping basket. She's what Denis would call a handsome woman.

'Hey, Annie, c'mere, I want ya to meet someone. Hilary, this is Ann Devine.'

'Hh–h— hello, Hilary.'

'Helluva story how it came to happen, but I asked Patrick Ignatius if I could help, ya know. Maybe help put a few people up because they got a shortage, ya see, with the whole lodgings situation, and we got plenny of room up at Tommy's house, God rest his soul. And then the funniest thing, I happen to mention that I got an interest in videography, so who do you think they matched me with? The videographer. Oh boy. I hope ya don't mind me sayin' so when you're standin' right there, Hilary, but you're a fascinatin' individual.'

Hilary smiles nervously.

'So, Ann, ya get anybody stayin' with ya?'

'Oh yeah, we got, I mean, we have a lovely fella staying with us – Declan. He's actually—'

'Oh my god, haha, Declan, oh boy, you got yourselves a real lucky dip there, Annie D. He's a doozy, oh boy. Good luck with that fella. Funny how things happen, ain't it?'

I just made one little mistake over that shagging field and it's like she hates me.

I go looking for the jasmine tea.

When I get back home Denis meets me at the door.

'He'll have to go, Ann. He's telling me now the wallpaper is crooked in several places.'

'Is it?'

'It is, but that's the walls in this house. You're not supposed to say that. Did you ever go to a B&B and say the wallpaper was crooked?'

I don't even tell him about Oona. He'd lose it entirely.

'We'll go on a cruise or something with the money,' I say, to placate him.

'Two grand? That'll be a ferry. One way, by the looks of things.'

36

COCKY OUT

'You're here at last, Ann.'

I find Flash Lordan sitting next to the window, looking very sorry for himself. There are bits of breakfast around his face. He's off the crutches now and well able to use his hands. The breakfast around the face is nothing to do with his physical ability. Flash can get down in himself.

'I suppose you're busy with all your protesting.'

I'm surprised at this. Flash is normally delighted to see me, but he's acting like Nonie.

'Ah, Flash, what's the matter with you? Are you sad about something?'

I get a J-Cloth and start wiping around his face. There's a bit of toast tucked into his shirt collar and I'm fairly certain it's from the day before because it's brown sliced pan and I know he goes every second day between the brown and the white and there was white on the table. He has a smell of underpants about him too.

'I'm an old eejit, Ann. Everyone is laughing at me.'

'You're not an eejit, Flash, aren't you the saviour of the place, warning people about speed vans?'

'I can't even do that now.'

'Well, you're retired from it. Anyway, you're not an eejit.'

'I am. Just a sad oul clown going around the place. Getting taken for a ride.'

'Who's hoodwinking you? Who's taking you for a ride?'

'That film crowd. And you too, Ann. Are ye having a laugh at me, I suppose?'

'What? No one's laughing at you.'

Except I *have* been. Laughing away over wine with that director fella.

'They said they'd give me a part in the thing. I might be a village elder. Or a blind Druid.'

'Why would they want you to be blind?'

'I don't know. I'd look wiser. That's a laugh anyway.'

'And did you want to be an actor, Flash?'

'I didn't think it until they offered it to me. For the field.'

'Oh, Flash, you didn't give them the field for nothing?'

He looks at his lap. 'They kind of caught me unawares. I wasn't expecting them, and then they all arrive in smelling grand and the beards and all, and they were saying what a great fella I was and how my field would be on the map. A grand little field. I usually rent it out to Andy Phelan for grazing or silage, but I said no to Andy, told him this year it's for the filming. He was mad about that. Then I said, "The next time you see me, I'll be a Druid." I was cocky out with him about it.'

'And are they going to make you a Druid?'

'Are they fuck. They've changed something. I don't know what. With the kibosh being on the filming they're changing things. Flash is the mug again. Just like when Linda left me. The whole village laughing at Flash with the wife gone. And I was looking forward awful hard to Denise seeing me on the telly. You know, my daughter, wherever she is now, I thought that she might get in contact. You put them on to me, Ann. So now I've no money and the land is in shite over their jeeps.'

'I'm so sorry, Flash.'

'Don't be sorry for me any more. No more stupid Flash. No one's going to be laughing at me.'

'Would you like me to help, Flash?'

'No need, Ann. I wrote to the paper about it.'

My throat goes dry. 'When did you do that, Flash? I could sort it for you maybe. Put a word in.'

'I sent it in last week, so it should be out today.'

Flash only gets the minimum of care from me for the next half an hour. I need to get a look at that paper.

I leave Flash's place and drive straight to Leona's shop. I grab the paper, shove some money at Leona and tell her I'm in a fierce hurry so I don't have to talk. Then I sit into the car and open it up.

Local Man 'Exploited' by Celts *filming* is the headline.

Local man John Flash Lordan is another who has suffered at the hands of the Celts *production ...*

It goes on to tell all of Flash's woes, that he feels cheated and betrayed. And then I see it. They've a few photos of him at the bottom, and in one of them he's posing next to one of the boats.

Oh God, they've roped me into it.

John's cause has been championed by local woman Ann Devine, who has pledged to help. Ann has been a thorn in the side of The Celts, causing production to be halted while investigations got underway into the financing of the TV series. And she's at it again ...

My phone beeps. Patsy. *So this is how it's going to be, is it, Ann?*

I lay my head back against the seat. I could nearly cry. How in God's name do I end up in these situations?

My phone starts to ring. My hand is shaking because I'm wondering if it's Patsy. But I don't recognize the number. It could be a death.

'Hello?'

'Hi, Ann, this is Andrew Kearns. I work for Mature Recollections Productions. We make the *Everyday Scandals* programme. You might have seen some of our investigative reporting on corruption in Irish public life.'

'You'll be never out of work so. Like the hairdressers.'

'Can I talk to you for a second?'

'I don't know. It depends what you want to talk about.'

'Patsy Duggan.'

'I'm saying nothing. I'm not talking about Cody Bryan or virals or *The Celts* or Flash Lordan or anything.'

'Who's Flash Lordan?'

See, that's the way you people catch me out. I'm not saying one word.

'Ann, hear me out. We've bigger fish to fry than the TV show. We saw the full video. What went viral was just a bit of you shouting at Cody Bryan. But I'm not interested in him. I'm more interested in what happened afterwards.'

'I don't care what you're interested in.' I don't hang up, though, because he has me half interested already.

'Do you remember when you went up to the Portakabin, there was Patsy Duggan and the director?'

'Maybe I do. I'm hoping to forget the whole thing.'

'Do you remember if there was a third man in the office?'

'There might have been. A fella with a smallish head. Sort of foreign.'

'Well, that foreign-looking fella is Ehsonallah Akaria.'

'Not a local name.'

'No, indeed. Ann, have you ever heard of Bin Jufali Imdad?'

'No, I haven't. They sound ferocious.'

'They are one of the largest property developers in the Middle East. They own shopping malls, skyscrapers and housing developments all over the world. And we think they're coming to Kilsudgeon.'

'Oh, I see. That'll be a boost for the local shop.'

'These lads don't mess around, Ann. If they're coming to Kilsudgeon, it'll never look the same again. The man in the Portakabin – Ehsonallah – works for them. When I was watching it, I thought I recognized him, but I couldn't place him. Then I remembered I'd seen him at an IDA conference for foreign investors. You see, Kilsudgeon is quite strategic. It's an underdeveloped little … what will I call it? … well, until your Tidy Towns group started up on it, it was a bit ramshackle. But when they're done with it, it could be sky-scrapers. Where would your fairy field be then? Now, they don't have planning permission or anything. It's just a bit of pie in the sky right now, but that's where Patsy comes in. He starts lobbying a minister. Maybe this one, maybe the next one. He'll play the long game. And then there's the land.'

'The land?'

'Well, the fairy field. If you look at it on a map, it's actu-ally part of a much bigger land parcel that was recently the subject of a rezoning. And guess who's backing that rezoning?'

'Patsy?'

'You got it in one. And Patsy is the director of a company called Pingo Investments, and do you know the other director?'

'Your man, the ayatollah that you mentioned.'

'Exactly. Patsy's carry-on goes way back. You might remember the Headage payments scandal a few decades ago?'

My mouth goes dry.

'Just to refresh your memory, there were tens of people claiming for cattle that didn't exist, and everyone thought Patsy was part of it, but it could never stick. Some other local slob took the rap for it. He had his day out in court.'

I remember who that slob was too.

'I don't know. It's not my scene. How would you want me to help?'

'We thought you might know something about Patsy. Just something that we can use to expose him. He's a crook, Ann. The evidence for the misappropriation of funds is right in front of you. His giant house with the big electric gates and the long driveway. Where do you think he gets the money for that?'

'I thought it was just the money from the Dáil.'

'That's ninety grand a year. Patsy's house is worth a million, even in Kilsudgeon. He's involved in property developments all around the country. He needs his wings clipped. Do you have anything at all on him you could give us? The tiniest tidbit.'

'I don't,' I lie to him. Anyway, what do I have? A bit of boasting in SuperValu about what he can do? Just pub talk or, rather, shop talk. 'No, I'm sorry, I don't have anything that would help ye. If I think of something ...'

'Are you sure, Ann? They won't stop here, you know. It won't be a few crushed chrysanthemums the next time.'

'I'm sure. Anyway, I'd never plant chrysanthemums.'

I sit in the car for a long time after he hangs up. My head feels crowded. News is coming at me from all angles. I was complaining before about being out of the loop. Now I know too much.

37

THE BOMB SQUAD

Home tomorrow.

Short and sweet. Like myself. I could have done with a bit more notice. That girl moves so fast, she expects everything else to move at the same pace. And in the same direction as her.

I have only a few hours to go at Rory's room, so. I could have put her in Kevin's, but Denis has turned that into a place for his 'things'. The poor man doesn't have much stuff, but what he does he minds. His coin collection and maps of local antiquities don't take up much room, but he's always buying broken clocks at jumble sales. Deirdre says, *Don't tell him about Ali Express*. I won't because I don't know what that is. Anyway, what he has in there should go in a skip by rights, but I wouldn't do that to him. If a man can't clutter an empty nest, what can he do?

And now that Declan is in Jennifer's room being strange, she'll have to go into Rory's. The sooner that filming starts up again, the better, because Declan's around the house nearly all the time. Looming. He's harmless enough but he sort of cramps our style a bit, if you know what I mean. We'd hardly be Samson and Delilah, but the empty house was nice again. You know, the kind of oddities you'd develop in that department over the years that if you told anyone else they'd think you were strange. Denis saying something silly like, *Well, are we on for an AGM this evening, Ann*?

And he sort of follows Denis around, asking him about his things and then telling him his things aren't very good. Although Denis brought him out in the lorry the other day and it shut him up. You can't argue with a lorry. And he's mad about engines. So they had a much better chat then. It turns out Declan's parents are in Dublin and the mother has a business of her own, though he wouldn't say what it was.

Hopefully, now, Jennifer coming home – a young woman – will scare him back into his room.

I text Rory to see if he minds me going through his room. I did it on the normal text so he wouldn't find it as early as the WhatsApp; that'll give me a chance to go through it anyway. I'm almost afraid of what I'll find up there, so I tell myself I'm not going to investigate much. When you're a mammy you want to know everything and you don't want to know everything at the same time. Because once you find it out, you have to do something about it, or at least be awake thinking about it. And I've found out enough things to keep me awake. So I wasn't going to go through anything, just a good surface clean.

Just as I'm about to do the top shelf of the wardrobe the doorbell rings. It's Skitchy Ryan on the doorstep.

'Mrs Devine,' he says. 'Rory's on the phone to me. Here you go.'

'Mam – Skitchy is just picking up a few things for me, all right?'

'All right so, love. What kind of things?'

'Ah, just some stuff I forgot to bring home the last day. All right, Mam, OK, grand so, I'll let you go. Thanks, Mam, fair play. That's great. Great stuff indeed. Credit to the parish. Good luck, g'wan.'

He always says this when he thinks I'm about to interrogate him. I hand the phone back to Skitchy and I see he has a big Kilsudgeon Gaels gearbag that's empty and he means to fill it. I follow him to Rory's room and then he, a bit more obvious than would be good manners, closes the door after him. He's talking to Rory on the phone inside.

'Up on top of the wardrobe, is it? I see it, bro. What's in it anyway? Holding out on me. I *won't*, I promise, OK.'

And then he comes out with a full bag.

'I'm taking this off to the bomb squad, Mrs Devine,' he says.

'Grand so, Skitchy. Don't be sending the bill here, though.'

I pretend like I don't care, but this latest mystery is loaded into my brain with all the other things to worry about. I should get a whiteboard. If it's drugs, they're out of the house now. They're all getting done for drug-dealing in college. Smart lads with solid families, everyone. My mind is going up to ninety again with the possibilities. I was nearly happier when I thought he was with the paramilitaries. At least they have a bit of discipline.

Declan wanders into the scene, eating some kind of a fungus or root or some odd bit of food out of a Tupperware. It turns out he has odd tastes in food. But I'm kind of getting used to him around the place all the same and I've started talking to him instead of talking to myself.

'What do you think of that, Declan?'

'Eh ...'

'Do you think it's something to do with drugs?'

'Might be.'

'Thanks, Declan.'

38

DISCUSSING HIS MERITS

She arrives at eleven, gives me a big hug as she gets out of her rented car and the very first thing she says to me: 'Sorry, Mammy, but you might have to do a bit of hosting this evening.'

She's organized a night out with the girls from school. It was the only night that suited between babysitters and husbands going training and various other commitments.

'I want to use the time to recentre and reconnect.'

I wish she'd centre somewhere else because I'm in no mood for entertaining. These are her schoolfriends, as opposed to her college friends, who are much nicer, but she's still sort of stuck with these when she comes home. I'm not sure if any of them like each other, but none of them wants to be the first to say it out loud.

'It's just a few of them in for prinks, Mammy.'

But it won't be just 'prinking'. They'll be primed by their own mothers to have a good look around when they're here.

They're probably trying to see did I get a wedge of money for going viral.

Jennifer and myself are having the tea in the sitting room. There's a thumping on the stairs.

'Is Rory back?' asks Jennifer.

'No, that's our new lodger. Here he is now. Well, Declan, how are you?'

'Hello, Ann. Is this Jennifer? Hello, Jennifer.'

Jennifer looks at me and then says hello to him. They are looking at each other for a bit.

'I hear the filming is stopped.'

'Yes.'

And he's still there staring at her.

'Any plans for today, Declan?' I ask, to break the silence.

'Not really.' And then he runs upstairs.

Jennifer looks at me. 'Your new housemate is different, Mammy.'

'He is.'

'He's a bit of a ride, though.'

'What?! Really? I never noticed.'

'Really, Mammy?'

It's true. I hadn't. I must get my eyes checked again.

'He is, if he had clothes that fitted him. Does he work out?'

'I hope he works out. I mean, it's working out grand.'

'No, I mean the gym. You can see it.'

'He says he does some sort of Brazilian thing. Capri sun or something. We heard him bouncing around upstairs and feared the worst, but Denis was walking past the door and he was waving his arms around.'

'Capoeira? Oooh, Mammy, curiouser and curiouser. Anyone I've ever seen do that has been Fit As.'

'Jennifer, don't be getting ideas now. I'm entangled enough with that crowd as it is.'

'Don't worry, Mammy. I'm not so starved that I'll jump on the first thing I see.'

They start to arrive around seven. Early. Or rather, on time, which is early. I still have the bags out for the nibbles, so now they know they're from Lidl.

But it's nice to have the house full again. There's something about the sound of talk all over the house and the bell going and coats all over the bannister. Even Denis was delighted to be scooting off upstairs again, away from *Sex and the Village*, as he calls them. But as I'm going in and out with bites, I could see there was a bit of 'positioning' going on.

It is three or four years since this gang got together, and they've moved on a good bit since. Most of them have babies. I stay out of it in the kitchen, but any time I go in Jennifer isn't saying much. She'd usually have been the big personality in the group.

Declan comes downstairs briefly and stands at the door then goes back up. There's a pause and shrieks of laughter after a while. I gather they are discussing his merits.

'Really? Do you think? I don't know.'

'Maybe.'

'If he cut his hair.'

'Or grew a beard.'

This brings them on to Jennifer as I come in with peanuts in a bowl.

'And how's the love life, J? Are you still free and single? Ann, is this one giving you any reason to buy a hat at all?'

'It's just really busy at work.'

'There must be tons of men in London, and all the billionaires you'd be working with.'

'The rabbit getting plenty of use, is it?' one of them says, winking at the others.

'Oh, Karen ... ya dirty bitch,' says another.

Jennifer is bright red and I decide to get out of the way. I don't think she has a pet at all. That's the last thing she needs now, to be getting overly attached to an animal. Time-consuming they are. But the way they're laughing suggests Muggins here is behind the curve. I don't want to know.

As I am leaving they start quizzing her again.

'But seriously, Jen, what's the story? Surely you're beating them away with a stick?'

'Some fellas might like that.'

'I know, you could be meeting Christian Grey.'

'Christian Doctrine more like,' says Jennifer, and tells them some story about a bad night out, but she seems to have avoided the questions. Then the conversation turns back on to one of the others and they let her be.

Strange out of her, not to go into detail. There's no mention of the cuddle workshops or the speed-dating. Not that she would have time to explain because any time the conversation dips they seem to be off talking about babies again. Kaya is 'gas, the things she comes out with', or Madison doesn't like her new playgroup. I only find this chat interesting about my own grandchildren, and even then barely.

I catch her eye the next time I'm in asking about refills, and I know by her she's bored silly.

It doesn't bode well for the night out down the village.

I don't know what time it is, but it's late. I'm coming down for Rennies for Denis. There's a fierce rattling at the door. I thought we were being broken into. It's Jennifer, struggling with her key. I let her in.

'I thought you were out with the girls and doing a sleepover.'

'Sleepover, haha. No, Mam, I'm not fourteen. No, I was going to stay with Breda, but I just came home to spend time with my beloved Mammaah.'

She is fluthered. I don't know when I've seen her drunk last.

'What about the girls? Did you get on OK afterwards? I thought myself they were a bit sly with you earlier. Asking you about your pets.'

'Pets?'

'Your rabbit.'

'MAMMY, YOU'RE A SCREAM!! HAHAHA. The girls are grand, Mammy. They were only teasing me. They're a good gang really and they know me well enough. It's only starting off that they're a bit, you know, but once you get them alone you can find out what's going on with them in their own lives. We're just at different stages. They're dying to talk to me about children, but then they're watching their words, so it's all a little ... you know, but ... still doesn't mean they don't bore the shite out of me, though, after a while. Non-stop giving out about childminders or the same teachers that used to teach them. But they're still my schoolfriends. And if I ever moved back, I might need them a bit more.'

'Moved back? What do you m—'

We're interrupted by a sound from the sitting room. We go in, and Declan is in there watching telly. I hope to God it's not something filthy. But it's not. It looks like a slow picture, though, with subtitles.

Jennifer, being well-oiled, decides now is the time to put talk on Declan.

'Oh, is that *Amour*? Oh God, I love that film, Mam.'

'I haven't seen it myself.'

'It was the best film in 2012.'

'What's it about?'

'Eh ... it's about this old man who kills his wife because she is sick and in pain.'

'Don't show it to Denis, so.'

Jennifer sits on the chair opposite Declan and they both start watching, him sneaking a look at her every thirty seconds.

'Do you like films, Declan?' she asks him.

I had never thought to ask him.

He launches into the longest spiel I've heard him say since he arrived. The films he likes and doesn't like. There are a lot he doesn't like, and he explains in detail why. He tells us how he's trying to get into movies by working on *The Celts*. The words are pouring out of him. All the time looking at the telly as Jennifer looks at him. He only looks at her when he knows she's not looking at him.

I don't know whether to stay or go. My dressing gown doesn't have its belt, so I could be exposed at any minute. I decide I'll leave them to it. Whatever *it* is.

39

THIS SHITE AGAIN

The filming has been suspended for two weeks now. The village is in a bit of a state. After the suspension, there seems to be a bit of bad blood now because there was no one turned up to the last clean-up, so it was back to a few of us doing it on our own. Today, it's just me and Freya doing a bit before I go up to Neans later.

'Why are we even doing this, Auntie Ann? Like, it's not even an official clean-up. You're obsessed, do you know that?'

'It's therapy, Freya. We'll just do a bit ourselves. I just need someone out there with me in the hi-vis so I don't feel like an eejit. You owe me in a way because of that video.'

'*I* owe you? *You* owe me! I've changed your life.'

'My life was fine before. Look, I'll bring you to a thing if you come with me.'

'What kind of a thing?'

'I don't know. A play or something like that. Something feministy.'

'Wow, Auntie Ann, have you been reading my diary? I literally just wrote about going to see something feministy.'

She's as *sarcastic*. How do they do that at that age?

We get a few beeps of the horn from people. Maybe they're supporting us. The twins stop. Here we go. But it's only to say, 'You're some woman, Ann Devine. Going up against a village. The outlaw Josey Devine.' And they drive off. We get back to work.

'People are filthy, aren't they, Freya?'

We're just after finding a load of cans. Freya is huffing a bit now.

'I'm going to need you to bring me to two feministy things, Auntie Ann. The price has gone up.'

Poor girl. Providing emotional support for a mad aunt is beyond the call of duty for her. We are out about an hour when there's a beep from her phone.

'Lossie,' she says. 'She's asking if I want to watch Netflix with her. Please, Auntie Ann, she has fibre?'

I let her go. I can't get in the way of her making friends with girls with fibre. She's done enough. And now it's just me. Alone with my thoughts. I'll just do this bit of road, I tell myself, and then I'll turn around.

But then I get carried away. That's the way with picking up rubbish. You end up trying to tidy up the world. I look down the road towards the Black Ditch and say I'll just do that. I get into a sort of hypnosis, where I'm talking to myself about the rubbish.

Stoop. Pick. Put in bag. Repeat. An empty packet of Meanies. Are they still making them? I remember Rory would go mad for them, and the smell of them. What beer is that? McGrourty's Goat? It must be a craft beer. But then there's twelve – no, thirteen – St Etiennes next to them in a bag. Why would you go this far and throw them out, and why there? Were they drinking them in

287

the car? I'll just do to the end of the road. A box of half-eaten curry chips? Now why would you eat along the road in the dark? I know you'd be hungry, but it's much more comfortable at home.

Before I know it I've four bags filled. I'm at the turn, and then I see it over the ditch, in an open gateway. Five bags of rubbish. I've seen them now, and I can't unsee them. I'm addicted to this. I'd better go back to the car to bring them up the road. That's the good thing about having a banger. You can put shite into it without feeling bad.

I get to the car and put my hand in my pocket for the car keys. No car keys. No sign in my jeans. What about the inside pocket? I felt something. Is that them? No, that's the house keys. *Ah, don't be doing this to me now and I trying to do something good.* I retrace my steps. Nothing. There's only one thing for it. I'll have to go along the road. The panic starts to rise in me again.

All the beeps of the horn and *You're some woman, Ann Devines* are forgotten. It's just me, late for going to Neans, and I can't find the car keys. I've to go back to the ditch. No sign. I cut my hand on a briar and my hi-vis gets caught in another. I go back to the bags and now I have to open them again to look if I can see the car keys. I check the phone. Nine per cent battery now. Should be enough to get me up to Neans and, once I'm there, I don't need to be anywhere else.

As I'm looking at it, the screen goes dark. What's that about?

The battery is gone.

'HOW ARE YOU GONE ALREADY, YOU BASTARDING PHONE? HOW DID YOU GO FROM NINE TO NOUGHT? WHAT ABOUT THE BITS IN BETWEEN?' I'm shouting at the phone on the side of the road.

I should have charged the phone in the car. This morning I had it charging, but the switch wasn't switched on. Because

Deirdre warned me about them catching fire and Jennifer's always telling me to let it go down before charging it because *you'll ruin the battery*. Well, that's no good to me now, daughters. I'm meant to be visiting Neans and I've no car keys and no phone.

Every decision today has led me to this. This is horrible. A car passes me on the road and I'm tempted to stop it, but then my hand has a bit of blood on it and I'm probably smelling of whatever was in the vet's rubbish bag. I press the On button. Wait! There's a flicker. Ah, it's the PLUG IN THE PHONE picture.

'FUCKIT,' I shout at a crow who's looking at me. 'You've no worries, do you, crow? Only waiting for me to leave your rubbish alone so you can finish the curry.'

After half an hour of looking I find the keys in the top of my wellington, in a fold of my jeans. 'HOW DID YOU GET THERE?' More shouting. I get into the car and the car won't start. I look at the lights lever. On full blast. *DENIS, YOU WERE SUPPOSED TO GET A NEW BATTERY*. Thanks be to God I've left it on a hill. I open the door and start rolling it and jump in and nearly knock a fella from the film set off his quad. I'm sorry it was nearly. But with the bit of a hill and a lifetime of starting bangers of cars, I turn the key at the right time and I get the car started.

I tear up the road to Neans. I'm a good hour late, between all the delays. I go in the door. It's open already. Oh God, there's a Dublin gang in there now, I bet you, and they've Neans tied up.

I run in, 'Neans, Neans!' shouting for her.

'She's in here,' says a familiar voice.

Tracy is here. Not one bit happy. Just nosing around. She has the nails of her left hand done. I go into Neans's sitting room.

Neans is looking sorry for me, as if she knows what's in store.

'You weren't here, Ann. I'm sorry I had to ring, but I was bursting and the bag was full. I had to, Ann. I wanted to wait and I told Tina to go away. Not that she was too keen to hang around even one second longer. That one only ever does the minimum.'

'If you don't mind, Mrs Malumphy, Tina is not the focus of this inquiry, so I'll thank you to leave her out of the accounts except to say she did all that was expected of her, according to her terms and conditions.'

Neans ignores her. 'Anyway, Tina left me. I knew you wouldn't let me down and I rang, but it went to your answering machine and it never goes to your answering machine. I said to myself, *Neans, Ann is in a car crash or a ditch or in hospital.* So I rang the emergency number.'

The call must have gone all the way through to Tracy.

'Where were you, Ann?' says Tracy, and she looks at my hi-vis still on me and I think there's still a bit of a smell off me.

I don't have to answer.

'Out with the Tidy Towns? Aren't you so noble-spirited now, helping the community? But that's not your job, Ann, is it? Not when you've someone to care for here. Now, are you going to look after Neans's sanitation needs?'

'Have you not looked after her already?' I say it before I think.

'It is not my job and it would be against regulations and it is *hardly* your place to question me.'

It was the nails, I suppose. She didn't want to ruin the manicure.

'She left me here stinking, Ann,' says Neans, but that's not helping matters.

Tracy looks at the two of us. She sees we're in cahoots. She doesn't like it.

'For your information, I was engaging with our overflow and disaster recovery system to see what contingencies we had for incontinence alleviation.'

I look at her.

'I was trying to get someone in to look after her bag because I didn't know if you were coming at all. Can you come out with me to the front room when you've sorted out Neans? Neans, do you mind if we use the front room?'

She doesn't wait for a reply and marches out to the room. I empty Neans's bag and clean her up and go in to Tracy. She sits on the chair facing the door and I sit on the couch.

'How would you describe what has just happened here now, Ann?'

This shite again. Asking questions. *What speed do you think you were doing?* They must have all learned it in the same book. Isn't it bleddy obvious what's after happening? I was late and I made a balls of the situation. But they want you to say it. As if you were up on the cross with your crime written over your head.

'I'm sorry, Tracy. The battery on my phone went and I wasn't able to ring and I didn't have the time.'

'You didn't have the time? You were so busy you didn't have the time?'

She's jumping on everything I say now.

'No, I mean I had no way of telling the time.'

'Ann, this is very serious now. Neans could have got a kidney infection. She could have got sepsis and we'd be dealing with a huge liability. I hope you realize the severity and the seriousness of the situation.'

'I do, Tracy, and it won't happen again. It was just a load of things that went wrong at the once. I lost the car keys and—'

'The picture you are presenting is not one that inspires confidence.'

I should stop talking, only making myself look worse.

'Ann, I will be including this on your Personal Development Milestone Management Document and ... well, the metrics are not best of breed. Informally, I would say that when we run the numbers you are likely to be one infraction away from a suspension. From now on I will *insist* on your weekly status metric Go-charts being filled out and posted to me.'

'I don't have a printer, Tracy.'

'I don't care, Ann.'

40

MENOPAUSAL, INDEED

I drive down to Neans for the first time since the incident. Early. Before Tina is gone. I send Tina away. I tell her to be sure and tell Tracy – if she's talking to her – that I was there early. Neans is watching me with a half a smile as I fill out the Go-charts.

'I'm sorry you got into trouble, Ann, but I'm glad to see you here early.'

On my way back there's another gang gathered outside Johnny's, drinking cans and pints. He sells the cans as well, so he doesn't mind. They have the dogs with them.

'What are these buckos up to?' I say to myself, but I'll pick my battles. I'll come back tomorrow and clean up after them.

As I'm driving out of town the car in front of me pulls in suddenly and I swerve around it, just about missing it. It must be strangers who had no problem getting into Kilsudgeon but are struggling to get out. I look in the mirror and I see three people getting out. A man with a tweed coat and two women. They look like retired teachers or librarians or ...

Inspectors!

Inspectors. The Tidy Towns people are here. And not a thing done around the place. Gordon said they don't do new villages until the end. Well, Gordon was wrong.

I do a U-turn like I've never done one before. I think the tyres squealed. The inspectors are looking at one of the boats, taking notes. At least that one's in good condition, since the lads are too lazy to drink anywhere else except outside Johnny's. Up ahead on the road I can see the party in full swing outside the bar. Ten or fifteen of them, and actually women too, as I get closer. The whole place looks like the hour after a concert. There are cans and plastic glasses and chip wrappers.

I pull in near them. I'm nervous approaching them, but I need their help.

'Lads.'

They don't notice me at first.

'LADS.'

'Oh, everyone, it's Queen Maeve.' They're laughing.

'Lads, can we clean up? The judges are here.'

'Ooh, it's Judgement Day,' says one of them.

'Please, just for a few minutes.'

I'm frantic now at this stage.

'ONE OF YE HELP ME.'

A couple of them start to vaguely kick cans under my car.

'Don't just kick them, pick them up. Look, put them in here. I have a few bags.' I go around distributing them, as if I were selling them raffle tickets. 'C'mon now, it's for a good cause.'

And what's this?

There in the flowerbed near Johnny's are bags of dog dirt. But they are the biggest dog dirts I've ever seen. They could only have come from one type of dog. A wolfhound. They'd gone to the trouble of picking up the dog dirt in a little bag, and then left it there! What kind of a bastard leaves dog dirt in a bright blue plastic bag in a flowerbed?

One of the dogs looks at me sadly. *I don't blame you, doggie,* I think. *You can only do what you have to do.*

I can see the judges approaching up the street.

'Look, can you please help me tidy up this bit? The Tidy Towns judges are just down there. If I can just do a little bit of cleaning, they'll think it's scheduled. C'mon!'

I fuss around them some more. A few half-heartedly start to help out.

'C'MON!' I say again.

'Listen, darling, there's no need to get all menopausal. Here, I'll see if I can land it in the bin,' says English tattoo man. He's supposed to be Denis's bosom buddy, but he's drunk now and has a harder look about him.

Menopausal, indeed. I'm long past that. Glad he thinks I'm still young enough to qualify, though.

He picks up a blue bag and throws it towards the bin, from about twenty feet away.

I don't know why it happens. Whether there's more in it than he expects, but the bag travels very well. Much further than he thought. It goes beyond the bin. By a good bit.

'Fack me,' says the Englishman.

The only small mercy I can be thankful for is that the bag doesn't burst when it hits Jeremiah Shannon, President of the Tidy Towns Judging Committee. The president doesn't go on every inspection. It's largely a ceremonial thing for a new entrant to the competition. I learn this later.

It doesn't burst, but it hits him right in the face. And the outside has soil on it, so it leaves a brown mark.

There's silence for half a second. Then the Berserkers all start laughing.

I rush to the car for a cloth. To help him tidy himself up. I'm apologizing all the time. He's not taking it well. He has a health-and-safety-officer look about him. Precise. Not a man who would have a high tolerance for having things thrown at him. The women with him – fair play to them – are smiling. I think they might be keeping in the laugh.

'This does not reflect well on the town, Mrs Devine,' is all he says to me, between deep breaths.

They get into their cars and leave. I do as well.

When I look back, the Berserkers are doing a bit of a tidy. Too little, too late.

'Have you seen it, Ann?'

Gordon must have got the email as well too.

'I think it might be the lowest mark ever in the history of the Tidy Towns, Ann. Thirty-four points. I don't know what they actually gave us marks for.'

'I know, Gordon. I think the Buddhist retreat got one for a bit of parsley outside the front door. And the only boat that wasn't knee-deep in cans.'

'They seem angry, Ann. I've never read a report like it. Usually, they'd put a positive spin on it.'

He's right. I'd been reading previous reports too. There could be ragwort growing out of a bin and they'd call it *an interesting display*. If the Tidy Towns went to Syria, they'd find something good to say about a pile of rubble or a burnt-out tank. But Kilsudgeon, according to them, *needs urgent attention. We would have concerns about antisocial behaviour which directly impacted on our President when a bag of faeces was thrown at him.*

And a final dig: *Kilsudgeon should look to its friendly neigh-bour, Drumfeakle, to see how they have really embraced the spirit of the Tidy Towns. Drumfeakle, in its fifteenth year of the process, has scored a very impressive 320 marks.*

'What are we going to do, Ann? We can't have this published. They give us the option of pulling out, but then what's the point of the committee? The town will be asking questions. They'll want to know what the money we raised from the table quiz was spent on. We might need Patsy to help us on that, so let's try to keep him on side.'

'It's a bit late for that, Gordon.'

'What do you mean?'

I'm looking at the latest issue of the *Kilsudgeon Sentinel* with the headline, *Bring back our* Celts*!*

'Nothing, Gordon. Yes, we need Patsy's help all right.'

Patsy wasn't messing about. It seems his man is back at the paper – and everywhere else too. No sign of the editor with the broken camera. The *Sentinel* and the Facebook page and the local radio are all campaigning for the filming to be restarted. There's an editorial from Patsy. And Patsy sticks the boot in.

Into me.

We are trying in our own small way to survive, despite the bias of the urban media against the rural communities. And we see this collapse in the collapse of values. We have recent incidents of the collapse of rural society – where a respected member of the Tidy Towns organization was assaulted with dog faeces in an altercation with someone from our own Tidy Towns committee ... In addition, we have several incidents of elder abuse in the community – an old woman was left unattended by her carer. This is not the spirit of Kilsudgeon.

He's blaming me for all of this but not using my name. He's warning me.

41

ALLEGEDLY, MY HOLE

Maybe it's the relief of not doing the Tidy Towns any more.
Maybe it's because I think things can't get any worse, but
I'm actually in good form when I go into Tracy's office with
my Personal Productivity and Effectiveness Programme
Report. What can you do to me now, Tracy? I've got your
precious paperwork. This is what you wanted all along. I
knock and walk in and hand it over, almost
triumphantly.

'Here's the report, Tracy, for my week, as requested. I had
to get it printed in the library, but I have to say, Tracy, it's
a help. It does focus the mind.' I'm licking up to her now,
but it's no harm, given what's gone on.

She doesn't look at the report, or up from her computer,
where I'd say nothing is happening.

'I don't need it, Ann. Please have a seat.'

Please have a seat – she never says that to me.

That's when I notice the other person in the room. He's
almost behind the door, sitting at the table in her office. Suit

with no tie. Cufflinks. He has a look of a salesman about him.

He springs up out of his chair and shakes my hand firmly. His hands are softer than mine.

Tracy gets up from her desk, goes to the table and sits down and waves at me to move from the wrong seat to the right seat, facing the two of them.

'Ann, I've brought Lee here to witness this. Lee is from GlobalHR.'

'GlobalHR are an outsourced HR function that handles some of the more involved aspects of the B2B and intra-B,' says Lee. He takes out a black folder, opens it up and starts writing on it. The name on the front of the folder is familiar, but I can't place it. I'm racking my brains when the printer starts going and I give a little start.

'Ann, we need to discuss Tommy Mullins. We received a complaint. An allegation that is very serious.'

'It's an allegation that would not correspond to the goals and ethos of the organization, Ann,' says Lee.

'An allegation?'

'An allegation that you attempted to interfere in a will.'

'Interfere in a will'. What could they be talking about?

'You allegedly' – she looks at Lee as if to say, *Allegedly, my hole* – 'interfered in Tommy Mullins's will.'

'I didn't. Tommy said he was going to change it for Noel, you see. He wanted us to use the field.'

'You were present during discussions about a will?'

'Only for a second, but then I said, "Lads, don't be getting me into trouble."'

'Did you document this at the time, in the P34 Patient Ancilliary Request and Incidental Narrative document?'

'The P-which? I didn't document anything.'

She knows well I didn't document anything.

'Let's look at The System and see what we do have on file.' She returns to her desk and makes a great show of looking at The System. 'Oh yes, now I remember it. I filled this out for you at the time and asked you were there any other details. So now we have' – and she starts typing and talking about what she's typing – 'withholding relevant details from supervisor.'

I can feel the jaws of a trap closing in on me. Lee is smiling still, but the eyes are snakey.

'It's not an optimal situation,' says Lee.

Fuck your optimal, I tell Lee in my head.

'I'm afraid we're going to have to issue you with a P23f, serving notice of temporary derosterization pending Structural KPI Inquiries.'

I look blankly at her.

'Suspend you, Ann.'

Lee clicks his pen. It's a *Patsy 2016* election one. I think I was meant to see it.

42

THE DOG WAS FIGHTING HIMSELF

im sorry ann

Just a text. Nothing else from Noel. I wait for a while, but there's nothing. I'm not even out of bed. I've no work and no children to mind. I've nothing to get up for. I'm tempted to ring him, but I'd sound like I was in bed. I'd need another half an hour to warm up, so I leave it and doze. But then another one arrives and wakes me.

don't ring me she'll be listening im in the toilet

I don't reply yet, as I don't know what's wrong with him. Noel gets maudlin, and he might have a few tins of beer in him. Even in the morning. Hopefully not in the toilet.

can you meet me in johnnys

I say no to that straightaway. I don't want to be going in there on my own meeting Noel. People would talk. Although what they would say I don't know. It would surely be the strangest match-up in the history of gruesome twosomes in Kilsudgeon, let alone an extramarital one. Whatever they'd be thinking about my capabilities, I don't know would anyone suspect poor Noel of having any kind of sexual thoughts at all.

that's the only place i'm allowed go or maybe mass

If that's the way with him, Noel's gone downhill. I mean, Tommy would have had him on a short enough leash, but he was protecting him in a way. His aunt, who he barely knows, dominating him like that, it's not right. She coming in out of America and pushing around a harmless poor fella like Noel.

I could meet you at confession

Whatever about Mass, I haven't been to confession in ages. I don't even know when it's on. I might bring Mam. I would *love* to know what Mam says in confession. Come to think of it, what am I going to say? Impure thoughts about Gordon? I try, but I can't think of a single one. Denis will be delighted. Arguing with my sister? Breaking my mother's heart?

I still haven't replied to him yet, but his texts keep coming.

Ive to go anyway ive a lot on my mind Thursdays usually are quiet

And that's why I'm now driving Mam to confession. She's delighted. I drive up to her little house and she's standing outside with her handbag and a coat I haven't seen before, ready to go. I get a little pang watching. She's some woman, living on her own still, with her group of friends and strong opinions. They can still surprise you, your parents, can't they?

'IT'S GOOD OF YOU TO BRING ME, ANN,' she says as I help her in on her side.

'Lift up the legs, Mam, and swing in around.'

'I KNOW HOW TO GET INTO A CAR, ANN, GIRL.'

Plenty of spirit left. We drive into the village, past the site, and it's still quiet, although all the film stuff is still there.

'I was thinking what you said, Mam.'

'WHAT DID I SAY?'

'When you said I was gone pagan.'

'DID I SAY THAT?'

'You did. And I was thinking, how do you stay praying with all that's happened over the years?'

'WHAT ELSE WOULD I DO?' And she doesn't say any more on the matter after that. She's not a heart-to-heart kind of person. Or maybe I'm not the one she talks to.

Confession is packed. Or at least packed for this day and age anyway. Here's the thing about Father Donnegan that would surprise you. He's always fundraising and going off coursing and golfing and what have you and people complain about him, but men go to confession to him. In other places confession is usually a line of perms and scarves waiting to tell the priest that they're troubled by dark thoughts about nieces stealing from them. But Father Donnegan has a way of talking to men. He doesn't put them off. He'll small-talk away to them about calf prices or the state of the road, and then they'll tell him things. Denis used to go into him for news, but eventually Father Donnegan said to him that he'd have to be bringing in some sins as well or the whole thing would be a joke. But a lot of these men would have no one to talk to, and wouldn't have one hundred euro a go to see a psychiatrist and another tenner for the petrol and where would you park a tractor now, with one-way systems all over the place? That'd make anyone anxious.

When we go into the church there's four or five people ahead of us, so Noel doesn't look out of place in the queue. Mam spots Bridie in another seat and shuffles up to her. I squeeze in next to Noel. He's left a gap to the fella next to him and we say nothing for a while. We hear a big laugh out of the confession box and a young lad – I think he's one of the GAA – stumbles out, too big for the step. 'G'luck, Father,' he says back in. We can hear 'G'luck, Barry' from the middle section. There wouldn't be much anonymous about confession around here. Barry heads straight out the door. I see Mam's lips pursed as she notices.

'A good crowd, Ann,' says Noel.

We talk without looking at one another. Denis would be better than me at this, from his days standing at the back of Mass. Lads standing there could nearly do the full *Hamlet* without anyone nearby knowing what was going on. I do my best.

'A good crowd. How are you, Noel?'

'Not too bad, Ann, not too bad. But bad enough too. It's not right, what's going on.'

'Which now, Noel?'

'That field should have been yours. Tommy said, *Mind the field, Noel,* to me. And that was why as well, Ann, I didn't call Oona home. I knew from when Tommy was better that he didn't like her one bit. She was only interested in money. But when he got close to the end he wanted her home. *She's all that's left of me, my sister, Noel,* he'd say to me. Tommy had been stone mad about the sister before she left, Ann. Ferocious fond. When she left, he was bereft. But she changed in America. And now he's gone ...'

He takes out a hankie and gives a big, wet, snuffly cough. I don't think anyone notices he's emotional because there's a good few coughs doing the rounds.

'She shouldn't be doing it, Ann. That lovely field. It's not right.'

'Is it not your field, or nearly anyway, when the probate comes in?'

'She changed it, Ann. She changed the will. She turned me out of the house one day. *G'way down to Johnny's, Noel,* she said, and gave me money, and I went, thinking maybe she wasn't so bad after all. I came back then and the solicitor was leaving and Tommy was out of it. And whatever was in that will before, now there's fuck-all for me in it after. And Patsy Duggan was there as well too.'

'Can you say anything?'

'I can't do a bit. She said she'd throw me out of the house, Ann, or have me put away. I just wanted you to know that I had nothing to do with it. Tommy always was doting about you, and he would never have changed it the way he did. The last few days he was out of it entirely. That will was changed, I'm telling you, Ann. In case you think we played a trick on you.'

'But what about the solicitor? Surely he can't be involved in that?'

'He's a cousin of Patsy's.'

'That's some story, Noel. Dan Brown wouldn't have it.'

'Dan Brown over in Flurt? Would he be involved as well? If he's anything to Val Brown, he might be. A reckless shower-afucks them Browns.'

'It was just a figure of speech, Noel. Don't mind me.'

'And Ann, they're out to get you as well. I hear them talking about you. Oona is furious with you all the time. *Do it, Patrick Ignatius*, she says. *You gotta teach that woman a lesson. She's always meddling in your stuff. In OUR stuff, Patrick.* The thing of it is, Ann, it's not even that that gets me the most riled. It's the other business.'

He leans forward now, elbows on his lap, and pauses as the fella next to him goes in. I'm all ears now. What could be worse? Noel gives another wet, snotty cough into the rag and puts it back into the pocket of his anorak and squeezes his nose and does a little sniff, the way men do.

He clears his throat again.

'They're going at it, Ann.'

'Who?'

305

'Patsy and Oona. One morning I came down I thought there was a burglar or the dog was fighting himself – he's not right since Tommy went – and I see Patsy on one leg, wearing Tom's dressing gown. The left leg was on the couch. I should have noticed it coming in the night before, but I was balubas. I sobered up fairly lively when I saw Patsy. In that bed, Ann. It's not right. I've to hear them, Ann.'

'Why doesn't she go up to his house with all the room there?'

'I don't think she thinks it's proper for a Christian woman to be going to a married man's house. Even though the wife is gone out of it a few years. Oona looks at me in the morning and says, *Are you listening in?* and *I bet you love that, don't you, Noel, you pervert?*'

The door creaks open and an oul lad comes out, looking a little less troubled. Mam is up on the other side and Noel is next to go in.

'Hup, this is me now.'

'Are you going to tell him all of this as well?'

'No. I'll tell him all the dirty stuff,' he says, and gives me a wink. Noel's not so helpless after all. I hope he gets out from under Oona's influence.

The question is, what am I going to do about it? I'll leave Denis out of it. He thinks I'm overreacting anyway. And Deirdre would only be all over me to do something and push me into a course of action like she was nominating me again. I love the bones of her, but she's a pusher, and this time I need to think. Sally? I might try Sally.

Sally is clear enough in her mind what I should do.

'Stay well away from it, Ann.'

We're sitting in her little kitchen. We can't go in the sitting room because Donal is *in there putting Google out of a job*, as

Sally puts it. I peeked in through the glass door. He was putting YouTube to good use anyway.

'Stay out of it, Ann. Do you hear me? You can't win with family. Tommy's people are a quare breed. And Patsy? You're talking about a mafia there, girl. Do you want to be mixing up with that crowd? You'd be better off with the IRA. They don't pretend to be respectable. Leave it, Ann. I'm telling you.'

But I ignore her and do the wrong thing.

I ring the telly man.

43

WE'RE ALL STARS NOW

'Ann? ANN?'

'What time is it? Hang on till I turn on the light.'

'There's no need to turn on the light. I was only looking for the Sudocrem.'

'What? What do you want Sudocrem for? What time is it?'

'Leave the light, it's fine.'

I've already reached for the switch.

'JESUS, DENIS! What happened your face?'

He has a scrape on his chin and his eye is looking puffy.

'You didn't drive home, did you? Sure, Denis, I'd have driven you. Lord God, if you've been caught ... Have you knocked someone down? DENIS, answer me.'

'Ah, Annie, relax. No, I walked away home.'

'Would Johnny not drop you? Doesn't he drop ye normally?'

'I wouldn't give that bastard the satisfaction.'

'What happened?'

'I don't want to talk about it.'

'Well, I do. I'm not going to sleep until you tell me.'

'There was talk.'

'Who was talking?'

'The Berserkers – the hairy lads, there were a gang of them.'

'You were fighting the extras?'

'I wasn't fighting. I fell over trying to fight them. They were lucky I didn't get to them. I still have a bit of go in me.'

'You do. What was the talk?'

'Ah, it was nothing.'

'Denis, you waded across a pub to start laying into a load of Celts. You haven't been in a fight since old money. What was it over?'

'You and Gordon.'

'Me and Gordon? Gordon Patterson?'

'No, fecking Gordon Lightfoot, they wanted to know if you liked his music. Yes, Gordon Patterson. They were slagging me off over it. *Poor Denis away in a truck while the two tidy the town between them on their own.*'

'*What?!*' Although a bit of me was half flattered. You don't get accused of having affairs at my age.

'They were saying things, you know. *She's fixed his picker. Watch out now, she'll bump you off. Like Catherine Nevin. You'll be put in the brown bin.* Then they said, *I wonder does she call him CAPTAIN?*'

'Where did they hear about that?'

He looks at me. 'Only one place.'

The penny drops. 'Declan! The little ... I'll throw him out. And what was Johnny saying?'

'He was laughing along with the rest of them. I lost the plot then. I went laying into them, but I tripped over a stool and sort of fell down by the table, and Johnny came around and helped me up and said to the lads not to be annoying

309

his regulars, even if they were acting the maggot. I thought that was a bit disloyal now myself.'

'Were there many there?'

'No, thank God. Be honest with me now, Ann.'

'For feck's sake, Denis, do I look like the type who'd have an affair?'

'Well, you'd be still tasty enough like.'

I think that's the most romantic thing he's ever said to me.

'So you're not having an affair?'

'Only with you. Come here, ya gobshite, and give me a cuddle. Defending my honour. Aren't you very chivalrous?'

He climbs into the bed and I give him a fierce tight hug.

'You're not the worst of them, Captain.'

'I bet Clooney hears that all the time.'

'He's married now to the solicitor.'

'He's sorted so.'

'Oh, Denis, what's going on with me at all, I wonder?'

'What do you mean?'

'All of this exposure.'

'I thought you don't mind exposure,' he says, and gives me a squeeze.

'Ah, stoppit now. I mean, all the viral stuff and losing the job. That kind of stuff isn't my style. We were never ones for notoriety and now every cornerboy and chancer thinks they know us, all over a few videos and hints in the paper. I feel so exposed. If I was on *Operation Transformation* in my bra and knickers being given out to by a lad in a tracksuit or the doctor I wouldn't feel as exposed as I do now. I don't like people having the advantage on me.'

'It'll die down after a while. Someone else will get into the *Guinness Book of Records* for Irish dancing in a tractor or something and they'll move on.'

'People don't move on out the country, though, Denis. They remember things for ages. You know that as well as anyone. Do you remember you didn't make your Communion until you were nine and they were talking about it at our wedding?'

'I think it's different now. There's so much happening that things move on much faster. They haven't time to be remembering. And, even if they do, people make comebacks. Sure look at Cody Bryan. I was reading he was caught somewhere with a loaded gun and a box of endangered tortoises. There's always a second chance now. Or more if you're a star.'

'We're all stars now, is that what you're saying?'

'I hope so anyway, otherwise they'll be talking about Denis Devine fighting in the pub.'

'You were always my star.'

I don't tell him about my next TV project.

44

THE HEEBIE-JEEBIES

Andrew from *Everyday Scandals* wants to meet after my revelations. I nearly suggest Thursday confessions.

I drive all the way to a layby on the motorway nearly twenty miles away. I've never done anything like this. I wear a headscarf, of all things. I haven't worn one in thirty years. Sitting there like Jackie Onassis. I should have a long fag hanging out of my gob and sunglasses. As long as Skitchy Ryan doesn't turn up on another errand I should be fine. I park behind Andrew's car and get out of mine and into his. I get the heebie-jeebies about being there.

'You came back, Ann.'

'I did. And I'm still not sure if I can help.'

'OK, well, while you're deciding, maybe have a think about this. We found out something else that might interest you. Remember I told you about the Saudis who want to turn Kilsudgeon into the Riyadh of the midlands? Well, right now in Saudi Arabia they're trying to get off oil and gas. They're hooked on it. So they're trying to diversify. And Bin Jufali

Imdad are one of most active. They are buying companies all over Europe. And they have also branched into another area, Ann. Elderly care. And one elderly care company, in particular, they've bought in the last few months. Mellamocare.'

So that's where I saw the name: on Lee's folder.

'And I'd be willing to bet that the fact you recently lost your job—'

'How did you hear that?'

'Your niece has put up several videos on Snapchat calling for justice for you.'

That'd be Freya all right.

'We've asked her to take them down. We need the element of surprise here.'

Element of surprise? I think. What kind of a situation have I walked myself into?

'We think you lost your job because of your viral video. It's put a halt to their plans. It's likely Tracy was asked to come down hard on you. There's a lot going on here, Ann.'

There is. I breathe heavily. I see a box of Silk Cut in the pocket of the car door.

'Can I have one of these? I don't normally smoke, but—'

'Yeah, I keep those handy. I find I need them a lot in this business when people want to talk.'

He lights it for me. I take a big drag. Oh, that's good. I'm nearly high with it. I take another drag and tell him my story. About how Patsy thinks he's the man to talk to if anyone wants to bring anything to Kilsudgeon, about how he'll fix it. And he'll do it all for money and the glory of Kilsudgeon and he doesn't see a problem with getting a bit of both. About the Dublin media, the carry-on with Oona, the solicitor, everything except the dressing gown and the one wooden leg. You'd have to have some respect for privacy.

313

Andrew is excited. He hugs me, which is a bit awkward in the car. He smells a bit of expensive deodorant.

'We have him, Ann. This gives us so many ideas. You've been a huge help. Finally, we'll take down Patsy Ignatius Duggan. And you can have your revenge.'

My revenge. It doesn't feel very sweet.

I should have knocked really. But why would I knock going into my own sitting room? And anyway, when I got home I was still in a fluster over all my conspiring.

I expect to see Jennifer. She's having a great time rebalancing and recentring on her sabbatical. I don't expect to see her doing her rebalancing and recentring on top of Declan.

They aren't exactly *in fragrante delicto*. The sofa wouldn't be comfortable enough. But Jennifer is straddling Declan, kissing him, when I go in. They are fully clothed. So I might only need the one year of therapy.

She turns around so she's sitting on his lap but doesn't seem too bothered. Oh, to have her lack of tizzy.

'I thought you were gone to town, Mammy.'

'I was, and now I'm back from town.'

'Mammy, this is Declan.'

'I KNOW THAT, Jennifer. I met him before you did.'

'Sorry. Yeah. I forgot. I mean, this is the real Declan.'

Declan gets out from under her. He is blushing like mad. For some reason, it seems stranger for me to see him up to something than her.

'Eh ... I was just ... Sorry, Mrs Devine. Jennifer said that ...'

'Jennifer. A word if you wouldn't mind.'

She comes out with me to the kitchen.

'Mammy, surely now you're not going to be all prudish about a bit of kissing? There's a lot more than that happened on that sofa. I know for a fact that Rory—'

'Don't tell me, Jennifer. Anyway, you'll need to do it some-where else because we are throwing him out.'

'What?'

'He told a load of his *Celt* pals some things that are private to this house and I won't stand for having my good name thrown around the street like a tramp.'

'What are you talking about?'

I am about to open my mouth but stop myself before I say anything. It's not the kind of thing a mother should be discussing with her daughter. No matter how 'cool' anyone is with that sort of thing.

'I'm going to find out eventually.'

'Lookit, all I'll say is that Declan might have overheard some things that I say to your father at a particular time.'

'You mean "Captain"?'

'Oh God, Jennifer, no.'

'We've known that for years.'

'IS THERE ANYTHING ABOUT MY LIFE THAT ISN'T COMMON KNOWLEDGE AROUND THE ROAD?'

'OK, so Declan was a bit indiscreet, but you know he's shy. I'm sure the lads were trying to get him to say stuff and maybe he was just trying to impress them.'

'I just don't see what the attraction is, Jennifer. He's very—'

'What, Mammy? Odd? I know, but maybe we're the odd ones and, honestly, the arseholes I meet in London are way more strange. They're actual psychopaths. He's kind and also, you have to admit, he has a lovely body.'

'And are you … like, is it serious? He's very into you, though. Always asking me, *Will Jennifer be around tomorrow? How long will she be here for?* I hope you're not giving him the wrong impression.'

'I don't know, Mammy. I don't have the answer to that now.'

'And I'd be grateful, if this goes any further, that you're not ... *active* in this house.'

'Mammy, you know we're all *active*. What difference does it make where it happens? And you're *active*. Why can't we all be *active*?'

'I just don't want to know. I don't want to think about it, OK?'

'Mammy, don't think about it and you'll be fine. Put it out of your mind.'

'I'm worn out. I don't have room in my mind to think about it.'

My fine daughter and Declan. You couldn't make it up. Can I just have one week without news?

45

LIKE IN *DONNIE BRASCO*

The days pass and there has been no news, no mention of *Everyday Scandals*. They must not have got what they wanted out of Patsy. I am relieved at the lack of news. No surprises, no one appearing in supermarkets, no 'viral' videos of me making a fool of myself. We've decided to stay out of the Tidy Towns for this year. I've stopped organizing clean-ups. It's no big deal. Voluntary things fizzle out all the time and no one bats an eyelid. There's a hullabulloo, a meeting and then there are cobwebs. This is just one of those things.

I'm still suspended, but Neans, Flash and the others have given me a bit of work on the sly. Even Nonie got Brian to ask me to come in for a couple of hours every week because Nonie got no pleasure from insulting a stranger. She wasn't herself at all, shouting at the girl from Dublin, because she caved too quickly, whereas she liked – this is Brian's theory – that I just let her bounce off me like a handball. All she's doing is venting. Well, we'll see. I still think, deep down, she's nasty. So that's the only bit of sneaking around I do now. Secretly visiting old people and giving them a wipe. That's some affair, isn't it? But I love it.

The filming got back up and running after Patsy got the minister involved and they leant on the council. The place is still a tip with the hairy lads drinking, but I don't care. I've had enough of interfering.

My peace of mind doesn't last long. One wet Wednesday morning Andrew rings. He has something he wants to show me. I should stay away but, when it comes down to it, I'm pure nosy.

An hour later I'm in his car on the side of the motorway again. There's a few trucks up ahead, but there isn't a peep out of them. A car pulls in behind just after I sit in. A man gets out quickly and runs to the back. My mind works overtime, imagining him to be a Patsy spy, a Saudi spy – any kind of spy. He wrenches the door open and, after frantically working something with his hands, hauls a small crying boy to finish getting sick on the road. I remember it well. I can't make up my mind if I'd swap with him now.

Andrew plays a video on the iPad.

'This is what we'll be showing in a couple of weeks' time, once the legals are fixed up and we've done a few more edits, but you're watching a preview of the programme.'

I take the iPad on my lap and press play.

There's Andrew walking down the road through Kilsudgeon. I don't know how people didn't notice him, but maybe they thought it was something to do with *The Celts*.

'We put a hidden camera on our reporter, who posed as a renewable-energy entrepreneur for a company called Solarwinds, their slogan "Energy Whatever the Weather". Patrick Ignatius Duggan has been a TD in this constituency for thirty years. A colourful character, known for his one leg, he has never let that affliction hold him back.'

There was footage of Patsy being held aloft in the election, when the leg wasn't on right, and him toppling off the shoulders of one of his hangers-on and the hanger-on still holding the leg.

'Duggan has managed to tread a fine line to ensure he's always at the centre of power. He has never been too rigid about a position and, appropriately, given what you are about to see when our reporter asks for help with a wind and solar farm, Duggan has always shown a keen sense for which way the wind was blowing.'

They had him talking about numerous referendums. *I would be against this 100 per cent*, and then in one case only a week later – *Of course, I would support this government's decision to have a referendum* – and a shot of a new library in Flusk.

While I'm looking at this, I'm thinking he has done a fair bit for the area. Looking at him on the telly, he does seem to be more 'one of our own' than the man sitting next to me.

Then the hidden camera stuff comes on. There's Patsy in tremendous form, talking to two men in suits in his constituency office.

'Lookit, I'm the man who fixes things around here. Do you see the *Celts* thing? Not a HOPE of getting that through without me. I run this council and I decide what goes through and what doesn't. Any minute I could have said, "No, ye can't go near that because it's a prehistoric monument or whatever," but no, I says I'll do it for the community. So, in exchange for administrative fees, I smoothed things over. We got planning for the thing through a loophole. Now I put a lot of work into that. That's local expertise. You can't buy that. But you can try. You need to do things fast or you'll lose it. That's my motto. Regulations and all that codology – that's for Dublin, where there's more people with shag-all to do to be worried about regulations. Fuckers reading the *Irish Times* with their green tea or whatever they drink. It's not that I want a cut. I just want a consideration. There is a different rule in these tight-knit communities – you have to pay into a club you want membership of.'

'What kind of fee are you thinking?'

'It'll have to be strong five figures, lads. That's all I'll say. I don't want to give too much away. Ye could be wearing wires, like in *Donnie Brasco*, hah?'

Patsy's laughing away and one of the reporters gives a kind of a nervous look in the direction of the camera. The camera was about waist-high, so he must have been pretending to fiddle with the zip on his coat. One of them speaks up.

'But *The Celts*, I mean, like, that would have gone through anyway, wouldn't it? Like, why would we need you? Sorry to play hardball, but how can we be sure that it'll actually help us?'

'Look, nothing happens around here without my involvement. Now, you must understand, tisn't a power trip. I'm not feckin Mugabe, but with the connections I have, with the way the Dáil numbers are, I'd always have a bit of pull at government level. And they'll elect me till doomsday because I get stuff done. So there's no sums done when it comes to coalitions without Patsy Duggan's name on the back of a fag box. J'understand me? It's not politics, just operational management, as I like to call it.

'We mightn't pay as much property tax, but you pay for your right to interact around here in other ways. Nothing's changed in the Irish country since the days of Hugh O'Neill, lad. You've the Pale with their ways and then you've the Tories out here in the country. The original Tories, not the other fuckers with their Lah-di-dah. No, the Irish countryside is still outlaws and we make do whatever way we can. Cutting deals to make our meals.'

'At this point, Patsy Duggan becomes more explicit about what it is he actually wants,' says the voiceover.

'Show me the money. I want all the money. I want to be able to retire and give back to the community even more than I've been giving before.'

'So you want a fixer fee to get the planning?'

'That, and as well as that you'll need to put this solar wind thing somewhere. I need to persude a few people. I have a farmer in mind.'

The voiceover says, 'The farmer he has in mind is local man John Lordan, an elderly farmer who lives alone in the area. Patsy Duggan tells our reporter that his land would be a prime location.'

Then they show them going in with Patsy to a yard that looks familiar. My heart gives an extra thump. It's Flash's house! Was the telly going to make another gom out of Flash?

'Well, Flash.'

'What do you want, Patsy?'

'This fella now'd be contrary enough. Let me do the talking. I know how to talk to these lads.'

You'd swear Flash was one of these tribes in the Amazon.

Andrew reaches across and presses Pause.

'We found Flash from the newspaper story. We called in and asked him if he wanted to be part of it. He jumped at the chance of a bit of acting. And, apparently, he has bad blood with Patsy from a few years ago. So he was perfect!' He presses Play again.

'Now, Flash, these are the people from the solar panels. Remember I was telling you about them?'

'Solar panels. Are they putting in new windows, Patsy?'

Patsy turns to the fake solar-panel people and whispers, 'This is what you're dealing with now, lads. He's worse than he normally is.' He turns back to Flash. 'Now, Flash, remember I talked to you concerning the High Field and solar panels for a few years? Guaranteed money. No need to be trying to get Andy to pay a few cents every year for renting the field.'

'Solar panels, Patsy. I see. And is there any sign of that chairlift for me? I was supposed to get a grant to put in, but now they're saying I've to do a means test. I don't want any money to tip me over the means test, you see.'

'I'll sort that out for you as well.'

Oh God, Flash. What'll they make of you now on the YouTube? You'll be torn apart by those smart alecs with their memes. You'll have a dancey song over you.

But then Flash plays a blinder. Acting like an eejit one minute and then being all cute the next.

'Are these lads anything to do with the stroke you pulled for the new houses, Patsy? Jayz, that was some going. Three housing estates built in a bog. How did you manage to swing that, hah?'

'Oh, stop now, Flash, you're an awful man. Anyway, all we're looking for from you today is just your signature on an expression of interest.'

'Signing my life away, Patsy, is it?'

Then the voiceover comes in again. 'Not quite signing his life away, but close. The agreement Patsy attempts to get Flash to sign is increasingly common in rural Ireland, where up to twenty-five years of a lease are signed away for money upfront but the farmer can't so much as plant a strawberry on the land or access it for that time. We put our findings to Patsy Duggan.'

'Patsy, one thing we should say. We are from *Everyday Scandals*.'

It was like a very angry *You've Been Framed*.

'Well, FUCK YE ANYWAY. That's entrapment. Shnakes. Who put ye up to it? Was it Cushin the Russian. Was it?'

I had to laugh at the idea that Gary Cushin was going to get more exposure in ten seconds than he'd got for the previous ten years.

'Why were you attempting to solicit bribes from our reporters in return for fixing a deal for solar-panel generation on a farm?'

'Bribes?! That is a scurrilous allegation. I was merely standing up for my local community.'

But as he protests more and more he looks a broken man.

There's a bit more background information on Patsy then. Some facts and figures about turbines and solar panels, a bit about *The Celts*, and that's it. I hand the iPad back to Andrew.

'We hope to interview Patsy in the studio. What do you think, Ann?'

'He'll be ruined.'

'That's the plan. Now we need a bit of local colour to back it up.'

'Do you have to show it?'

'What? Do we have ... what do you mean? Why wouldn't we show it?'

'It's just that ... well, he does do a lot for the area.'

'Are you fucking serious, Ann?'

'He has fierce energy. The other three in the constituency are useless. At least he cares, even if he does take his cut.'

'Are you getting cold feet, Ann? You know he's a crook, don't you? You know about the signposts and the dodgy developments? He's taken far more than he's given. We are looking for some local opinion to back it up. We already have Flash giving out about him. We have a few others. And, might I add, we're planning also to look into Oona Beauregard – or Oona Valdez, or whatever she calls herself now. What a piece of work she is. There's some stories coming out of the States about her. But you, viral Ann

323

Devine, who lost her job because of him, you'd be the icing on the cake.'

I shake my head.

'I want no part of it. You TV people are the same as *The Celts*. You come down the country for a bit of a story and make us out to be eejits and then feck off again. You won't be around for the fallout. I have to live around here. Do you think I'll be talking out against neighbours? You've another think coming. Good luck to you.'

'It'll be shown anyway, Ann, with or without you. Like it or not, you helped it happen,' he says as I take off my seatbelt and get out.

'YOU'RE JUST HELPING KEEP THE LIKES OF HIM IN POWER,' he shouts through his window as I walk away. He's right, but I can't do it. Country life lasts far longer than a television show. And the likes of Patsy recover from being in a spot of bother all the time. And when they do, they go looking for whoever put them in that spot.

46

SOMETHING THAT'D BE ON CHANNEL 4

'... and the collection today is for the Pope's Intentions. Last week's total for the priests of the parish was three hundred and forty-two euro twenty-nine cents. Thank you for your generosity.'

He almost spits out the word 'generosity'. Father Donnegan thinks there should be more of a return out of us. *It was twice that during the recession,* he said one day, according to Mam.

I'm back at Mass with Mam. She has no one else to bring her at the moment because the woman who normally takes her is laid up.

'And now we'll have the Prayers of the Faithf— Oh, hang on a second. I forgot this. Gubu Productions are delighted to welcome you to a special – it says here *rough cut* – screening of a promotional video of *The Celts*. This will be taking place in the parish hall on Wednesday night. Might I say as well that they have been very generous in their donation to the parish hall for the purpose, so it would be great to get a good turn-out.'

I won't be going to him for confession so.

'You can bring me along to that,' whispers Mam. 'Nora's gone to a home with her ankle.'

I go, even though I've a bad feeling in the pit of my stomach. The hall is full. We have to check-in our phones to stop us recording anything. Even Mam starts fussing and takes one of the ones with big buttons out of her handbag and hands it over.

'Since when do you have a phone, Mam? You told us they were a curse and not to bother getting you one.'

'Bim Geraghty gave it to me.'

'What's your number?'

'I don't know. Bim has it.'

Bim Geraghty. A bit of a quare hawk, not much older than me, sniffing around Mam in the last few years. She's never clear on what the story is with Bim. But I'll find out when I get a chance. That fella could be taking advantage of her or trying to get a hand on the house. Maybe I shouldn't have been so hasty with Andrew. If he can bring down Patsy, he'd make mincemeat of Bim Geraghty.

We take our seats – Mam, Denis, me, Deirdre and Jennifer. *Girls' night out*, says Jennifer. Nosey wans' night out, more like it. There's a lot of talk around the town now about what in the name of God are they actually making up there, because anyone who went up to do a bit of acting at it seems to be confused.

There are none of the bigwigs from the production here tonight. It's just Man Bun, but he seems different. He turns his head and I see he has lost the man bun. I don't know what to call him now.

'So this is just a little thank you to Kilsudgeon as we come close to the end of our pilot filming. First, you'll see a little taster of what it was like to film here.'

'This looks like a charm offensive, Mam,' whispers Jennifer.

The screen goes black and a little message appears. WE'VE HAD A LOT OF FUN HERE, it says.

There is a behind-the-scenes video showing the filming of a crowd scene. Half the village is in it as extras and there are shouts all over the hall as locals spot themselves.

EVEN THOUGH WE'VE HAD OUR UPS AND DOWNS.

Then it's my turn to cringe. They play a video of me shouting at Cody Bryan. There are cheers for me and a few boos because they still think I got money out of it. Patsy appears on the screen then, looking all shifty, talking to the Saudi lad.

'G'wan the Patsy!'

'Just doing my bit,' shouts Patsy from the side.

There's no mention of Solarwinds, but I'd say, if there was, he'd get even more cheers. He's pure Teflon, that fella. But knowing what I know, I think I see him worried in the eyes. Maybe I'm imagining it.

BUT THE GOOD TIMES HAVE BEEN MORE THAN THE BAD.

There follows a few seconds of Cody Bryan singing in Johnny's, talking about how he had found peace here, and then they cut to him wrestling in the back of the pub. I don't know who he is wrestling at first, but as I look at it for a few seconds I know I'd recognize that back anywhere.

'DENIS, IS THAT YOUR GOOD JUMPER?' I shout-whisper at him, while everyone cheers.

'I told you you should have come with me that night.'

There were a few more minutes of Kilsudgeon: Father Donnegan horsing around with an axe, Cody Bryan drinking shots, the dog from the Welcome Festival barking at the Berserkers, a baby asleep, the usual St Patrick's Day news report. Then the screen goes black again. More white writing appears.

CONTAINS STRONG LANGUAGE AND SCENES OF NUDITY.

'Hup, yah biya,' shouts out one of the twins. 'You might see yourself in this, Nuala.'

'Nuala Costigan is supposed to be in this, Mam,' Deirdre says, 'as a serving woman.'

'She won't like serving anyone.'

The writing goes across the screen: THE YEAR IS 3000BC. THE ANCIENT TRIBES OF EUROPE ARE GATHERING FOR A BATTLE AGAINST THE EVIL THAT LURKS IN THE DARKNESS ...

There are images of fellas with masks and curvy swords and a tiger on a leash.

'WHERE DID THEY GET THE TIGER AROUND HERE?'

'CGI, Nan.'

'I DON'T KNOW THAT PLACE.'

THE MYSTERIOUS ISLAND OF IRELAND, ON THE EDGE OF THE ATLANTIC, A LAND OF MAGIC AND HEROES, IS THREATENED BY MARAUDING TRIBES FROM THE EAST AND TWO RIVALS MUST UNITE TO FIGHT THE THREAT – CÚCHULAINN AND FIONN MAC CUMHAILL. WAR AND LOVE ARE TWO SIDES OF THE SAME COIN ...

'Fionn, she is here,' a fella with a big wolf's-head cloak says.

Cody Brian appears. He looks hungover.

'Bring her to me.'

The accent was cat. I don't know if it was meant to be Irish or not, but he was woejus.

The warriors brought in a young wan wearing some sort of leopardskin-bikini thing.

'Who are you?'

You could hear the crowd in the hall murmuring, 'Iseult Deasy.' She's gone fierce grown-up looking. The hair was up and fairly soon everything else was down.

'Tlachta, daughter of Ubrug, king of the Formorians. Why do you come here, to Tara, the seat of my kingdom?'

'I want to know the greatest hero of all.'

'Know means yes,' says Cody with a smile.

And then they started going at it in front of us. Like something that'd be on Channel 4. Father Donnegan's face was a picture, although he wasn't telling anyone to turn it off.

'That's the stuff!' someone shouts. I don't know who shouted it. I'm too transfixed. In fairness, Freya was right. What did she call it? Fighting and fff— Anyway, they soon switch to a big scene in the daytime. A huge fight with axes between Cody Bryan and the fella playing Cúchulainn. They had yer man from the North, Samuel McTaggart, playing Cúchulainn.

'He's an Orangeman,' says Denis to me. 'They would have been delighted with him as Cúchulainn.'

Shelf McKinnon makes a brief appearance to warn Fionn to be careful. I don't know whether she means about the girl, Cúchulainn or the tiger.

Nuala Costigan arrives in a big shawl carrying wine. A big cheer.

'Are you going to *know* him as well, Nuala?' shouts one of the twins.

And then it ends rather suddenly. It was no more than a trailer, really. There's no sign of Man Bun any more. And there's certainly no guacamole on offer, or nice bread. We're just left to our own devices.

'Will we go for a drink after, Mam?' says Jennifer. 'Just the women? Nana, what do you think? Will you come with us to Johnny's?'

'INDEED AND I WILL NOT,' says Mam. 'IT'S TOO MUCH DRINKING WOMEN DO NOW. DENIS WILL BRING ME HOME. I'VE TO TAKE MY TABLETS.'

We walk with her to the car and stroll down the village to Johnny's.

329

We say nothing for a while in the pub until Johnny brings the drinks and the crisps over.

'Well, that was, how shall I say it, *shit*, Mam,' Jennifer says after a big slurp of beer.

'You say it as if it was my fault, Jennifer. All I did was eat a few sandwiches.'

'Could you not have put in a word, Mam, when you were on the set, what with you being an influencer?'

'Don't talk to me about influencing. I'd rather it was influenza.'

I don't say anything about Andrew or *Everyday Scandals*. You get used to keeping things from your children when you have to.

'Iseult Deasy did well out of it,' says Deirdre. 'Now might be a good time to book in the NCT, while the father's in a good mood.'

'There's something odd about that whole film production,' says Jennifer. 'With my evil corporate hat on, they look like they're up to something. If they look like they're up to something, they mustn't be doing it very well. I must have a root around.'

I feel a bit sick.

Deirdre has more important things on her mind.

'What's the story with Declan, Jennifer? Mam was saying he's pure odd.'

'Jesus, Deirdre, come straight out with it, why don't you? And what if I like him a lot? Will you tell me he's odd then too?'

'Now and again. You're like Auntie Geraldine for strange men, only you've a bit more choice. With the money.'

'He's not after my money. Anyway, he's not as strange as some of the others I've dated over the last while. And what would you suggest? One of Hughie's brothers, I suppose?'

'You could build a house next to us. The children would be cousins.'

Deirdre is joking, I think. She knows this would be Jennifer's worst nightmare. Jennifer puts her fist in her mouth.

'Which brother, though?'

'Leonard,' Deirdre says. 'The other fella needs his mammy too much. Leonard would be solid enough for you. It's your destiny, Jennifer. Marry a solid man like Mammy and me did.'

'Or I could have a fling with a gobshite and produce a possible genius like Freya.'

'Are you saying my children aren't geniuses?' Deirdre says.

'Are they?'

'No.' She laughs. 'Bless them. I think they might be solid too. Fiftieth percentile of everything all the way up. But c'mon away home, though, Jennifer. I miss you. You should move back home anyway. Open up a financial company here.'

'Go into competition with Kevin's father-in-law?'

I let them at it. It's nice to see them snipping away at each other like when they were small.

Deirdre brings things back to basics. 'So what *is* the story with Declan? Are you and him ... you know ...?'

'Will I go?' I say. I'm like Denis now. 'I don't need to be around for this bit.'

'And I thought you were going to throw him out, Mammy?' Deirdre says, stirring.

'Mammy and I had a little talk.' Jennifer tells her about the Captain incident. Deirdre throws her head back.

'Oh God, I thought I'd blotted that out of my mind. Remember when we both heard it together? What age were we? Old enough to know what was going on anyway.'

'Can we *please* stop talking about that? I don't know what your fascination is with me and your father. You know how ye got here. Do you think we just stopped?'

'I'm just happy you and Daddy are … you know … still *active*. I hope you're taking precautions. The rate of STI among the elderly is—'

'STOPPIT!'

They're dreadful slaggers, but they took my mind off other things anyway. When Johnny shouts, 'Last orders,' we're all hammered. We should do it more often.

47

A LITTLE SCATTER-EYED

'We're off, Mam.' Jennifer and Declan are at the door of the kitchen.

'Where are ye going?'

'Just for a drive. Maybe we'll have a picnic. What's up, Mammy? You look like you haven't slept.'

'I'm fine, pet.'

'OK, Mammy, we'll be back later.' She kisses me on the forehead. It hurts after the night before.

Geraldine rings me as Jennifer closes the door.

'Ann, you're there.'

'Nowhere else to go at the moment, Ger. Do you want Freya minded or something?'

'Ah, Ann, I'm not always looking for something from you. No, you see the thing is, I was just up with Patsy—'

'Oh, right.' I'm trying to hide the catch in my voice.

'Yeah, I wanted him to see if he could help me with my wellness-retreat plan.'

'I thought it was yoga?'

'I don't want to specialize too much yet. The thing is, it's all forms and health and safety and bullshit, so I wanted to see if he could hurry it up in some way. I put on a bit of lippy and a low-cut top. You know the story, Ann.'

'Don't tell Freya.'

'I know.' She laughs. 'She'll say I'm *part of the problem*. But listen, about Patsy, he's not himself. Very shook, he was. And he asked me if you were about, said he might call up to you for a chat. So just to give you a bit of a warning.'

I feel cold, like someone has left a window or a door open. Patsy wants to talk to me? This is it. The jig is up.

The doorbell rings at that very instant.

'There you go now,' Geraldine says. 'That must be him. You might want to slip a bit of brandy in his tea. Looks like he needs it.'

She's right. He is fairly shook-looking. The hair is a bit unkempt. I'm dreading what he wants to say.

'Can I come in, Ann?' He comes in and sits down. He's a good bit slower than before.

No word out of Patsy as I boil the kettle, make the tea and put a few biscuits in front of him.

'How's Rory?' he says.

I was thinking I should have asked him that question, that he'd know more.

'I left him alone for his exams. But I might have a job for him in Cork,' he goes on.

If this was any other time, I'd get upset that he's managing my son's life again, but with all that's going on and him so quiet, I'll leave it go.

'There you go, Patsy. And how are things with you?' I ask, as if I haven't seen him being caught rotten on camera.

'Have you any fags, Ann?'

'I don't, Patsy.'

He doesn't pursue it. He says nothing for a while but eats a digestive. This lack of small talk with a neighbour is stranger than anything that's happened.

'I made a balls of the whole thing, Ann,' he says eventually.

'What thing, Patsy?'

'You see, I was caught on the hop.'

I think he's talking first about the filming, but no.

'I let her in too close. She ran rings around me, Ann. I wasn't thinking straight.'

'Who, Patsy?'

'I was awful lonely. You wouldn't think it, would you? But I was. Ah, she's gone now anyway. And left a right mess after her. They were always a quare lot, them Mullinses. You never knew Tommy in his prime. People were afraid of him. The real talk about that fairy field is that there might be someone buried in there, you know. Going back years. But no one knows for definite. Neans might, but the people who know things are dying. And maybe that's not such a bad thing. A lot of things are better buried.'

'Oona?'

'It was personal with her, Ann, you know. I'm a practical man. I do my few deals and I get things done and I take a percentage. 'Tis only capitalism, isn't it? We all take our slice along the way, don't we? Except the likes of you, Ann. Helping old people for small money. You don't take any slice. You just do the job. The nurses and the carers, ye're pure saints.'

'We're not saints, Patsy. We're flawed enough too, if we're tired or the old people are in bad form. Nothing saintly about it. Only a lot of mess and smell and then the odd squeeze of the hand or a smile to make you feel good about it. It's the people looking after their own I feel sorry for. They never get a break. They've no shifts.'

'I've no one to look after me, Ann. Not since Ursula left. I don't blame her. The hours weren't fair on her. And … I might have been a bit of a bold boy as well.'

I let him talk. It isn't like him to be so open, but maybe everything is going to be exposed so he doesn't care. I clam up. I look at him now. He seems a smaller man. Tapping away at his leg.

'Where's she gone, Patsy?'

'I don't know, Ann. When the TV crowd came sniffing around me—'

'What TV crowd?' I'm cute enough to pretend not to know what's going on.

Patsy tells me the story I've already heard from Andrew, but the way he tells it he's being ruined by jealous people locally. I blow my nose just to have something to do with my face, in case it gives me away.

'Janey Mac, Patsy. What are you going to do?'

'I don't know. I've never been caught out like that before. I wasn't thinking straight. Are there any more biscuits?'

I go up to the press and all I have is Rich Tea, but he hardly notices the difference.

'She says, *Patrick, I can't* – and he puts on a kind of cod American accent – *I can't have this in my life right now. I can't deal with this kind of attention. It's not a good look for me.*'

'I see.'

'But she … it was personal. She hated you, Ann. She wanted me to name you in the paper, you know. That time. Like, I wasn't even going to go on about it, but she was over my shoulder saying, *Do it, Patrick Ignatius, she's got it coming to her*. But I said no. I put my foot down – the good one, haha. I told her the libel laws were something fierce here.'

'But why does she hate me, Patsy? I only mentioned the field by accident to that fella at the *Sentinel*. I wouldn't dream of presuming anyone's land.'

'It was Noel told me one night. He was warning me off her. Can you believe it? Poor ould Noel wouldn't hurt a fly. He was worried enough about me to tell me to keep away.'

'Noel has hidden depths all right, Patsy.' I was thinking of his confession-box caper.

'You see, she was ... is a troubled woman, Ann. Noel said that one night they were putting Tommy to bed and Tommy was asking where you were and Oona said she was looking after him now and Tommy – it must have been during one of his clear moments – started shouting at her. *I know what you did*, he says. *You're a bad one, Oona, you always were. Mammy said it too, you know. There's something wrong with you and that's the truth of it. Ann Devine is a good woman. You'll never be like her. You'll never mind me like she would. I know ye stole the field. You and Patsy.*'

'What do you mean, Patsy?' I act all innocent again. My brain is *creaking* with the weight of the secrets I'm trying to keep.

Patsy looks a little scatter-eyed.

'The will, Ann. I ... well, it was Oona really. She said she wanted to change the will. Asked me how she'd go about that and, well, it was the night we first clicked. I told her a few things about my plans for the area that I wouldn't normally ... I suppose I was trying to impress her, and she says, *Patrick, we'll change the will. The jerk wants to leave it to Noel, and Noel is simple, but you can never tell what he might do.* After that I got on to the cousin, and we changed the will. It was the most foolish thing I've ever done. I'm telling you, I wasn't thinking straight. She was some woman, Ann. She could do things. I was lonely. There now, I said it. They can all pick over the bones of me, but that's what I did.'

He takes a big slurp of the tea. Patsy in love? I'm not sure I believe that. He loves money anyway, I know that. And money never treated him badly. Maybe he's getting his story ready for when the whole things breaks. If he cries for the telly, they'll love that.

'That's grand tea. I want to make it right, Ann.'

'The tea?'

'No, I mean make it right with you. I don't want bad blood.'

'Why would you care about us, Patsy? I mean, like, we're hardly the mayor around here.'

'Rory, Ann. That young lad is a real treasure. I'd like him to work with me and I can't do that if I'm at war with his mother. And you're a good woman. You've an awful habit of getting involved in things that are not your business, by accident. I don't know whether you're lucky or unlucky, but whatever way this whole thing falls out, you're a good woman, and I'm sorry about the paper and I want to make it up to you.'

I don't mention losing my job, and he doesn't either. He's not laying himself completely bare, so I'm still cagey around him. I don't want to get Noel into trouble. One secret at a time.

'So we need to fix this. I'll get you another go at the Tidy Towns. I know Jeremiah. He's not as squeaky clean as you might imagine.'

'He isn't now anyway, with dogshit on his head.'

He laughs. 'I can see where Rory gets the sharp wit too, Ann.'

It's the first time we've bonded over Rory.

'Anyway, Jeremiah has benefited from a bit of – shall we say – untidy towns over the years. You get to see a lot of derelict sites in his game and get in on the ground floor in a few places, and sometimes you need a man in the

338

department to look at things for you. So I think he owes me a return visit anyway. So ye'll get another go. "Watch this space," as the fella said.'

He stands up with a little bounce. He seems lighter after telling his story, or some of it.

'Right so, Ann. Come what may, it'll get a little hairy around here for me over the next while, so can I count on your support?'

'I suppose you can, Patsy.'

And he goes out. I feel rotten, though. All the biscuits and tea and thanks, and I helped land him in it. I wonder does he know what exactly is coming down the line at him?

I haven't slept the last three nights with the worry. A couple of weeks, the producer said it would be, before the legal eagles would have a chance to look at it. I don't know if I can bear it. What will the place make of its leader being torn down? God, he looked awful pathetic in the TV show, and then being so trusting of me and me like a snake. Saying nothing.

But the funny thing is, there's no mention of it at all. Normally, when they've a scoop they're all over the place. NEXT WEEK WE LIFT THE LID on so and so and TONIGHT HIS NIBS HAS BEEN UP TO NO GOOD. But there's nothing.

I'm all ears for it, and then I catch it. Only a snippet of news after a murder and before a strike.

'An investigative journalist has been accused by a number of women of inappropriate sexual advances. It is alleged that Mr Andrew Kearns, who is a director of the production company Mature Recollections, groped a number of colleagues and engaged in a campaign of bullying when his advances were refused. Some of the incidents are said to have taken place during the filming of the company's flagship show *Everyday Scandals*. As a result, RTÉ has announced that it will not work with the company until allegations are addressed, and the current series will not be shown. Mr Kearns has issued a statement denying all allegations.'

I stare at the screen as they move over to the sports correspondent, but I don't see anything. There's a sort of noise in my head. The other side of the room seems far away. Like a dream.

When you're small, you think life is going to be like a western, with the good fellas and bad fellas, but then you get older and you start to see the other side of everyone's story. It sometimes turns out the bad fellas are actually not the worst of them when you get to know them and where they're coming from and might even do you a favour the odd time and you can't hate them like you used to. And the fella you thought was sound out was up to something behind your back. I hope Freya never finds out about this. To think that one bad fella should be let off the hook by another bad fella, I don't know … It's an awful depressing lesson to learn so young. She should at least have a bit of a chance at idealism. Yer man was supposed to be the good cowboy coming in, but what is he now? And is it OK to feel happy that Patsy will be able to do whatever he wants as long as my name is left out of it? God, I never knew it was so hard to have principles. But then, if you look hard enough, a lot of us are hypocrites, aren't we?

What do you think of that, Ann? An awful story, but it looks like I'm off the hook! I'll get your Tidy Towns thing sorted now, says a text from Patsy no more than five minutes later. Glue wouldn't stick to that man.

EPILOGUE

NO SENSE OF ANY MAGIC

It's all change around here now. The TV show packed up and left in less than a week. The extras were gone overnight. They left a pile of rubbish. They left the huts and most of the stuff behind. I wasn't blamed, thank God. They ran out of money. Patsy's Arab lads got the heebie-jeebies with all the attention. Then, according to the *Sentinel*, the film crowd didn't have a whole lot of money anyway. They never had it. They were hoping to run on fresh air until the money came in.

There were a good few stung. Johnny had allowed Cody Bryan to run up a tab that was into the thousands. Farmers weren't paid for the use of cows. They didn't even pay their electric. The whole thing was a hames. The only one who got paid, as far as I can see, was Patsy. Even Father Donnegan now has to raise money for the broadband from his roof, which has replaced the fund for fixing the roof itself. But it's the best collection ever since attendances went down.

'It seems Kilsudgeon may have had a lucky escape,' said the *Sentinel*, with a report on another TV show they'd started, done one series and left everyone even more high and dry than us. I'm glad to see the back of them, to be honest. The place is back to normal, and that suits me fine.

We did a massive clean-up before the Tidy Towns visit. We never explained fully why it was on again, off again. People aren't interested in the ins and outs of that. Just give them a thing to turn up to and some of them might turn up. You have to be a special type of person to go on a committee and argue over tiny things. And I still don't know if I'm that type of person or not. But it was the clean-up to end all clean-ups.

Patsy fixed it with Jeremiah that their surprise visit would be the following Monday. A big crowd turned out. A speech from Gordon and Patsy with a megaphone about the importance of community. We were just about to set off from the car park with our bags and our pickers when an old minibus with HARD BASTARDS ON TOUR written on the outside of it roared up the street. With another one after it, and another. As soon as I saw the first tanned, sandalled leg and hairy head come out, I knew who they were. Forty hairy men and women and two big wolfhounds. My friend – the fella who'd thrown the dogshit at the president – was there, holding a tray of bedding plants.

'To say sorry,' he said to me. Now the plants were fairly miserable, but I didn't say a word, only thanked him.

We didn't have enough pickers to go round, but those hardy bucks would nearly pick glass with their teeth. With such a gang, we cleaned the town from front to back. People from every walk of life picking up the rubbish of people who'll never know what it is to have a bit of pride in their area. The fuckers. May they never have any luck either.

And to cap it all off we had tea in the sun outside Johnny's, which escalated into cans and chips. Five o'clock I went home. Mouldy.

'You can't be getting drunk on every clean-up now,' said Denis. 'You'll end up on the scrapheap.'

The Tidy Towns came along on the Monday and we pretended we didn't know who they were, but everyone was winking away like mad at each other. They gave us 185 points. Last in the region, but it will do for a first time.

'We recognize the great strides Kilsudgeon has taken in the past year, despite a number of well-publicised challenges. The community spirit is admirable. We note a number of areas for improvement, including a scrap yard on the edge of town that could benefit from ...' they said in their report.

I'll take 185. Drumfeakle only got 180 in their first year, and that's all that matters. A nice quiet start and no more spotlight on the town.

So that was the Tidy Towns. And now I'm back at home, tidying there too. Freya and Lossie walk into the kitchen. They're making one of their *Culchie Feminist* podcasts. They just sit and talk about absolutely everything that happens in their lives in the tiniest of detail. They do it here because Lossie's house is smaller and, as she says herself, 'full of people who won't shut up during a recording'. I listened to one, and it was about me hanging out the washing and how I was trapped. It turns out Lossie is very good at talking. She out-talks Freya. Or they just talk at the same time. They haven't gone viral, but they don't seem disappointed. I leave them to it. I go out to the car and get in and drive out the gate.

There's a place I have to go back to. To get *closure* – isn't that what they call it on telly? By myself. No children or niece. I drive along the bendy roads, enjoying the feeling of the traffic being back to normal, and no quad bikes or Northern-reg jeeps to be seen.

I get out of the car and go up to the fence. I look in through the broken plywood. The fairy field is still a bit of a mess. A lot of the metal has been stripped out by the kind of lads who would strip the metal out of your fillings. There are a lot of cans in there. We told the Tidy Towns that, strictly speaking, the field was in the townland of Branaphuca on some old maps, and so it wasn't in our jurisdiction. But when we get our town park we'll get new maps and bring it back into the fold.

I push open the fence gate. Someone else is in there already, walking around. As I get close I see that it's Noel. There's a new spring in his step since Oona went.

'It's in a state, isn't it, Ann?'

We look around at the rubbish. Thankfully, they haven't gone near the gateway to the underworld, or two white-thorns, depending on your point of view.

'I got a solicitor, Ann. We're going to challenge that will. Patsy is helping me out with it.'

'No sign of Oona?'

'Gone completely. Back to America. She's a conwoman, Ann.'

'I hope you get the field back now, Noel. It would be nice to have the town park all right.'

'Well ...' Noel takes a drag on a fag he had behind his back. 'I don't know what we'll have in it yet. A lot of demand for houses around here, Ann.'

The Mullins is coming out in him at long last. I don't think we'll see a park. I won't be saying a word anyway. I'm happy with what I have.

I walk around for a bit, but there's no sense of any magic in the air here. Just crows giving out on a June day. A bit of peace. I'm going to take it nice and handy now, plant a few shrubs, try and get my job back, keep Denis out of fights, and get Rory through his next year in college after he pure scraped the bare minimum to pass this time, while his mother was neglecting him.

Boop boop beep.

Facetime call from Jennifer Third Child. (Rory put in all the names. He put himself in as Favourite Child.) Accept or reject?

'Hang on there, Jennifer,' I shout at the phone. 'I'll go up to Dooney's Turn. See you again, Noel.'

'Bye, Ann.'

We are back at Dooney's Turn. The receivers took the internet gear out of the church last Tuesday. Father Donnegan wanted to give them a cheque from the collection, but the legals were so complicated he couldn't find anyone to give it to, so the internet had to go. Funnily enough, it was the only protest anyone could ever remember in Kilsudgeon. There must have been a hundred people trying to prevent the bailiffs from dismantling it. Lads were there with laptops overnight, downloading every dirty film, I'd say. The receiver won't get much out of the gear. Kilsudgeon wore it out.

Patsy's promising a rural broadband scheme, so we'll see where that ends up and how much ends up in his pocket.

I pull in to Dooney's. It's busy here again and the chip van is back.

'OK so, pet. How are you adjusting after your sabbatical? Me and your dad are missing you.'

'Well, I have some news that'll cheer you up so, Mammy. I'm moving back to Dublin. With a Saudi bank. They're opening an office in Ireland because of Brexit. So it looks like we're just as evil over there. But seriously, it'll allow me to get out of it with a bit more planning, you know. An exit strategy. And I'll get to see more of Declan.'

347

'Declan? Is it serious?'

'You thought that was just a fling?'

'So you did fling. After what I said.'

'Don't worry, not in the house. I couldn't anyway. Not with that new wallpaper. Listen, I thought it was a fling too, but … I missed him. I think I might love him, or really like him anyway. I dunno, it's early. But I'm not telling him that yet. I don't know has anyone told him that before, so I think he might need a bit of advance warning. Who knows? I might even move in with him. He has a place, and it's so hard to find somewhere to live in Dublin, you know.'

'I see.'

'Mammy, will you at least pretend to be happy?'

'I am happy. I mean, I suppose, like … and do you know him well enough? It's just not like you to jump into this kind of a thing. I mean, you took so long to get as far as you've got I just didn't think you'd go to the next stage as quick.'

'Mammy!'

'No, I'm happy for ye, honestly. Just a bit surprised.'

'No, the moment's gone, Mammy. Too late.'

'Jennifer …'

'My battery's going anyway, Mammy. Love to Daddy.'

I drive out of Dooney's Turn. A fella is thumbing up ahead. I wouldn't dream of stopping normally. But then I see it's the Buddhist lad, Tim. The one who wasn't a ninja in *The Celts*.

I stop and lean over to wind down the window.

'How's Ann? I'm out of petrol. Would you give me a lift up to the filling station?'

'Jump in, Tim. Maybe you can help me too. I've a lot to meditate on.'

ACKNOWLEDGEMENTS

Thanks once again to Faith O'Grady and all at Lisa Richards for being the professionals they are in removing worries from my plate and replacing them with excellent biscuits and advice.

To Brian and Eoin, who gave me the 'start' in books back in 2012, the first people to believe I could string more than a few hundred words together and who were instrumental in getting Ann to tell her story. I learned my trade writing to make you laugh.

To Mairead Lavery at the *Irish Farmers Journal*, who gave Ann a column a few years ago and allowed me the time to build Kilsudgeon without planning permission or functioning broadband.

To Ivan McMahon, Ciaran O'Kelly, who told me a few stories about film sets to get me started. Even though I'm sure there's nothing like *The Celts – Hound of Destiny* in operation anywhere.

To my family of brothers and my own mother Eileen, who continues to watch and support with love and care and advice as she navigates life without Dada (the late Patrick O'Regan), a man who, while on his walk around the block, never passed a hedge-discarded chip wrapper without picking it up and putting it in the bin at home.

(And to all in Dripsey Tidy Towns who keep the lane even more spotless since. Kilsudgeon Tidy Towns isn't based on you, don't worry. You're a far more professional outfit.)

To a lovely woman called Nuala from 'up the country somewhere', who one day, out of the blue, wrote me a funny, touching letter about life as a carer.

This is also a tribute to anyone who's ever donned a hi-vis jacket, stood on the edge of a road picking rubbish, directed cars for a 'thing that is on', opened a parish hall, raised money, organized a raffle or just generally done any bit of voluntary work at all for the people who live around them.

Thanks to my darling wife, Marie, who has put up with my 323 bouts of self-doubt and imposter syndrome, while still providing funny ideas and inspiration and crucial edits. Marie does most of the minding of our two daughters, Lily and Ruby, and that means I have time to do my work. I love you very much. Thanks to Ruby and Lily for your mostly unconditional hugs and a sense of comic timing that is pure and natural. (burp)

To Fiona and Rachel, my incisive, intuitive and generally superb editors, who put in so much work to make this a book that made sense and could be read by humans. They separated the wheat from the chaff, milled the wheat, made bread out of it, the whole shebang.

To illustrator Ollie Man and to the wonderful Transworld team in Ireland and in the UK who brought Ann into the book world with such enthusiasm, skill, creativity and warmth: Patricia McVeigh, Aimee Johnston, Brian Walker, Sophie Dwyer, Tom Hill, Ella Horne, Kate Samano, Josh Benn, Cat Hillerton and Beci Kelly.

He had a good job and a degree and everything, but Colm O'Regan gave it all up to try and be a comedian. He is also a columnist, broadcaster and anything else that will keep the wolf from the door. He heard there was fierce money in books so he has written four – the three best-selling books of Irish Mammies and also *Bolloxology*, a title which neatly sums up his skillset. From Dripsey in County Cork, Colm now lives in Dublin, but he's up and down that road a good bit – especially since they put in the motorway.